DON'T OVERTHINK THIS

KELLY PIAZZA

Foxglove Publishing LLC

foxglovepublishing.com

Foxglove Publishing paperback edition 2022

Library of Congress Cataloging-in-Publication Data

Names: Piazza, Kelly, author.

Title: Don't overthink this / Kelly Piazza.

Description: First Edition. | Missouri: Foxglove, 2022.

Identifiers:

ISBN: 9798985067408 (paperback)

ISBN: 9798985067415 (ebook)

Subjects: GSAFD: Love Stories.

First Edition: March 2022

Printed in the United States of America

1st Printing

Dear Reader:

The book you hold in your hand is a story that has been living in my heart for a long time. It has lived in the back of my mind, scribbled into pages of notebooks, typed out in drafts, and lost on long-forgotten hard drives. It wasn't until a draft that vaguely resembles the book you are now holding came together that this story finally found its footing. In every version of this story that has existed, one thing has always been true:

This is a love story.

These pages are full of all of the beautiful moments that come with falling in love; moments that I couldn't help but smile at as I wrote them. I *love* love stories. There was a version of this story that was lighter, fluffier, and full of only good feelings. But something about that didn't sit quite right with me as another thing has always been true of this story:

This is a story about addiction.

A story about addiction that only highlights light, fluffy, good feelings isn't a story about addiction at all because addiction is devastating. Addiction can destroy families, friendships, relationships, and lives. In no way did I want to sugar-coat that reality when writing this story. I built this love story around the damage that addiction can cause, the levels it can sink to, and the impossible struggle to overcome it.

But the truth is, not every story of addiction comes with a happy ending. While I did not shy away from telling some truths about addiction, I know that for some, the devastation it causes goes so much deeper than the rose-colored version of detox and sobriety that are depicted in this story. To those of you who have been affected by addiction or the opioid epidemic, I hope that I have done you justice on the pages to follow. I hope that I have honored your experiences.

In order to tell a full story about addiction, this story features some beautiful moments of love and redemption right along side the struggle and darkness. Addiction isn't a supporting role in this story. Our protagonist, Matty, struggles with addiction. Along with it comes depression, anxiety, panic disorder, and thoughts and descriptions of suicide, as well as the loss of a loved one, on-page drug and alcohol use, and the spiraling mind of an addict. Never are any of these potentially triggering elements intended to simply shock, but are rather used to give a realistic representation of addiction and mental illness.

If any of this subject matter is triggering to you, please read with caution. Take care of yourself first and foremost. The following resources are available to anyone who might need them:

Crisis Text Line: https://www.crisistextline.org;
or text HOME to 741741

National Suicide Prevention Lifeline: 1-800-273-8255

Samaritans Helpline (call or text): 1-877-870-4673

Substance Abuse and Mental Health Services Administration
(SAMHSA): 1-877-726-4727

Find substance abuse or non-emergency mental health help near
you: https://www.findtreatment.gov

All of my love and support to each and every one of you.
Thank you for being here,

Kelly Piazza

PART ONE:
ELMWOOD, MISSOURI

I

Wednesday, April 18th

The peak of my existence came the year I turned twenty-three. Or maybe it was even earlier than that. It feels really pathetic to say you're at the *peak of your existence* when you're also clinically depressed. Maybe my real peak came at thirteen, before any of this started.

Either way, my life fell off a fucking cliff at twenty-six, figuratively speaking of course, and my crumpled, pathetic self has been lying at the bottom ever since, waiting for the day I'm lucky enough to not wake up.

The thought of killing myself comes to mind often, but my crippling anxiety keeps me from following through with it. I imagine my parents finding me the way we found Keelie's dad, and there's no amount of depression in the world that brings me more pain than the thought of inflicting all of that on someone else. Instead, I let the pain engulf me. I absorb it and wait to die.

Two years of lying at the bottom of this cliff have gone by, and now I'm twenty-eight. There are days when I fall down this rabbit hole of suicidal fantasies—usually before my first pill of the day—and today death by starvation seems most promising. It wouldn't have the same gut-ripping effect as your traditional suicide. Sure, they might still call it a suicide, but my family could say things like "He was too depressed to get out of bed" instead of having to say "He took a shit ton of pills and never woke up." That's how I would do it though, if there weren't other people to consider. I would take a hearty handful of oxycodone, fall asleep, and never wake up. Blissful euphoria until my last conscious breath. *Peaceful.*

But the reality is that once your brain falls asleep, your body still tries to save you. You gasp for air, your stomach rejects the pills, your heart stops. And it's only then that your family finds you lying on the floor, lips turned blue, covered in your own vomit. Maybe it's your mom or your dad. Or *maybe* it's your two young kids and their best friend, who walk home after school one day to find you like that. Looking familiar, and yet completely unrecognizable, all at once. It's an image they'll never forget. At least, I've never been able to.

That's why death by starvation seems promising. It would be less painful for everyone involved. My starvation fantasy hasn't taken me as far as Googling what happens to someone as they starve to death, but it's on my to-do list. I have to be sure it's nothing like what happened to Rich.

These thoughts of death come to me only when the pills wear off. When I'm high, suicide is far from my mind. At least, it used to be. Pills used to make me feel good, but now I take them to not feel bad.

When I wake up this morning, my brain pulses with pain, and my eye sockets are sore. It's the beginning of a hangover, mostly. That is, until the skin of my arms starts to crawl, until my hands start to shake. That's when I know the withdrawals are settling in.

The skin crawls are the absolute worst part about taking pills. Usually, I avoid these at all costs. I do whatever I can to keep the pills from ever wearing off. Except for today. Today, I want the crawls to come, to see how bad things have gotten. To see how long it takes to get from my last taste of oxycodone to the first sign of nausea. What I did not anticipate when making this plan was the possibility that I might wake up horribly nauseous. *Miserably nauseous.* It isn't the pills yet. My stomach is churning with the grumbling aftershock of all the alcohol I drank last night. At least, I'm pretty sure that's what it is. The crawls will let me know for sure. Going out with June always seems to blur the line between hangover and withdrawal.

June is a *friend.* To call her my girlfriend would be a staggering overstatement, even if we see each other a few times a week now. Most days she picks me up and we go to a dingy dive bar across town. She has to pick me up because my license was suspended just over a year ago, after my second DUI. It's not so bad not being able to drive. Even if I could, I wouldn't have a car to drive after I clipped a curb and crashed mine straight into a streetlight at full speed. The entire passenger side of my car was completely annihilated. I woke up in the hospital without a scratch on me, or a clue about how I got there. The ER nurse said I was lucky to be alive, and even luckier to be completely unharmed. Had there been someone in the passenger seat, they would have been declared dead at the scene, if there was anything left of them at all, and I would have spent the rest of my life in prison.

I try not to think about that day. Whenever I do, I think about how it could have been Keelie in the passenger seat. The impact of the light pole tearing her apart. Her unidentifiable remains left at the scene while I got rushed off to the nearest hospital, completely untouched. My stomach swirls at the thought of it. Her family and mine would have gladly seen me rot in prison after that, a place where killing myself would be an even more unattainable fantasy than it is now. That day was the only time in my life I was actually happy about being alone.

Whenever June picks me up, she parks a few doors down, then creeps along the side of our house and knocks on my window to let me know she's here, as if we're a couple of teenagers sneaking around. Not that I have any idea what that's like. My parents never gave me a reason to sneak around. They were pretty hands-off with me. Especially after Rich died and I started taking antidepressants. After that, I was too fragile to parent. They were afraid they might break me.

As soon as June's knock raps on my basement-level bedroom window, I bolt up the stairs to meet her. By now, my parents are so annoyed with me, they rarely acknowledge my existence. Every once in a while, I call out "Sto uscendo!" as I leave, which translates to *I'm going out*. Some days they'll reply with "Ti voglio bene," which means *Love you*. But most of the time, we ignore each other all together.

Last night, they were watching a crime drama on TV when I left. I thought I had snuck out unnoticed, quietly latching the front door without stirring their attention. But as soon as the storm door shut behind me, Dad flipped on the porch light so they wouldn't have to worry about me tripping on the stairs when I stumbled home drunk. The last time I shuffled up those three small steps in the dark, I smashed my face on the metal door frame and split my lip wide open. My parents paid out of pocket for the four stitches it took to fix my gushing split lip because I don't have health insurance or a dime to my name. I don't even have a bank account anymore.

As I jump into June's car, she passes me a pill bottle and says, "You owe me big-time for this one." Twisting the cap off and peering inside, I determine that, yeah, I owe her big-time. My favorite little green tablets fill the bottle all the way to the brim. Tapping the pill bottle against my palm makes three pills cascade into my hand. Etched into each pill is a tiny *15* on one side and a bold *M* on the other. Fifteen milligrams of oxy. The chemical flavor stings my tongue as I toss the first pill into my mouth. I grind it up between my teeth so the effects take hold of me quicker.

June cringes as she says, "I don't know how you do that." She says that every time. We're getting to that point where we're starting to repeat ourselves. Cringing at my pill chewing is a constant for June. That and saying things like "You owe me."

It isn't an easy taste to swallow. It has a bitter, chemical taste, and it makes my whole mouth dry. A few years ago, I would have filled my mouth with water to avoid the taste. But now I crave it. I dream of it. I can taste it even when it isn't there. A phantom chemical flavor pangs my tongue whenever it's been too long since my last dose. It was hard to get used to at first, but now there is no better taste in the world.

"Take a left at the end of the street," I instruct June as I pocket the rest of the pills.

She gives me the side-eye, still keeping most of her attention on the dark street in front of her.

"Why?" she asks hesitantly as she adjusts her grip on the steering wheel so she can make the left turn one-handed, holding out her other hand to accept a pill from me.

"Shortcut."

She turns more fully my way, studying me, her eyes only briefly flashing to the road as she tries to get a better idea of what I'm up to. She bites the pill between her front teeth, careful not to let it touch her tongue.

Avoiding her look, I contort my body across the center console and fish her water bottle out from behind her seat, flip the straw-top open, and offer it to her for a drink. She briefly allows the bitter taste of the pill to dance across her tongue as she leans her head toward me to grab a sip from the straw. She gulps down the pill with a blissful smile.

"Thanks, baby," she coos in a way that makes my skin crawl quicker than the withdrawals.

"Take a right at the next block," I say, ignoring her.

"Matt, I've been here a thousand times. This isn't a shortcut. Tell me where we're going or I'm turning around."

"I want to check on something," I grumble as she makes the right turn.

My eyes snap to Keelie's mom's house as though they've been drawn by a magnet. Keelie's car is parked in the driveway. It's *still* parked in the driveway. It has been for weeks. I gaze out the window as we drive by. June slams on the brakes when she notices where my attention is.

"Don't stop!" I hiss.

"Whose house is that?" She barely takes her foot off the brake, slowly coasting by. The front window has the blinds drawn, the room behind it fully illuminated. Someone is home. I hold my breath, as if doing so will prevent anyone inside from noticing the slow-rolling car outside.

"Drive," I beg.

June shifts her foot back to the gas pedal and accelerates as she asks, "Is that Keelie's house?"

"No." I cringe, not wanting to admit that the actual answer is maybe. Hopefully. But I don't actually know where Keelie lives. I haven't for a long time. She stayed in our apartment for a while after she kicked me out. I knew where to find her when she lived there. I could see her, I could talk to her, I could explain to her how things had changed. But I never had the courage to do any of that sober, and she could recognize that the instant she opened the door, every single time. She would tell me to leave. Ask me not to sit outside of *our* apartment waiting for her. Tell me to get help. And then one day I knocked on the door and she was simply gone. A new tenant had moved in, and I didn't know where to find her.

The only place left to look was her mom's house. I didn't knock on the door there. I never wanted to make contact. Her mom never really liked me, even before we started dating. I can only imagine her distaste for me now.

"Whose house is it then?" June demands.

I toss the last pill into my mouth and chew it. Through clenched teeth, I huff out, "Her mom's."

"That's Keelie's mom's house?" June groans back, mouth agape. "Stalking your ex-girlfriend's family is next-level crazy. You know that, right?"

I glare at June, allowing the bubbling saliva to coat my tongue with the bitter taste of oxy.

"I'm not *stalking* her," I defend. "Just checking in. That was her car in the driveway. It's been there for a while and I'm worried something is wrong."

"Have you tried calling her?"

A burst of laughter escapes my lips. "She doesn't answer my calls."

"If she doesn't want to talk to you, you should leave her alone," June states plainly.

I sink down, heavy in my seat. *Why did I let June know about any of this?*

June drives us to the other side of the city, to our usual grimy dive bar. The drinks are cheap, and the bartenders don't ask too many questions. Which is good for June because she doesn't use her real name when we go out. *Stephanie*—that's what she calls herself. She says she uses a fake name because of her job, because she has a reputation to maintain. And she says it's because her kids go to a nice school where all the other parents are snobby and would judge her if they found out she spends her Tuesday nights getting stoned at a shitty bar with a guy twenty years younger than her. It seems a little farfetched, but I bite my tongue and don't ask questions. If I say the wrong thing, she might take the pills away.

Inside the bar, a man with tightly coiled hair raises a hand to wave at us as we approach.

"Hey, Dale." I wave, sitting on a stool in our usual spot.

"Hey there, Matty," Dale hollers back, already grabbing a glass for my usual double pour of Jim Beam Black. I don't have any reason to use a fake name, so I've always just been *Matty*.

Tonight, June is drinking vodka Red Bulls because she thinks she sounds young when she orders them. It takes every ounce of my energy not to tell her that drinking Red Bull fucks with her high. But as long as she keeps paying for it, she can waste her oxy however the hell she wants.

After a couple of hours slowly sipping her drinks, June topples off her barstool, leaning her body against mine and pressing a finger to my lips. She whispers in my ear, "Meet me in the bathroom in two minutes," and a chill pulses through me.

"No," I snap back in vain, already knowing exactly what she is going to say in reply.

I have to shove the glass of bourbon to my lips to keep my mouth from mimicking her words as she says, "Matt, you owe me."

Tilting my head back, I toss the rest of the bourbon down my throat in one swift motion. "Right."

I lift a hand to flag down Dale, but he's already read my mind, pouring me the shot of vodka I was about to order. He knows our routine. I quickly toss it back, hoping that today could actually be the day I have too much in my system to get an erection, but I'm never that lucky. I've been alone for too long. After less than a minute, I follow June's trail into the bathroom, ready to get this over with.

For all the discretion that June thinks she's using when we make our way into the bathroom, she shows little interest in actually being secretive about what we're doing. She shouts at an unnecessarily loud volume as I fuck her on the bathroom counter, a noise so deafening it is likely heard in every corner of this small bar. She follows me closely as we return to our barstools, proudly adjusting her clothes and passing a flirty smile to the old guys sitting in the corner, who are gawking at what they witnessed. Every. Fucking. Time.

Dale has a fresh pour of bourbon waiting for me. I nod a thank-you in his direction, but his kindness makes me feel worse about myself. It confirms that I look as pathetic as I feel.

June switches to coffee after that. Me? I double down. Once June stops drinking, I drink more, quickly losing count of how many I've had. It's enough that I strain to even lift my head. A massive weight settles in my face, preventing me from keeping my head upright. My eyes blink independently of each other. The entire room around me is fuzzy.

It's possible that I drifted off to sleep, only for a second, because I am jarred back to life when Dale sets a glass of water on the bar next to my half-full glass of bourbon.

"You okay, Matty?" he asks kindly.

He's standing right in front of me, but my eyes still pan the room in search of him, unable to snap onto his position. I nod my head a few times, my mouth too heavy to form words. I take another sip of bourbon, ignoring the water entirely.

"Hey, Stephanie!" Dale shouts out to June. "I'm closing you out. Matty's cut off."

A blur at the corner of the room lifts a hand in our direction and gives a thumbs-up without saying a word. I might not see her clearly right now, but I know what she's doing. She's saddled up next to some guy she's not even interested in, leading him on. She's brushing his arm, laughing at his horrible jokes, letting me fade into the background as if she doesn't know I exist. I'm supposed to keep an eye out for her signal. A quick itch along her jawline means "Get me out of here." Then I jump in and rescue her, preventing her from ever having to break the news to the schmuck she's flirting with that this is all a big game to her.

The only problem is that tonight my eyes won't focus on anything. I can't see June or her signal. I throw back the last of the bourbon and push myself away from the bar, the stool teetering backward and knocking me into a standing position. Stumbling, I brace myself against the bar as the stool goes clattering to the ground, my foot twisting up on one of the barstool legs. I lean further against the bar's edge, trying and failing to lift my leg high enough in the air to get my foot untangled.

"I've got it," Dale calls out, running to lend a hand.

I attempt to mumble back a thanks but there's no sound; my lips are weighted shut. I stagger in June's direction, bumping into a couple of chairs on my way across the room. With two hands planted on her table, I blink a few times to bring her into focus and then mutter out, "Let's go."

"Hold on a minute, champ," the guy sitting across from June spits back. "The lady and I aren't done with our conver—"

"Stephanie!" I shout to June, interrupting him. "Let's go."

"That's my cue," June drawls back in a horribly fake Kentucky accent.

June snatches my arm and leads me toward the door, across the parking lot, into the car. She slams her door on the driver's side and shouts out, "What the fuck, Matt? I've been begging you to get me out of there for the last twenty minutes."

Ignoring her, I press my forehead against the cold glass of the passenger-side window. I pinch my eyes shut, trying to stop the world from spinning around me.

June drives me back to my parent's house, helps me to get up the stairs at the front porch, helps me step over the metal door frame, guides me down the stairs back into my room in the basement. She fixes her eyes on a photo of Keelie and me that I have on the dresser. She's probably seen it at least a dozen times before, but this time she stares at it a little longer.

"Who's Val?" she asks, reading the *I love you, Val* that Keelie scribbled in Sharpie, right onto the glass.

"Me," I mumble back, stumbling as I step out of my shoes.

"How do you get from Matthew to Val?" she asks as she flips the photo facedown. She does that every time she's here, flips it facedown and tells me it's time to get rid of it. She doesn't mind talking about Keelie, but she does mind that I refuse to let Keelie go, even after two years.

"Matteo." I mutter, chin to chest, trying desperately to unbutton my jeans.

"What?" she asks with a laugh, coming to my rescue.

She pushes the button through its respective loop like it's nothing.

"It's not Matthew, it's *Matteo*," I inform her, marching in place and stepping on the bottom of each pant leg with each stride to pull my jeans off me, hands free.

June contemplates this for a second before asking, "Okay. How do you get from Matteo to Val?"

"Arvali." I remind her of my last name as I fall onto my bed.

June cocks her head. "So then it's pronounced 'vol,' like volleyball?"

"No. It's *Val*." I scrub a hand across my face and mutter, "Val Kilmer."

"Those vowels don't even—"

"I don't know, June!" I snap. "How about you don't call me that, and then it doesn't fucking matter how the vowels are pronounced?"

"Touchy subject. Got it." She takes two steps toward the door. "Aren't you a little young for Val Kilmer?"

"No one's too young for Batman."

"Right," she'd said, unimpressed. Without another word, not even so much as a goodbye, June had shut off the lights in the basement and taken off up the stairs, out the front door, and into the night, leaving me alone to fall asleep before the alcohol had worn off.

And then I wake up this morning, alone again, feeling like shit in more ways than one, waiting for the nausea from the withdrawals to overpower the nausea from drinking all night. Soon, I'll have the answer to my stupid experiment, and then I can take a pill again.

Once the chills settle down the length of my spine and my arms feel jittery from my fingers to my shoulders, I know it's time to call it. Nine hours and thirty-six minutes. Not so bad.

My clothes from last night are thrown all around the room, which is often the case when I come home drunk. Frantically, I search for my jacket, throwing back the sheets and looking in drawers for the brilliant place I thought to stash it while inebriated. It's hung up in my closet, all the way in the back. The pill bottle is still in the pocket. A sigh of relief escapes my lips as I twist off the cap and pop my first pill of the day.

An angry pounding at my door makes me jump. I shove the pills back in my jacket, the jacket back into the closet, and listen, convinced that it was in my head. But then the knocking comes again, even louder.

"Cosaaaaa?" I whine. *Whaaaaat?*

"Svegliati!" the voice barks back. *Wake up!*

"Chris?" I mutter, surprised.

Equally surprising is that I have actually said that out loud. I thought the words stayed inside my head, but then Chris replies, "Who else? Get the fuck out here."

"Ostrega, un minuto!" I snap. *My God, one minute!*

"Be upstairs in three or I'm coming back down," Chris threatens.

And then what?

Chris is my brother. He lives over an hour away, so unless it's a holiday, he usually only shows up when I'm in trouble. Like after both my DUIs, and when Keelie kicked me out. He's happy to be the bad guy. Especially with me. Despite that, he's also gotten me out of a lot of bad situations recently. Namely, his connections kept me from going to jail. Twice. I'm not sure what it is this time, but judging by his tone, he's likely here to rescue me again.

My jeans are shoved completely under the bed when I find them. My shirt is hooked nicely on a knob of my dresser. The photo of Keelie and me is facedown from when June flipped it over last night. I stand it back upright. It's one of my favorite photos of us. Keelie stands behind me, her arms wrapped around my shoulders, and my head is turned to kiss her. We are frozen in time with huge laughing smiles plastered on our faces. The words *I love you, Val* scrawled across my shoulders. Looking at that photo makes me smile. After taking enough oxy, I can actually feel myself back in the joy of that moment.

Chris's heavy feet barrel down the steps. As I flip my shirt over my head, I fling open the door to keep him from pounding on it again. Upstairs, my parents sit together on the couch, a chair from the kitchen table pulled up nearby. Mom looks as though she's been crying. *Oh good, an intervention.* Chris tells me to sit down, and I reluctantly oblige, slouching down in my chair, crossing my arms over my chest, and digging my nails into the crawling skin of my left arm. *Ten more minutes.* If I could have had ten more minutes for this pill to kick in, this whole thing would be infinitely more bearable.

"Diglielo," Chris says to my parents. *Tell him.*

Mom immediately starts crying. My foot taps impatiently, waiting for them to get this over with. They'll tell me to stop; I'll agree and then cut back for a few weeks to show them I'm okay. We've been here before.

Then Mom whispers, "If you keep living like this, you're going to die. Do you understand that? We can't keep supporting you and your addiction. It's going to kill you." She's so painfully rehearsed. "You can't stay here anymore. I won't watch you kill yourself."

She knows full well how deeply a phrase like "kill yourself" burns me. She chose that phrase intentionally, knowing it would make me think of Rich.

"Non possiamo aiutarti, Matteo," Dad echoes her thoughts. "Non più." *We can't help you, Matteo. Not anymore.*

"So what?" I snap back, a light laugh twisting through my response. "I can't live here, so you want me to go live on the streets?"

"If that's what you want." Chris takes over the conversation.

"No," I mumble back my reply.

"That's good," he assures me, clapping a firm hand onto my back, which feels more like a harsh slap than a comforting grasp. "Then you're going to come stay with me."

I laugh at him. "I'm not moving to Elmwood." I turn back to Mom and repeat the same thing I've said a thousand times. "I can stop, Ma. *I will.*"

"That's not how it's going to work this time, Matteo," Chris cuts in, slapping my back again, this time so hard it makes me wince. "My car leaves in twenty minutes and you're either in it or you're not, but you're not allowed to stay here anymore."

Mom sucks in a sharp breath of air, as if Chris's words prick in her side. She won't meet my eyes. I plant both my feet firmly on the ground, jumping out of my chair and storming off back to the basement.

"Twenty minutes!" Chris yells after me.

The soft, fuzzy effects of my first pill kick in as I run down the stairs. Perfect timing, as always. When I yank my jacket out of the closet by its sleeve, the pill bottle rattles as it hits against my leg. I twist off the cap and tap more pills into my hand. I want to feel numb to all of this. Numb to the change, numb to the disappointment. Blissfully unaware of all the expectations I once had and how far I've strayed from that version of myself. I throw back two pills. Forty-five milligrams pulsing through my bloodstream should be enough to erase all of this.

Crouching on the floor, I dig an old duffel bag out from under the bed. *Arvali* is embroidered on the side of it, along with the numbers *02*, a remnant from when I was an athlete. Those days are long behind me.

I shove whatever clothes will fit into the bag, unconcerned with what I'm packing and whether any of it will be of any use at all. All I'm concerned with is jamming enough stuff inside to protect the things I really need to pack: a large bottle of cheap bourbon and my stash of oxy.

I don't know where I'm going to go, but I can't go to Elmwood. There's nothing for me there; although there isn't anything for me *here* either. Most of my friends have moved far away. My best friend, Josh, is in Los Angeles. His sister Lex lives in New York. Our friend Jess moved back to Cleveland. Even my sister lives in North Carolina now. With Keelie and her family out of my life, the only friend I've got left here is June. If I can even call her a friend at all.

Maybe I could move in with June for a bit, at least until I get back on my feet. But the thought of spending any more time with June is repulsive. I got to know what a great relationship felt like when I was with Keelie, and whatever is going on with June definitely isn't that. I'm not sure I want her help anyway; I'd hate to *owe her* anymore than I already do.

In my top dresser drawer, I dig out the only pair of red socks I've ever owned, balled up and shoved all the way in the back. A layer of sock hides a pill bottle with my name on it, allowing me to pass it off as a prescription in a pinch. Two pills rattle around inside. One is an extended-release eighty-milligram tablet; the other is a bright yellow forty-milligram tablet I've been saving for a special occasion. *This might be the day.* I tap them both out into my hand and shove them in my pocket, then pour the bottle from June into the one with my name on it. Before putting the lid back on, I tap out three more pills into my hand and shove those into my pockets, too. Just in case. Rolling the pill bottle back inside the red socks, I shove this bundle deep into my duffel bag, hidden far from sight.

The photo of me and Keelie draws my eyes one last time. The pills boost the buzzing feeling this photo gives me. Overwhelming joy takes over my brain. No matter where I go, this photo is a necessity. Placing it gently on top of everything in the duffel bag, I give it one last longing look before zipping it inside.

By the time I'm done packing, I can hardly feel the ground beneath my feet. My hands grip tightly onto the railing as I float back upstairs. I don't say goodbye to my parents on my way out the door. I don't even think to. My floating takes me to the front porch step. There I take in a hearty breath of fresh air, and then another. Every breath that fills my lungs feels like the most refreshing air I've ever tasted. A smile creeps across my face for no reason at all, just because once again, it actually feels good to be alive.

Out here, everything becomes crystal clear. I don't have to give up the pills. I have enough to last me a while, and I'll keep them hidden from Chris. Once I run low, I can figure out what I'm going to do next. I'll figure out how to get more, I'll figure out where else to live.

Chris comes striding out a few minutes later, jumping into his car and starting up his engine without saying a word to me. My body swirls as I build up enough momentum to stand and follow him. The driveway keeps rotating long after my body is vertical, and I lean sideways to counteract the rotation. I lean so far, I bump right into Chris's SUV. It takes a few swatting attempts for my hand to find the door handle, and when I make contact and yank it open, the door gives me a hearty shove backward, sending the driveway back into orbit around me.

My feet are as heavy as two cement blocks. They might as well be a part of the driveway, too. I can't lift them high enough to reach the step up into the tall vehicle. Instead I place each knee on the step, gripping one hand tightly onto the center console and the other onto the edge of the door to propel myself into the car. When I land, the duffel bag wedges between me and the seat, the bourbon bottle stabbing into my ribcage.

"You can put that in the back if you want," Chris offers without asking for any explanation about my decision to join him.

My eyes hardly stay open, but I turn to him anyway, crinkling my brow in confusion.

"Your duffel bag," he clarifies.

I shake my head a few times, twisting the bag back to my front and hugging it tightly to my chest, settling down into the soft leather seats.

With a heavy sigh, I mumble out, "This feels amazing." I settle even further into it, feeling it hug my sides. I fumble with the handle on the side of the chair to recline it back.

Chris glances at me out of the side of his eye and lets out a pitying laugh. "How much did you take this morning?"

"Just enough," I reply with a blissful sigh.

"How much?" he repeats himself, a little more forcefully.

"Forty-five."

"How much do you have left?"

"That was the last of it." I blink slowly and turn back to staring out the window.

Chris laughs again, much more friendly this time. "Bugiardo del cazzo." *Fucking liar.*

My mouth isn't able to reply. My brain isn't able to form words. I can think only about this soft leather seat. We ride in silence. I blink hard to focus on the road ahead of us, my eyes searching for the skyline, trying to make out buildings in the distance. I do anything I can to hold my focus in the present, to prevent myself from nodding off, but no matter what I do, this perfectly formfitting leather chair calls me to relax deeply, and I slowly float away.

It feels as if with one blink, the car is suddenly stopped, and Chris is shaking me awake from the passenger-side door. I pry open my eyes, and Chris's small country home stares back at me.

He presses the seat belt release for me and pulls my arm free. My vision pulses. My eyes aren't able to focus on anything. The world around me is a complete blur, until they finally settle on Chris's face. His angry look has softened.

He taps my hand a few times and then says slowly and deliberately, "I need you to get up. I'll help you. Grab on." He pats my hand once more until I understand and latch onto his hand. He wraps my arm around his shoulder and taps my leg a few times. "Standing, okay? We're going to stand up."

"I know how to fucking stand," I sputter back at him, using the arm that was draped around his shoulders to push him away.

He takes a step back. I grab the handle on the car's ceiling to hoist myself up. My foot slowly taps around in the air, searching for the step. My body twists around awkwardly as I find the footing to step out of the car. The world around me spins when my feet hit the ground. I take a few hard blinks, willing my swaying vision to snap back into focus. Chris tugs on my arm to steady me. I take a couple of shuffling steps, my feet kicking up dust from his gravel driveway.

Each of my eyes functions independently of the other. There are two driveways, two houses, two sets of stairs, two front doors. As I walk forward, I don't know which version of the world in front of me to aim for. The ground has seemingly vanished from beneath my feet. There's no feeling left in my legs. It's hard to tell whether I'm walking on my own, or if I'm being lifted and carried into the house by Chris. It becomes painfully obvious that I'm doing my own walking when my toe smashes into the step at his front porch and my body flies forward. Chris catches my fall, preventing my collapsing body from making contact with the ground before I even recognize I'm falling.

"Rallentiamo, va bene?" *Let's slow down, okay?* Chris says, taking a handful of fabric from my jeans, right above my kneecap, and lifting my leg high enough to find the next step. He's twice my size; he'd be better off carrying me up these stairs. My mouth twitches as I attempt to form the words to say just that, but no sound comes out.

He grabs another handful of fabric from my other leg and hoists it up onto the next step. My feet feel like rocks. My duffel bag is weighing me down. If I could take the bag off my shoulders, I could make it up these stairs on my own. I pull my arm off Chris and tug at the strap, but Chris snatches my arm and wraps it back around his shoulder.

"Come on, Matteo," he says kindly, bouncing slightly to shift my grip higher across his back.

"Merrvaluof faa," I mumble out in reply.

"What?" Chris asks. But I've already completely lost the thought. *What was I trying to say?*

Chris opens the screen door, leans his body against it to hold it open, then pushes open the front door and guides me inside. I'm completely lost in the entryway. I have fallen so deeply into the tunnel vision, I can't figure out where I am. Chris grips a hand onto each of my shoulders and leads me into the room on the right, allowing me to collapse into a large recliner tucked into one corner.

"Sleep it off," he instructs, but before he gets the chance to finish his words, my mind is already nodding off to sleep.

When I wake up, Chris is sitting on the couch on the opposite side of the room from me. He has his head down, reading a book. The house is quiet. Everything is quiet. It's so eerie.

"Where is everyone?" I ask, coughing to clear my throat after my words can barely escape.

Chris lifts his head, surprised to see me conscious. "Staying with Michelle's parents for a few days while you get settled in."

He has a wife and two young daughters. Chris doesn't let me see them anymore. It's been at least a year since I've seen Michelle, and probably at least two since I've seen my nieces.

"Why?" I ask in place of my real question, which is *How long do they plan on avoiding me while I'm living in their house?*

He shakes his head in disbelief. "Are you really asking me that? You know what you're in for."

I have an entire stash of pills in my bag and five more in my pocket. It will be a few weeks before I have to worry about withdrawals.

Then, ominously, he asks again, "How much do you have on you right now?"

I throw my head back and recline in the chair, muttering, "I told you, I don't have any more."

He stands, holding a hand out to me, nodding his head toward the kitchen. I take his hand reluctantly, allowing him to pull me out of the chair. He takes off for the kitchen, expecting me to follow. The thought of lying back down and ignoring him crosses my mind, but I've already made it past the point of being able to fall back to sleep, so I follow him.

Chris sits down at the kitchen table and motions for me to do the same. I slump down on the chair across from him, forehead braced in the palm of my hand, elbow stabbed into the table. After taking a moment to get grounded, I let out another huge exhale and meet his eyes.

He stares at me for a second before repeating, "How much do you have?"

"How many times are you going to ask me that?" I snap. "I don't have any more *fucking* pills."

He slams a pill bottle down on the table, bolting me upright. He presses it between his fingers and the table, the old worn-out label with my name on it staring back at me.

"Here's a tip for you, Matteo." His stare burns through me. "It's a lot easier to hide something when you're conscious."

My eyes snap to the duffel bag, which I had ditched at the front door, then turns back to him with a glare.

"Bourbon's gone, too. Dumped it. It was terrible shit anyway. No loss there."

I hold his stare, burning with anger. My foot is twitching uncontrollably under the table. I can't tell whether it's the beginning of withdrawals or the rage building up inside me. But either way, it gets faster and faster and faster as I stew over what to say. Finally, I settle on the only thing I can think of.

"Are we done?" I snap at him, childishly.

"For now," he growls back. "Come find me when you start feeling sick."

I retrieve my bag from the front door, casually placing a hand on my front pocket as subtly as I can to feel the pills still hiding there. I have five pills to get me through this. Slinging my bag over my shoulder, I turn to Chris for directions, and he points a finger down the hall on the first floor. I don't wait around for him to say anything else, striding off confidently toward his point, searching for a room that looks unoccupied.

Once inside, I close the door almost all the way shut, but not far enough that it latches, the same way I would at Mom and Dad's. The kind of silent movements that make it easy to disappear.

I dig the pills out of my pocket and count them all. One green-coated tablet, *OC 80*. One bright yellow tablet, *OP 40*. Three beautiful little green tablets, all with the familiar bold *M* on one side and a small *15* on the other. My happy little family.

I toss the duffel bag on the bed and unzip it. The photo of Keelie and me is still at the top. I place it next to the lamp on the side table, then carefully line all the pills up behind the photo, where they can hide in plain sight. Everything else stays in the duffel bag, which I toss onto the floor. I don't intend to unpack it.

Still feeling the soft, buzzy remnants of the pills from earlier, I gaze at the photo of the two of us and smile. This one photo makes me crave a look at more of the memories we've created together. I tap open the photo app on my phone and search through all the albums of the places we've been and the things we've done. I flip to a video from when we hiked to the top of Forney Ridge Trail in the Great Smoky Mountains. The video took a panoramic sweep of the colors shifting in the sky at sunrise, the low mountains turning bright shades of maroon in the distance. The end of the video reveals the edge of Keelie's face as she turns to look at me. With her face glowing with pure, unwavering awe, she smiles and says, "This is absolutely incredible."

My throat catches as I choke back tears. Suddenly, I don't feel so blissfully happy anymore, but I still crave another look. I want to hear her voice again, to hear her laugh again. I flip through every video I have, settling on one from college when we were at a house party with friends. She's singing along to a song she hardly knows the words to, her favorite song she assures me. Then she reaffirms this to the camera when she realizes my phone is out. "My favorite!" She sings along again, completely flubbing the words. She buries her face in her hands and lets out the tiniest snort, a sound that melts my heart in an instant, and then the loudest, drunken belly laugh.

I watch it once more as a large lump takes form in my throat. It makes it hard for me to swallow, chokes me. Tears well up in my eyes and a heavy weight settles in on my chest, crushing my lungs and making it even harder to breathe. Every breath I take is shallow and empty. My heart rate rises in panic. I can't catch my breath. I sit up in bed, the video still stuck playing on a loop, driving me deeper into this billowing cloud of anxiety.

I hold my breath for a moment, pressing my tongue to the roof of my mouth, taking a deep breath in through my nose into the back of my throat. The air doesn't get far. My throat clenches tightly shut. I exhale the small bit of air and repeat the process.

The chemical taste of oxy pings my tongue, reminding me another pill is the calming boost I need to get out of this panic attack.

This could be so much easier with one more pill.

But I know I shouldn't. Not yet. I can do this. I can breathe. It's one of the few things in life I can still do. Just breathe. Inhaling another deep breath into the back of my throat, more air sneaks in this time. Even more comes in the breath after that.

Panic attacks aren't new to me. I've been having them for years. Fourteen years. They were better when Keelie was around to comfort me. They were better when I actually took antianxiety medication. But they're also better when I take oxycodone, at least for a few hours.

The panic gets worse once the oxy wears off. So much worse. And it gets worse when I think about Keelie. It's worse when I think about failure. It's worse when my brain cycles through the endlessly crushing thoughts that fill my head. After fourteen years, I have simply accepted that panic and spiraling thoughts are a part of my life. All I can do now is take pills to try to make it more bearable.

Three Years Ago

Thursday, December 31st

"Someone's here!" I yelled out to Keelie after the knock on the door.

"I'll be out in three minutes!" she hollered back.

Anxiety pulsed through me as I hesitated to answer. My stomach dropped. I hated making small talk; it didn't matter who was on the other side of the door. Starting a conversation with anyone without Keelie there made me anxious. She was the people person, and I was the one who made smart jokes and otherwise tried to be invisible.

I patted my front pocket, feeling the three round pills stashed inside. They were supposed to be for later, but I could really use a bit of their calmness now. Just knowing that one would kick in soon would be enough to lower my blood pressure, allowing me to relax long enough for Keelie to join us.

Fishing one out of my pocket, I took a second to admire the small pink pill. *K 56* etched into its surface. Ten milligrams of oxycodone—enough to make the first part of this night better. This party was for Keelie, not me. Ever since we moved into our first apartment together, she'd been talking about hosting a New Year's Eve party with our friends. This was our fifth year living together, our second apartment together, but the first time we'd been able to make it work.

I didn't want to have this party. I'm not a fan of being a host. And Keelie knows that, which is why she'd never been too pushy about it. But this year, I owed her so much. I relapsed twice this year, and I haven't had the guts to tell her I've started taking pills again for a third time. Not all the time, it's not a full relapse. Just occasional use. Like during New Year's Eve parties.

I ground the pill up between my teeth and swallowed the chemical powder as I answered the door, the grit still lingering in the back of my throat. Our friend Jess was on the other side, a bottle of booze in each hand.

"Happy New Year, Matty!" she shouted. Jess has been a friend of ours since we were fourteen. Eighth grade. Her family moved to St. Louis six months after Rich died. She was the first person who cluelessly asked why Keelie and I got a sympathetic free pass from practically every teacher in school. The first person we had to explain things to.

"Hey!" I yelled back at her excitedly, making note of the guy standing beside her who I knew was Dan, but hadn't met yet.

Jess leaned in to give me a quick kiss on the cheek, pressing a bottle of alcohol along each of my arms as she did. "This is Dan."

"Matty," I replied, careful to break it up into two distinct syllables, *Mat-tee*, so that he didn't decide it was okay to call me *Matt*. I extended a hand to him. "It's good to finally meet you."

Jess had been dating Dan for just over a year, ever since she moved to Cleveland. She was back in town only for a short amount of time, spending the holidays with her family and introducing him to everyone important to her. Jess coming to town had really sent Keelie buzzing to make plans to host a party this year.

"Keelie will be right out." I nodded in her direction down the hallway as I shut the door behind them.

"I'm here!" Keelie shouted back at us, emerging a moment later from our room at the end. She yelled out "Jess!" as she met the eyes of our old friend.

Jess tossed the booze into my arms and ran to greet Keelie, diving into a hug and rocking back and forth excitedly in each other's arms and mumbling "I've missed you so much" into each other's ears. I eyed up the labels on the alcohol bottles. One was my favorite kind of wine, a Chianti, which I knew Jess had picked out intentionally. The other one was—

"Jess says you guys really like bourbon," Dan offered as a conversation starter. "I'm more of a beer guy myself, but I've heard this one is fantastic."

I read over the other label. It was scotch, but I raised the bottle toward him in appreciation anyway.

"Thanks, Dan," I said. "We've got tons of beer in the fridge if you want one, or we could crack this open right now if you're curious to try it."

I was hoping he would say yes to a glass of scotch so I could have some for myself. I didn't love scotch, but I'd gladly accept any opportunity for a quicker, alcohol-fueled assist to ease into conversations with strangers.

"A beer would be great," he said, rejecting the latter offer.

I pointed him toward the fridge, and with a smile said, "Help yourself. No strangers here."

Before he could grab a drink, Keelie approached, jumping at him with a warm and friendly hug. "Dan, I'm so glad you could make it!" she said excitedly. "We've heard so much about you!"

She jumped into conversation with him like it was nothing, because for Keelie, it *was* nothing. I admired how easily she could talk to someone she had only just met, how easily she remembered small details about him from conversations she had with Jess over the past year. I wished Keelie would have given him time to find a beer before they started talking though, so that I wouldn't have to be the first one to start drinking.

"Do you guys want to toss your coats in our room?" Keelie offered.

Jess nodded, showing Dan the way.

Keelie turned to me with a huge smile. She let out a big exhale. Excitement radiated off her. While I was less than thrilled about having so many people piled into our apartment, I loved seeing Keelie like this. She was in her element, and the happiness that sprung from her was enough to make me feel slightly better about this party. Keelie's enthusiasm mixed with the calming sensation of the pills to create a euphoria that simmered inside me.

I placed my hands on Keelie's hips, brushing a thumb against the soft fabric of her billowy, low-cut shirt. I would absolutely steal more than a few glances down that shirt throughout the course of the evening, but right now I couldn't take my eyes off her glowing smile. The way the corner of her mouth curled with enthusiasm, the way her lips parted to reveal her teeth, the way creases formed in the corners of her eyes.

Pressing my forehead against Keelie's, I whispered, "Mia, you look amazing."

She grasped my forearms tightly, giving each a squeeze and then inching her hand under the edge of my shirt to trace a line with her thumb along my hip bone. She closed her eyes as she melted into this moment.

As I was about to kiss her, Jess's voice came echoing around the corner. "This place looks so great, you guys!" she shouted. "I think the last time I was here you only had the couch."

Keelie gave my arms one last squeeze, a disappointed smirk spreading across her face. She whispered, "Midnight," and then turned her attention to Jess.

One word was all I needed to understand everything she was thinking. That's the beauty of being with someone for so long. After nine years of being in love with Keelie, I could easily crawl into her thoughts.

No matter how chaotic tonight gets, we can still look forward to our midnight kiss.

There was another loud knock at the door, but without waiting for it to be answered, Keelie's brother Sam stepped inside.

"Just me!" he called out. I let out a heavy sigh of relief. Sam's arrival and the soft buzz from the pills meant I could finally relax and enjoy this party.

"Where's Brooke?" Keelie demanded as her brother approached without his girlfriend in tow.

"She'll stop by later. She had another party with her friends," Sam replied, "but I told her I didn't want to miss New Year's with you guys." He turned to me with a sly look on his face and whispered, "Also, I didn't want to go."

I raised an eyebrow at him knowingly. Sam also wasn't particularly fond of meeting new people, so we tried to stick together at parties like this one, staying out of sight as much as possible. Sam passed a friendly wave to Jess, introduced himself to Dan, and begrudgingly accepted an enormous hug from Keelie.

Without waiting for small talk to begin, Sam made a beeline for the fridge, where he immediately cracked open a beer and passed it straight to me. I graciously accepted it with a huge gulp. He opened a second one for himself, taking a drink and then placing it on the counter. Then he offered one up to Keelie, only opening it for her after she accepted.

Sam pointed to Jess and Dan next. "Beer?"

Dan accepted, but Jess pointed to a bottle of wine we had on the counter.

"Moog! Bust open the wine, will ya?" Sam shouted at me. "It's only a party once Sam shows up, huh? Come on, guys, let's go!"

More people filtered in as the night went on. Friends from Keelie's work. Jess's friends. Friends I hadn't seen in so long that they felt more like acquaintances. There were at least thirty people crammed into our cozy apartment, and I only knew a handful of them. The rest were small talk waiting to happen. I took another drink of beer and reminded myself how happy it made Keelie that we finally did this.

It was encroaching on ten o'clock, and Sam's girlfriend still hadn't shown up. Sam approached with two plastic cups and handed one to me.

"This scotch is terrible," he said, tapping his cup to mine for a cheers. "Drink up."

The heavy, peaty taste lingered in my mouth far too long for my liking, but I replied that it wasn't so bad to ensure that Sam would bring me another one.

"Where's Brooke?" I asked, now that we were far from the prying ears of his sister.

"I don't think it's going to work out" was the only information he offered. Sam was very selective about what he shared, even with me and Keelie. He'd tell us eventually, but it had to be on his terms. Pushing him for more information before he was ready made him push back harder.

"More scotch then?" I asked, releasing him from his fear of further questioning.

"That should do the trick."

I threw back the rest of what was in my cup and handed it off to him as he left to get more.

I looked out at the room full of people. After taking a second pill, I was having a hard time keeping my focus on any one of them. The whole room swayed slightly. Everyone's features were fuzzy, as though everyone was moving past me too quickly, and I was sitting watching them all buzz by in a blur. But when Keelie caught my eye, I could make her out as if she were the only one in the room. I smiled at her, maybe a bit too big of a smile, and she laughed to poke fun at me for having too much to drink.

"Hey," she leaned into me, wrapping her arms around my neck and sitting across my legs. I placed one hand low on her back, the other gripping the inside of her thigh, leaning my face even closer to hers, our noses hovering right at the edge of a kiss. But as I was about to press my lips to hers, she got a whiff of my breath and pulled back slightly, laughing in surprise. "Are you guys drinking scotch?"

"Sam's getting us more right now if you want to try some," I slurred.

She nodded, then pressing her forehead to mine, she asked, "Could you go grab a game out of the closet?"

"Which one?"

"Whichever one will get you and Sam to stop hanging out over here and come join the party." Then she whispered, "Pick one that will let me be on your team."

My entire body pulsed toward her in a quick twitch. Even a few inches was too much space between us. As my hand inched further up her thigh, she brushed her thumb softly behind my ear, melting me into her. She was so completely irresistible, I had to—

"Gross," Sam yelled out with a smile, jarring our attention and jolting us apart. He shoved the refilled plastic cup in my face, and I immediately passed it to Keelie for a taste. She wrinkled her nose as she drank it and then coughed out a quiet "nope."

Keelie kept her eyes fixed on me as she slowly stood up. The slight crinkle in her nose made me want to put my hands all over her. Would anyone notice if we disappeared for a few minutes?

"Midnight," she whispered to me apologetically, nodding her head back toward the party.

Sam returned to his spot on the chair next to me. I threw a light tap against his shoulder and said, "Don't sit. Keelie wants us to pick out a game."

I jumped up, placing my hand on the back of Keelie's head and pulling her toward me. With my lips pressed to her forehead, I returned her promise in a soft grumble, "Midnight," before leading Sam to our room, where we kept the games.

Throwing open the closet door, I said, "Top shelf. Whatever you want to play." I flopped down onto our bed as the room spun around me. No matter which game Sam picked, Keelie *would* be on my team. I'd be sure of that.

Sam stared into my closet for a long time before I realized he wasn't looking at the games. He turned around slowly, narrowing his eyes at me, his look burning into me furiously.

A nervous laugh escaped my lips. "What?"

He plunged a hand into a pocket of one of my jackets hanging in the back of my closet. My stomach lurched. I knew what he found. Sam flipped the pill bottle in his hand to inspect the label. The name on the bottle was mine, but the prescription was dated almost ten years ago. He unscrewed the lid and peered down his nose to the contents inside. As he suspected, it was full.

"Thought you were done with these," he grumbled.

I nodded. "I am. I only take them when I need them."

"Which is when, exactly?"

"Hardly ever," I promised, even though we both knew that was a lie.

"Tonight?"

I nodded cautiously. "Before everyone started showing up." It didn't feel necessary to mention the second one I had taken an hour ago.

He copied my nod, understanding what I meant. "And one more tomorrow to help with the hangover, maybe another tomorrow afternoon when you're still feeling shitty, another tomorrow night to help you sleep . . ." He smiled sarcastically. "I get the idea."

"Not that often," I offered in a whisper, "but usually to help me sleep."

He took a slow, menacing drink from his scotch, and without looking at me, he asked, "Does Keelie know?"

His face was hard for me to focus on, but his fury was unmistakable.

"Yes," I lied again, hoping that by saying so he wouldn't feel the need to tell Keelie about it.

He stared at me for a moment longer before returning the bottle back to the jacket pocket where he found it. A silent sigh of relief escaped my lips.

"Let's do that one," he said, pointing to a game on the very top of the stacks.

I nodded, grateful he was willing to drop it, even if it was only for the moment. I set my drink on the side table and retrieved the game. He didn't wait for me before bolting out of the room.

Sam stayed close to me for the rest of the night out of habit, but the conversations were much stiffer after that. He stopped offering to grab me drinks, and when I offered to grab him one, he declined, as if proving he had more self-control than I did. I brushed it off, but then thought better of it. Maybe I should show a bit more restraint. I blinked a few times, trying to force my eyes to focus. The drinks were going to my head. The drinks *and the pills* were going to my head. Tunnel vision settled in. I couldn't see anything I wasn't directly and intently looking at. I could hardly focus on anything at all.

It was almost midnight. Keelie had bottles of prosecco and plastic champagne flutes that she wanted to pass out. She popped open a bottle, letting out a little yelp as the cork jumped out, laughing to herself as she handed me the bottle. I used all my energy to focus on the lip of the bottle and the rim of the glass, making sure the two were perfectly aligned before pouring.

"Matty!" she cried out with another laugh, noticing before I did that prosecco poured across my hand. She snatched a towel, wiping it up before I even had time to react. "You're drunk," she teased, leaning in close to me.

"Sorry." I frowned.

Once the icy coolness of the prosecco touched my hand, chills overtook my whole body. I felt a tugging at my chest that felt like anxiety but quickly grew into the familiar swell of nausea, which would soon hitch its way out of my stomach.

I ran for the bathroom and shut the door, not turning the light on. The light would make it worse. It would give my eyes the chance to focus on the things in the room that were spinning around me. It was better when I wasn't able to see.

Tossing up the toilet seat, I heaved out the contents of my stomach. I hadn't eaten anything all night, afraid to let anything mess with my buzz. That might have been a mistake. As our friends began their countdown to midnight, I heaved into the toilet once more. Time didn't wait for us. *Midnight* didn't wait for us.

Lifting my gaze caused the room to spin, so instead I stretched my arm across the cold porcelain bowl and rested my forehead against it, keeping my eyes fixed on the water below me.

A light knock vibrated against the door. "Val?" Keelie whispered as she cracked it open. She flipped the lights on as she crept inside, softly closing the door behind her. She sat down on the edge of the bathtub behind me, stroking a hand across my back.

"What time is it?" I grumbled into the toilet bowl, already knowing the answer would be a disappointment to us both.

"Twelve ten," she sighed back.

"I'm sorry, Mia. I shouldn't have had all that scotch."

After a long, agonizing pause, Keelie whispered back, "Sam told me about the pills. What happened, Val?"

What she wanted to ask was, *What the hell is wrong with you? Why are you taking pills again?* I chewed on the inside of my lip, hoping the pain of each bite could bring me closer to sobriety. I wouldn't be able to have this conversation with Keelie if I couldn't get my focus back.

Tears welled up in my eyes, then spilled out until I was full-on sobbing on the bathroom floor. Embarrassed, mostly. Ashamed I got caught. I buried my face in her knee, and she placed a hand on the back of my head. Even when she was undeniably furious with me, she was still kind.

"Mia, I'm so sorry," I mumbled through tears.

She didn't reply, allowing her silence to echo the hurt she was feeling. The pain I caused her. That's the trouble with being with someone for so long. Even when she didn't say anything at all, I could still hear each and every horrible thought pulsing through her mind. *You've ruined this again. You're so unbelievably infuriating. You are such a disappointment to me.*

"Are you feeling better now?" she asked impatiently, burying everything that was going on inside her head.

I nodded, slowly lifting my gaze to meet hers.

"Do you want to go lie down?" she offered.

I shook my head. "No, I'll come back out so we can play that game. Just give me a minute, okay?"

She kissed me on the top of my head and stood to leave. "Light on or off?"

"On is fine," I croaked. Then she was gone, and I was alone.

I stuck to drinking water for the rest of the night, doing the best I could to sober up so I could have a clear enough mind to talk to Keelie whenever she was ready. She swallowed up her emotions horrifyingly efficiently. She didn't let any of our friends in on what was going on. Even Jess, who knows all about my previous relapses, was left clueless enough to make a joke about me having too much fun at the party. I agreed with her, laughing at her assessment, trying my hardest not to give any indication that I had something to hide. Trying my hardest to cover up my secret from as many people as I could.

The next morning, my mouth was so dry I had to peel my tongue off my teeth. There was a dull, throbbing headache building in my temples. My eye sockets felt bruised. I shuffled out of bed and dug around in my closet for the pill bottle hiding in my jacket pocket, stopping when I remembered Sam predicted this would happen.

I released the pill bottle and took a few steps toward the door, not wanting to prove him right, but then I doubled back, fixing my eyes on my closet. If they're already going to assume that I've taken a pill, what will I prove by *not* taking one? Digging the bottle out of my jacket pocket once again, I tapped one pink pill into the palm of my hand, chewing it up before swallowing it.

Keelie was brewing a pot of coffee in the kitchen when I emerged from the hallway. I wrapped an arm around her waist and gave her a kiss on the top of her shoulder. She glanced my way as she closed the water chamber of the coffeemaker and pressed the Start button. She spun around where she stood, turning to face me, leaning against the counter and smiling at me as if she was never mad at all.

"How long has this been going on, Val?" Keelie whispered so softly that I could hardly hear her words, even standing only a few inches from their source.

"A couple weeks," I lied, only because I was ashamed that the actual answer was a couple of *months*, and she thought I had been *off* them for three months. I hadn't lied when I told Sam I wasn't taking them that often, though. Twenty or thirty milligrams a day at most—and that wasn't even every day of the week. I was a long way from where I was before, but I knew that *balanced* was not what Keelie thought I should be aiming for. Still, I felt good about this usage. I decided when I wanted to take them, and I could decide when I didn't want to take them. I was in control. She just didn't understand the difference. She didn't understand what it felt like to be in control or to be out of control. To her, it all looked the same, but this time, for me, it was a choice. I was going to make better decisions. I was going to keep pills in my life, but I wouldn't let them take over. I could do this.

"Why didn't you tell me?" she whispered.

"I didn't want you to worry," I assured her. "I'm in control of this, Mia. I'm taking care of it."

She studied me skeptically. "How, exactly?" With that question, her voice was a little firmer, a little less kind and soft.

"How am I in control? Or how—"

"How are you taking care of it?" She bit her teeth into her bottom lip. Her voice sounded calm, but her cocked head and wide eyes told a different story.

I brushed a hand along her hairline, settling in with a cupped hand against her cheek. Then, in the most sincere, calm, loving voice I could muster, I lied right to her face. "I've got an appointment with my doctor next week," I promised her. "Thursday at two," I doubled down.

She let out a soft laugh, like maybe she *had* gotten a little too worked up about all of this.

I pressed my forehead to hers. "I told you, I'm taking care of it. I didn't want you to worry about me for nothing."

She brushed her thumb along my side, reminding me, "We don't keep secrets from each other."

"I'm sorry," I answered quickly. "Now you know though, okay?"

"Can I come with you?"

"On Thursday?"

She nodded.

"If you want to," I replied confidently. Far too confident for someone who had a fake doctor's appointment. Then I whispered softly, "We know everything they're going to say, right? Not much point in us both being there. But you can come if you want to."

"At least let me drop you off."

"That'd be great," I conceded. "We can check out that coffee shop they put in down the street afterward."

"It's a date." She raised a flirty eyebrow at me, but then her expression settled on something a bit more suspicious. "Can I see your appointment confirmation?"

I laughed casually, as if I didn't know why she was asking for that, as if it was an absurd question to ask. "You don't believe me," I stated as an accusation.

"I want to believe you," she pleaded.

I smiled at her suggestively, leaning in close to her, my cheek against hers, my mouth whispering into her ear, "Then believe me." I pulled away, my eyes fixed on her lips, set on flirting my way out of this line of questioning.

Her eyes glistened as she held my gaze. I thought my distraction tactic was working, but as she wrapped one arm around my neck, softly brushing at my hairline, I realized she was throwing that move right back at me. *I see what you're doing, and it's not going to work.*

"Show me the confirmation," she said firmly.

"Come on," I begged. "Why do you need that?"

"You know why," she spoke harshly.

I let out a long, heavy sigh. "Look at me," I said, widening my eyes at her. "I'm not high. I've got no reason to lie to you. I need you to trust me."

The bubbly calm of oxy that settled into my body at that moment helped me feel less horrible about lying, or rather, made me feel less bad to be lying about lying. *Everything is fine. Everything is good. Keelie trusts me. Keelie believes me.*

But that blissful feeling came crashing to a halt. "Show me your appointment confirmation and we can drop this."

"No," I stammered. "Why can't you trust me on this? What the hell do I have to do? I go three months without pills, and I have one slip up, and suddenly I'm not *trustworthy* again? How long are you going to keep punishing me?"

Deflect. Avoid. Reroute. I expertly turned any conversation around. Dispersed any blame, no matter how well deserved it might have been. Avoided all accusations that called my decisions into question.

Keelie's expression dropped. She had a frown so long on her face it looked almost unnatural. She saw right through me, and it pained her I wouldn't admit it.

"If you don't have an appointment confirmation to show me by this time tomorrow, I'll call your doctor myself, alright?" Her low, threatening grumble sent her message loud and clear: *I'm not fucking around. Stop trying to lie your way out of this.*

"Okay." I admitted defeat, my whole body deflated. "I'll call this afternoon."

Her lips tightened into a small, thin line. Her mouth almost disappeared entirely. She had been hoping I was telling the truth, but instead she confirmed her suspicion that I was a liar.

And I was a liar the next day, too, when I tried to convince her again that I had booked an appointment when I still hadn't. She called my bluff immediately, and as soon as I tried to fight her on showing her the confirmation, she pulled out her phone, dialed my doctor's office, and put it on speakerphone.

"BHN Counseling Services, this is Cara," the chipper voice on the other end answered.

"Hey, Cara, this is Matteo Arvali. I'm calling to make an appointment with Dr. Neals."

"Hi, Matty. While I get your account pulled up, can you answer a few questions for me?"

"I am not feeling depressed or having suicidal thoughts, I am not experiencing the symptoms of an overdose, and I know that if I were experiencing either of these things I should hang up and dial 9-1-1."

Keelie rolled her eyes at me, not amused, but the small smile that cracked across her face soon after suggested otherwise.

"You're making my job easy today, aren't you?" Cara replied kindly. "How soon would you like to come in?"

"Do you have anything available Thursday at two?" I asked, not letting my voice betray the silent laugh that blossomed across my face as Keelie gave me a soft slug to the shoulder.

"Sure, I can get you in with Dr. Neals on Thursday, the seventh, at two."

"Thanks, Cara. I'll see you then."

Keelie glared at me as I hung up. "You probably could have gotten in sooner than Thursday."

"Probably," I replied smugly.

My phone chimed with the sound of a text message. I turned my phone to Keelie to reveal a text confirming my appointment.

"I'll still take you, if you want," Keelie offered, "and then we can get coffee afterward."

"That'd be really great, Mia."

We lay outstretched on the soft rug in the center of our living room. Keelie held a hand out to me, and I held on to it with a tight squeeze.

"What happened, Val?" she asked me again.

I rolled over onto my back, stretching out my arm, inviting her to lie on my chest. She curled up into the crook of my arm, one hand resting against my sternum, the other pressed to the top of my shoulder. I took a deep breath, breathing in the soft smell of coconut that always lingered in her hair.

"I don't know," I sighed. "I've been worried about going back to school, I guess."

She tilted her head to look up at me. "What's your real reason?"

I laughed. "What? That's not a good enough reason?"

"Maybe it is for someone, but that's not what's going through your head."

"Okay," I gave in. "I've been spiraling about all the amazing things you've been doing. And I feel like I keep falling further and further behind in life. I don't think that finishing my degree is going to help me get any further ahead, and I'm afraid I'm always going to be stuck right where I am."

Keelie took a long moment to contemplate this answer. So long that it started to make me analyze the things I had said, trying to find the point where I said something I shouldn't have.

"So don't go back to school," she suggested, like the solution was obvious.

"And then what?"

She propped herself up on her elbow so she could look me in the eyes. "Matty, you love what you're doing right now."

"Yeah, I guess."

"You guess?" It was her turn to laugh. "You love it. Don't give that up to go back to school if you think going back to school is going to make you feel miserable and you're happy doing exactly what you're doing. I want whatever is going to make you happy."

"I don't want to be a disappointment to you." I sighed.

She wrapped her arm across my torso and gave me a tight squeeze. "How could someone that makes me so happy ever be a disappointment to me?" Then she pressed a soft kiss to my lips that took every ounce of fear away.

II

Wednesday, April 18th

The crawling settles in on my skin again. Ten hours have passed since Chris picked me up. That's more time than I usually get before the crawl, even though the high wears off long before then. Chills settle down my body, concentrated right behind my shoulder blades, pulling my body tightly into itself.

I slide off the bed and slink back out into the kitchen, where Chris is still sitting at the table. Sitting on the chair across from him, I announce, "I feel sick."

He stands, shakes out a pill from a nearby pill bottle, and places it on the table in front of me. It's round and smooth, light yellow in color, but I can tell before I even touch it that it isn't oxy. I pick it up and examine it. The letters *DRA* are etched into the top.

"What the hell is this?" I demand.

"When's the last time you've asked a question about a pill someone's handed you?"

I furrow my brow at him. "I *always* ask questions before I take a pill I don't recognize. I'm not stupid."

"It will help with the nausea," he says shortly.

"A fucking Dramamine, Chris? Dramamine isn't going to help me. You're going to kill me, you know that?" I plead, hoping he can look at this logically.

"You won't die from this, Picco," he says calmly. He calls me Picco, short for my family nickname, Piccolo. *Little one.*

I shake my head rapidly, swallow hard, then whisper, "Per favore, Cristiano. dammene uno." *Please, just give me one.*

"Take the Dramamine, Matteo," he says, "and give it ten more minutes."

"And then what?" I ask greedily.

"And then we'll talk about getting you another pill."

I snatch the Dramamine off the table and throw it into the back of my throat in one quick swoop. It's so small, I hardly have to make any effort to swallow it. But my brain already knows a Dramamine isn't what it craves, and I'm hit with even more crawling skin as punishment. I dig my nails into the soft underside of my forearm, doing everything I can to make it stop.

"It's going to get worse before it gets bet—"

"Can we save the inspirational pep talk for when I don't feel like I'm going to puke my guts out?" I beg. Closing my eyes, I take a deep breath to tamp down the nausea. "Sorry, I can't fucking see straight right now, and I don't need a lecture."

Chris nods and jumps up to pour a glass of water for me.

I shake my head. "I don't want it."

"You need to stay hydrated," he says calmly, sitting back down across from me. Then he starts in with a line of questioning. "How much are you taking?"

I lean back in my chair and don't meet his eyes. "A day or at once?" I ask.

"Both." He matches my lean with one of his own.

I look to the ceiling, as if I'm searching for my answer up there, as if I need to think about how much I take. I let out a sigh. "Sixty or eighty. Half when I wake up, half to go to sleep."

He shakes his head at me, disappointed. I know what he's thinking. I was completely off them a few months ago. *What the hell happened?* I know what happened. My court-ordered treatment ended, and I didn't have the threat of jail time to keep me sober. I told myself I wanted to stay sober after that program was done. I thought I did. I really believed it. I only started taking oxy again to help me sleep. Sleep is the last thing that comes back after you get clean. You don't sleep for months, *years* maybe—if you ever get that far. It wears you down. But once I told myself I could have one taste, I was back to taking them all the time. I couldn't remember why I had ever stopped.

"I have a friend I want you to talk to," Chris says.

I roll my eyes as a reflex. I can't help it. We've had this conversation before. It's not a friend he wants me to talk to; it's a therapist.

Chris jumps in, reading my mind. "I know how you feel about it, so save it. It's not up for negotiation. You can't beat this without getting back on antidepressants."

Of course, that would mean I actually want to beat this, and I don't. Nothing good comes out of getting sober, just my sad, monotonous life. I'd play along with Chris's plan long enough to get back on my feet, and then I'd be back to my pills.

"What's their name?" I ask, humoring him.

"Adam," Chris replies without hesitation.

"So he's actually a friend?" I ask slyly. "You didn't pull that off a bio on a website?"

"He's actually a friend. I used to work with him."

"He got sick of a bunch of messed up seventeen-year-olds trying to choke him out at work?" I throw back at him, knowing full well I'm pushing his buttons. Chris works for a juvenile detention facility. He's told us a handful of stories about terrifying encounters over the past ten years, but those are rare in comparison to all the happy stories he has to tell about the kids he works with.

"That's enough," his voice booms angrily.

I stop antagonizing him, but I don't flinch. I don't blink. *You don't scare me.*

Then Chris laughs—not the reaction I was expecting. I furrow my brow in surprise. "Do you think you're somehow better than those kids, Matteo?" he asks. "Because you're not. You're exactly like them. The only difference between you and them is that you've got a family that keeps fixing your problems. Not everyone has that."

"I never asked for your help."

"If you don't want my help, say the word, and I'll drop you off anywhere you'd like and never bother you again."

"Would you give me my pills back if I decided to leave?" I ask.

Another disbelieving laugh escapes his lips. "No."

That's fine. June will have more; she always does. She'll pick me up, let me crash with her, get me more pills. June can fix this.

"Matteo," Chris says softly, "if you keep doing this, you're going to lose our family just like you lost Keelie."

Sometimes, I allow my brain to forget that Keelie ever left. I let myself believe she's gone *for now* and will return soon, like she's taken an extended weekend trip. A weekend trip that never fucking ends. Hearing Chris mention out loud that she's gone forces me to remember that it's not just for the weekend. It makes all of this real.

"That's a really shitty thing to say," I growl at him threateningly.

"It's the truth, and you need to hear it while you're sober enough to understand it," he snaps back. "You've lost Mom and Dad. They're done with you. You're running out of people to fall back on. I'm all you've got left, and I have my own family that I have to look out for. I can't put them at risk for you. Your only option here is sobriety. Take it or leave it."

I could do this for a while. I could pretend. Fake it until I find another option. Until I find another place to live. Until I find a job that can support me being on my own. I'll find a way to get pills without Chris knowing until then. I can cut back to smaller doses so he doesn't notice. I can outsmart him.

"Alright," I say in a soft whisper. "I guess I'm in."

"Good." A kind, welcoming smile spreads across his face. "I was hoping you'd say that."

My stomach churns. I'm not sure how much longer I'm going to be able to sit at this table with Chris before I actually get sick. He must be able to see it on my face, the color draining from my cheeks, because without saying anything, he gets up to find another pill. I hold my hand out for it, and as it falls into my palm, I can tell without even looking at it that it's not the one I was hoping for. It's a small oblong green pill with a line down the middle on one side, making it easy to break in two. On the other side, it says *L 2*.

"Loperamide?" I ask, disappointed. Chris nods. "So that's it then? You're not even going to let me taper off of it?"

He pushes out his lips into an unsympathetic frown. "Not when you're coming down off of sixty. Probably even less than that, right? You wanted your taper dose to start higher. You're taking what, forty, maybe? You can handle coming off forty."

"So you're saying I should have been taking *more* oxy? I'll remember that for next time," I say with a grin.

"There's not going to be a next time, Matteo."

I throw the loperamide into the back of my throat and swallow it down, accepting my fate. Dramamine and loperamide, anti-nausea and antidiarrheal medicines. A couple of over-the-counter pills don't stand a chance against this. The chills and the crawls I can handle, the rest I can manage, but the worst part about detoxing is the mental withdrawal symptoms. The overwhelming sadness that overtakes your entire body when the euphoric drugs leave. I'm not equipped to handle that again. Not all at once. If I am going to detox this time without any help aside from a few low-level drugstore pills, my body is going to full-on revolt. Chris has to know that.

"So what's your plan then?" I ask him.

"Lock you up in here and hope that your heart keeps beating," he says. I can't help but get the feeling that he isn't totally joking.

"Where's the closest hospital?" I ask for good measure.

"About twenty minutes away," he replies, "but *Michelle* is only ten minutes away, so you'll probably be fine."

His wife, Michelle, is a physician assistant. Chris had medical training for his job, too. Still, there's something incredibly unsettling about the nonchalant attitude he's taking toward all this. *You'll probably be fine.*

I shake my head in reply. "You can't just cut me off," I try begging again. "You're going to kill me. I need to taper off of them."

A look of pity floods his face. "You don't."

"Yes, I do," I yell. "You don't know what you're fucking talking about. I wasn't lying. I'm at sixty a day. I need a taper."

He nods. He's so calm, it's irritating. "I know that you're clinging to anything you can to get another dose. And I know that even if you agreed to tapering right now, we would have to go through this same negotiation every time I tried to cut you back because your body is scared to let it go." He leans forward, resting his chin on his fist. "It won't get easier by putting it off."

"It *is* going to get easier by putting it off," I snap back. "That's exactly what tapering does."

Chris shrugs. "It's not up for negotiation, Matteo."

Fine. I jump up from my seat at the table and storm off through the kitchen and back toward my room. This time when I retreat into my room, there's nothing secretive about it. I don't slowly shut the door; I give it a full-bodied slam. Then I take a few breaths and I suddenly feel remorse for the outburst, but it's too late. I sit on the edge of my bed, burying my face in my hands. My skin is alive. My stomach does somersaults as it tries to decide in which direction to spew bile first.

I slowly lie down on the bed and scroll through my contacts until I find the one listed as *Stephanie / June*. I call her, knowing she won't answer. She always lets my calls go to voice mail.

"Hi, you've reached Juniper Nelson at Remington Realty. I'm sorry I missed your call. Please leave me a detailed message, and I'll return your call as quickly as possible. Thank you." I don't have any other phone number for her, only her work line. Her voice mail beeps, demanding I start talking.

"Hey, it's me." My voice sounds pathetic, lacking any confidence. I hate talking on the phone sober. "I might need your help. I'm fine, I just—I'm staying with my brother for a bit." Do I want June's help? Do I want to *owe her*? "I guess I just wanted to let you know I won't be around for a while. I'll call you when I'm back."

I hang up, lying on the bed and letting my unconfident words cycle through my head, letting the words antagonize me. She's going to listen to that and think I'm an idiot. Why did I leave a message? Maybe I should call her back and—*No*. It's done. I lay my phone on the side table next to the framed photo of me and Keelie before I'm able to change my mind.

I study the photo for a second, tracing with my eyes the intricate wood carving that makes up the frame. I nudge the frame aside and retrieve one of the fifteens. I need one of these now so I can stop thinking about how stupid June will probably think I sounded. So I can stop thinking about Keelie being gone. I pop it into my mouth and start to chew it—

Just as Chris opens up the door.

"Who are you—"

I jump, trying to shove the photo frame back into place as quickly as I can before Chris can see what it's hiding. *Too late.*

He takes long, barreling strides for me. Frantically, I dive my hand behind the frame, protecting the last of my pills. I'm in such a hurry, my hand knocks the frame right off the table. It goes crashing to the floor, landing on its corner. The edges of the frame crack away from each other and the glass breaks. My heart drops.

Chris snatches my wrist and forces me to release the rest of the pills. As I drop them into his hand, I notice the yellow one isn't among them. I try my best not to let my eyes wander around the room, not drawing attention to it. It has to be here somewhere, and wherever it is, I'll find it.

Chris lifts my arm forcefully, turning my body so that I have no choice but to meet his eyes. He glares at me for a second, then releases my wrist from his grasp.

"Go sit in the kitchen," he growls.

Fifteen milligrams of oxy wouldn't be enough to numb the growing sinking feeling inside me. The frame itself is just a memory, a souvenir Keelie bought from a trip we took to Sedona, but the glass where she scrawled out *I love you, Val* is irreplaceable. Looking at it makes it easier to pretend she's still here.

"Can I—" I start, gesturing toward the broken photo frame. Chris shoves the last of my pills in his pocket as he kneels down to the ground to pick up the remains of the frame. The yellow pill isn't among the broken pieces.

"We'll get you a new one," Chris offers. He picks up a large shard of glass off the ground, the letters *ou, Val* permanently written on the glass. Chris thins his lips at the realization of what was lost. "We'll fix it," he assures me. But we both know it's too late to repair the damage I've done. To this and every other part of my life.

After almost an hour of rummaging through every inch of my room, Chris emerges empty-handed, aside from the few pills I already surrendered.

He sits with me at the table again. "You're only going to make this worse by prolonging it fifteen milligrams at a time. Please, be honest with me, was that all of it?"

I nod slowly, defeated.

"Empty your pockets," he demands.

I don't fight him anymore. I sigh, stand, and turn my pockets inside out.

"Give me your phone," he instructs. But this time, I have to push back.

"I'm not giving you my phone."

"It wasn't a question," he challenges me, folding one arm over the other. His forearms are bigger than my biceps. I feel completely drained of any confidence I felt in confronting him earlier.

"Everyone who is going to be looking for you already knows you're here. Even Keelie," he says in a calm, stern voice.

"Keelie knows I'm here?" I ask quickly.

Chris cringes as he replies, "She does."

"Did you talk to her?"

"It doesn't matter, Matteo."

But it *does* matter. If Chris is reporting back to Keelie, that changes everything.

He leans his body toward me, staking his claim as the boss. One more time he repeats, "Give me your phone."

I pull my phone out of my pocket, power it off, and slide it across the table to him. I want Chris to tell Keelie I'm cooperating. Doing what I can to get sober and get her back. Proving that I can do that for her.

"Thank you," Chris says softly, and then hardening his voice, he asks, "Who were you talking to earlier?"

"June." I don't offer more information, hoping he drops it. I should have known better.

"June . . .?" he asks, placing my phone closer to his folded arms, just out of reach from me.

"She's a friend."

"The one you're always sneaking around with?"

"That's her." I lean back in my chair, the oxycodone fully settling in. It's not enough to feel high, but enough that my stomach settles and the crawling stops. Enough for me to feel normal.

"What do you know about her?" he asks.

"Not much," I reluctantly reply. "Divorced, two kids. She's a realtor. She lets me talk about Keelie and doesn't get mad."

"Have you been seeing her long?"

"I don't remember," I admit.

All I remember about meeting June is what she's told me. I don't remember meeting her; she was just there one day. We met at some point in the months that followed Keelie kicking me out, but I was taking enough oxy at the time to be sure I blacked out each and every one of those days. I didn't want to face her leaving.

I let myself stay like that for months, but once I started waking up in places I didn't recognize with people I didn't know, I got freaked out enough to cut back to just the essentials. Only what I needed to function. Enough to wake up in the morning and not immediately get sick. Enough to sleep at night. Enough to make me forget I couldn't stand being left alone with myself.

My phone would light up with names I didn't recognize, people I didn't remember meeting. One day, someone named Twig sent me a text: *Hitting the H again tonight. Come hang.* My eyes immediately began scanning my arms and legs for track marks. Did I let a guy named *Twig* shoot me with heroin?

The same afternoon that the text from Twig came through, I got a call from someone else saved in my phone as *Stephanie.*

"Matt, it's June," she said in a voice that made her sound as though she worked for a doctor's office. Calm, professional, safe.

I blinked hard and looked at my phone screen to be sure I had read it right.

"June?" I asked, confused.

"Yes," she said with a laugh. "I got what you asked for. Can I see you tonight?"

I tried to remember who she was, what I had asked for. It didn't matter. Her soft voice felt much safer than texts from Twig.

"Sure, where?"

"I'll come pick you up as soon as I can," she promised, then hung up. She knew who I was, she knew where I lived, but I had no memory of her.

It took a long time before I admitted to June that I didn't remember meeting her. She laughed about it, and said, "That makes sense, I guess," as though she could tell I was outside of myself when we met. I never asked her how she got oxycodone. I didn't want to know. As long as she could keep getting it, I didn't care where it came from. Especially when all she asked for in return was someone to mess around with, someone to control. She delighted in telling me what to do and reminding me that if I didn't do it, she might take the pills away. Companionship was a low price to pay for never having to worry about meeting up with people like Twig.

Whenever June called, I said yes. And as long as I kept saying yes, I kept getting pills. And as long as I kept getting pills, I kept being able to forget about this horrible fucking life I had. All I needed was to take a pill and forget all about it. Instead of dealing with my emotions, I buried myself deeper and deeper, and hoped that no one would notice as I slowly disappeared.

Seven Years Ago

Tuesday, March 15th

Keelie didn't hear the door open when I came home that evening. I tossed my duffel bag down on the ground, thinking she would hear it hit the floor, but she didn't turn around. She had her earbuds in and had been on a true crime podcast kick. She was likely sucked into the gory details of an unsolved murder.

I watched her bounce from one side of our small kitchen to the other, bowls and ingredients littering every available surface. I snuck up behind her, placing a hand on her waist to catch her as she dove over to the kitchen sink. She jumped out of her skin at my touch, then laughed out a sigh of relief when she realized I wasn't a serial killer.

"Just me." I chuckled into her ear.

"Val, you scared me," she said, removing an earbud as she gave me a quick kiss. "How was work?"

Instead of answering her question, I took the earbud from her hand and popped it into my ear so I could hear what she was listening to.

A deep male voice crooned through the earbud, "A che ora parte il prossimo autobus? A che ora parte il prossimo autobus? *What time is the next bus?*"

I smiled at her, plucking the earbud out of my ear. "You want to learn Italian?"

She shrugged as if the thought embarrassed her.

"I'll teach you," I said enthusiastically.

"You're going to teach me?"

"Sure, I'll teach you shit you'll actually need to know how to say. You're never going to need to know how to say 'When's the next bus?' Because you're going to look it up on your phone. Just like you would here."

She removed her other earbud and narrowed her eyes at me. "Fine. Teach me something useful."

Standing behind her, I wrapped my arms around her hips and placed one hand in each of her front pockets, scratching the fronts of her hips through the thin fabric of the pocket lining. She picked up an egg, cracking it on the edge of the bowl.

I rested my chin on her shoulder and whispered in her ear, "Uovo."

"This?" she asked, holding up the eggshell.

"Quello, sì." *Yeah, that.*

"Uovo," she repeated with pride.

"Bene," I nodded, then pointed to the other objects spread across the counter. "Farina, sale, patata, burro . . ." *Flour, salt, potato, butter.*

She repeated the words back to me. I pressed my hands into her hips and turned her body slightly, directing her eyes to mine. I eyed her suspiciously and asked, "What are you making?"

"In italiano," she reminded me.

"Cosa stai cucinando?" I repeated.

She scrunched her face at me as she thought about her response, then hesitantly replied, "Sto cucinando gnocchi della nonna." *I'm making your grandma's gnocchi.*

My heart fluttered. All I could do was gape at her magnificence.

"Your dad gave me the recipe." She explained, "I stopped by there this afternoon."

I shook my head at her, completely in awe. Breathlessly, all I could say was "Keelie Mae."

She shrugged like it wasn't a big deal. Her selflessness was that second nature to her.

"What can I do?" I asked, but she stared at me cluelessly until I repeated it in Italian. "Cosa posso fare?"

"Niente," she replied confidently. *Nothing*.

She'd heard me say that to my mom countless times when we were younger. It didn't matter what the question was. "What are you doing?" "What did you do at school?" "What do you want to do this weekend?" My answer was almost always a snarky "niente." Keelie picked that one up quick.

She spun around to face me, placing her flour-coated hands against my chest and repeated her earlier question. "How was work?"

I shrugged. "Good."

"Is that Tyler kid still being a shithead?"

I was working at the rec center, coaching youth sports leagues. Before they started drug testing me. Back when they still trusted me.

I pressed my forehead to hers and whispered, "He's the fucking worst."

"I can come with you tomorrow and rough him up if you want? Maybe shove him in a locker?"

"That would be great, thank you."

She squeezed her hands on each of my forearms and sucked her lips into her mouth for a second, releasing them with a *pop*. "How are you feeling?"

I took a deep breath and let it out in a sigh. "A little jittery."

"Do you want your pills now?" she asked, as if it were a lifesaving medication and not a tapered dose of oxycodone.

Recently, I had taken the jump from thirty milligrams to twenty and my body felt the absence this time, like it did every time I dropped dose. But tonight, I was going to push through it. "I'm okay for now. Later."

Satisfied with that answer, Keelie grabbed my wrist with one hand, pulling my arm outstretched so she could place the roll of parchment paper in my grasp.

"Then let's get started," she declared.

When Keelie put her mind to doing something, she did it. We ran through Italian vocabulary together for the next few months and she picked it up quickly, which shouldn't have surprised me. She's been surrounded by my Italian-speaking family her entire life. We went over to my parent's house one day that summer, and on our way there, she nervously announced, "I want to try speaking Italian to your parents."

I nodded, and then somewhat sarcastically added, "I bet they know enough to understand what you're saying."

She flashed a quick scowl my way to show that she didn't find my joke the least bit comical. So I doubled back and added encouragingly, "They're going to be ecstatic, Keelie Mae."

When we walked through the door, I announced our arrival by shouting, "Buonasera!"

Mom came running to the door, excited to see us and saying, "Buonasera tesori miei!" *Hello, my treasures!* Then she turned to Keelie and said, "Good to see you, dear," and gave her a kiss on the cheek.

I threw a glance at Keelie. I knew she knew how to respond in Italian, but she clammed up and instead said, "Ciao, Arianna." I glared at her for chickening out and she passed an apologetic grin my way.

Chris, Michelle, and my sister, Ellie, were all seated around the table. I wrapped my arms around Ellie's shoulders from behind, planting a big, over-the-top kiss on her cheek. She snarled her lip at me.

"Where's Nick?" I asked her.

"He's back in Raleigh," she sighed.

"So then, you're probably moving back there pretty soon, huh?" I joked.

Michelle grimaced, like I just uncovered a terrible secret. Mom stared in our direction, suddenly very concerned about hearing Ellie's answer. Ellie scowled at me and said, "No, Matty. I'm not moving back to Raleigh."

I raised an eyebrow at Ellie as a symbol of my briefest apology. Then I stood between Chris and Michelle, pulling them both toward me for a tandem hug, and whispered, "Oops." Michelle stifled a laugh. Ellie wouldn't take her eyes off me, so I flashed her another apologetic smile before shouting to the room, "Where is she?"

"Sleeping," Chris snapped back almost immediately. "So shut the fuck up."

I turned to Michelle. "Wake her up? Please?"

"No," Chris grumbled before Michelle had the chance to answer.

My niece, Luci, was born a couple of months earlier, and I couldn't get enough of her. She was the most amazing little creature. I wanted to hold her in my arms and touch her soft little hands any chance I could.

Keelie wandered her way into the kitchen and said hello to my dad, then added, "Cosa stai cucinando?" *What are you making?*

Instead of replying, my dad cocked his head and stared at her, as if he might have heard her wrong.

Chris, Michelle, and Ellie all turned to stare, too. Keelie's expression dropped, embarrassed. She looked to me for assurance and whispered, "Cosa?"

"You're speaking Italian, that's *what*," Ellie pointed out, as if Keelie might not have been aware.

I nodded to Keelie encouragingly and then said to my family, "Abbiamo fatto allenamento." *We've been practicing.*

A look of pride blossomed across Dad's face as he slowly replied to Keelie's original question, overpronouncing each syllable for her. "Cucinando carbonara."

"Profumino delizioso," Keelie replied. *Smells delicious.*

"Grazie, amore mio."

"What else does she know how to say?" Ellie asked excitedly.

"She's not a dog, Elle." Chris laughed.

"Not much more than that." Keelie shrugged. She turned her eyes up toward the ceiling, searching her brain for the words she was looking for. "Non più di quello."

"I love this," Ellie enthused in my direction before turning back to Keelie. "My Italian commentary is a real treat. I'm glad you'll be in on it. Matty, why didn't you teach her sooner?"

"It was all her idea," I replied with a gesture in Keelie's direction.

"You guys can cover the basics. I'll teach you how to say all the important stuff," Ellie promised.

"The important stuff? Like what?" Keelie asked, throwing a smirk my way as she noted my look of protest.

Ellie leaned in to whisper in Keelie's ear, and Keelie's smile grew wider by the second as Ellie taught her all kinds of new phrases that Mom would be mortified to hear her say.

Keelie turned to whisper something back to Ellie, and Ellie said, "Oh yeah, definitely." Keelie drew her lips into a straight line and flashed me a flirty wink.

A soft cry from Luci echoed from down the hallway. My ears perked up. I snapped my eyes to Chris. "Can I get her?" I begged.

"Knock yourself out, Zio Picco," Chris said, relieved.

I bounded toward her small, crackled cry. Scooped her up into my arms. Held her tight. She calmed down quickly, her beautiful big eyes staring at me as she sucked on her hand. I wiggled my pinky against her fist and she clung to it. She was so fucking small. I walked back out to the kitchen with her, grinning from ear to ear and softly touching her cheek with my index finger.

"She's the coolest," I said, admiring her.

"I can tell you how to get your very own one of those if you want," Chris offered.

Keelie immediately protested with a laugh. "No, that's okay."

"Matty has to figure out how to take care of himself first," Ellie helpfully added.

"Vaffanculo, Eleonora," I huffed. *Fuck off.*

"Matteo," Mom snapped at me, giving me a glare. *Watch your mouth.*

Ellie and I exchanged glances as I sat down next to her, as we did when we bickered as kids and got in trouble.

I mumbled an apology. "Scusa."

Keelie leaned against my shoulder, gazing at Luci. She gently ran a finger down Luci's soft, chunky arm, allowing another finger to gently brush my hand as she passed it. I turned a quick smile to her.

"Is it alright if we call you Zia Kiki?" Chris asked, jarring both of our attentions from Luci for a split second.

Keelie beamed at the sound of it, her smile stretching from ear to ear. Then, her eyes panned back down to Luci as she said, "I'd love that."

Luci crinkled up her face, scrunching up her lips enough to show off her gums, and then wailed. I briefly tried to soothe her. When that didn't work, I jumped out of my chair and immediately handed her off to Chris. *Your problem now.*

III

Thursday, April 19th

The fifteen milligrams of oxy I had yesterday afternoon were hardly enough to carry me through the night. I usually need oxy to sleep. It used to be because I had nightmares, mostly about Rich, and the pills messed with my brain chemistry enough to block them out so I could sleep. But eventually, I became too dependent on them. I couldn't sleep without them. I couldn't do *anything* without them.

Last night, I stared up at the ceiling for what felt like hours before I finally fell asleep. And without oxy in my system, the nightmares came back.

My dream started out happy. I was back with Keelie in our cozy apartment. We sat, with her body leaning against mine, each one of our appendages intertwined. It was the kind of dream that wrapped me up in an unmistakable warmth. The feeling that radiates through me long after I wake up. I wish it had stopped there so I could take that feeling with me. But it never stopped there.

A cold, angry voice barked out, "Keelie! Matty! Get the fuck over here!"

Keelie tilted her head to face me, passing me a glance that said, *Oh boy, here we go again.*

With her arm wrapped around me tightly, Keelie gave me a quick squeeze as she jumped off the couch and skipped innocently off toward the sound of the angry voice.

"Mia! Don't."

She tossed a playful glance my way, then said, "What?"

"You know what," I begged her. "Please, stop."

Without listening to my warning, she walked down the hallway. I sat on the couch, clenching my eyes as tightly closed as I could, waiting for the familiar moment when I heard her scream. But instead of the familiar, something unfamiliar happened.

"Where the fuck is Matty?" the voice barked at Keelie. "Is he coming or not?"

She laughed slightly and said, "Yeah, he wants to come. I'll go grab him." Keelie's voice was light, happy. Keelie popped her head around the corner and said, "Val, come on."

I stared at her for a second, trying to figure out what was happening. She patiently stood in the walkway, waiting for me to follow. Reluctantly, I stood up from my spot on the couch and followed her, as I had the day we found Rich.

She led me down that familiar hallway. The door at the end cracked open, afternoon light beams shining toward us, showing us the way.

I stopped in my tracks, trying once more to end this. "Mia, please don't," I begged, hoping this time she would stop, but it was too late. She turned her head slightly to flash a smile at me. I pinched my eyes shut, fighting against my dream, hoping it would let me forget.

Keelie pressed a hand against the door and nudged it open.

"Dad?" she called, and my stomach sank as I braced myself for what came next.

The scream that has been echoing in my head for fourteen years.

I jolt awake, a soft yell escaping my lips. My body is coated in a cold sweat, and darkness surrounds me. I sit up, holding on tightly to the blankets beneath me, grounding myself as I look around the room. *I'm in Chris's house. I'm okay.* I repeat that to myself over and over, trying to catch my breath as the familiar nightmare subsides.

I'm not going to be able to get back to sleep after that. I never can. I would need another pill if I were ever going to fall back asleep. *The yellow pill.*

I'll find it and take half. Half will be enough to keep my skin from crawling. Enough to fall asleep.

I slide out of bed and stand in the middle of the room, studying the table and the lamp where the picture frame sat. I imagine my hand sweeping across the side table, trying to picture where the pill might have gone.

The door gives out a soft creak as it swings open behind me. I jump, and when I do, chills overtake my body. The same terrifying image of Rich I see in my dreams flashes to my mind. Irrationally, I imagine him walking through the door. But then a soft voice whispers out, "Matteo, stai bene?" *Are you okay?*

The door swings open more aggressively once Chris realizes I'm not in bed. When he sees me standing in the middle of the room, relief washes over his face. I feel calmer, too, when I meet the eyes of my brother, instead of the haunting image of a dead man.

"What's going on, Picco?" he says in his full voice.

"I couldn't sleep."

"Come on." He nods his head toward the door and bounds out into the kitchen.

I laugh after him. "What time is it?"

"Doesn't matter," he yells back, then quiets his voice once I'm in sight. "You're up, I'm up. What the hell difference does it make what time it is?"

I take a seat at the table as he fills a glass with water and places it on the counter closest to me.

"Drink this," he says. I roll my eyes at him, retrieving it off the counter. He springs to his own defense. "Michelle is not coming down here to plug an IV in you because you refuse to drink water."

"Well, I know that's not true." I smirk. "If you guys weren't interested in saving me from my stupid decisions, I wouldn't be here."

Off his glare, I put the glass to my lips and obediently take a big gulp.

"When do the girls get back?" I ask him, shifting the conversation.

"Monday." He presses Start on the coffeemaker. "Michelle has to go back to work."

"And you?"

"I took two weeks off to be here with you," he says, then adds, "unpaid," to remind me how much of an inconvenience I am. "We'll figure it out from there."

"Luci and Katy coming back on Monday, too?"

"*Luciana* and *Katya*," he corrects my unwanted nicknames for them, "will be back on Monday, yes."

"It's been a long time since I've seen them," I accuse him. "I wanted to, but you never let me."

"You're right," he replies coldly. I suddenly feel a switch in his voice; he's turned on therapist mode. "And why is that?"

"You tell me," I snap back, not playing into his games. But his burning stare makes me feel guilty for my sharp reply, so I sigh and double back. "Because I'm high all the time, and you don't want me tripping on your toddlers?"

Sitting across the table from me, he says, "They're hardly toddlers anymore. Luciana is *seven*."

"Cavolo." I gape in disbelief. *Shoot.* A prick crawls across my arm. I snap my hand to swat it away out of reflex, and dig my thumbnail into my forearm to make it stop.

Chris immediately notices. "Come stai, Picco?" *How are you feeling?*

"Una schifezza." *Like garbage.* My skin is crawling all over. The chills haven't left. I feel exhausted already from the horrible sleep I got—the best sleep I will get all week, I'm sure. But above all else, I am completely weighed down by the thought of the misery of sobriety. My life is happy with pills. Why do I have to change that?

"What do you want to do to keep your mind off it?" he asks optimistically, as though I am going to have a lot of free time over the next few days between bouts of spewing my guts out.

"Eat candy and watch movies," I answer confidently.

Chris laughs. "Somehow that's almost the exact opposite of what I was going to suggest."

"Which was what?"

He pours us two mugs of coffee, handing one to me, as he replies, "Making *real* food and going outside."

"Can we make gnocchi della nonna?" I ask excitedly.

Chris smiles. "Sure."

We are the only ones at the grocery store when we arrive at six, as they open. Our shopping cart is piled high with all the ingredients we need for gnocchi della nonna and everything that I deem to be a detox necessity: ice cream, soup, large bags of candy. Chris, on the other hand, adds in more practical detox items like plain crackers, unsalted nuts, and Gatorade.

As we make our way to the checkout lane, the crawls take over my entire body. I pinch the skin behind my neck, digging at a particularly irritating spot, clawing into it in an attempt to remove the creature living beneath the surface. The slight pain I feel as my fingernails dig under layers of skin is a welcomed relief from the crawl. The more I scratch into it, the less power the crawl has. If I scratch a little further, it will—

"Matteo," Chris says softly, placing a hand on my elbow. "It's not real."

"It doesn't matter," I scoff back. "It's the only way to make it stop."

I slowly transfer my dig to a spot on my forearm, a particularly irritating crawl I can pick at without Chris noticing. I half-heartedly attempt to help Chris pile things onto the conveyor belt, only able to move one thing at a time, always keeping a fingernail digging into my skin.

A bolt of pain surges through my abdomen. I double over, bracing myself on the edge of the conveyor belt table.

"Stai bene?" Chris asks.

"No," I mumble back in a groan.

"Che c'è?" *What's wrong?*

I slowly turn my head to glare at him. "I need to leave."

"Less than five minutes," he promises.

"Now."

"Matteo," he tries to reason, gesturing toward the pile of food the cashier still has yet to scan, "just take a breath. We'll be gone in a few minutes."

"You're not getting it," I start to explain, but I don't get to finish my thought. Fiery bile threatens my esophagus, my clenching stomach rising higher and higher within me.

I close my eyes and swallow a few times, willing my stomach to stop churning, begging my body not to do this now.

"I'll be at the car," I state, taking large strides toward the front door.

Chris hollers after me, but I ignore him. I need air. I need anything that will keep the nausea from spilling over. After only three steps out the front door, my body hitches again. I'm not even going to make it to the car. I double back, punching the lid off the trash can, and heave the bile of my stomach inside. I haven't eaten anything substantial for a couple of days except for a few delicious bites of oxycodone. There's nothing in my stomach to come out.

Leaning against Chris's car, pressing my forehead to the cold glass of the window, I wait there for him. The locks of Chris's car shift open as he emerges from the store with our cart full of groceries.

I brace one hand on the top of the door frame, the other on the top of the open door, as I hoist my body up into the tall vehicle. Sinking into the leather seat doesn't feel so comfortable anymore. Nothing about this feels comfortable. As I sit down, my stomach swirls again. I lean out the open car door and puke onto the ground once more as Chris loads the groceries into the back.

Once my stomach settles, I ease the passenger seat back as far as it will go, lying flat and stretching the tense muscles of my heaving stomach.

When Chris jumps into the driver's side seat, he passes a bottle of ginger ale my way. I accept the gesture but don't drink it. I can't lift my head without puking.

Chris drives carefully the entire way home. Each press of the gas pedal is subtle, each tap on the brake soft and only when absolutely necessary. He turns into his gravel driveway, and the sudden movement of the car bouncing against rock stirs my stomach again. As he throws the car into park, right up against the front porch, I lurch forward, swing open the door, and heave. Only this time, there's nothing left.

Chris rushes to my side of the car, offering his arm, helping me climb out. Out of instinct, I apologize to him. He nods and gives me a soft pat on the back. My stomach clenches tighter and tighter and tighter, sending a sharp pain through my abdomen. I close my eyes in a cringe, then soften my face long enough to climb the stairs and make it back inside.

These withdrawals are the worst I've ever experienced. I pick apart every inch of my crawling skin, and ache as if knives are stabbing me right through the bone. I heave and sweat, and I convulse with chills. I am so sick I'm barely conscious, and yet I can never actually fall asleep.

On day three, my body temperature runs so hot that I hallucinate. Keelie is standing a few feet away from me as I drift back into consciousness. She's on the other side of the room, talking to Chris. No matter how real she looks, I know she isn't here. This image of her my brain is crafting isn't real.

But then this hallucinated Keelie steps closer to me. She grabs my arm and whispers softly, "Hey, Matty. How're you feeling?"

"Mia Mae," I whisper back with a grin that swallows up my entire face.

Keelie snaps a device onto my arm. It slowly clamps down on me with a loud humming sound. Blood pressure monitor.

"What did he say?" Keelie turns to ask Chris.

"'Mia Mae,'" Chris repeats back to her. "That's what he calls Keelie."

Keelie turns back to me with a kind smile. "Matteo." She laughs lightly. "It's Michelle."

I blink hard a few times, trying to get my eyes to focus on the person in front of me. My eyes flick around uncontrollably for a second, a cloudiness taking over my vision. And then, with one last blink, it all comes into focus. *Michelle* comes into focus.

The device on my arm beeps. Michelle snatches it off and announces, "Pulse is a little high. Blood pressure's still good."

She pops a thermometer into my mouth next. I scrub a hand across my face and press the palms of my hands into my cheekbones, looking to relieve the pressure that's built up in my sinuses. I pull the blanket up to my chin as shivers take over my entire body.

Michelle returns with an ice-cold wet towel and places it across my forehead. I toss it off immediately, chills surging through me again as the cold towel touches my fingers.

"I don't want that," I snap at her as I bite down on the thermometer between my teeth.

The thermometer chirps, and Michelle plucks it from my lips.

"Your temperature is one-oh-two," she informs me. "I'm going to have to take you in if we can't get it down under a hundred."

"It's too cold," I plead.

"I need you to fight through it, okay, Matty?" She over annunciates each word. "I need your fever to come down."

I lay my head back down on the pillow and allow her to place the icy towel across my forehead once again.

Chris shoves a sparkly purple straw-topped cup in my face. "Drink this, Picco."

I snatch it from his hand, taking the smallest sip. He offers me a closed hand next, and when I hold my open palm out to him, he drops a handful of pills in it. I lift my gaze briefly to look at the pills provided, but none of them are the relief I crave. I toss them back and swallow them dry.

By the fifth day, I'm much more lucid. I can sit up, look around, move without fear of upsetting my stomach. Chris spends most of the afternoon sitting in the recliner at the foot of the couch, where he can alternate between watching the Cardinals game and offering up conversations with me. After an inning of listening to the quiet commentary of the announcers, I shove a few pillows under my back to prop myself up on the couch to get a better view of the screen.

At the end of an inning, Chris suggests, "Let's go for a walk."

I laugh at him. "Vaffanculo." *Fuck off.* He has to be joking, right?

He laughs too, recognizing why his request sounds ridiculous to me, but then he defends it by saying, "I'm serious. It will make you feel so much better to move."

"That's not possible," I groan. "Everything hurts. I can't move."

"Yep. Come on." He jumps out of the recliner and holds a hand out to me. "We'll take it slow."

I glare at him. His warm smile is irritating. If I were in any position to move my arms, I would smack that smile right off his face. *That* would make me feel better. He tosses the comforter off me and holds his hand out once again. I slap it as hard as I can to express my distaste for this, but my entire body is weak, and it doesn't come off as a slap so much as a firm and eager grasp.

He drags me up off the couch, and once I am standing he asks, "Stai Bene?"

I shake my head and keep my stare fixed on the floor.

"Che c'é, Picco?" he asks. *What's wrong?*

I shake my head again and take a deep breath. "I'm fine."

Each step sends a fresh surge of pain through my body. My muscles tense with each stride. But when we get to the porch and the sun warms my face, my muscles release. Each step pumps blood through my veins and renews my energy. Chris was right, unfortunately. Moving does make me feel better.

We walk in circles around the fields of green grass behind his house. I try to focus on keeping my breathing slow and even, but the air is jittery as it fills my lungs. I shuffle my feet slowly. The grass pricks against my legs. Chris holds my pace, even when I hardly move at all.

"I made you an appointment with Adam tomorrow," he says casually.

I shake my head. "It's not happening."

"Sure it is. You're doing a lot better today, and you need to see him as soon as possible."

I need to see him before my mind takes a jump off the deep end—that's what he means. There's an overwhelming hopelessness that comes along with detoxing. Especially when you've already failed so many times before. There's a sense that nothing in the world will make you feel better than you are when you're high, and that's not the addiction talking, it's just the honest truth. There's no better feeling in the world. And when you take that away, you're left with *nothing*. It's dreadful. And in this case, I actually have nothing. My mind tells me I'm hopeless and my reality matches. Chris wants me to trade in one drug that tricks my brain into thinking I'm happy for another. Antidepressants won't make my life better. They'll just black out the part of my brain that can recognize how shitty it is.

"It's not going to make a difference, you know," I point out glumly.

Chris shrugs. "Well, if it's not going to make a difference, then it's not going to hurt anything either. What the hell else do you have to do?"

That night, I'm finally able to eat all that food we bought. That *Chris* bought. I hardly have an appetite for the things that I thought I would eat, and go for more of the plain crackers and unsalted nuts that Chris picked out. Feeling optimistic about my appetite, I ask if we can make some gnocchi della nonna for dinner. Chris lets me roll out the dough and press each one with a fork, but my hands are still so jittery that he doesn't trust me with a knife. We have every surface of the entire kitchen covered in parchment paper, and every inch of parchment covered in tiny balls of dough. It's like we used to do it when we were kids—no surface went uncovered.

Most of it ends up in the freezer. "I don't know when we're going to eat all this," Chris says with a laugh, but then I assure him that Mom and Dad would probably love to take some off our hands. Dad would beam with pride, knowing he was able to successfully pass something on to us.

Chris fries up a generous portion of gnocchi with butter and sage on the stove, while I stay slumped at the table, my elbows carefully placed between two sheets of drying gnocchi, my face buried in my hands. My foot twitches and my body aches all over. I take a calming breath deep into my stomach and tell myself I'm not going to get sick. I'm going to eat this, and I'm not going to get sick anymore. I'm done being sick.

"Can I have another Dramamine?" I beg him, hoping that it will help my stomach enough to eat this delicious meal.

"When was the last one?" he asks, but we both know full well he already knows the answer to that question.

"It's been four hours," I lie.

He turns to glare at me. "It's been three."

"Then why did you ask?" I snap back. "It will take an hour to take effect anyway. Please?"

He sets down the wooden spoon, turns down the burner heat, and turns to face me, carefully placing two hands on the counter between trays of gnocchi so he can lean in to get a better look at me.

"It's about controlling the urge to fix your problems with pills," he explains. "And taking medication as directed."

I let out a frustrated groan, like an angsty teenager instead of an adult that should be incredibly grateful to his brother for all that he's doing. "How is taking an anti-nausea pill when I'm feeling nauseous *not* taking medication as directed?" I whine.

He narrows his eyes at me and then turns back around to continue stirring our dinner. *You know how.* With his back still turned to me, he calls out, "Hey, package up the gnocchi on the table and stick it in the freezer."

He pulls open a drawer and places a box of gallon-sized bags on a small corner of the counter. As I bag them up, one by one, I ask, "Why aren't the girls back yet?"

Chris laughs. "You're not ready for them yet. Trust me."

He dishes our gnocchi della nonna out onto two plates, and hands me one in exchange for a bag of gnocchi. He tosses the bag into the freezer before joining me at the table with his plate.

I already have a bite in my mouth before he even has the chance to sit down. For the first time all week, I have an appetite. Actually, probably the first time in *months*. A soft *mmm* escapes my lips with the first bite. It tastes even better than I remember it. The smallest hit of euphoria surges through my body at the delicious taste, and then it's gone so, so fast. *That* feeling. That hit of pleasure that lasts only a second when it comes from food, a minute when it comes from sex, or hours when it's captured inside a pill. That's the feeling I'm constantly after. It's the feeling I've spent the last five days trying to forget. And now that I've had the smallest taste again, I need it back. *I need to find that yellow pill.*

Six Years Ago

Thursday, July 19th

Keelie's grip clenched onto my hand as though her life depended on it. My cousin Luca sped around the narrow, twisting streets of the small Italian village that my family originated from. His car came to a screeching halt next to a tiny structure made of cement blocks and covered in a stucco roof that was missing more than a few tiles. Inside the small structure was an even smaller wooden bench held up by more cement blocks. This seemingly abandoned bus stop had seen better days.

"Quand'è il prossimo autobus?" I asked Luca as Keelie tossed open the passenger door. *When's the next bus?*

"You told me I'd never need to know how to say that," Keelie scoffed under her breath. I flashed a guilty smile and squeezed her hand as my reply.

"Dieci minuti." *Ten minutes.* Luca turned fully around to us, a mischievous look on his face. "O forse venti." *Or maybe twenty.* "If you are here longer than thirty minutes, call me."

"So, whenever he feels like showing up, huh?" I laughed.

"Calmatevi, americani." Luca grinned. *Calm down, Americans.* "He'll get here when he gets here. Enjoy Venezia."

"Grazie, Luca," Keelie called back to him, dragging me out of the car.

"Grazie, cugino," I reluctantly replied as I closed the door. *Thanks, cousin.*

Luca cut his wheel hard to the left and pulled off the curb, spinning his car back in the direction we had come from a moment ago. Keelie stood next to the cement structure, gazing out into the vastness of nature in front of us. Tall, overgrown shrubs surrounded most of the bus-stop structure. Beyond that, rows and rows of tree-covered hills. Even farther back, a series of tall, snow-capped mountains pierced the skyline. A warm Mediterranean breeze brushed against our skin, and our ears filled with the white noise of rustling branches.

I wrapped an arm around Keelie's shoulders, pulling her close to me, kissing her on her temple so I wouldn't interrupt her awestruck gaze.

"Imagine how plain the rest of the world must look when *this* is your ordinary," Keelie sighed, her eyes tracing the peaks of every mountain before her.

"Only you could make a bus stop poetic," I mumbled appreciatively into the top of her head.

She turned her gaze up to me and teased, "And only *you* could be in a place surrounded by the most beautiful trees and mountains and warm Mediterranean sun and see just a bus stop."

I pointed, drawing her attention to the bright blue sign with an image of a bus only a few feet from where we stood.

"Well then," she sharply replied, "it's the most beautiful bus stop I've ever seen."

"You're right about that, Keelie Mae."

Keelie flipped her backpack off one shoulder, unzipped the front pocket, and fished out a piece of paper that she and Luca had taken turns scribbling on this morning. A pros and cons–styled list that they had worked on over breakfast. The headings at the top were labeled Must See and Must Skip, with the list of must-see spots significantly longer and more refined, and the must-skip column mostly filled with sarcastic comments, like "Skip all tourist-covered bridges" and "Don't even think about visiting Piazza San Marco between the hours of eight and eight."

We had only the weekend in Venice. We were in Italy with my family, but this was Keelie's first time visiting, and I wanted to show her more of Italy than the hillside village my family called home. Venice was the closest big city to their town, so that's where we went. Keelie insisted on one day of seeing each and every hokey tourist attraction the city had to offer. After getting all the tourist destinations out of the way, we would spend the rest of our quick trip living like locals, visiting cafés in cozy alleyways, and drinking our weight in wine.

The bus rolled up to our tiny shack of a bus stop after fifteen minutes. On board, we immediately stood out as tourists, every pair of eyes from the handful of people on board glued to us as we shuffled our way to the first pair of open seats.

An old woman across the aisle, with leathery, tanned skin and braided gray hair, kept her eyes fixed on us long after we took our seats. I nodded a hello and quickly added, "Buonasera, signora."

The soft wrinkles of her face folded into a warm smile as she replied, "Buonasera," and turned her attention away from us.

Keelie nestled her face into my shoulder and whispered, "Is it that obvious that we don't belong here?"

"There aren't a lot of unfamiliar faces around here," I explained.

"Next time we should make shirts that say *Arvali* so everyone knows who we are."

The hotel we booked was close to Piazza San Marco, and boasted of gorgeous views of the Grand Canal and the city skyline, with a small balcony for us to enjoy the Mediterranean sunsets. When we finally checked in, we were utterly shocked by how incredibly tiny our room was. It was so small that I could touch the closet door while lying on the bed. And Keelie could draw the curtains with her head still buried under the comforter.

Keelie held my hand in hers and snorted as she wondered, "Can we touch both ends at once?"

Instead of reaching for the opposite wall, I extended my arm straight up in the air, noting the exceptionally high ceilings. "It might be taller than it is wide."

I took to the closet, intending to toss our backpacks inside. Instead of an actual open closet space, there was an oversize dresser shoved behind the closet door. The dresser was so large, the drawers couldn't fully open without the folds of the accordion-style closet doors getting in the way. I had to give both of our backpacks a hearty shove to get them to fit inside the drawers through the small opening.

Keelie let out an audible gasp as she opened the doors to our balcony.

"What horrors await us out there?" I shouted out to her.

"Val," she whispered, as if she were trying not to alert a predator to her position. "Come look at this."

"Do I have to?" I cringed.

"Yes!" she snapped back, disappearing behind the flowing sheer curtains and fully stepping onto the balcony.

Pushing the curtains aside, I ducked my head through the unnaturally low doorway and stepped out onto the balcony behind her. Keelie leaned over the ledge. A canal stretched across our view, crossed with bridges every few blocks. The tall stucco buildings lining the canal were vibrant shades of yellow, orange, and pink, each with balconies at every window, for taking in the view. The red-tiled roofs of each building painted the ground as far as our eyes could see. Every once in a while, a church steeple or dome broke up the sea of red.

She turned to look at me, face glowing with excitement. "Can you believe this view?"

Before I could respond, she'd twisted back around, taking it all in once more. I wrapped her in my arms, nuzzling my face alongside hers. "It almost makes the cardboard box we're staying in worth it." I smirked and planted a kiss on her cheek.

"We're going to be spending all our time out here anyway," she said, eyeing up the woven chairs sitting on one side of the balcony.

Down below, gondolas with small lanterns attached to their noses wound their way through the ever-darkening canals. A few gondoliers shouted back and forth to each other as the tourists in their boats snapped photos of the light rays from the setting sun shining across the canal.

"Aren't they supposed to be serenading the riders with beautiful Italian ballads?" Keelie wrinkled her nose, unable to take her eyes off the bustling city.

"You probably have to pay extra for that," I informed her, "and even when you do, I bet they're not happy about doing it."

"That's disappointing," she said. "Luckily, I have you to serenade me with beautiful Italian ballads during our ride."

"I'd be happy to." I buried my face into the sweet scent of her hair and whispered in her ear, "For fifty euro."

Keelie busted out a laugh. "You think they'd charge fifty euro for that? That's absurd!"

"I don't know. It's a tourist trap, Keelie Mae. They'd charge you for the water you're floating on if they could."

"Yeah," she sighed, a longing look taking over her face as she continued to watch the commotion of the canal.

I pulled her tight into my side. "Let's go find one."

"No," she replied sharply. "Tourist day isn't until tomorrow."

"But I want to go now."

"No, you don't." She laughed, graciously extending me the option to back out of my offer.

"Okay, but you do. So that means I want to." I laced my fingers through hers. "Please?"

"As long as the record can reflect that the hokey gondola ride was completely your idea."

"I will take full credit for the tourist-trap boat ride."

We took to the cobblestone streets outside of our hotel and were welcomed by shoulder-to-shoulder crowds of tourists. Keelie grabbed my wrist as she stepped out into the crowded street. I returned the wrist-clamped hold, solidifying our grip. Winding through the field of people, Keelie propelled us to the opposite side of the street. After breaking free of the crowd, I spun her into my arms and held on to her tight.

"This is absolute madness." Keelie relaxed into my arms.

"Tourist day is going to be like this all day," I reminded her.

"I'm ready for it." She nodded confidently.

"Ehi! Americani! Hello!" A man in black pants and a black-and-white striped shirt shouted at us from under a green awning. "Come take a ride, eh?"

"Quanto costa?" I hollered back over the noise of the crowd. *How much?*

"Cento euro."

Keelie's jaw dropped. "Grazie, no."

"Keelie Mae." I nudged her. "Come on."

"Matty," she snapped, "he said one *hundred* euros. We aren't doing that."

"This tourist trap is my idea, remember?"

Without waiting for her protest, I clung to her wrist and dragged her toward the awning, handing the striped-shirt man my credit card. The man's welcoming expression completely dropped. He angrily shouted toward his coworkers, swiping my card without another word, and ushering us toward an empty dock, instructing us to wait for the next group to return.

"Sono americani," the one who took our money shouted out to the gondolier as he docked his gondola and unloaded his previous passengers.

"Ciao. Hello, americani!" he shouted at us. "English, sì?"

"Sì, in inglese per lei," I replied, nodding my head to Keelie. *English for her.*

"No, non serve," Keelie said confidently. "Van bene in italiano." *Italian is fine.*

"Okay," he said, ignoring her request, "get in."

"For one hundred euros, he should carry me onto this boat," Keelie scoffed under her breath.

I wrapped my arms around her waist and lifted her up into the air. "Val, stop!" She screeched out a big laugh.

"I want to be sure you're getting all that you paid for." I planted her feet right at the edge of the dock and held out a hand to help her balance as she stepped on board.

I sat next to her on the bench inside the gondola, wrapping my arm around her shoulders, taking one of her hands in mine. The bright Mediterranean sunset reflected in the water of the Grand Canal, surrounding us in vibrant shades of pink, orange, and purple. Every dock had a glowing black lantern, and café lights were strung across the canal way, lighting our path like stars in the sky.

Hundreds of gondolas filled the waters of the canal, and plenty of motorized boats added noise and pollution to the already crowded and noisy streets along both sides of the water. Gondoliers held full conversations with one another from opposite sides of the canal, further breaking the peace.

"It's not quite the grand romantic experience I had envisioned," Keelie sighed, "but it sure is beautiful."

I pressed a kiss to her temple, then leaned my head against hers as we admired the view. "Yeah, it is."

"Hey, americani!" the gondolier called out. "Where are you from? New York?"

"No." I laughed. "Di St. Louis."

"Di San Louis?" he asked. "Mai sentito." *I don't know it.*

"È nel mezzo," I replied. *It's in the middle.*

"Come mai a Venezia? Turisti?" *What brings you to Venice? Tourists?*

"No, faccio visita ai miei parenti." *Visiting family.*

"E questa bellissima signoria? È tua parente o è la tua ragaz-za?" *And the beautiful lady? Is she your family or your girlfriend?*

"Lei è tutta la mia vita." *She's my whole life.*

Our gondolier put a hand to his heart and clicked his tongue a few times against the roof of his mouth. "Che bella." He dug his stick deep into the canal and gave us a slow push forward. "Bellissima Ragazza," he said to Keelie, simply calling her *Beautiful Girlfriend.* "Do you know what it is he says of you?"

"Yeah," she replied, her gaze clinging to me. "I know what that means."

"Siete così carini," he staccatos softly. *You are so cute.* "How long are you together?"

"Eight years," Keelie replied with a laugh.

"Eight years," he gasped. Then he yelled to me, "Ehi, rubacuori! Ha detto otto anni?" *Hey, lover boy! Did she say eight years?*

"Sì, otto anni," I confirmed.

"Dio mio," he scoffed under his breath. "Uh, listen to me, Bellissima Ragazza. If you ever are tired of waiting for this rubacuori to marry you, please, you give me a call. You are too beautiful to be with someone who will not marry you."

Keelie snapped her gaze to the gondolier with a menacing grin. "What makes you think he won't marry me? Maybe I won't marry him."

"Ostrega. Come with me, Bellissima Ragazza, and I will give you a beautiful life."

"I already have a beautiful life," she said confidently, turning her attention back to me. "Tutta la mia vita." *My whole life.*

We returned to our hotel room with a full bag of snacks that we picked up from a grocery store. Meats and cheese, olives, fruit. We both carried a bottle of wine in each hand. Keelie passed one of hers off to me to tuck into my arm as she dug the room key out of her pocket. She wasted no time breaking the foil of the bottle of prosecco she had in her grasp, twisting the metal ring that caged the top of the cork and giving it a soft tug until it busted off with a loud *pop!*

I scooped up the two glasses the hotel provided us, offering them up to Keelie one at a time for her to fill. She poured the first one so heavy-handedly that bubbles immediately jumped to the top of the glass. I knocked her hand back and pressed the glass to my lips to sip down the bubbles. Her second pour was more steady.

With her filled glass, she made her way out onto the patio and settled into one of the wicker chairs to watch night fall over the busy city. I brought the bottle of prosecco with me as I stepped out onto the patio behind her, and Keelie chastised me when she saw I had only one of our bottles in hand.

"I thought you wanted to have a good time in Venezia? Go get the rest of them!"

"You want all four?" I raised an eyebrow at her. "What am I going to do with you, Keelie Mae?"

"Drink wine. I thought I made that abundantly clear."

I ducked back into the room, needing only two strides to reach the remaining three bottles of wine.

"Are you trying to get me drunk, Bellissima Ragazza?"

She topped off my already plenty-full glass with another pour from the bottle of prosecco. "Yes, I am."

As the sun sunk deeper and deeper beyond the horizon, a chilly breeze overtook the canal way and our balcony. A brisk breeze that not even the warmth of a few glasses of prosecco or Chianti could cure. We retreated to the room and curled up at the head of the bed, backs pressed against the headboard, the wine causing our shoulders to slump closer and closer together until we practically depended on each other for support.

Keelie leaned her head against my shoulder, whispering softly into my ear, "What's on your mind, Val?"

I smirked at her. "You telling that flirty Italian guy you didn't want to marry me."

Keelie leaned away from me so she could let free a full-bodied laugh. "You say 'flirty Italian guy' like that doesn't describe you to a T." She swayed back, her head falling to my shoulder once more. "You've never asked me to marry you, Val."

"Why would I ask you that?" I teased.

She pulled her face away, giving me a scowl. Her blood turned to a boil so quickly I could see a soft shade of crimson flood to her wine-warmed face. "Oh, I don't know," she snapped back defensively, "maybe because you love me and you want to spend your life with me."

"That's true. And you feel the same. So why would I ask you a question I already know the answer to?"

Her scowl softened slightly as she studied me.

"I'm going to marry you," I assured her. "I don't need to ask if you want to because I know you do. And someday I *am* going to marry you. And then I'm going to buy you a beautiful house. Something that's close enough to your family so they can stop by whenever they want, but somehow also far enough from my family so my mom doesn't move in."

She snorted out a soft laugh.

"And whatever we find, we have to be sure it has an identical house next door for Sam to live in."

"I would love that," she admitted.

"I know you would. I know everything about you, mia vita. I'm going to give you everything you want and more."

Keelie twisted her legs into a pretzel knot as she turned her body to face me, as if she was about to say something deeply meaningful. Instead she said, "*Mia Vita* would be a great stage name. I'm using that if I ever become famous."

"To the rest of the world you'll be Mia Vita, but you'll always be Mia Mae to me."

"Mia Mae and the Rubacuori." She smirked.

"Do you know what that means?" I demanded with a glare.

She contemplated. "No, but if a flirty Italian man said it, it must be true."

"He means it to be like a heartbreaker. A ladies' man."

"That sounds like you."

I squeezed her hand in mine. "Just the one lady for me. It's always been you, and it always will be you."

She leaned in close to me. Close enough that I could study the stripes of color that made up her beautiful eyes. Her bottom eyelid pinched inward, only slightly, challenging me as she added, "And yet for some reason, you won't ask me to marry you."

I sprung off the bed and retrieved the metal ring from our first bottle of prosecco. Sliding it onto her finger, I stubbornly replied, "You're going to marry me, Mia Mae. Not a question."

She narrowed her eyes and said "If it's not a question, then I don't have to give you an answer" as she twisted the metal tab a few times, tightening the metal ring to the correct size. She held out her hand to examine it, then with a sarcastic grin she said, "It's beautiful, Val."

"Only the best for you."

She stole the almost-empty glass from my hand and let the last of the wine from the bottle next to her *glug glug glug* into my glass until the steady stream of wine filled it almost to the rim. She licked a drop of wine rolling down the neck of the bottle suggestively, then giggled as she placed it down on the floor and returned with an unopened bottle.

I skimmed a large gulp of wine off the top of my glass before placing it on the table on my side of the bed so I could uncork the next bottle.

"I can't believe this wine was five dollars," she said through purple teeth, aggressively passing the unopened bottle to me. "We should bring this back with us. All of it. Suitcases full of wine."

"Imagine the baggage fees," I posed.

She scowled. "I didn't think of that."

Pulling her glass from her grasp, I filled it to the top.

"Maybe that's because this is our third bottle of wine, Mia."

She snorted. "Is it really the third one?" She leaned off the edge of the bed to check out the "floor cellar," as she called it, below. When she snapped back upright, her face glowed with surprise. "When did that happen?"

"About ten seconds ago."

With the most serious expression she could muster after four hearty glasses of wine, she said, "Bring it on."

"This is your last one," I informed her as I pressed the cork back into the bottle. My firm tone was betrayed by my love for her. I couldn't even pretend to be mad.

"No," she replied innocently, "we have the rest of that bottle and still one more after that."

I squished her cheeks between my hands and pressed my forehead to hers. Creases at the corners of her eyes accompanied her guilty giggle.

"No more wine," I scolded, kissing her purple-hued lips.

"Fine, but first thing tomorrow we're finishing them." She raised a glass to me. "You know what they say, Quando sei a Venezia . . ." *When in Venice . . .*

"O come cavolo è." *Or something like that.* I tap my glass of wine to hers.

IV
Wednesday, April 25th

Tonight's dream starts as a beautiful moment spent with my family, but it slowly melts into this same horrible nightmare I've had a thousand times before.

But for the first time, I am completely alone as I walk down the hallway. Keelie isn't with me. I press open the door, worrying that I'll find her inside instead of Rich, but he's still the one who is there. I've been here so many times, I've grown numb to this image of him. But yet, I feel a pang of anxiety surge through me. Without Keelie, this is unfamiliar territory. This is not the dream I usually have. This isn't how it happened.

I take slow and steady breaths as I walk toward Rich. He looks back at me, awake, his eyes pleading with me. Something isn't right, but I can't figure out what it is.

Then Rich stands. He reaches his hand toward me. His arm stretches out to a length only possible in a dream. He points a finger at me, then touches my nose. When his icy finger makes contact with my skin, my body realizes there is something in the real world touching my nose, too. This touch jolts me awake.

When I open my eyes, two small eyes are staring back at me. I let out a breathy yelp and the little eyes retreat with a giggle. Chris's booming laugh surges from the doorway. I take a few deep breaths to calm my heart rate, then look around, trying to decipher what is going on.

"Scusa, Picco," Chris apologizes. "She was excited to see you"—he turns to Luci—"but I told her not to wake you up."

She giggles again mischievously.

I rub my eyes, trying to ground myself back into reality. I sit up. The nausea sways my stomach slightly, but it feels much more in control than it had a few days ago.

"Luci, come here," I say sternly.

She looks up at her dad, pleading for protection, but he flicks his hand in my direction, telling her to go. She slowly creeps toward me, her head tilted down so she can look up at me with her beautiful big eyes. She stands at the side of the bed, afraid she's about to be in trouble.

"Do you know what I do to people who wake me up when I'm sleeping?" I demand.

She shakes her head bashfully.

I hold my hands up like claws and lunge toward her, shouting, "I tickle them!"

A smile bursts across her face. She shrieks and runs away laughing. As she shouts her way back into the living room, a second tiny voice joins her in the screaming.

"Luciana! Katya! Stop screaming!" a third groans. Michelle.

I exchange glances with Chris, the excitement on his face echoing what I'm feeling inside.

"By the way, the girls are coming home sometime this morning." Chris laughs. "I'll let you know when they get here."

He ducks back out into the hallway, grunting as he scoops up one of the screaming creatures he's inflicted on the world. Another shriek of laughter erupts. I get up and find Michelle slumped over the table in the kitchen, a mug of coffee clutched tightly in her hand. Chris chases Luci and Katy around the house, threatening to blow raspberries on their bellies if he catches them. "Mind if I join you?" I call out as I make my way to the table.

"As long as you promise not to scream, be my guest," she mumbles. Then she brightens her tone to add, "It's good to see you, Matty."

"Were you here a couple of days ago?" I ask as I sit down next to her.

"I was." She studies me. "You gave us a bit of a scare. Glad to see you're doing better."

"Much. Thank you."

Michelle runs through a series of questions to gauge how much concern she should continue to exhibit. Nausea? Exhaustion? Sleeping any? I tell her I'm feeling much less nauseous, but I'm not sleeping much and I'm so fucking tired.

Katy lets out another loud shriek. Michelle groans. "Me too. My parents spent the whole week getting the girls wound up and then passing them off to me."

"Thank you for letting me stay here," I say. "I'm sorry to put you out."

"No!" she replies, already more energy in her voice. "Don't mention it. That was stupid of me to say. Of course you're welcome here, anytime."

"Zio Piccolo?" Luci squeaks from behind me.

I turn around to see her standing in the doorway, with Chris right behind her.

Despite the brain fog and the slight ripple of dizziness that hovers inside my body, I put on my best happy face to invite her to speak.

"Do you want to play a game?" she asks nervously.

"I'd love to, Luci. What do you want to play?"

"Scopa," she says very matter-of-factly.

I look to Chris for an explanation. He shrugs slyly, as if he doesn't know where she could have learned it from.

"Will you remind me how to play?" I ask Luci. "It's been a long time."

She agrees, then runs off to find the deck. The game has its own special deck of cards, with its own suits: coins, clubs, cups, and swords.

It's mostly a game of counting and basic math. And gambling. That was always Nonna's favorite part.

"How do you know how to play Scopa?" Luci asks me as she deals the first round.

"My nonna taught me," I tell her, "same as your dad. We used to play with her when we would visit her in Italy. Way before you were born."

"You go first, Zio Picco," Luci instructs excitedly.

My hands jitter all the way to the table. When I try to pick up the three cards she's dealt me, my fingers jump away from them in a violent shake. It takes multiple attempts for me to get them off the table, and even then, I'm only able to get them in my hands by sliding them across the table's surface and over the edge into my palm.

As I rotate my cards to study them, one slips right through my shaking fingers and onto the floor.

"Luciana," Chris nudges her toward my fallen card.

"I don't want to cheat," she whines in protest.

"I've got it," I reply confidently, leaning over to grab the card. When my leg presses into my stomach, I'm hit once again with rising nausea. I take deep breaths, pushing past it, fighting through it, but it isn't enough.

I toss my cards down on the table and bolt toward the bathroom without offering an explanation.

As I heave into the toilet, there is a light knock on the door. I feel a sense of déjà vu. All the times I had too much to drink, in combination with the pills I had taken, and lost control of my stomach. But this time, the knock on the door comes from Michelle, not Keelie.

"Matteo?" she calls quietly. "Are you okay?"

I wait a moment to make sure I'm not going to vomit mid-sentence before replying, "Yeah."

"Can I come in?" she asks. When I don't answer, she opens the door and lets herself in. She sits on the edge of the bathtub behind me, the same way Keelie used to do. She offers a glass of water and then says, "Have you had a Dramamine today?"

I shake my head. "I thought I was done with the nausea."

She holds out a pill to me. "Maybe tomorrow."

I take it from her graciously, feeling terrible that she has to take care of me on her declared day off from parenting. I'm an adult. Why haven't I figured out how to take care of myself?

As Michelle retreats to the kitchen, she says "Zio Picco is going to be fine" in a confident tone, assuring Luci that my sudden bout of sickness is nothing to worry about. I glance up just long enough to see Luci peeking around the door frame at me, witnessing firsthand how pathetic I really am.

By the time I return, Chris, Luci, and Katy are curled up on the couch. Chris has his tablet leaning against his knees, and the girls are taking turns shouting over each other on a video call. Chris beams, resigned to letting them ramble and shout.

"Zia Ellie! I have a loose tooth! Do you want to see?" Luci asks, attempting to wiggle a tooth that is nowhere near moving.

"Wow! Look at that!" Ellie replies enthusiastically.

"Eleonora?" I shout excitedly, scooping Luci up off the couch, taking a seat next to Chris, and plopping Luci down on my lap.

Ellie and Nick are on the other end of the video call. It's been a long time since I've seen either of them. Ellie looks so different. Her brown hair is sun-faded with soft golden edges. It's wavy and slightly frizzy like beach hair, even though they live at least two hours from the ocean. Her olive skin is deeply darkened by the sun, and she wears layers and layers of necklaces, some tight on her neck, others hanging long and out of frame.

Nick, on the other hand, looks the same. His hair closely cut on the sides, longer and twisted into short curls on top. His cleanly cut beard frames his bright white teeth, which are practically luminous against his dark skin. His slightly sloped eyes make him look as though he's permanently smiling, even when he isn't.

"Ciao, fratellino!" Ellie screeches back. *Hey, baby brother!* Then she adds, "Wow, you look awful."

"You should have seen him three days ago," Chris helpfully adds.

"Vaffanculo. Both of you."

"She knows what that means!" Michelle shouts from the kitchen as Luci giggles guiltily.

I tilt my gaze down to Luci. "You don't know what that means, do you?"

"I know it's a bad word." She snickers.

"Who's teaching you bad words?" I demand.

"Daddy." She smiles slyly at Chris. Chris gives her a playful glare. *Oh whatever.*

"And probably Zio Picco," Ellie adds.

I feign offense. "Never."

Michelle emerges from the kitchen, her position having been revealed, with a steaming cup of coffee. She sits on the other side of Chris, and Katy crawls onto her lap, goofily hanging across both of her parents.

"Hey, guys," Michelle says casually, as though they have this chat daily.

"You don't look so good either." Ellie's eyes grow wide as she examines us more closely.

Michelle leans her gaze across Chris right to me, making sure her annoyed expression translates clearly into the camera's view. "Wow."

"Sorry, it's true," Ellie teases. "What the hell is going on over there?"

"I've been spewing my guts out for the last six days." I sigh.

"It shows. Majorly."

Nick laughs. "Why are you so mean to your family?"

"I'm not mean! Just honest. I don't want to lie to them. If they look like spazzatura, I'm going to tell them." Ellie turns back to us. "Detto con tutto l'amore del mondo." *I say it with all the love in the world.*

"Come potremmo dubitarne?" I grumble back. *How could we doubt it?*

"How's it been going this time around, fratellino?"

Horrible. Miserable. Awful. "Good."

Chris snorts in disagreement.

"È una gran rottura di coglioni," I amend my reply. *It fucking sucks.*

"Michelle, what's your excuse?" Ellie asks.

"I've been taking care of two crazy kids"—she gives Katy a big kiss on her cheek—"all by myself while my husband ditches me to hang out with his brother."

"Oh, yeah. We've been having a blast," Chris scoffs.

"Is it weird that I wish I could be there?" Ellie asks.

"Next time I relapse, I'll be sure to detox at your house so you don't miss out on the fun."

"No next time," Chris reminds me again.

"Sorry, Elle. You missed your shot."

"That's okay, fratellino. I'd rather have you healthy."

"Yeah, we all would," Chris says, elbowing me in the side.

I run my fingers through my hair, buying myself a second of time. One moment where I don't have to quickly answer with a lie. "I'm working on it, alright?" I promise them, but I don't mean it. I would stay sober as long as I had to, and eventually I'd get back to pills. There wasn't anything to *work* on. I knew where I'd rather be.

Fifteen Years Ago

Wednesday, August 13th

The music was cranked up loud, just loud enough that we could drown out the sound of the exceptionally loud car muffler of Rich's beat-up sedan. Rich was in the front seat. On his bad days, he made Keelie sit in the passenger seat next to him because, as he said, "I'm not your fucking chauffeur." On his good days, he let Keelie sit in the back seat with me because "it's cool if you want to hang out with your friends more than your dad."

On good days, Rich was one of my favorite people to be around. He was laid back, fun, adventurous. We went to museums, landmarks, roadside attractions. He took us to his favorite restaurants, places he went to as a kid, places he heard about an hour ago and couldn't possibly rest until he saw. He was always on the move on his good days. He was excited about everything and wanted to share it all with us.

We usually didn't see Rich on his bad days. He'd lie on the couch, or he'd retreat into his room. Some days, he would leave all together and stay with Grandma Linda, Rich's mom. Some days, Keelie and her siblings would all get shipped off to live with their grandma for a week while Rich "figured things out."

I liked the days that Rich had to figure things out because Keelie's Grandma Linda lived in the house directly behind my parents. I'd scale the fence that separated our yards, and we'd stay outside until it was too dark to see. My dad would yell out "Matteo, adiamo!" to tell me it was time to come back home

If we did see Rich on those days, he usually said things like "Fuck off, I'm sleeping," even when we knew he was awake. Then Keelie's mom would get angry at him. Rich would reply, "She's heard me say it a thousand times already. What's one more going to hurt?"

Today was a good day for Rich. He was fixated on a sandwich place he had been to one time six years ago. He found out they were still open, and he suddenly had to have it.

"Do you remember when we went there?" he asked Keelie.

"No?" She rolled her eyes. "I was seven."

"Man. You fucking loved it. We should go again."

While Good-Day Rich said, "We should go," Bad-Day Rich would have said, "Get in the fucking car." Either way, as soon as he decided he wanted to go somewhere, we went.

Keelie asked if she could sit in the back seat with me, and Rich said, "Of course," as though it were the stupidest question he'd ever heard.

"I think I'm going to find us a place to go camping next weekend," Rich said out of the blue as we pulled off the highway.

"Ugh. Camping?" I groaned.

"Yeah, what's wrong with that?" Rich met my eyes in the rearview mirror.

"That sounds super boring," I scoffed. "I hate the outdoors."

He locked eyes with me. He was no longer looking at the road as we propelled forward.

"What did you just say?" he snarled.

"I don't know," I backpedaled. "Nature's just really boring. Can we do something at Forest Park instead?"

I didn't fully believe what I was saying. The truth was, I knew Rich spent a lot of time exploring the city, and I thought *he* hated the outdoors. I said what I thought he would say because I wanted to be just like him.

Rich kept his eyes locked on me as he yanked the steering wheel hard to the left and whipped the car across three lanes of traffic to put us in the opposite direction. A car horn honked violently, but we were unscratched by the stunt. He pressed hard on the accelerator and we sped off back toward the highway.

Wide-eyed, Keelie looked to me as if to say, *What did you do?* And then she smiled because she knew we were on another one of her dad's spontaneous adventures.

After forty-five minutes of driving down the highway at the fastest speeds I'd ever traveled in a car, Keelie leaned her head to the front seat and said, "Dad, where are we going?"

He held up a hand to silence her and said, "You'll fucking see. Just wait."

The roads were getting more hilly, the ground more tree-covered. Houses became more sporadic, tucked away between the tall trees that could only be found on the outer edges of the city.

Another thirty minutes and we were on a two-lane highway, a tall canopy of trees creating a tunnel across the road. I glanced at the speedometer and saw that Rich was driving almost ninety miles per hour. His car shook violently any time he took it over eighty, which he rarely did. But this moment called for some serious urgency, so he ignored the car's shaking to get to our destination.

"Dad?" Keelie pleaded. "Will you tell us where we're going?"

"Five minutes, Keelie Mae." This time he almost sang his words. His face lit up with excitement.

Eight minutes later, he slowed down his speed and came to an almost stop as he carefully pulled into a gravel driveway of a parking lot tucked right off the highway. A sign at the entrance read Elephant Rocks State Park.

He put the car in park and looked at us through the rearview mirror.

"Alright, let's go."

"Where are we going?" Keelie asked, but Rich didn't answer. He got out of the car and slammed the door behind him, taking off toward a nearby trailhead.

Keelie and I exchanged confused glances. She shrugged, and we both got out of the car and chased after him.

He charged along an easy hiking trail for what felt like miles when we weren't sure where we were headed.

He led us to a spot on the trail that was lined with large rock walls. A narrow pass between two of them seemed to be his destination.

"Go on," he said, gesturing to the space between the rocks.

Keelie looked to me and then back at her dad. "What is it?"

He glared at her. "Do you trust me?"

"Yes," she replied without hesitation.

Then he turned to me. "Matty?"

I nodded, though I wasn't nearly as confident about it as Keelie was. "Yeah," I replied.

He clapped his hands together one time, encouragingly. "Okay, then. Go climb to the top."

Keelie turned her smile to me, then poked her head through the pass between the rocks. I followed closely behind, and Rich behind me. At the top of the tiny climb, we were on a completely level, completely smooth rock surface.

In front of us were the most enormous boulders we had ever seen, placed precariously on the edge, seemingly ready to roll away at any moment. There were dozens of them, all lined up on this granite tabletop. It was as if someone had intentionally piled them all there.

Keelie and I stood in awe of these giant boulders, but Rich strode right past them, finding his home on the opposite side of the largest one. He sat on the ground, his back up against the rock. He looked out into the sky before him. Miles and miles of trees rolled across the skyline in front of us in every direction. The sun was getting ready to set, and Rich had planted himself there to watch it.

Keelie sat down next to him. He put an arm around her shoulders. When I sat down next to Keelie, he extended his arm to lay his hand on my shoulder.

"Give it an hour, and your mind is going to be blown," he promised.

Rich took a deep breath, taking in the nature that surrounded us. Then he nodded his head, like he decided he'd seen enough. He shifted his body, lifting one leg off the ground slightly and leaning into Keelie, which pushed her into me. He slid a small black notebook from his back pocket, then dug into his front pocket for a pen.

He carried this notebook with him everywhere, scribbling down secret thoughts whenever the urge struck him. "This notebook is the only thing keeping my head on my shoulders," he'd often say, tapping on its worn front cover. As he flipped through it in search of a blank page, I had my first and only glimpse at what went on inside.

Some pages were full of small, neat letters, written in perfectly straight lines. The words so tiny, they were impossible to make out. Other pages were filled with deep, angry lines. Lines so deep, they'd cut through the paper, straight through to the page behind it. Jagged lines, abstract drawings, and hateful words spread, in no particular order, all over the page.

The last occupied page had one word scribbled in the middle. Rich flipped past it so quickly, I couldn't make out what it said, but the lines had been pressed so heavily into the page that it passed through multiple pages. Rich flipped past a few more blank pages until he got to one that wasn't damaged by pen strokes ripping through. He passed the notebook to me.

"Draw what you see," he instructed. "And *only* what you see. It'll make you better. Remember that pen trick I taught you?"

I extended my arm straight out in front of me, closing one eye and leveling the pen with the skyline.

"That's right," Rich said proudly as I transferred the angle of the pen onto the page in front of me.

As I drew, I studied the paper carefully, trying to make out the word that had left an indent on it. I picked out an *E* as I traced the line of the horizon. The *N* as my pen followed the outline of the granite cliff edge. As I dotted the speckles of the rock onto the page in front of me, I could see a *D*. I found the letter *I* as my pen mimicked the long, wispy clouds that zigzagged across the sky. And as I started shading in the dark leaves of the trees, scratching the rest of the word out of recognition, I realized the last letter was a *T. End it?*

"You know that red cobblestone down by the Arch that you love so much?" Rich asked Keelie, their conversation pulling my attention away from the letters pressed into the page.

"Yes," Keelie remembered.

"They got all that rock from right here," Rich said, pointing a finger to the ground below us.

"From the Elephant Rocks?" Keelie asked, appalled. "You mean there used to be more of these, and they chopped them up for roads?"

Rich shook his head violently. "Not from these rocks." He lifted a hand and smacked the rock he was leaning up against for emphasis. "Rock from the quarry."

Keelie crinkled her eyebrow; she didn't understand what he meant.

"You know what a fucking quarry is, Keelie Mae."

"Yeah, I know what a quarry is, Dad," she grumbled, offended. "But I don't see one here."

Rich extended his hand out to his right, closing one eye to better see what Keelie's view might have looked like. "It's right about there," he said, sweeping his point in a circle on the horizon. "Matty, make sure you get that in your drawing, okay?"

"I can't *see* the quarry," I snarked back. "You told me to only draw what I could see."

"Use your fucking imagination." He laughed. "Then you'll see it clear as day."

As the sun set, the Elephant Rocks glowed pink with the reflection of the sky. The three of us sat, watching in awe as the bright summer sun finally fell behind the horizon. It was spectacular.

"Hey, Matty?" Rich called. "Don't you ever let me hear you say nature is boring again. You got it?"

I smiled. "Yeah, okay. This is pretty awesome."

"Yeah, it's fucking awesome," he confirmed. Then he tilted his head to Keelie. "What do you think? Did I do good or what?"

"Yeah, this place is really cool, Dad."

He gazed out at the darkening sky, a look of pride pricking at his cheeks. "Yeah." He waited a moment longer, contemplating his next move. "So I'm thinking of finding us a place to go camping next weekend. Are you guys in or what?"

"Okay." I laughed.

"I think we'll bring Sam with us, too. He's old enough. Just the four of us. Does that sound good to you, Keelie Mae?"

She nodded, resting her head on her dad's shoulder.

"Of course I have to buy some camping stuff first," he pondered. "I bet your grandma still has a tent lying around. Do you like s'mores, Matty?"

"Sure." I shrugged. "S'mores are good."

"And I'm bringing lots of whiskey," he said. "I'll let you have some if you don't tell your mom."

Keelie scrunched her face. "I don't know."

"You'll love it," he promised. "Someday."

It was almost pitch-black dark on our walk back to the car. I didn't want to say anything, but every noise that rustled in the woods beside us completely terrified me. I wasn't even fully sure we were on the right trail. The small sliver of moon was the only light we had guiding our way.

"Guess I should have grabbed a flashlight, huh?" Rich considered. "There wasn't any time for that, though."

If it weren't so dark, I knew I'd see Keelie locking eyes with me so we could laugh about this later. Her dad never thought through any of his plans. It was getting darker by the second, and our hike went on for much longer than it had on our way to the Elephant Rocks; I was sure of that. We finally stumbled upon the trailhead and our car, alone in the parking lot.

Rich jumped in, and Keelie occupied the front seat next to him because she loved being around him when he lit up this way.

He couldn't stop talking about camping the entire way home. He talked about where we could go, what we should see. He walked Keelie through how to start a fire and promised she was going to be an expert at it by the time we were done. He drove much slower now, enjoying every curve of the road on the ride back home.

After well over two hours of driving, we pulled onto Keelie's street, and Rich immediately let out a "motherfucker" when he saw a police car parked on their driveway.

Rich turned to Keelie. "Your mom called the fucking cops," he scoffed. "Be cool, alright?"

When we stepped inside, my parents, Keelie's mom, and two police officers were standing around the table.

"Oh, thank God," Keelie's mom, Makaela, sighed when we walked in the door. She pulled Keelie in for a hug.

"What's going on?" Rich asked cluelessly.

"Where have you been?" Makaela demanded.

"We went hiking. Is that what this is about?"

"It's almost midnight!" Makaela yelled. "You've been gone for over fourteen hours."

My mom wrapped an arm around my shoulder and kissed the top of my head.

"Stai bene?" my dad asked. *Are you alright?*

"Siamo bene," I replied with a huff. *We're fine.*

"Sir, would you mind stepping outside for a minute?" one officer asked.

Rich held both his hands up in the air. "Fine."

He turned on his heels and headed back out the door.

The officers checked with both of us to make sure we were alright. They asked where we went, asked why, asked if we ever felt threatened. They seemed a bit confused by the starkness of our answers, but they didn't know Rich. Nothing he did ever made sense—that's what made him fun.

"Keelie can come stay with us tonight," Mom offered. "That way no one wakes up at Linda's house."

Makaela nodded. "That would be great, thank you."

When we went outside, Rich was sitting on the front step smoking a cigarette. He immediately stamped it out when he heard us step behind him. He hated that he smoked, and he always told us how stupid it was, even when we knew he snuck off multiple times a day to do it.

Rich stood and addressed my dad first. "Ben, I'm really sorry about the confusion."

Dad nodded with a warm smile.

Then Rich turned to Mom. "You guys know I'd never do anything that would put them in danger, though, right? I fucking love these kids."

Mom matched the warmth of Dad's smile, placing a gentle hand on his shoulder. "We know, dear."

Rich nodded, satisfied that he was absolved.

He pressed his forehead to Keelie's and said with a grin, "You leaving me to clean up this mess by myself?"

Keelie playfully patted her dad on his cheek. "I'm afraid so."

"She's going to go off on me, isn't she?" he asked.

Keelie scrunched her face and nodded.

"Wouldn't be the first time. Don't worry, I'll take care of it. I love you, sweetie. I'll see you soon, alright?"

He pulled her in for a big, crushing hug and gave her a face-squishing kiss on her cheek.

"You too, Matty." He extended his arm to me, scooping me into an equally enormous hug.

We said goodnight, and Rich sat back down on his step, waiting until we were almost gone from view to light up his cigarette again.

Chris and Ellie were both awake when we got home, sitting in the living room, anxiously awaiting an end to the excitement that disrupted their night.

"Dovresti essere a letto," my dad scolded as he walked through the door. *You're supposed to be in bed.*

Ellie's look pleaded for an exception.

"Va!" he instructed. *Go!*

She scurried off.

My parents didn't say anything about Keelie or me, so we sat down on the couch next to Chris. He was twenty years old and home from college for the summer.

"Where the hell have you been?" he whispered to me, hoping to be out of earshot of our parents.

"We went to Elephant Rocks," I said smugly.

"That place is like two hours away. What were you doing down there?"

"Going on an adventure." That's what Rich liked to call them. *Adventures.*

"An adventure?" he replied dubiously.

"Yes," I said, annoyed. "Because Rich is fun."

"You think Rich's adventures are *fun?*"

"Yes," I repeated, stepping up the hostility in my voice to express my unruly thirteen-year-old discontent.

"So the next time Makaela calls and says Rich is having a manic episode and she doesn't know where you guys are, you want me to say. . . 'It's fine, Mom. Matteo is probably having fun?'"

I rolled my eyes at him. "Whatever."

"No, I'm being serious. Everyone was freaking out, and you think that's fine because it was fun? You could be in *actual* danger when he's manic. You know that, right?"

I narrowed my eyes at him.

"You don't know what that means, do you?"

"I know what that means," I pushed back, even though I most certainly did not.

"Manic. Like the spontaneous Rich that takes you somewhere two hours away without telling your parents? Acts Impulsively? Dangerous maybe?"

The Good-Day Rich.

"But I bet you don't notice when he's manic as much as you notice when he's *not* manic. When he doesn't get out of bed. When he's mean. Does that one sound familiar?"

Bad-Day Rich.

"Rich isn't like this because he's *fun*, Matteo. He's like this because he has bipolar disorder and refuses to take his medication."

Keelie and her siblings stayed at their Grandma Linda's house for two weeks after that while Rich, once again, had to "figure things out." When we were allowed to see him, he was different. He usually was after he figured things out. He was back to being mean, hiding in his room.

One day, when I was at their house after school, he shuffled out of his hiding place and sat down on the couch. He motioned for us to come sit by him, so we did.

He held out a bottle of pills and said, "I'm going to be dull for a while. Your mom is making me take these pills that make me *boring*. I fucking hate them. But if I don't take them, I don't get to see you, and I love you so much." He turned to look at me. "Both of you. We'll get back to having fun again soon. I'm only going to be like this for a little while. Just until this all passes.

Then I'll ditch the boring pills, and we can go on that camping trip I promised you. Okay?"

We both nodded, and squeaked out, "Okay."

"Good," he replied, pleased, before he slumped back into the cave he had crawled out of.

A few weeks later, he stopped taking the pills that made him *boring,* but he never returned to his non-boring self. He never got to take us on the camping trip he had been planning. He slipped further and further into a dark, angry depression and killed himself two months later.

V
Friday, May 11th

"You smile a lot talking about Rich," Adam points out before taking his first sip of his espresso shot that is surely cold by now.

Adam is a different kind of doctor, more laid back than I'm used to. Maybe it's because he is friends with Chris and feels he can be more casual with me, or maybe he's this way with everyone. Either way, I actually enjoy talking to him most days.

He runs his practice out of an old home on Main Street in Elmwood. The space that was once a living room in this old house has been converted into a reception area, but I've never seen anyone else here besides Adam. At my first visit, Adam was seated at the front desk when we arrived, feet propped up on a filing cabinet, leaning way back in his chair. As soon as he saw us, he jumped to his feet and greeted Chris before introducing himself to me.

Instead of sitting in two opposite-facing chairs to start our session, Adam walked straight into the kitchen, where he had a Nespresso machine proudly displayed on the counter. "You like coffee, Matty?" he asked. He was buzzing as though he had already had more than a few shots from his Nespresso machine that morning. He showed me how to make it work, then took his tiny shot of espresso and casually sat at a table nearby without offering an explanation. He didn't say anything to officially start our session; he just started talking to me. I leaned against the counter for a while, expecting that eventually we would move elsewhere, but once it became clear he had settled in, I joined him at the table.

Every visit to Adam's office felt that informal. He didn't have a notebook anywhere in sight. He never wrote anything down, at least not in front of me, and yet he somehow always remembered everything I said. I felt more comfortable talking to him than I did other doctors like him, but despite Chris's insistence, I still didn't want to talk to him about Rich.

Until today, on my fourth visit with him. I can't stop thinking about Rich or the day we visited Elephant Rock.

"You don't talk about him much, do you?"

"Never," I reply immediately. "Not anymore."

"Only with Keelie?"

"And Sam, yeah." I sigh. "So, no one."

"Why's it so hard to open up about him?"

I shrug. "He doesn't exactly come off as a good guy. I get that now. It's easier to keep those memories to myself than to risk any more light getting shed on them. I just want happy memories to stay happy, and I don't want to think about what it looks like to anyone else."

Adam nods slowly. "Like how your Elephant Rock story could have been a happy memory if Chris hadn't told you why it should have made you scared?"

I shrug.

Adam smirks. "You can tell me to fuck off if you think that wasn't accurate."

I laugh. "No, that's pretty spot on."

Adam nods again. "Bipolar disorder is hard to understand. Even when you're close to it."

"Yeah," I reply shortly with a quick puff of air that comes out like a laugh. "I was so close to it, I couldn't even see it."

"You were young," Adam excuses it. "Most adults aren't able to detect the warning signs, even when they're obvious."

"Even when the warning signs are as obvious as scribbling 'End it' in a notebook?"

"Even then," he assures me. "What could you have done differently if you had recognized that as a warning sign?"

"I don't know." I shrug. "Tell someone?"

"Your parents?" Adam asks. "Makaela? They knew, Matty. And you know they knew because you've told me you used to hear them talking about it while he was still alive. Everyone did everything they could. Sometimes mental illness still wins."

I nod a few times, eyes fixed on the ground, contemplating what he said. It feels like I could have done more. Like I *should* have done more. But maybe the reason I feel so much guilt over this, fifteen years later, is because even if Rich had told me directly what he was planning, I wouldn't have done anything differently. Even if I had known without a shadow of a doubt, I still wouldn't have told anyone. Because telling someone would have felt like a betrayal to Rich.

Adam senses the drop in mood and tries to lift the conversation back up to something constructive. "Is Rich the reason you got into graphic design?"

"Not directly," I answer, a smile forming across my face, "but indirectly, probably. He was constantly pushing me to draw."

"Because he saw your talent," Adam informs me. "He knew you could do something great."

I scoff at this. "Yeah, I'm doing really great."

"Is there something you could do to get back into that? To graphic design?"

I laugh. "Not anymore."

"Why not?"

"I burned all those bridges. I let down people who were counting on me, because I was high."

"You could build those relationships back up, you know. Ask for forgiveness, start fresh?" Adam cranes his neck at me, encouraging me to challenge him on this. When I sit silently, contemplating his suggestion, he continues. "Like, what about that branding work you did for Delizia? There are thousands of small businesses like theirs you could work with. Build *new* bridges."

"How do you always remember this stuff?"

"Remember what?" he asks genuinely. "Your work with Delizia?"

"That. Graphic design. Any of it."

"I listen to you, Matty." He states plainly, "You told me, so I remembered."

"But I say a lot of things, and that was such a small piece. It's incredible you can remember it, that's all."

"It might be a small piece of your whole story." He nods slowly. "But it was your first professional design job. And that was huge for you. And whenever you land the next one, your *new* first, I'll remember that one, too."

"A new first, huh?" I laugh, doubtful. "That feels like more than I can take on right now."

"Why?"

I sigh, reluctant to offer an explanation with more depth than *I don't want to*. Adam would never allow such vague statements of disinterest to come to pass. "Because I haven't even been sober for a month, and restarting a career feels too daunting."

Adam cracks a smile. "I'm not asking you to relaunch an entire career. All you need to do is take the first step."

"Which is *what* exactly?"

"You tell me," Adam replies, infuriating me with his own vague suggestions. "You're the expert in that field."

I shrug.

"Why not just start drawing?" he suggests.

Luci is lying on the floor in the living room when we get back from my session with Adam. She has pieces of papers thrown all around her, markers lying haphazardly so she can quickly pick up a new one as her creative flow changes direction. I sit down next to her cross-legged and peer over her shoulder at the drawings she has around her.

"What are you drawing, Luci?"

"Mia famiglia," she drones back, not looking up from the work in front of her.

"Can I draw with you?" I ask, then repeat in Italian, "Posso disegnare con te?"

"Sure." She shrugs, stabbing a series of violent dots of color onto her portrait.

I look over her shoulder. There are five people in her drawing —the five of us. "Chi sono, Luci?" *Who are they?* I ask her, feeling wrapped up in warmth from her inclusion.

She points to each person and says, "Me. Mommy. Daddy. Katya. Zio Picco."

"Thanks for putting me in your drawing." I grin. "Dove sono tuoi nonni?" *Where's Grandma and Grandpa?*

"They don't live here," she says matter-of-factly. *Of course not.*

I grab a clipboard off the ground and lie down on the rug across from her. Taking one of the many thrown-about markers off the floor, I draw. My hand is shaky, and my lines are wobbly, but I still create. I start by drawing a cartoon version of Luci, giving particular attention to drawing the crazy bloom of hair spilling out of her ponytail in every direction, her long, soft eyelashes that are directed down toward her own drawing, and the ocean of papers surrounding her.

"What's your favorite animal?" I ask.

"Penguin," she drones back, an automated response.

"Un pinguino?" I repeat back to her, adding tiny penguins to all the pieces of paper in my drawing of Luci.

"Yeah," she says, "like at the zoo. They're funny."

Once I finish the drawing of Luci, I pick up another piece of paper and draw a penguin, like the big emperor penguins we have at the zoo, with bright orange and yellow chests. I draw the little rockhopper penguins with their tufts of bright yellow feathers poking out of their foreheads like large, bushy eyebrows. I even draw a couple of puffins with their bright orange beaks. I cover an entire page with a wallpaper of penguins. I am so lost in drawing that I don't even notice when Luci stops.

"Whoa!" she exclaims, looking over my shoulder.

"You like it?"

"Yes!" She beams.

"Bene," I reply, "it's for you."

She jumps on my back, pushing a puff of air out of my lungs. She wraps her arms around my neck as she watches me put the finishing touches on her collage of penguins. When I tell her it's finished, she snatches it from me, clipboard and all, and takes off running, screaming out, "Mom! Look what Zio Piccolo did!"

Michelle takes a few fearful strides from the kitchen, worried that Zio Piccolo did something dangerous. When Michelle meets Luci in the entryway, the worry on her face melts into relief as she sees the penguin drawing in Luci's hand.

"Hang it on the wall!" Luci screams with delight.

"Please?" Michelle scowls at Luci.

Luci grunts, not sure why her mom doesn't understand the urgency of this situation. "Please, can you hang it on the wall?" Luci drones back, less enthusiastically.

That weekend, we take a drive to our parents' house. It's been a month since I've seen them, and I am a little afraid they won't want to see me. After we pull into the driveway, I help Luci get untangled from her booster seat, grabbing both her hands so she can jump out of the tall vehicle by herself.

Anxiety pulses through me as we stare down my parents' front door. I'm not sure what I'm expecting to happen, but I want to have Luci close by in case I'm not well received.

I push open the front door without knocking. They always leave it unlocked when they're expecting someone. I hold on to Luci's hand firmly so she can give her best leap up the top step into the house, the one I had split my face open on last year.

"Pronto?" I ask Luci. She nods, I count us down so Luci and I can shout out our greeting as we had rehearsed. "Tre, due, uno." But then I yell out "Buongiorno!" in a booming voice, and Luci leaves me high and dry, looking like an idiot.

I give her arm a soft tug to say *What gives?* and she smirks at me and says, "I forgot what to say."

I sigh, "Ripeti." Luci counts down with me this time, and we both shout out "Buongiorno!" together. Dad emerges from the hallway with a look of pride after our second attempt.

"Ciao a tutti!" *Hey, everyone!* He beams, mostly in Luci's direction. I flash him a nervous smile when he catches my eye. He bends down to scoop Luci up into a hug. She dives into his arms, much less terrified of him than I am.

"Ciao, Picco," he says stiffly, after Luci runs off to find the secret stash of toys that are only at Nonni's house.

"Hey, Dad," I reply solemnly.

"Hi, Ben!" Michelle says as she steps through the door behind me, saving me from having to say anything more. Dad gives Michelle a big hug, as though it's been years since they've seen each other. My parents love Michelle. Much more than they love me right now, and maybe even ever.

"Buongiorno, tesori miei," Mom chimes as she emerges from the hallway next. *Hello, my treasures.* Chris pops in through the door with Katy, who's fast asleep, slung over his shoulder.

"Put her in Eleonora's room," Mom says to Chris as she turns to meet Michelle. "Hello, dear. You look fantastic."

Michelle's expression melts. She's completely touched by the compliment she receives from Mom almost every time she sees her. "Thank you, Arianna. Good to see you."

Michelle strides into the house confidently, following Luci in search of the toys. I'm the last one standing. Alone in the doorway with my parents, who have every reason to hate me. I suck in a sharp breath of air in anticipation of harsh words as Mom approaches me.

"Come stai, amore mio?" she whispers, placing a hand gently on my face.

"I'm good, Ma," I reply, fighting back a sea of emotions that floods into me with her kindness. "Thank you," I choke.

She pulls her mouth into a long, straight line. She nods slowly and says, "I am very happy to hear that."

I owe her a groveling apology, and a much bigger thank-you than the one I gave, but she seems content to leave it as it is for now. She wraps me up into a large, much-needed hug and holds me in her arms for a long time. Heat pricks at my eyes as I'm unable to fight back a few stray tears that have bubbled to the surface.

Without another word, Dad resumes his ritual of peering into the oven every four minutes, and Mom follows Luci and Michelle. Things have seemingly reverted back to normal. I take this as the opportunity to duck into the basement in search of some things I had left behind.

Everything about my room still looks the same, even down to the clothes on the floor. It's been completely untouched from the moment I left it, and yet it looks completely unfamiliar to me, as if I'm seeing it for the very first time. I pick a shirt up off the floor and fold it, laying it on the bed. Out of instinct, my brain pulls my eyes to the top of the dresser, where the photo of Keelie and me once stood. It's jarring not to see it there, even when I see it every day at Chris's house.

I kneel on the floor and retrieve my laptop and Wacom tablet from under my bed, which are both coated in a thin layer of dust from months, or maybe years, of being unused. I set them onto a pile of things I'm going to bring back with me.

Chris quietly appears in the doorway, arms crossed. He leans against the door frame to watch me.

"Need any help?" he offers.

"No, I'm fine."

He keeps his eyes fixed on me as I turn back to my drawer to dig out more things to bring back with us.

"Are you supervising?" I ask, eyebrow raised.

"Something like that," he admits. "You've probably got some more pills stashed around here somewhere, right?"

"I don't know."

He scoffs, "You know."

I dig out another pair of jeans from my drawer, an oversize hoodie I've been missing from the closet, and a handful of other things. I can think of a couple of places I might have a few pills stashed away, ones Chris hasn't taken yet, but it's too dangerous to look for them now. Chris will take them from me if I find them. He'll search me as soon as we get home. I need to keep them hidden for the day I ultimately wind up back here.

I lift the small pile of personal possessions off the floor and gesture the stack toward Chris. "Do you want to tear through my shit now, or are you saving that for later?"

"Later is good." He claps a hand firmly on my shoulder and leads me up the stairs.

Once I have my equipment back, I spend every free moment drawing again. It's nice having this to focus on instead of the cravings that still ping my mind. I'm not feeling particularly inspired, so I work on creating things for Luci. One day while Luci is at school, I design an entire penguin-shaped font for her. Every press of the keyboard makes a different penguin shape. She laughs for hours as she smashes on the keys and watches all shapes and sizes of penguins appear.

We make a ritual out of doing this together. Every night, she perches on top of my legs at the kitchen table and we draw. Some days, I draw as she barks out orders of what she wants to see next. Other days, I let her take control of the "magic pen," as she calls it.

"Hold it like this," I instruct her, placing it gently in her hand. She taps it on the surface of the tablet and watches as color explodes onto the screen.

She turns to look at me, joy in her eyes. She scribbles all over the tablet, creating an angry rain cloud of lines. Then she accidentally clicks the button next to her thumb, and a sea of color swatches pops up on the screen.

"Whoa!" she exclaims.

"Quale colore?" I ask her. *Which color?*

"Green!" she shouts back.

"Verde," I repeat back to her in Italian.

I show her how to select the green swatch, and she continues her vicious scribble, creating a cyclone of green.

When it's my turn to draw, she crosses her arms and lays her head on top of her stacked hands, watching the colors dance before her. Her favorite thing to have me draw is a portrait of one of her many imagined penguin families. She has me put them in purple, blue, and red sweaters. Every time she says a color, I repeat it back to her in Italian. Viola, blu, rosso. Then she repeats the words back to me.

After a few weeks of taking turns drawing with Luci, she says things like "Il mio pinguino ha bisongo di un maglione rosso," and I draw her a little penguin with a red sweater, without needing to translate for her at all. Once Chris hears her speaking full sentences in Italian, he practically begs me to draw with her any chance we get.

Not that he needs to beg. I love spending time with her. I love being a part of her family again. *Our* family again. I love having a purpose, even if it is as small as Italian lessons disguised as drawing with my niece. Even if it is small, it's something I can hold on to. That I can look forward to. I haven't had anything like that in a long time.

Four Years Ago

Saturday, June 7th

"Do you ever wonder how the hell Dad could decide to do something last minute and have it all work out? *We* try to actually *plan* a trip"—Keelie slammed her car door, giving up on her search—"and we can't even remember to bring along the tent poles."

Sam cracked open the first beer of the weekend. "Kiki, when are you going to figure out that when shit went wrong for Dad, he just pretended it was exactly how he had planned it?"

"I'm going to find a Walmart and buy us a new tent!" I suggested for the third time.

"I *know* I packed them!" Keelie insisted, opening the trunk again and pulling out the storage totes one by one.

"You've already looked in here," I reminded her, taking the first tote from her and placing it on the ground behind us.

She violently turned around to look at me, flapping her arms at her side. She furrowed her brow in anger, then her bottom lip quivered as she stifled a cry.

"Hey." I pulled her in for a hug. "It's okay."

She kept her arms stiff at her side, but buried her face into my shoulder to cry. I kissed her on the top of her head. She mumbled something that I couldn't quite make out.

I pushed her away slightly so I could look at her. Tears poured down her cheeks. She sucked both her lips in and bit down on them, then she whispered, "No, it isn't."

I placed my forehead on hers. "It can be," I said, diving a hand into her sweatshirt pocket and trying to fish out the car keys, "if you will let me go buy us a new one."

"I know I packed them," she whispered again.

"Hey, did you guys pack a lighter?" Sam shouted from the fire pit.

I spun around and glared at him. "Not a great time, Sam!"

He took another sip from his beer. "So do you want us to stare at each other for a couple more hours, or . . .?"

I threw my head back in frustration, then stomped over to him. In a low voice, I said, "Keelie is freaking out right now, and you're not helping."

"I can see that," he whispered back, "but I'm not going to stand around waiting for her to stop freaking out to do literally anything else."

"Please." I made my eyes wide at him. "Don't ask her for anything right now."

"Hey, Kiki?" he called out. I let my eyes go wider still.

Keelie stopped her frantic digging and poked her head out from behind the car.

"Are you sure you didn't put those in *my* car?"

Her frustration melted, and she turned up the corners of her mouth with a smile. "In the trunk next to the trash bags," she remembered.

I narrowed my eyes at him and held out my hand for his keys. "How long were you going to let her look for those?"

"I was thinking about telling her after you left to go buy a new one."

He dug his keys out of his pocket and held them in the air, offering them up to me.

"You're the worst," I said, ripping the keys away from him and turning to toss them to Keelie.

She caught them and strode over to Sam's car to unlock the trunk. "Ahhh! I found them!" she yelled out.

"Now what about that lighter?" Sam shouted back.

He piled up wood and twigs and newspaper, in no particular order, in the fire pit.

"Doesn't matter where the lighter is." I laughed at him. "That's never going to catch."

"That's what I told him," their younger brother, Jake, groaned.

"What do you know about it?" he snapped back. "Looks good to me."

I flicked a hand in Sam's direction, waving him off. Jake had wasted no time opening a book in a lawn chair nearby. Placing a hand on his shoulder, I pleaded, "Will you show him how it's done?"

"You bet." Jake jumped up and immediately started rearranging the sticks in the fire pit in a way that might actually result in a fire getting started.

Keelie was the oldest of four. Jake was a few years younger than Sam. He was a smart kid, really quiet, but in a lost-in-thought sort of way. He rarely had anything to say, but when he did talk, it was brilliant. "No wasted words," he liked to say.

Their youngest sibling, Emmy, was a miniature version of Keelie in absolutely every way. Independent, strong-willed, rebellious. She was almost eleven years younger than Keelie and I were. I remembered the day she was born, and not because I heard about it from the adults my whole life and committed it to memory. I truly remembered it. By the time she was born, I was so inseparable from the Santiago family that I *was* another sibling to Emmy.

I grabbed the tub where we had stashed the weekend's portable bar. Mostly our favorite types of whiskey, just as Rich had planned.

I set the booze tub on the picnic table and rummaged through it. Holding up two different bottles of whiskey in Keelie's direction, I asked, "Which one?"

She pointed to the one on the left, so I cracked it open and poured it in a cup before opening the one on the right for myself so she could steal a taste. Em jumped over to my side and straddled the seat of the picnic table, facing me.

"Can I have a beer?" she asked quietly.

I glared at her, and then with a slight smile, I said, "You're asking the wrong person, and you know it."

Em groaned. "But Keelie's going to say no."

"Then I guess you have your answer."

"Come on, Moog. Just *one?*"

"If you ask Keelie, I'll back you up," I offered, "but that's the best I can do."

She slumped her shoulders and grumbled, "Fine."

I closed our portable bar tub and joined Keelie at our tent construction site. I palmed both cups in one hand so I could scratch her back with the other.

"Here," I instructed. "Whiskey first."

She gratefully accepted the cup. "Just like Dad would have wanted." After taking a sip, she added, "I'm glad we're finally doing this."

"Me too, Mia."

"Hey, Kiki!" Em shouted out casually, catching Keelie at the perfect moment for her anticipated question. Keelie turned her attention to her.

Em skipped over so she could ask in a low voice, quiet enough that the other campers couldn't hear her, "Can I have a beer?"

Keelie crinkled her nose but then turned to look at me for my opinion.

I narrowed my eyes at her, and with a slight smirk, I asked, "What would your dad have said?"

The corner of Em's mouth twitched into a smile for a second, and then she straightened her face out coolly, waiting for Keelie's response. We all know exactly what Rich would have said.

"Fine," Keelie huffed at her sternly. Em took off running toward the cooler, but Keelie called out, "Hold on!" stopping Em dead in her tracks.

Em threw her head back and drooped her shoulders, then she turned back to Keelie. *Whaaaaat?*

"Matty can get them for you. Stay out of the cooler."

Em put her hands on her hips. "Why?" she asked with a thick layer of sass.

I shook my head at her, begging her to stop while she was ahead. "Because that puts me in charge of making sure you don't get sloshed."

"I'll just wait for *you* to get sloshed first," she snarked.

I held in a laugh, turned to Keelie, and said, "Is she really stupid enough to start trash-talking the only one here who's got her back?" I turned back to Em. "Tell me you're not that stupid."

Em gave me a huge, cheesy grin and said, "Moog, can you grab me a beer?"

I wrapped my arm around her shoulders and led her over to the cooler. "Yeah, you little shit, I'll grab you a beer."

I dug a beer out of the cooler, stuck it in a koozie, and opened it for her.

"Hold on a minute," I added as I ran over to Keelie's car to find a Sharpie she had stashed in the door pocket. I snatched Em's wrist and gave her arm a quick tally. She scowled at me, and then with a suspicious curl of her lip, she said, "Can I see that for a second?"

I handed the Sharpie her way, and she snatched my wrist and gave my arm the same tally. I let out a laugh and said, "Thanks for looking out, Em."

She clipped the arm of the Sharpie to her sweatshirt collar, anticipating needing it for my next tally sooner than I would need it for hers.

"What are you guys doing? Trying to see who can drink more?" Sam joked. "Moog is going to crush you, Emmy."

"He's only allowed to drink whiskey," Em shot back, "to level the playing field a bit."

Sam smirked. "I still don't like your odds, kid."

"You can hold your own, right?" I lifted my cup to cheers her.

"You're about to find out," Em joked in reply, tapping her can to my cup.

"I've got my eyes on both of you!" Keelie shouted out from the other side of our campsite.

Once all the tents were set up and the fire was built, we sat in our lawn chairs and shared stories about their dad. It was his camping trip, after all.

"Do you guys remember the water park?" Keelie reminisced.

I let out a huge belly laugh when Sam, reading my mind, replied, "I remember getting super fucking sunburned because Dad didn't bring sunscreen."

I did my best to impersonate Rich. "Twelve dollars for a bottle of sunscreen? I'm not paying for that. I'm going to teach you guys something about a thing called highway robbery. That's what the fuck that is."

Sam busted out laughing. "Spot on!" He shook his head. "Learned all the important life lessons from Dad."

"Bet you've never forgotten to pack sunscreen again," I said to him. "Keelie hasn't."

"I have two bottles of it in my car right now," she confirmed.

"I've got one in the passenger door," Sam agreed.

Keelie leaned in to tell the story to Jake and Em. Jake had been too young to join us, and Em hadn't even been born yet. "We stole sunscreen from people, one handful at a time." She shook her head and laughed. "All those cubbies at the bottom of the rides? We had to peek in for people who had sunscreen and squirt a bit in our hand and run off. Anytime we got on a ride, we would have to look for sunscreen before we got in line."

Sam jumped back in. "Matty, tell them about when you got caught."

"I forgot about that!" I laughed. "So this lady caught me with my hands in her cubby, and she yelled out, 'Hey, what do you think you're doing?' And I panicked! So I started speaking Italian to her."

Em cracked a smile.

"Mi scusi, pensavo fosse il mio," I whined to mimic myself. *Sorry, I thought it was mine.*

"And then what happened?" Sam egged me on.

I laughed again. "And then your dad comes running up behind me and starts *screaming* at me. '¡Matteo, tuyo está aquí!' And then he turns to the lady and says, 'Lo siento por mi hijo estúpido,' and makes these big sad eyes at her, pleading for her forgiveness. And all she can do is nod because she doesn't understand a word we're saying. Which was incredibly lucky for us because your dad and I weren't even speaking the same language. Once we were far enough away from her, I turned to him and said, 'Dude, that was Spanish.'" I grinned, thinking about it all over again. "And he replies, 'Well, who the fuck knows how to speak Italian? That's useless.'"

"Sorry, Dad." Keelie shrugged.

"Do you guys remember the aquarium?" Jake chimed in.

Sam laughed. "Shedd Aquarium, or the fish tank thing?"

"When we drove to Chicago," Jake confirmed, "and got there right before they closed."

Keelie let out a soft snort.

"Yeah, when Dad decided we shouldn't have to pay full price because they were almost closed, and we only needed a 'quick peek' at the sharks?" Sam scoffed.

"And then the woman at the ticket booth told us to come back tomorrow"—Keelie laughed again—"and Dad said, 'We can't come back tomorrow. We live in St. Louis. Do you know how long of a drive this was for us?'"

"At least we got to visit the gift shop, though." I smirked, then pointed to Jake. "And you got that giant stuffed shark that hardly fit in the car."

"I still have it!" Jake replied proudly.

"What was the fish tank thing?" Em asked.

Sam replied, "We used to have a fish tank in the basement at the old house"—he shook his head as he thought about it—"for like a day, and then all the fish died because Dad didn't know you couldn't just fill it up with tap water."

I remembered, "We filled it up with the hose, fed it through the basement window." Then I turned to Keelie. "There was that tiny hole in it you had to plug with your finger the whole time."

"Yeah, but Dad still got mad at me for letting the couch get dripped on."

"Couldn't have been too mad, though, or you wouldn't be laughing," Sam added glumly.

Keelie let out a noise that sounded like a soft, disbelieving laugh as she suddenly remembered all *those* times. "He definitely wasn't mad like that."

We sat in silence for a minute, the flames flickering light on our faces while all of us simultaneously thought about the not-so-funny moments. The holes punched in walls, broken light fixtures, microwave doors ripped off. Being woken up at three in the morning because he was convinced something terrible was about to happen but didn't know what. Having the electricity shut off for hours while he disassembled every outlet in the house, searching for "the bad one." Asking questions about his irrational behavior made us "part of the problem," so we sat silently and waited for these moments to pass, or for Makaela to get home and put a stop to them. It was easier to forget about those times and hold on to the funnier memories instead.

I placed a reassuring hand on Keelie's forearm, and she shifted her sullen face into a fake smile, then took a deep breath to wash all the thoughts away.

"I wish I could remember him," Em sighed, adding fuel to the increasingly somber mood.

"I wish you could, too, sweetie," Keelie replied, sounding exactly like her mom.

Em tilted her head back and finished the contents of her can, then stood up from her chair and said, "Moog, can I have another beer?"

I flagged her over to me and she held out her arm, then I plucked the Sharpie off her shirt collar and popped the cap off. "What time is it?" I asked Keelie.

"Eleven forty-five," she replied.

I gave Em's arm her fourth tally mark and popped the pen back on her shirt. Then I jumped out of the chair and dug another beer out of the cooler for her. I grabbed a bottle of whiskey off the table and gave my cup a heavy pour.

Em let out a little "ahem," and I turned my arm out to her. She took a peek inside my cup, raised an eyebrow at me, and then gave my arm a sixth tally mark and a shorter half mark.

"Oh, whatever!" I fired back at her in protest.

Without responding, she capped the marker, put it back on her collar, and strode back to her seat by the fire.

I put my drink in the cup holder, then kissed Keelie on the top of her head and kept my lips pressed into her crown as I asked, "Can I grab you something?" She held her cup out for me to take. "Same one?"

She tilted her head back to meet my eyes and said "Yes, please" with a straight-line grin.

"Get me one, too, Moog!" Sam called out. "With ice!"

"Jake, do you need anything?" I asked, maximizing my servitude.

Jake shook his head, raising the can of soda he had in his grasp.

As I walked toward the picnic table lined with bottles of alcohol, Sam's next words to Em were barely audible. "Dad was crazy about you, you know. He had this sweatshirt that he slashed a hole in so he could carry you around right up against his chest with only your head sticking out. And he wore it everywhere."

"Everywhere!" Keelie confirmed. "And he'd press his mouth to the top of your head and talk to you. All day long. He'd whisper things to you that no one else could hear. Just you and Dad."

I passed Sam a plastic cup with a heavy pour of whiskey, then handed the second one to Keelie as I took a seat next to her. Em stared at the fire, not saying anything for a long time, her eyebrows crinkled in confusion as if she might try to dispute what Keelie and Sam were telling her.

"He was singing," Em whispered finally, so quiet it was almost impossible to hear her.

"He was singing?" Keelie repeated louder.

Em kept her crinkling stare at the flames as she nodded, then slowly looked to Keelie. "He sang songs," Em confirmed. "Or like, one song mostly. I get it stuck in my head all the time."

Keelie let out a tiny puff of air like a quick sob, and she clung to my hand. "What song is it?"

"I don't know what song it is." Em shrugged. She blinked her gaze back to the fire and softly sang the song from memory.

Keelie let out another sobbing breath as her eyes welled up with tears. "That's an incredible memory to have of him, Em."

A heavy silence floated across us, before Jake found his appropriate window to jump in and add, "That's a Tom Petty song." He tapped on his phone a few times to confirm his suspicion. "'Wildflowers.'"

He handed his phone over to Em, and she tapped play. An upbeat acoustic guitar strummed, followed by words that Em had previously only held in her head. A blissful happiness washed across her face as she listened to the words as though they were all brand new to her. When the song ended, she played it again, leaning far back in her chair, her eyes turned up to the sky.

VI
Saturday, July 21st

Why am I doing this? Really, what's the point? I've been staring at the ceiling for hours this morning, not ready to get out of bed, not ready to face another monotonous day sober. I don't know why I even—

"Zio Piccolo!" Luci yells at the top of her lungs, jarring me from my morning spiral.

I'm not ready for her energy yet, for her enthusiasm about life. I'm not equipped to handle any—

"Zio! It's for you!" she persists.

I pretend to be asleep, yelling back as if she had woken me up, just like Rich used to do. "Luciana! Sta zitta!" *Be quiet!*

She tries again. "Zio Piccolo! Adesso!" *Right now.*

"Cristiano!" I shout out for Chris to stop this.

But instead, Chris knocks on my door and says, "Hey, she's not messing around. Someone's here for you. Get up." Almost as quickly as he arrives, he vanishes.

Someone is here for me? Who knows I'm here? My mind jumps to the only obvious answer. *Keelie?*

I retrieve yesterday's clothes from the floor, before slowly lurking down the hallway. The voice talking to Chris and Michelle isn't Keelie's, but it is familiar. As I peek my head around the corner, I immediately recognize the face. My oldest friend, Josh Parker. He looks different from the last time I saw him, but then again, so do I.

He was once tall and lanky with the long, flippy hair so iconic of our childhood. Now he is full all over. His forearms are muscular, his stomach round. He has a tattoo on his arm that barely shows itself from under his rolled-up sleeve. His full, scraggly beard makes mine look like stubble. Only someone from California could get away with something so seemingly unkempt. He has long ago ditched the long, flipping bangs; his hair is a few inches long and swept up and sideways in a way that looks hurried but composed. Despite all the differences in appearance, there is no mistaking him.

"Holy shit." The words escape my mouth before I can reel them back in. Katy and Luci giggle.

"That's a bad word," Luci reminds me, turning to her mom to see her reaction.

"Yeah, come on, Zio Piccolo. Try to set a good example for the kids." Josh grins, holding his arms out wide.

I quickly run to accept his embrace. "What are you doing here?"

"I wanted to come check in on you. No one's heard from you in a few months. So I put in a couple of phone calls and—" He gestures his arms as if to say, *Here you are.* "I'm only here for a few hours. I have to stop by Mom's yet, too, you know. But I thought we could catch up, if you're not busy."

"That would be great."

Josh turns to Chris. "Mind if I break him out of here for a bit?"

Chris hesitates before reluctantly agreeing. "Where are you headed?"

"Not sure yet," Josh says. "What's good?"

"Merle's," Michelle suggests without hesitation. "Little diner down on Main Street. Excellent coffee."

"Let's go to Merle's!" Josh says excitedly.

Merle's is not what you'd expect of a small-town diner. The corner shop's brick exterior is painted crisp white on the outside. A modern cursive font made of hot pink neon light scrolls out *Merle's* above the front door. A matching vinyl sticker is pasted on the glass.

The interior is the same crisp white. Modern subway tiles, quartz tiled floors, white Formica countertops and tables. There are accents of chrome and hot pink throughout. It has a slight fifties-diner vibe, but in the way that modern design tries to mimic vintage.

"Did you know this was here?" Josh asks, studying every corner of the diner.

I shake my head. "I don't leave the house much."

We order coffee at the counter and take a seat at a table in the corner.

"So, you really came all this way just to stop by?" I ask.

He shrugs. "Yeah, like I said, you and Mom."

"How long of a flight is that?" I press. "Like four or five hours?"

"Actually," he looks down at his hands to break eye contact as he says, "it's only about an hour and a half."

"No shit." I narrow my eyes at him. "So you didn't come from LAX, then."

"No," he hesitates, "Cleveland."

"What the fuck were you doing in Cleveland?" I ask. "Jess lives in Cleveland. Did you see her while you were there?"

Another long pause lingers in front of Josh's reply. "I live in Cleveland now."

"You?" I laugh. "You moved to Cleveland?"

A young woman wearing black jeans and a black button-down shirt brings over our coffees. The name tag on her shirt reads, Yes, That Merle. She is much younger than I'd expect someone named *Merle* to be. Her hair is dyed a deep brown color that is almost black. She has one lone streak of hot pink on the back of her head. Her earlobes are stretched with large gauges, and she has piercings all over. How did someone like Merle end up opening a shop in a place like Elmwood?

"She's your type." Josh nods in her direction, solely because she bares the slightest resemblance to Keelie.

I shake my head. "Doesn't matter," I reply, tilting my chin toward the large, muscular man, with an equally large beard, who is taking orders behind the counter. Merle gingerly touches one of his tattoo-covered arms as she walks by.

"Have you been seeing anyone?" Josh asks, moving completely off the subject of Cleveland.

I shrug. "Not really." Then I add, "I've had a casual thing going. Haven't talked to her since moving here, though."

"What's her name?"

"June."

"Tell me about June," he presses.

I look over at Merle and her burly colleague. She leans in close to him, their faces practically touching. I don't even know them, but I envy them.

"There's nothing to tell," I say, distracted by the chemistry that passes between them. I miss that.

"Well, who is she?" he continues to prod.

I turn my attention back to him, flash a desolate, insincere smile, and admit, "She's just a friend." Then I correct, "Barely a friend."

"More like a friends-with-benefits?"

I nod along with Josh's assessment, knowing full well that we're talking about two very different types of benefits that stem from my friendship with June.

"Can we go back to that Cleveland thing?" I ask, desperate to change the subject. "What made you move to Cleveland?"

He chuckles nervously, then says, "God, it's so good to see you."

"It's been a long time," I agree. Why is he so expertly dodging this question?

"Can I be honest with you, Matty?" he asks. When I nod, he leans in, propping his head up on his elbows so he can look at me more intently. "The last time I saw you, you were like *maybe* thirty-five percent there." He sighs. "And that sucked. It was hard to even tell if you could understand what I was saying, you know?"

He leans back in his chair, crossing his arms over his chest, examining me as a full picture now. "I can't even begin to tell you how great it is to just be able to fucking talk to you again, man." He smiles on one side of his mouth, still inspecting me as he speaks. "And you look great. Alive. Vibrant. It's so great to see you like this again."

I shrug. "Thanks." But hearing him talk about how great it is to see boring, sober Matty in a coffee shop in a small town reminds me of how fucked up I let things get. This boring version of me is the one people are excited to see? *Great.*

"I mean it," he assures me. "I know it must have been hard for you to get here."

I nod. "It fucking sucked."

I stop short of telling him that this sobriety is temporary for me. That it sucks for now, but not forever. I don't have any reason to stay sober anymore.

"How did you find me out here?" I ask.

"Keelie told me where you were." He scrunches up the corner of his mouth in a sympathetic frown. "She got me in touch with Chris."

I sigh. "How is she?"

Still with his sorry-for-you look scrunching one side of his face, he says, "She's good, Matty." He nods his head a few times before adding, "She's glad you're here. We all are."

"So, what, you call her up to talk about me then?" I tease.

"No," he pauses, lets out a deep breath, then continues, "Jess asked her, actually."

"Do you see Jess often then?"

He smiles widely, almost suspiciously happy. "Yeah, all the time."

"What does that mean? 'All the time'?"

He doesn't reply, instead staring at his hands again, a big stupid grin wiped across his face.

"Are you going to make me drag this explanation out of you?" I smirk at him, getting a sense of what might be going on.

"What explanation?" he asks coolly, before his composed look collapses into embarrassment.

I laugh. "What the fuck is going on with you and Jess?"

I wouldn't have thought it was possible, but his smile grows even wider. I've never seen him like this before. I'm hit with a bubbly gladness for him and a sinking pity for me all at once.

Instead of offering an answer, he beams with excitement. "I have so much to tell you."

"Why don't you start by answering the question?"

He thinks about it for an extra second, probably searching for a way to evade the question again entirely. But finally he says, "We're getting married, Matty."

My eyes grow wide and my jaw drops. *Married?* I didn't even know they had been in touch beyond high school. They lived on opposite sides of the country. *Married?*

I can't find the words to say anything. The only thing my brain allows me to croak out is, "Cazzo." *Fuck.*

Josh laughs.

"Okay, rewind," I say, my tongue finally forming words. "What?"

He nods. "Yeah, so that's why I live in Cleveland now," he draws out every syllable in a singsongy way, as if that will somehow make the jolting response easier to digest.

"When did you start seeing Jess?" I ask, finding my words again. "*How* did you start seeing Jess?"

He holds a fist up to his mouth, pressing his face against it for support, a pseudoshield. Then he moves his mouth away from his hand, only slightly, and replies, "Just over two years ago. I got sent to a work conference in Cleveland. I called her up the first night I was there. We went out for drinks and hit it off."

"Two years?" I practically shout. Then, softer, I say, "You and Jess. Wow."

"She's so fucking great, Matty," he sighs, and for some reason, hearing him say these words stabs me right through the heart. *I should be this happy with Keelie.*

"I'm really happy for you guys," I say genuinely.

"Yeah, um"—he pauses—"there's more. But I'm going to go grab another coffee. Can I get you one?"

I nod appreciatively. As he walks to the counter, my brain spirals, thinking about what more he could have to tell me. I feel a sudden heaviness. The weight of my failure drops on me. I'm almost thirty and don't have anything to show for it. I didn't graduate from college. I don't have a job. I don't have any idea what I'm going to do with my life. I don't have a house of my own. I don't have anything that's just mine.

Josh places a fresh cup of coffee on the table in front of me. I throw back the last gulp of my first, wishing I was throwing back whiskey.

"What other surprises do you have for me today?" I ask.

"There's actually a reason I came to see you," he starts.

"Really?" I feign a sarcastic surprise.

He nods. "We're getting married in September. Jess and I both want you to be there."

"Of course," I reply quickly, "I wouldn't miss it."

His hands steal his attention once again. "There's more to it than that," he says, before meeting my eyes.

"Okay . . ." I invite him to continue.

He sighs and sinks his head into the palm of his hand. "Jess and I both really want you to be there," he repeats, trying to find the next words in a sentence he likely rehearsed, "but only if you're sober."

I nod slowly to show him I'm giving his request the thought it deserves. Even though I know there is nothing in the world that would keep me from missing this day with my best friends.

When there's nervous energy in the air, Josh can't help but to fill the space with more words, so he continues talking. "And I know that's a really shitty thing to ask of you. And really shitty of us to make that decision for you. Especially when there's going to be an open bar and you're supposed to get super drunk at weddings and have a good time, and it's—"

"Josh!" I cut him off. "It's not a problem."

"You're sure?" he asks nervously.

No, of course I'm not sure. It probably will be a huge problem for me. But I can't miss it. So I'm going to have to make it work. Or at least keep it hidden.

"Absolutely," I reply confidently.

"Good." He claps his hands together once, an electricity surging through him. "In that case, would you be my best man?"

My eyes go wide. "I'd be honored."

"Okay," he says flatly, all his energy completely dropping under the weight of another catch coming on. My heart flutters with anxiety. He says quietly, "Keelie is going to be in the wedding party, too. And I know that makes things super fucking complicated, so if that's not—"

"I can handle it," I say with a slight laugh, betraying the choking feeling rising in my throat. *I can't handle this.* "Are you sure she's okay with it?"

"We asked her first," he gives me that pitying look again. "You know we had to."

My heart gushes in big, heavy, pounding beats as I think about seeing Keelie again. Even if we don't talk much, seeing her smile, hearing her laugh, that would be enough.

"There's one more thing," Josh adds. "And I definitely drew the short straw having to be the one to fucking tell you this."

He locks onto his coffee cup, tracing the rim with his eyes. Anything to keep from looking at me.

"She's, uh," he mutters, "bringing someone. To the wedding." He rapidly picks up the pace of words, letting them fly out of his mouth. "And listen, Matty, if that's going to be too much for you to handle, we completely understand."

I shake my head, searching for the words I'm trying to say, but nothing comes. I'm stuck shaking my head in disbelief.

"Who?" is the only word I can spit out.

"His name's Logan," Josh says sympathetically.

Logan. I scowl. "When?"

"Maybe a year ago." Then he jumps in with a defensive "I was fucking furious when I found out nobody had told you. Ask Jess."

Anxiety pulses through my body in the form of a painful chill on my neck, a lurch in my stomach, a weight pressing down on my chest. If I'm already afraid of what it will be like to see her at the wedding, how much worse is it going to be to see her arm in arm with the guy who has everything I destroyed? And to be around everyone else there who knows that I am the one who ruined my life and hers, with nothing to show for it? I'm going to look pathetic.

"But hey, listen. If you want to bring June or whoever," he starts, then loses steam as he adds, "it might make it a bit easier."

It's safe to say that having June by my side could make me look significantly less pathetic. She is charismatic, attractive, and wears expensive clothes, so everyone knows she is, in fact, the whole package. If I could persuade June to come with me, I could gain a serious edge on my status. After all, how could I be just some sober, lonely schmuck if I'm with someone like her?

But could I handle spending an entire weekend with June? A long weekend, no less? I haven't spent more than a few minutes around her sober. Ever. She lets me talk about Keelie, but she gets mad if I even mention her ex-husband or her kids. Our conversations have always been shallow. Drinking, pills, sex. Nothing more than that. I'm not sure I could handle spending multiple days in a row with June, but could I handle being there alone?

I shrug. "I'll think about it."

Josh smirks. "She can't be that bad."

"She's not that bad, but she's not . . ." I trail off. *She's not Keelie.* That's what I want to say.

Josh draws his lips into a thin line and nods sympathetically. "I know," he replies, reading my mind.

"Fuck, man," I whisper. I try my hand at saying his name out loud. "*Logan.* What's he like?"

Josh eyes me suspiciously. "Are you sure you want me to answer that?"

I nod slowly. Although I wish he would stop asking me that. He's known me long enough to know that I've never once been sure about anything. But I want to know what I should be expecting if I'm going to have to see him at the wedding.

Josh shrugs. "He's nice. And Keelie seems to be really happy with him."

I feel like he's holding something back, so I press into that a bit. "But . . .?"

"But what?" He laughs. "That's it. I don't know him that well, I guess. I've only met him once, and he seems nice and makes her happy."

I nod again, this time much heavier, disappointed. The air has fully evacuated my lungs, and I can't seem to get it back. I forcibly pull air into my mouth, but my throat is closed off, and my breath stays shallow. I feel like I'm about to pass out.

"That's great," I choke.

"You're a terrible liar." Josh smirks. "Next time try not to sound like you're swallowing glass when you say that."

I let out an airy, pathetic laugh. I want to be happy for her, I do. But I don't have the energy to be happy for her today. Today I want to feel sorry for myself. Tomorrow I can work on being happy for her.

"Why couldn't you be a friend and tell me he's fucking awful?"

"I can do that," he offers. "Do you want me to lie to you like everyone else?"

I slump down in my chair and let out a dramatic sigh. "No."

He flashes a comforting smile. "You'll probably like him, Matty."

"I don't want to."

He nods. "I didn't either."

"Who the fuck is *Logan*?" I yell at Chris after Josh drops me back at home.

Chris holds up his hands, palms toward the ground, gesturing that I need to calm down. He takes a seat on one of the nearby patio chairs, but I stay standing. I'm fuming.

"Why the fuck didn't you tell me?" I demand.

He studies me, not replying. I widen my eyes at him. *Well?*

"She asked me not to," he mumbles.

"Keelie?" I snap. "Keelie asked you not to tell me?"

Chris nods.

"Why?"

"I didn't ask why," he snarls, his tone echoing mine. Angry, frustrated. "I just agreed not to mention it."

I shake my head, convinced I surely must be misunderstanding this situation. "So you've talked to her about him?"

"Yes," he says, more sternly now.

"When?" I demand.

Instead of responding, he motions to the patio chair beside him, inviting me to sit. I reluctantly pull out a chair, but sit close to the edge, not ready to settle in for a calm conversation yet. He leans far back in his chair as though he is about to take a nap.

"When?" I repeat louder, more sternly.

"I don't know *when*," he mocks, as if it's ridiculous for me to expect him to remember when he spoke to Keelie last. "We all still talk to Keelie. All the time."

"What do you mean, you '*all* still talk to Keelie'?" I turn to look at him now, but he fixates on something off in the distance.

"Me, Michelle, Mom, Dad, Ellie." Then he turns to meet my eyes and grinds me right into the dirt with his words. "She didn't break up with the rest of us."

"Why would you do that?" I grumble.

"You're the only one who fucked up here, Matteo." He states bluntly, "We shouldn't have to live with those consequences."

"I would think my family would be on my side."

"If I wasn't on your side, you would be in prison. Don't you fucking forget that."

How could I forget? He never lets me, not even for a second.

"You destroyed Keelie's life. We didn't abandon her because she wanted it back."

"I didn't *destroy* her life."

"Right. Just lied to her constantly, burned through her savings, and damaged her relationship with her family," Chris says. "You would have gotten her evicted, too, if Mom and Dad hadn't helped her pay out the lease."

"What happened with her family?"

"She stood up for you when she shouldn't have," he grumbles. "They're good now, as far as I know."

The familiarly bitter chemical taste comes seeping into my mouth, sticking to my tongue. I need them right now. I need to find a few strong pills and fall asleep. With enough pills, I could fall asleep and never wake up.

No. I shouldn't even think about that. Who would find me like we found Rich? It might be Luci. Would she ever get that image of me out of her mind, or would it follow her for the rest of her life?

"I think you should give Adam a call," Chris sighs.

I'm suddenly aware of my jaw clenching tightly, my eyebrows furrowed, my hands gripping the armrests.

"I want to call June."

"Absolutely not," he replies without giving it a second thought.

"Okay." I swallow hard. "Then I'm not calling Adam either."

"Please don't do that," he begs. "Don't use your therapist as a bargaining chip."

"It's the only thing I've got left to bargain with."

And that's the sad, pathetic truth. There's nothing left of the life I once had, so why would I fight to claw my way back to it? Back to nothing. Sobriety won't fix this. It will only force me to live in a world where I have to acknowledge how shitty my life has gotten.

"Why do you want to call June?" Chris asks softly, giving a little ground.

"I can't handle being there alone," I choke.

I can't get the image out of my mind. Keelie and *Logan*. Her beautiful smile directed toward him. Smart remarks whispered in his ear. Secret jokes only they understand. Holding and kissing and loving and all these things that I had. That I should still have.

A lump forms in the back of my throat, making it hard to breathe. I try to fight it off, just as I try to fight off the images of them. But they stick in my mind. A pain digs its way into my chest as I think about all the days I've had waking up next to her, smelling her hair as I kiss her temple, then her lips. Running my fingers down the length of her side.

Suddenly, I picture *Logan* there instead of me. *Logan* kissing her lips, smelling her hair, running his fingers down her side.

Logan gazing into her beautiful amber eyes. Tears pool into my vision. I try to blink them away, taking in a deep breath to erase the thoughts that brought them on.

"I can't," I choke out once more.

"And there's no one else?" Chris asks kindly.

I shake my head.

He reluctantly stands without another word, walking inside. He comes back a moment later with my phone in his hand. I stand as I take it from him, heading toward the door, but he holds out a hand to stop me and points to the chair across from him as he sits back down. "Right here."

Then he nudges his head toward the chair to further demonstrate that this part will not be up for negotiation. I sit down and power on my phone. A flurry of notifications fly in, but I ignore them all, instead tapping into my contacts to dial June's number.

The phone rings four times. Her voice mail message starts, "Hi, you've reached Juniper Nelson at Rem—"

"Matt?" her voice cuts in with a whisper.

"Hey," I reply softly, my voice cracking. I try to silently clear my throat, to remove the weight of emotions from my voice.

"So great to hear from you. Thank you so much for returning my call," she says in her fake professional voice. I hear her office chair make a soft punching sound as she stands up. Her heels click on the floor as she goes to shut her door. Then the real June speaks. "Baby," she says breathlessly, "what happened to you?"

"I'm fine." That sums everything up as concisely as possible. I need to get right to the point. "Listen, I don't have a lot of time right now." I glance over at Chris, and he raises an eyebrow suspiciously. "I can explain everything, but I have a huge favor to ask of you, and I really need you to say yes."

"Anything," she purrs. She's just as fake with me as she is with her coworkers. She has her fake professional voice when she talks around them, and she has her soft seductive voice that she puts on when she's around me. I hate it. Especially once I figured out it was all for show. She doesn't sound like this when she drinks. When she drinks, her real voice comes out. She becomes more of her real self. I prefer that June. I prefer that Matty, too.

"I've been invited to a wedding at the end of September, and I need you to be my date."

Silence from the other end of the phone. The kind of silence that comes before a stark *no*. But I hold out, waiting for her to say it.

"Oh, Matt," she sighs. "I don't know . . ."

"Keelie is going to be there," I explain. "I really need you to come."

"Where is it?" she asks begrudgingly. Her suave voice wavering, the realest version of June surfacing now.

I wince. "Cleveland."

"Cleveland?" She almost sounds happy that I said it. As if the thought of traveling to Cleveland with the guy she doesn't want to even admit to seeing would be the perfect plan. "When?"

"September twenty-second," I offer. "And maybe a day or two before."

"That's a Saturday?" she asks.

"Yeah." I listen intently to the clicking of keys on her keyboard, as if it might indicate what she is doing on the other end of the phone.

"I would have to move some things around . . ." she trails off.

"So is that a yes?"

She hesitates. "I could probably make it work. Can I call you back tomorrow?"

"I'm not sure when I'm going to be around tomorrow," I reply. "Leave me a voice mail. You don't have to say anything but yes or no if you want. I'll know what it means."

"Okay, baby," her seductive voice is back. "Tomorrow."

Then she hangs up.

"Why the secrecy?" Chris questions.

"What do you mean?"

"'You don't have to say anything but yes or no if you want,'" he repeats. "What's that about?"

"It's just how she does things," I defend her.

"It's a little weird, that's all."

I shrug instead of replying. Why would I ask questions when *not* asking questions makes things so much less complicated? It doesn't matter what June is hiding. June has pills. Nothing is more important than that. And in two short months, I will have them back again.

My mouth waters as the phantom flavor floods in. Two months until I can taste them again.

Chris grabs my phone off the table, powering it off once more. He turns his phone out to me, Adam's number already queued up on the call screen. He passes me a stern glance as he takes off with my phone, leaving me here. Alone.

I tap the green button to dial Adam's number.

Thirteen Years Ago

Saturday, October 8th

"Why don't you stop staring at her and go ask her to dance, dude?" Josh said in a hushed tone as he leaned over my shoulder.

"I wasn't staring." I played it off coolly. "Just spacing out, I guess."

He clutched both my shoulders and stared me firmly in the eyes. "You're full of shit."

As I was denying it, I was still looking over his shoulder at Keelie.

"Come here," he yelled over the loud music, pulling my arm toward the hallway. Most of the school was blocked off to prevent anyone from wandering into classrooms to hook up, but one hallway was kept open for anyone looking to escape the noise.

"What's going on, man?" he asked, sliding his back along the wall and sitting on the ground.

I sat next to him, looking for the right words. The truth was I didn't know what was going on. I couldn't stop thinking about her. I couldn't stop noticing every brush of her hand, or touch of her leg. Every nice thing she said suddenly set my heart on fire.

Any time I started to feel that way, I pushed it out of my mind. She was my best friend. She was practically my sister. I knew she didn't feel the same. I knew her heart couldn't possibly skip a beat every time I talked, the way mine had started to whenever she spoke. I knew she didn't think anything of our knees touching when we sat by each other at lunch. I knew it because up until about a month ago I didn't think anything of it either.

"I don't know," I said finally. It wasn't the answer Josh was hoping for. Frankly, it wasn't the answer I was hoping for, either. I wished I knew.

"You've got a major crush on her," he said. I couldn't tell if he was asking me or if he was telling me, so I didn't reply. He continued, "What changed?"

"I don't know," I said again, defeated.

"How long have you been feeling like this?"

"Maybe a month or two?"

His eyes got wide, and he turned to me as if I had insulted him.

"A month or two?" he demanded. "You've been wanting to hook up with *Keelie* for *a month or two* and you didn't tell me?"

I shrugged. I wanted to tell him. I wanted to tell everyone. But I worried about what would happen when I told her and she didn't feel the same way. Then what? Would we still be able to be friends after that? I wasn't sure. It wasn't worth the risk.

"You should make a move tonight," he encouraged. "I mean it."

I laughed. "No."

"Why? What's the worst that could happen?"

I didn't even need to think about it. I knew exactly the worst that could happen. "She doesn't feel the same way, and it ruins our friendship," I recited back, immediately regretting how quickly I had responded.

"Matty, I promise if she decides she doesn't want to be friends with you anymore, I will do everything in my power to make her be friends with you again."

"It will be weird," I whined. "I'll make it weird."

He stood up, holding a hand out to me, ready to pull me up to his level.

"You're overthinking it," he stated, then challenged, "If you don't do it, I will."

"You'll do what?"

He shrugged. "I'll ask her to dance. I'll make a move on her." He curled the corner of his mouth into a grin. "I'll be the one making out with her at the party tonight. Is that what you want?"

"You're so full of shit."

"Watch me."

"You're not going to do that," I called his bluff.

"Okay, no," he wrapped his arm around my shoulder. "I wouldn't do that to you. But someone will."

Before I could say anything else, Ellie came stumbling over with some of her friends in tow. They were dressed in jeans and hoodies. They were seniors and thought it would be incredibly uncool to miss their last homecoming dance, but equally uncool to look as though they cared about it while attending.

"Hey, Matteo!" she shouted.

"Eleonora!" I yelled back in a hushed tone. "Che cazzo vuoi?" *What the fuck do you want?*

She ran to approach me, her arms and legs flailing more than usual. She stopped right in front of me, putting her face inches from mine. She was plastered, and whatever she had been drinking was bright blue. Her whole mouth glowed. Alcohol practically evaporated off her tongue.

"Can you be kind to me for once in your life?" she whispered.

I smirked. "I'm always kind to you, Elle."

"I mean it. I'm here, humbly asking you for a huge favor, and I need you to be cool, alright?"

"What?" I groaned.

"Doug's parents are out of town this weekend, so we're going to have a party at his house tonight," she began, "but I need you to tell Mom and Dad that I was here all night and that I went over to Chloe's house after. Chlo-eeee. Got it?"

"Chloe's out of town, and you're going to Doug's? Got it."

Her whole body drooped. "No! Come on, Matty, be cool!"

I conceded. "You stayed until eleven thirty and then Chloe's mom picked you up. Just you and Chloe?"

"And Megan."

"You. Megan. Chloe. Chloe's mom. Eleven thirty," I repeated back to her. "I've got you, Elle."

She beamed, giving me a hug, screeching out, "Matty, thank you!"

She ran away to go tell her friends the good news.

I yelled after her to give a word of sound advice. "Eleonora!"

She turned back to look at me, her smile fading a bit as she thought about the possibility of me taking it all back.

"Non fare stupidaggini!" *Don't do anything stupid!*

Her grin grew even bigger than before. "No, mai!" *No, never!* Then she added, "Ti voglio bene, fratellino!"

"Tanto bene," I replied. *Very much.*

I stared straight ahead, hoping Josh had forgotten all about our previous conversation. I knew if I talked to him for too long, he could convince me I should make a move on Keelie. My mind was filled with pinging thoughts of all the new things I wanted to do with her. To her. And I couldn't stop it. The harder I tried to push it out of my head, dismiss it as *we're just friends*, the more I wanted her.

"Stupidaggini," Josh repeated with mock-Italian accent. "God, I love Italian." When I didn't react to his joke, he put his arm around my shoulder again and gave me a friendly shake. "You're thinking about it, aren't you?"

"I'm thinking about how *stupidaggini* it would be."

"It might be," he said, "but what if it isn't?"

We rejoined our friends, but between the loud music and the spiraling thoughts, I couldn't focus on what anyone was saying. All I could think about was Keelie. I tried to hide it the best I could, moving along to the music with everyone else, but Keelie noticed I wasn't all there. Of course she noticed. That only made me want her more.

"Did you let him smoke too much?" Keelie elbowed Josh, eyeing me suspiciously. She thought I was acting weird because I was high. At that moment, I wished I were.

Josh held up his hands to say *wasn't me* and shook his head. I was grateful the music was too loud for the conversation Josh actually wanted to have with her. *He's acting weird because he's in love with you.*

A slow song came on, and out of habit, everyone who wasn't there with someone vacated the dance floor. Our friends all drifted to the outside edges of the room, making excuses about grabbing water or finding another friend. When Keelie walked to the outside edge, I followed.

Suddenly, courage flooded up inside me as I looked at the clock. It was a quarter past ten. If I was going to do this, I needed to do it. And I needed to do it now so I had enough time to deal with the rejection.

"Keelie," I called out after her, immediately regretting opening my big stupid mouth.

She turned to look at me, unaware of the colossal way I was about to change our friendship forever. I held out a hand to her. My stomach lurched, and my whole body tingled with pings of anxiety. The back of my neck surged with an icy coolness of fear. I tried to mask my terror with an air of overconfidence. Nodding my head back toward the spot our group had retreated from, I said, "Come dance with me."

She pinched her eyes at me, skeptically. "Why?"

"Because I want you to."

She looked me over, trying to figure out my game. When she couldn't figure out the ulterior motive, she took my hand. My stomach lurched again as her fingers touched mine.

With her right hand in my left, she placed her other hand firmly on my shoulder, her arm running alongside mine. I was hesitant to put my hand on her waist. A few weeks ago, I wouldn't have thought anything of touching her, but now it suddenly meant something. She probably wasn't thinking about it like that. I placed my other hand high on her waist. Electricity surged through me, jolting up my arm as I came into contact.

"What's on your mind, Arvali?" She pierced her gaze into mine. It was dark, but we stood so close together that I could still make out every wave of amber in her eyes.

"I just wanted to dance with you."

Her attention floated down to my lips as I spoke, which made me want to do the same. But after only a couple of seconds of tracing the soft hills of her lips, she pulled them tight and flat into a slight smile.

"What?" she asked, breaking my stare.

I met her eyes again. Was it possible that we had gotten even closer together since the last time I looked into her eyes? Her hand slid from resting on the top of my shoulder to running fully across my back. Now she was definitely closer.

"I've been keeping a secret from you," I admitted with a shrug. My heart raced a thousand miles a minute, fluttering with the regret of starting this conversation.

"Tell me," she demanded, her eyes widened, as if I needed to update her on gossip.

"I like you," I sighed and waited for a reaction that didn't come. The pace of my heart beats doubled as I waited for her reply.

She scrunched up one side of her face, confusion taking over her expression. Her mouth pushed her cheek so far up her face that one eye was almost closed. Then she let out a soft laugh. "I would hope so. It would be kind of weird for us to hang out every day if you didn't."

She was deflecting, giving me a chance to change course. One last opportunity to laugh it off and say, *Yeah, that's what I meant*. But it was already too late. She knew what I meant, and if I didn't get it out in the open now, it would hover around our friendship forever and slowly cause it to decay. I needed to tell her.

I pressed my forehead against hers, as I'd done a thousand times before without thinking twice. Now, I was suddenly very aware of how close this move made her lips to mine.

"You know what I mean," I said in the quietest voice I could over the sounds of the loud music.

She dropped her expression, fixing her eyes to mine, her face completely blank. *Say something.* I imagined the message being passed from my brain to hers. *Say anything.*

"Can we talk about this later?" she said finally, and my heart dropped. *Of course.* I have officially ruined everything.

I nodded slowly, our foreheads still pressed together, and every nod drew her lips closer and then further from mine. She raised her eyebrows, and I felt as they pressed further into my forehead. She gave my hand a soft squeeze that was either meant to assure me that everything was okay or comfort me as she let me down easy. I wasn't sure which one she had meant it to be, but if she had meant it to be a rejection, she had a strange way of showing it.

She gave my hand a tighter squeeze as she studied my lips again. Had it been anyone else, I wouldn't have needed a clearer signal than that, but with Keelie, I was terrified of anything that might jeopardize our friendship. When she raised her gaze back to mine, the look she gave me was different than before. Curious almost. Then she shifted her hand further up my shoulder and brushed her thumb softly over the exposed skin of my neck, right behind my ear and *that* was the clearest signal I could have ever asked for. She might as well have been holding a sign that said *Just do it already.*

I moved my hands from her waist to the small of her back and pulled her body even closer. I hesitated for one final moment, giving her one last chance to warn me if I was making a huge mistake.

She kept her eyes fixed on mine, leaning into me, her soft touch on my neck assuring me that this would all be okay.

And then I kissed her.

She pressed one hand along my cheek; the other gripped into my bicep. Her lips, firmly on mine, sent a surge of electricity through me. Just as quickly as it started, she rolled her forehead along mine, pulling her lips away, ending our kiss. Her teeth peeked out from her still-parted lips as she gave a soft, guilty laugh.

The slow song ended, and a loud beat replaced it. Keelie pulled away, but still allowed her finger to brush softly against my neck.

Through her curled lips, she said, "Let's definitely talk about this later, okay?"

I blew a puff of air out of my nose like a quick laugh. "Okay," I agreed, even though I would much rather talk to her about this *now* so I could kiss her again. And again.

She ran her hands along the lengths of my arms, giving my hands a quick squeeze before she stopped touching me entirely. She tilted her head toward the other side of the room, where we had just come from, and I gave her a nod. She gave me a soft kiss on the cheek, hovered her face close to mine like she was going to give me a *real* kiss, but then she changed her mind, instead leading the way to find our friends.

Mom picked us up after the dance. Eight of us piled into her crossover built to seat five. We didn't have far to go. I sat in the passenger seat. Josh, Zach, and Dylan piled into the back seat, Josh's sister Lex, Jess, and Jess's friend Rachel all piled in on top of them. Six people sitting in three seats. Keelie came running over from the group she was chatting with and peeked into the back seat.

Josh yelled out, "Go sit by Matty."

And without thinking anything of it, Keelie popped open my door and climbed inside. She sat with her legs across my lap, knees facing Mom.

"Can you buckle in if you guys are going to do that?" Mom kept her voice light, probably not wanting to lose her cool-mom image by asking us to do something responsible.

Keelie leaned into my shoulder as she reached around me to pull the seat belt from its place on the side of the car, her thighs grinding into mine as she twisted from her right to her left, strapping us together. I exhaled a slow and steady breath to keep myself grounded, stretching an arm up to the roof and bringing it to rest right behind the headrest, out of sight of Mom and Keelie, as I flipped Josh my middle finger. He accepted the fuck-you gesture with a flick. The smallest yelp escaped my lips as I pulled my hand back from behind me. Keelie eyed me, concerned, but I shook my head to say, *It's nothing*.

On the first turn out of the parking lot, Keelie's body shifted, and she slid away from me slightly. To stabilize, she wrapped an arm around my shoulders, bringing my mouth perfectly level to hers. I locked my gaze to the speedometer and watched the tiny red arm raise and lower with the press of the foot pedal. Anything to keep my mind, and eyes, *and mouth* off Keelie.

"Did you guys have fun?" Mom asked, taking a quick glance at me.

"Huh?" I mumbled, jolting my attention to her.

Keelie released a soft laugh. "We did."

"We did what?" I demanded nervously.

"Ho detto, 'vi siete divertiti?'" Mom repeated suspiciously.

"Oh," I sighed. "Yeah, it was fun."

"Keelie," Mom scolded, "has Matteo been getting into trouble tonight?"

"No," I snapped back instantly. "I'm just tired, I guess."

"I haven't let him out of my sight all night," she promised, which was only mostly true. "He's just being weird."

Keelie gave me a pinch behind my shoulder, telling me to knock it off. But how could I when all I could think about were Keelie's legs pressing into mine, or how the hell I would stifle the beginnings of this hard-on threatening to poke her in her upper thigh? Nothing about this entire situation was normal, so how could I pretend it was?

I occupied my mind by looking forward, thinking about the rest of the evening, about hanging out with our friends in the basement and drinking beers that Mom "accidentally" left for us to find. I thought about how Josh would likely be making out with Rachel by the end of the night. But then I thought about making out with Keelie, and suddenly I was right back to where I started, thinking about Keelie sitting on my leg, thinking about the seat belt pulling her into my chest, thinking about her arm wrapped around me and my hand resting on her knee.

When did I do that?

My parents had a few rules for having friends over to drink. I had to pretend as though they had no idea what was going on. Which meant no loud music, no yelling, no one puking in the upstairs bathroom. Everything had to be cleaned up the next morning, as if I were trying to hide it. But more importantly, no one was allowed to leave unless they were picked up by their parents.

And because it was an official sleepover, everyone brought comfy clothes to change into after we got back. Out of habit, Keelie had tossed her stuff into my room, and she followed me in when I went in there to ditch the formal wear.

"Help me with this?" Keelie asked, turning around and pointing to her zipper.

My cheeks lit up bright red, and I bit the inside of my lip to keep myself from thinking about unzipping her dress and gliding my mouth all over her body.

"Can we talk first?" I pleaded.

She shook her head. "We can talk once I'm wearing sweatpants."

I gulped hard. I kept my eyes turned away as I unzipped her. Stealing a peek would be a bad idea. Unless, of course, I wanted to start the I-don't-feel-the-same-way-about-you conversation with a full hard-on, and I was certain I did not.

With my back turned to her, I stripped down to my underwear and switched into lounge wear. When I turned back around, Keelie was sitting cross-legged on my bed, as she's done a thousand times—only now it knocked the wind out of me to see her there. She patted the spot next to her. I thought about grasping her shoulders, tossing her backward onto the bed, and pressing my body against hers. Instead, I sat down on top of my hands to resist the urge.

"I don't know what to say," she started. It sounded like the start of a let's-just-be-friends conversation to me. I felt my entire body deflate.

"It was dumb. I shouldn't have said anything. Can we—"

She held up a hand and shushed me. I felt taken aback by her shushing and made a face that matched the confusion.

"I want more time to think about it," she said. "Five hours ago, kissing you had never crossed my mind. But now it has. And I want to give it more thought."

"What are you going to do, make a pros and cons list?" I teased.

"I might." She shrugged. "Huge pro: you're already my favorite person in the world. Con: I don't want to mess up our friendship."

I nodded. "I know what you mean."

"Pro: on the same page."

"Another pro?" I offered. She nodded, allowing me to add an item to her list.

I leaned across the bed and kissed her again. She kissed me back, placing a hand on my arm for balance and gripping onto it tight.

She pulled back, contemplating. "It's very presumptuous of you to put that on the pro side"—she tilted her head—"but currently it does seem that the pros are coming out ahead."

I let out an airy laugh. I wanted to kiss her again, but I knew I shouldn't, not yet.

"I want to think about it, okay?" she said. "I want to be sure."

"Okay," I deflated.

We agreed to go back to the party as if nothing happened. "We," of course, being Keelie. She wanted us to pretend like everything was normal. I wanted to hold her in my arms and kiss her forever, but I agreed to normal for now.

The basement living room was surrounded by old couches on all sides, and yet we still sat on the floor. Keelie sat next to me all night long. She kept her body in contact with mine at all times. Our knees touched when we sat cross-legged; her foot brushed mine if my legs were stretched out. At one point, she placed the tiniest surface of her pinky finger up against the side of my hand to discreetly maintain contact.

I couldn't decide whether she had done this intentionally, until she brushed her finger in a soft swirl on the side of my hand before changing her position. That move made me sure she had been holding contact intentionally. I added that to my own personal pro list.

The more we drank, the less Keelie seemed to care about hiding our secret from our friends. She would do things like laugh and then lay her head on my shoulder for a second, and she had moved from a secret pinky touch on the side of my hand to placing her hand completely on top of mine. I was pretty certain I was visibly sweating about it. My face felt hot. Maybe that was from the vodka that Josh had smuggled in. But Keelie touching my hand likely had something to do with it, too.

Around two in the morning, Lex suggested we play a game of Never Have I Ever, which was easily my least favorite drinking game. I could never think of anything that wasn't completely stupid to say, and I usually spent an entire round trying, only to come up empty-handed.

Lex laid out the ground rules, but the most important rule she directed at Josh. "No targeting"—no saying something that would only take out one specific player. Josh and Lex often liked to ride the line on targeting each other when we played this. They had a relationship not unlike the one I had with my sister. Unending amounts of giving the other grief for stupid decisions they had made. It was likely part of the reason Lex suggested the game in the first place.

I didn't pay much attention, preferring instead to focus on Keelie's hand resting on top of mine.

On Josh's turn, he leaned into the center of the circle and looked me dead in the eye, squinting.

I lifted my two fingers up confidently and raised an eyebrow at him. Externally, I was challenging his move. But inside, my stomach clenched thinking about what he was about to call me out on.

"Never have I ever . . ." he started, acting as if he were thinking. I could tell he knew what he wanted to say, but he was trying to decide to what level he wanted to fuck with me. "Never have I ever kissed Matty Arvali."

"Targeting!" Lex cried out before I had a chance to react.

"That's *not* targeting," he retorted, shaking his head in her direction.

"Oh my God, it so is," she screeched back. "Who the hell else would that one be for? I'm the only one who's dated Matty."

"I didn't say *dated*," he turned his eyes back to me. "What do ya think, Matty? Is it targeting?"

"It's a gray area," I decided. "I'm Italian. I've probably kissed everyone here. Except for maybe Rachel"—I looked to her—"because I don't really know you yet"—I looked back to Josh—"but, like, everyone else, I'm sure."

Josh rolled his eyes at me now. "You know what I mean." Then he stuck out his tongue and swirled it in the air a few times to demonstrate.

"Yeah, so then that's targeting!" Lex shouted again. "So you drink!"

Josh didn't let up. "Matty?"

"Why are you asking me? I've never kissed Matty Arvali." I tried one last time to use vague statements to get him to drop it.

"Yeah, but you know the answer, right? So tell me I'm targeting, and I'll take my point and drink."

I raised both my eyebrows at him, pleading for him to drop it, but that only made him stare at me more harshly. The corner of his mouth curled into a smile. He waited.

Keelie finally reluctantly put up her first finger and took a drink. Josh flashed a big, stupid grin. Lex raised an eyebrow our way. Jess covered her mouth in surprise.

"I also would like to throw in my vote for targeting," Keelie chimed in.

"It's not targeting if I get more than one person," he replied sharply. "Fucking drink, Alexis."

Lex took a drink from her glass. "Okay, but can we talk about that?" She pointed a finger in my direction.

"No follow-up questions," I snapped back. "That's against your rules."

Keelie stifled a laugh and buried her face into my shoulder to hide it. Her complete lack of composure made me laugh, too. Josh's new stare signaled that we would definitely be talking about this later.

Keelie was even less secretive about coming into contact with me after that, which I really enjoyed. She leaned her body fully against mine. She didn't worry about hiding when she touched my hand, and felt free to lay her head on my shoulder whenever she wanted.

The more everyone drank, the more energy was drained from the room. It was well past four in the morning when Dylan suggested a round of *Mario Kart*. Jess, Zach, and Lex joined as the other three players. Josh took it as an opportunity to make a move on Rachel. Jess was a great wingman for him. It seemed she always brought along the friend most likely to fall for Josh's moves.

He always started the same way—casually sitting next to her at a respectable distance so that he doesn't look as though he's trying to make a move. He'd lean back, extending his legs out toward her.

He'd ask a generic question like "So, Rachel, how do you know Jess?" to get her to talk. It didn't matter what the answer was; Josh could always start a conversation with it.

She'd say something like, "We're on the tennis team together."

And Josh would ask more and more questions until he found something to compliment her on, something real. He'd be sure to sit up and lean toward her once he had entered the compliment phase. Something like, "You're on the state team? You're so incredible. That must have taken years of hard work."

Keelie leaned closer to me and whispered in my ear, "I bet it takes him two minutes to mention the beach." Then she pulled back with a smirk. *What do you think?*

"I'll take the under on that," I whispered back. "He's overdue for some beach talk."

Josh wasted no time working it in. "There are these amazing tennis courts by Venice Beach. In Los Angeles. My dad lives a few miles from there."

I extended my fist to Keelie, and she bumped her knuckles against mine, acknowledging my win. Josh gave us a quick glare, silently letting us know we needed to fuck off.

That Los Angeles line worked particularly well on Rachel. "You're from LA?" She sighed. "I'd love to go there. It looks so glamorous."

Josh's dad's house in the Los Angeles suburbs was anything but glamorous, and it might be an hour away from the beach on a bad day. He'd be the first to bash the busy city, but never when he was trying to make a move.

"It's great. I miss it so much." He sighed. "I haven't been in almost a year."

"It must be hard being away." She put her hand on his as he continued his charade.

Keelie stood up and loudly asked if I could show her where the Sprite was. And we both knew that she knew exactly where the Sprite was, so I took that as a signal and got up to show her.

She used my arm as support as she stumbled over to the corner of the room where the fridge was tucked away. When we got there, she winked at me and then gave me a sloppy, drunken kiss that I gladly accepted before adding, "You need water before you make another drink."

She sneered at me, opening the fridge and pulling out a water bottle and a can of Sprite. She tucked the Sprite under her arm, opened the water bottle, took a huge drink, and then handed it to me. She poured two cups half full with Sprite and added almost an equal portion of vodka to the first cup before I grabbed her hand to cut her off.

"That one's mine," I said, laughing and taking the bottle from her hand to pour another hearty, but not quite as stiff, drink for her.

She took the bottle back from me and leaned it over her cup again.

"Keelie!" I scolded.

She giggled as she added the tiniest drop of vodka to her cup before placing the vodka back on the counter so I could put the cap back on it.

"Can I have *one* sip of the first one?" she begged. I knew I would regret it, but I reluctantly handed it over to her anyway. She took a large gulp, and I quickly pulled it back to trade in the cup with the less strong pour.

She cackled. I got up in her face, and with a smile I whispered, "Hey, you're drunk."

She kissed me in reply, sending electricity through me again. I was about to reveal to her exactly how smitten with her I was because, as she kissed me, I hardly even noticed that she was also attempting to loosen the cup containing the strong pour of vodka from my hand. Once I felt her tug it free, I immediately lunged my newly empty hand toward her and gave her side a light squeeze where I knew she was incredibly ticklish. She let out a loud yelp of laughter that froze both of us dead in our tracks.

Wide-eyed, she gritted her teeth and whispered, "Sorry."

I looked up at the ceiling, as if staring at it would help me hear whether my parents were getting up to investigate the noise. When I didn't hear anything, I placed a hand on the back of her head, pulled her ear to my mouth and whispered a soft "Shush" in her ear before giving her a kiss on her temple.

She wrapped her arm around my waist for a hug that's main purpose was to keep her stabilized. I pulled her with me back to the couch where we were sitting a moment ago. Josh and Rachel were no longer there.

"Where's Josh?" I demanded. I looked around, but no one replied. So I repeated, "Yo, Lex. Where's Josh?"

"He's with Rachel, *chill*," she said, her eyes glazed over as she rounded the curve of the road on the game.

"Yeah, where?"

She turned to look at me this time. "I don't know, Matty," she snapped.

I blew out a dramatic breath of air and flopped down on the couch. Keelie sat down next to me and looped her arm through mine.

"Do you want to go look for him?" Keelie asked, concerned. She was too drunk to put the pieces together.

"No," I sighed. "I know where he is."

I flopped my head sideways to fix my eyes on my closed bedroom door, then flopped my head back to Keelie and raised my eyebrows at her. *Get it?*

"Oh," she said, surprised. Then more forcefully as she finally put it together, "No! I was going to sleep in there!"

I laughed, nodding my head. Then I pressed my forehead against her temple and whispered, "We can sleep upstairs if you want to."

She nodded. "Right now?"

Her eyes blinked slowly. She hadn't even touched the drink she *had* to have a minute ago, and now she was ready to fall asleep.

"Do you want to right now?"

She nodded again. "Five minutes." Then she held up her drink to explain the rest of her thought. She peeked over at mine, still mostly full, too. She pointed at it and then at me. *Drink that.*

I raised my cup to hers and gave her one last cheers before taking a big gulp. She did the same. I finished mine first, and then we took turns taking large sips of hers until Keelie paused, took a look at the contents of her cup, and threw it all back.

She giggled. "That was probably a bad idea."

"You can't go upstairs if you're going to be sick."

She shook her head. "I'm okay." She nodded once more to convince herself it was true. "Walking is my biggest concern presently."

"I'll help," I assured her.

I stood up and announced my departure to the four who were still drinking and playing video games even though it was approaching five in the morning. I placed a gentle touch on Keelie's arm and nodded my head toward the stairs. She clung to me tightly as she swayed down the hallway. Unfortunately, I was not the same reliable stabilizer I had been a few moments ago. The large amounts of vodka we downed were settling in. We bumped into the walls a few times on our way to the open bedroom upstairs. Each time, I shushed Keelie as she stifled a giggle.

At the end of the hallway was my parents' room on one side, Ellie's room on the other. I carefully, silently unlatched the door to Ellie's room and ushered Keelie inside, closing the door before turning on the lights.

Keelie flopped down on the bed and buried her head in the high pile of pillows at the headboard.

"Is that where you're staying?" I laughed. "I'm going to turn off the lights."

She lifted her arm in the air, giving me a thumbs up as she nodded her head deeper into the pile of pillows. I shut off the light and lay down next to her, pushing all but two pillows off my half of the bed, bringing my eyes down to her level. It was too dark to see her, but I knew she was there.

"Hey, Matty?" she whispered.

"Yeah?"

"I think I've had enough time to think." She extended her neck, uncovering her head from the pillows. Placing her hand gently on the side of my face, she circled her face near mine a few times, trying to touch her nose to mine in the dark. Once the tips of our noses touched, she hovered there for a few seconds before kissing my nose. Then she gave me a kiss goodnight, and I could feel her lips curling into a smile as they pressed against mine.

VII

Friday, August 10th

With the wedding a little over a month away, I spend a lot of evenings sitting at the kitchen table with Chris nearby for supervised phone conversations while I get wedding plans figured out. I have to call the suit rental company with my measurements. I have to call Jess about the hotel reservation. I need to call June, during business hours, of course, to give her the details about where to go. I call Mom to keep her updated on everything that's going on, happy she wants to hear from me at all.

Having to remember anything feels foreign to me after all this time, but now I am making to-do lists and writing out itineraries and following up when I say I will. Basic responsibilities bogged me down a few years ago. Doing something as simple as waking up when an alarm told me to get up, or remembering to set an alarm at all, was more responsibility than I could handle.

Now suddenly I am back to being driven by a list of tasks. Adding something to the list means I have someone relying on me. Jess is an obsessive planner, and she has gotten used to me being unreliable, so I want to make sure I let her know I am following through on the things I say I will do as often as I can.

The first time I call her about wedding plans, she ends our conversation by saying, "Hey, hold on a minute. Josh wants to say hi."

I know the whole reason for the lists of tasks and phone calls is ultimately for Josh and Jess's wedding, but it isn't until I hear her whisper "it's Matty" as she hands the phone over that I finally connect the synapses in my brain.

"Matty!" Josh shouts through the phone.

A quick laugh escapes my lips. "I'm still not used to that."

"What's that?" Josh returns my same light tone.

"You and Jess in the same place."

"Me and Jess, or me and Cleveland?" he jokes.

"You love it here," Jess reminds him from a distance.

"I love it because *you* love it," he croons back to her, so blissfully in love it makes my heart ache.

"I can't wait to see you guys." I dart back into the conversation. "You guys *and* Cleveland."

After I hang up with them, I pan through the streets of downtown Cleveland on Google Maps, figuring out where everything would be. Luci hops into the kitchen and yanks my arm out of her way so she can climb onto the chair and sit on my leg. She scrunches her face at me when she sees I'm looking at a map and not a blank canvas on my screen.

"Zio Piccolo?" she pulls my attention.

"Pinguinetta mia?" I've started to call her *my little penguin*.

"Ti va di disegnare con me?" *Will you draw with me?*

I smile at her. "Due minuti." *Two minutes.*

She slumps into a puddle on the table, chin resting on her arms, eyes transfixed on the screen, waiting for me to click off of this map.

We are working on our latest creation when Michelle comes into the kitchen, visibly deflated as she pockets her phone.

"Mom had to cancel tonight," she whispers to Chris. "Can you call Taylor and Abby, and let them know we can't make it?"

They had plans to meet up with their friends in the city for dinner and drinks. Michelle's parents were going to watch the girls, and I was going to be trusted to stay at home by myself late into the night.

"I can watch them," I interject. Luci's face lights up, and she rapidly nods in her mom's direction.

Chris and Michelle exchange glances, neither wanting to respond to my offer.

"I can do it," I repeat confidently.

"I don't know," Chris groans.

"Why not?" I demand, knowing exactly why not, but wanting to make him say it.

"Because we don't want to leave a drug addict alone with our kids, Matteo."

"Do you have any painkillers in the house?"

"No," he replies sharply.

"Any alcohol I'm not aware of?"

"Not currently."

"Then what's the problem?"

He lets out a sigh. "You can't drive, for one."

I hold up a finger to say *just a minute*. "I *can* drive. I'm a great driver. And if anything were to happen—which it won't—I am more than capable of driving, regardless of whether I have a license."

Chris looks to Michelle, who is doing her best to completely avoid eye contact with me.

"Please, let me do this for you guys," I push. "I want to. I can do this."

"Okay," Michelle mumbles, her gaze still fixed on the ground. She looks up to Chris, shrugs, and says it again, more confidently. "Okay."

"You're sure you're okay with that?" he asks her.

"Yeah," her words fall out of her mouth like a sigh, "it's only a few hours."

A smile spreads across my whole face, one I quickly share with Luci.

When it's time for them to leave, their parental panic settles in again. I've been living here for four months, but suddenly it is imperative that I know where the circuit breaker and water shutoff valves are. I am given a whole list of emergency contacts in town "just in case." It is brought to my attention that we have a first aid kit in the cupboard above the microwave. I am given specific instructions on how much Tylenol I can administer to each of my nieces.

"You guys!" I laugh, as Chris drills off one more thing. "It'll be fine!"

Chris reluctantly holds out the keys to Michelle's car.

"Emergencies. Only." He narrows his eyes at me and whispers, "I fucking mean it."

"I promise," I say, reaching for the keys.

He doesn't release them from his grip, his stare still burning a hole through me.

"I'm not going to let you down," I assure him.

He softens his glare and releases the keys to me. "Okay."

I place them in the center of the counter so I know where to find them.

Michelle is wearing a long flowy dress, big earrings, lipstick. She is a completely different person than her ponytail-and-a-baseball-cap normal. Chris looks the same as always, only everything he is wearing is nicer. He's wearing his good dark denim jeans. He has on a high-quality button-down shirt. The sleeves aren't rolled up, but he still won't tuck it in, not in a million years, not even if Michelle asked nicely. He shaved. He's definitely wearing cologne.

"You guys look nice," I tease in a long, drawn-out song.

Michelle beams. "It feels like it's been ages since we've gone out anywhere."

"Have fun."

"Thank you, Matty. Call us if you need anything, okay? My phone is on," Michelle says frantically.

"I'm not going to call you because everything is going to be fine." I call out for Luci. She comes running into the kitchen, her arms and legs flailing like a goof. "Tell your mom we're going to have fun tonight," I instruct her.

"Yeeees!" She jumps. "So much fun!"

I gesture my hands toward her, offering this as evidence to Michelle that everything will be fine.

"Okay," she sighs. "We should be back by eleven."

"I remember that from when you told me the first time." I grin at her.

"But Luciana is going to be in bed by eight thirty"—Chris lowers a stern look to her—"and she's going to be a good listener to Zio Piccolo, mi lo prometti?" *Do you promise?*

"Prometto," she echoes back her assurance with a slight pang of annoyance.

He nods his approval, then waves a hand to her, signaling for her to come here.

She hops over to him. Chris scoops her up and starts by giving her one quick kiss on her cheek, but then he erupts into big goofy kisses all over her face, her neck, her belly. Luci screeches with laughter. Chris passes her off to Michelle so she can do the same.

"Katya!" Chris yells out.

Katy slumps in, her arms crossed across her chest, an angry look on her face. Chris's expression melts. "Why are you mad at me?"

"I don't want you to leave," she huffs.

"You're going to have fun with Zio Piccolo," he offers, but she shakes her head violently. Chris kneels down to her level. "You're right. He's no fun," he says, matching her grumpy face.

Katy's glare softens. She looks a bit confused as to why her dad is suddenly agreeing with her.

"He's probably going to make you play with toys and watch a movie and read you bedtime stories. That doesn't sound like fun at all, does it?"

Katy shrugs, worried her interest might be misconstrued as enthusiasm.

Chris turns to Michelle. "What do you think, Mom? Should we stay home so Katya doesn't have to play with toys and read bedtime stories?"

Michelle contemplates the thought, very melodramatically.

"No!" Katy yells out before Michelle has time to answer.

Michelle laughs, "Oh, so now you want to stay with Zio Piccolo?"

Katy nods her head excitedly. Michelle bends down and extends her arms out for Katy to give her a hug. She creeps over to her mom and wraps her arms around her neck. Michelle gives her a quick kiss and says, "I love you." Chris does the same, but saying, "Ti voglio bene."

In her anxious floundering, Michelle had decided she needed to have dinner ready for the girls, all sliced up and portioned out so all I would have to do is open containers, pour it onto a plate, and pop it in the microwave, because apparently the thought of me using a stove is too terrifying.

I call them over to eat and put two plates on the table. Luci immediately giggles, making a face at me.

"Che cosa?" I demand, worried I did something wrong. *What?*

Luci points to Katy, who is gripping her fork right down by the prongs, and says, "You're not supposed to give Katya a big fork." She giggles again, mocking me. "She's too little."

Katy screams at this insult, "I am not!" Then she proceeds to stab her food violently with the adult fork.

"Maybe I can get you a purple fork instead?" I offer, hoping to persuade Katy to release the puncture wound waiting to happen.

"No."

"Okay," I sigh. "Just promise you'll be careful?"

Katy replies by stabbing her plate again at full force, the tiny bits of food jumping in every direction. Meanwhile, Luci stares at her plate, not touching any of it. When I ask her what's wrong, she finally admits, "I don't like this stuff."

"Bugiarda," I scoff at her. *Liar.* Her plate is filled with things I've seen her eat dozens of times. But tonight, she is going to cause trouble about it. "You have to eat at least some of it."

She shakes her head. "Can I have an Oreo?"

"Luciana, no! Eat this or your dad is going to be mad at me," I plead with her the only way someone her age can understand.

"*One* Oreo?" she begs.

"I want one," Katy immediately pipes in, stabbing a single noodle with her fork so violently the noodle is completely split in two.

"No, no Oreos," I say.

Katy lets out an angry shriek and flings her plate from the table, adult fork and all. It goes clanging down onto the floor. It's something she wouldn't have dared to do around Chris, but now she wants to be the one in charge.

"Katya!" I snap at her. Luci jumps up to clean it, anything she can do to procrastinate. "Luci, I'll get it. Please, eat your dinner."

She lets out a huff, then picks up her fork to eat.

Katy, forgetting all about her Oreo outburst, points to her stuffed dog lying on a chair and asks, "Can I go play with Pickles?"

"No, wait for Luci."

Katy replies by crossing her arms and furrowing her brow.

I pick up the plate from the floor, placing it and the fork on the counter. I collect what is left of the food, although it isn't much. One bean somehow rolled all the way to the air vent, sitting between two of the grates. As I retrieve it, I notice a couple of other things have been lost down the vent. A penny, a bobby pin, a button.

Then it occurs to me. *I know where the yellow pill is.*

Once Luci finishes her dinner, I cave and give them one Oreo each. I can't afford to be on Katy's bad side any more than I already am. Besides, they're not my kids. I'm supposed to be the fun uncle, not the mean babysitter. But the small dose of sugar mixed with their full bellies leaves them fueled up and completely chaotic, and I immediately regret it. They run laps around the house. Through the entryway, down the hallway where it passes my room, in the back entrance of the kitchen, and back through the dining room where it connects back to the entryway.

"Zio Picco, come on!" Luci calls out as they run past.

"Aspetta!" I reply, poking my head into my room in search of a vent. *Hold on.* As I suspected, there is one directly behind the side table. A smile washes over me, and I'm filled with the sense of calmness that only pills can provide.

I shift the side table, carefully pulling it away from the vent for better access. Luci comes running into my room. She grabs hold of my arm and gives it a tug.

"Zio Picco, adesso!" she yells. *Right now!*

"Aspetta!" I repeat.

"Katya! Help!" Luci yells out, giving my arm another firm tug. Katy comes running into the room, too. Luci shrieks, "Get his other arm!"

Katy squeals out a laugh as she mimics Luci, pulling on my wrist.

"Alright!" I raise my arms up in the air, lifting them both off the ground. Their roaring laughter becomes contagious.

"Zio, chase us," Katy giggles. I lower them back down to the ground, and they take off running. I pull the socks off my feet for better traction on the hardwood floors, then take off after them. Katy screeches when she turns around to see me coming. As I run through the kitchen, Luci jumps off our track and runs to another part of the house.

"Hey, Katy," I whisper. She giggles again, not trusting that I'm not up to something. I put a finger to my lips and make a quiet *shhh*, then signal for her to get close. "Where's Luci?"

Katy shrugs with another giggle.

"Let's go get her," I suggest.

Katy nods excitedly, the first time she's ever shown any kind of interest in anything I've had to say. I instruct her to tiptoe, and she follows suit behind me. We search the living room first, overturning pillows and peeking behind chairs. Luci isn't here.

Katy loses interest quickly, instead cradling a doll she finds in a pile of toys in the corner, smoothing over her hair, and handing it to me.

"Can you brush her hair?" Katy asks.

"We're looking for Luci, remember?"

"I don't want to," she whines.

Luci's feet patter down the hallway.

"There she is!" I say excitedly, trying to get Katy back into the game. Katy glances up over her doll, showing interest. So I add, "Which way did she go?"

Katy sprints off down the hallway, yelling out, "She went in here!"

She turns on a light in the hallway and then again in my room, convinced Luci is hiding inside. She sets off on searching through my dresser drawers, all of which are much too small for Luci to be hiding inside. I lie down on the floor next to the side table, making it appear that I am searching under the bed, but then as Katy overturns the pillows, I take a glance into the air vent behind the side table in search of the yellow pill. It's so dark, I can hardly see past the grates.

A clank comes from the kitchen, and Katy takes off into the next room, continuing her search for Luci. I flip on the lamp and rotate it slightly so that it now shines directly onto the floor behind the table, lighting up the vent. I lean my head to one side, then the other, trying to get my eyes on every inch of the inside of the vent. Then a flash of yellow catches my eye.

I found it.

"I found her!" Katy shrieks out.

Luci takes off running once again. She sprints out of the kitchen, her feet pattering down the hallway. She lets out a screeching laugh as Katy takes off after her. Wedging a finger under the edge of the vent grate, I shimmy it off and lift it out of place. I have a clear view of the yellow pill now. My mouth waters.

A loud thud comes from the hallway and jars my attention back to the girls. I set the vent cover off to the side, then stand. Before I even get my feet planted back on the floor, Katy lets out an ear-piercing wail that sends me running into the hall.

She is sitting on the floor, face already turning bright red from screaming. Luci locks eyes with me, terrified.

"What happened?" I shout, diving to Katy's side.

"It was an accident," Luci says.

"Luci pushed me!" Katy screams between sobs.

I snap a glare in Luci's direction, waiting for an explanation. Luci shakes her head violently and defends herself. "It was an accident."

"Tell me what happened," I soften, picking Katy off the ground to comfort her. Instead, this only makes her wail louder.

"Katy was chasing me around and around, so I tried to go the other way, but she kept going this way"—she spins her hands to demonstrate the directions—"and then I bumped into her. But not on purpose! I couldn't see her! It was an accident!"

Luci, overwhelmed with emotions, starts crying, too. I pull her head into the side of my leg for a quick hug, brushing a hand through her hair.

"Okay, okay," I plead for her to stop crying. "It's okay, Luci. It was an accident," I confirm. Then I try to convince Katy. "She didn't mean to hurt you. Are you okay?"

Katy screams even louder. Luci apologizes profusely to Katy, offering anything she can to help her calm down, but Katy doesn't want to hear it. I pace around the room with Katy on my hip. Luci follows closely behind me, her face completely washed with guilt. I should be the one feeling guilty, though. This might not have happened if I hadn't left them alone. All because of the yellow pill.

"Katya," Luci pleads, "do you want your boo-boo buddy?"

"No!" Katy shrieks back.

"What's that?" I ask.

"Umm . . ." She doesn't understand why I don't know what she's talking about, so she repeats, "It's a boo-boo buddy."

"Show me?"

Luci leads me to the kitchen and slides open the freezer drawer, pointing to some frozen stuffed-animal ice packs that are tucked away on the top shelf. A penguin, a rhino, a giraffe. I beg Katy to pick one. She, of course, settles on the penguin, which makes Luci mad because that one is hers. I ask Luci to let Katy borrow it, and she scowls as she reluctantly agrees.

"Luci, can you go put on a movie for us?" I nod a head toward the living room. Luci takes off running, then picks up the remote and flips through the apps on the TV as though it's second nature to her. She pulls up a streaming service, clicks through until she finds what she's looking for, and turns it on. Her speed is incredible.

Still holding Katy, I take a seat in the big puffy recliner and invite Luci to join us. The three of us snuggle up in the chair together and watch most of the movie before they drift off to sleep. When it ends, I give Luci a kiss on the top of her head to wake her up.

"Let's go get ready for bed," I say.

She rubs her face groggily and nods.

We walk upstairs to their rooms. Without turning on the lights, I tuck Katy into bed. She is still firmly grasping onto her boo-boo buddy, even after the rest of her body has gone limp.

Luci grabs my hand and walks me down the hallway to her room. She turns on the lights and excitedly opens one of the dresser drawers to pick out her jammies. She hands them to me, then climbs onto her bed and starts jumping. I scoop her up midflight and squish her in my arms.

"I know your mom and dad would not want you jumping on the bed," I remind her.

"It's okay," she lies, trying to wiggle free.

I shake my head and eye her suspiciously. "You're a stinky liar."

She lets out a loud giggle.

"Can we go brush our teeth?" I ask her.

Luci nods. "You have to, too."

"My toothbrush is downstairs." I plead for an exception, but she won't hear it.

We retrieve Luci's toothbrush and toothpaste and walk back downstairs. I look at the clock in the kitchen as we pass. It's already past nine.

I offer my toothbrush out to Luci, and she squeezes a large glob of bright pink, bubble gum–flavored toothpaste on it. She does the same to hers. After brushing our teeth, she insists on brushing her hair to further stall her bedtime. Reluctantly, I agree, ushering her up to her room immediately after.

She climbs onto her bed and starts bouncing again. This time, I have to be the bad guy. "Luciana," I snap in a hushed voice, "jammies. Let's go."

She takes one last big rebellious jump, crosses her legs midair, then flops onto her bed. I walk through each body part I need her to move to get her jammies on. "Arm. Other arm. Foot." I tuck her under the covers and give her a kiss on her forehead.

"Ti voglio bene, pinguinetta mia."

"Ti voglio bene, Zio Picco."

I turn off her lights and head back downstairs. My brain pings back to the glimpse of the yellow pill tucked away inside the vent. The lamp is still on, the vent cover still removed. I lie down on my stomach and peer down into the vent.

I carefully reach in with a thinned hand, tweezing the pill with my two longest fingers. *Don't drop it. Don't drop it.* I cup a hand under it as my fingers surface from the vent and drop it into my palm to get a better look at it. Etched into the top is the most beautiful thing I have ever seen.

OP 40.

My entire mouth waters to prepare for swallowing the pill. I can already taste the comforting bitterness at the back of my throat. But instead of a calmness taking over, panic settles in. My heart races faster.

Just fucking take it.

And then what? Then I would want more. Then I would need more. How long am I going to keep letting this stupid fucking pill control me?

Not stupid, beautiful. Captivating.

Crushing. It's never going to stop. It's always going to be my top priority. It's always going to run my life. Where does it end?

"Zio Picco?" a soft voice whines from upstairs.

I shove the pill in my pocket and take off running up the stairs.

"Luciana, what's wrong?" I whisper to her in the dark.

"Can you read me a story?" she pleads. It's nine thirty. An hour past her bedtime. But Chris and Michelle won't be back until eleven. They'll never know.

They will never know any of this.

"Pick one out," I say, lifting her off the bed and placing her down on the floor. I flip on the lamp at her bedside and sit on the bed, my back pressed against the headboard. She scurries over to her books, quickly plucking one from the shelf, and runs back. She tosses the book on the bed before gripping her hands firmly onto the comforter and pulling herself up.

The book she hands me is titled *Stella e le Stelle*. *Stella and the Stars*. A small girl dressed as an astronaut is on the dark cover, surrounded by hundreds of sparkling stars. I trace the sparkling texture with my hand, captivated by the design.

"Luci," I ask with pride, "do you know what this says?"

She nods. I place an arm around her shoulder and pull her in tight, giving her a big kiss on the top of her head. I open the book to the first page. It is *all* in Italian.

"Luciana, è tutto in italiani. You know all these words?"

She nods again, then nuzzles up against my side, waiting for me to read her the story of Stella, the small girl who keeps watch on the night sky through her window, learns to use a telescope, and imagines becoming an astronaut one day.

Once we finish reading the book, she still isn't quite ready to sleep. I tuck her in tight and sit on the side of her bed, slowly running my fingers through her freshly brushed hair.

"Vuoi fare l'astronauta?" I ask her softly. *Do you want to be an astronaut?*

"No," she sighs, very matter-of-factly. But she doesn't have the energy to tell me what she does want to be. She slowly drifts off to sleep.

I softly press one last kiss on the top of her head. Tears well up in my eyes as I look at her. It took a lot for Chris and Michelle to trust me to take care of them. Was I prepared to give that up? To wind up back at square one?

They'd never know.

But what if they did? I'd really have nothing left after that. I can't keep doing this.

I flick off the lamp in Luci's room and pull the yellow pill out of my pocket as I head down the stairs. I hold it in my hand, tracing the *OP 40* with my thumbnail.

One last time. My mouth is watering. The phantom flavor coats my throat.

I turn the lights on in the first-floor bathroom, where Luci and I had brushed our teeth less than an hour ago. The dreamed-up taste of oxycodone has completely drowned out the bubble gum flavor. I roll the pill across my fingers, then turn to look at myself in the mirror. I lean in close and lock eyes with myself.

Fucking do it.

I flip open the toilet lid and drop my last beautiful pill inside. It makes a soft *plink*. A tiny bubble floats to the surface in its place as it sinks to the bottom. I give my precious yellow pill one last look, then press down on the handle and watch it swim around as the water rushes in and pulls it down the drain. It's gone forever.

PART TWO:
CLEVELAND, OHIO

I
Thursday, September 20th

Chris drops me off at the airport on the day I'm set to head to Cleveland.

Everything I needed could have been packed into my one duffel bag—it was only a weekend trip after all—but Michelle insisted I couldn't pack a suit in a duffel bag.

"You're going to ruin it with wrinkles," she'd scolded. She asked me if I wanted to borrow a garment bag from her dad, and I had to admit to her that I didn't know what that was. Also, I didn't want to say yes to anything that left me indebted to her parents. They weren't fans of mine.

Chris told me that Michelle's mom lost her mind when she found out I would be living with them. "Think about your kids," she'd said.

Even five months later, even after the house had not burned down with me there—so far anyway—they still reminded Michelle that it was a bad idea to have me around. So the thought of Michelle asking them for something on my behalf was completely mortifying. They probably would assume that any self-respecting twenty-eight-year-old who didn't have their own carry-on, rolling garment bag must not be very successful. They'd be right about that, though. I wasn't. It wouldn't do me any good to point out that neither Chris nor Michelle owned a coveted garment bag, either, because their success could be measured in other ways. I didn't even have the kind of success that could be measured in frivolous luggage.

Despite my incessant protests, Michelle eventually asked her dad if we could borrow the carry-on, rolling garment bag he hadn't used in the better part of a decade. We picked it up from them while we were out picking up the rented suit that would be put in it. Her dad asked *Michelle* what I would use it for, because he wouldn't direct any questions to me. He asked as if he was convinced I was going to fill it with cocaine and smuggle it across the border. "What exactly will he be using it for?"

Michelle laughed at the question, but when she realized he was serious, she explained that I was going to a wedding. This time, it was her mom's turn to insult me. She turned her body away from me as if she could disguise her question, perhaps blame it on someone else. "Do you think that's a good idea?" she'd asked.

"It'll be fine, Mom," Michelle assured her. Michelle had so much more confidence than I did on the matter.

When we were in the car, driving back home, Michelle apologized for them. "They're a bit freaked out by the whole thing," she explained. "I was, too, at first." The difference, of course, being that after five months, Michelle had changed her mind about me, but her parents still had not.

Michelle was eager to help me pack the bag as soon as we got home. She started by showing me how to lay out the suit inside so it didn't get wrinkled, then she tore through each drawer of my dresser to find what she thought I should wear, passing it to me and supervising as I packed the bag to make sure I hadn't done anything to wrinkle the suit.

The next day, I give Luci a big hug and a lingering kiss on the top of her head. Katy is in another mood and refuses to even look at me, but she does allow for one very brief fist bump to supplement before burrowing her face into Michelle's neck.

Michelle says, "Have fun, Matty. We'll talk to you soon!" She gives me a side hug, with Katy still clinging to her other side, and a big kiss on the cheek to prove that she is, in fact, a member of the Arvali family. The three of them stand on the front porch to wave goodbye as we leave, as if I am leaving for months instead of a few days.

The drive to the airport takes almost forty minutes. Chris quizzes me on everything that's happening this weekend. He asks more questions about June. He tells me I have to check in with him at least once every night by midnight so that he knows I am doing okay. And of course, by "doing okay" he means these calls serve as a sobriety checkpoint, and I better not miss them.

He swings his car into the Departures parking lanes, then jumps out to give me a big hug. A worrier like Mom, he asks whether I have everything, running through the list of things I may have forgotten. Passport? . . . Boarding pass? . . . Money?

I don't have a dime to my name, but Chris and Michelle had decided to sponsor me on this trip. Chris begrudgingly gave me cash for emergencies and a prepaid credit card for everything else. My parents paid for my flight to Cleveland and our hotel room. I feel incredibly guilty accepting this kindness from all of them after what I put them through.

Chris pulls my phone out of his pocket, and as he hands it to me, he reminds me, "Call Mom when you land, too." Once I power it on, I am officially on my own. It's weird to have this small freedom back after so long. I hardly feel as though I've earned any of this. Chris gives me another huge hug before I leave, instructing me to call him at any time for anything, no matter how small. I promise him I will. Then we part ways, and I'm at the airport. Alone. Free to do anything I want.

Free to escape. Free to find pills.

This is going to be the easiest part of my weekend, and I'm already not feeling up to the task.

Downtown Cleveland is a twenty-minute car ride from the airport. My brain nervously spirals with anxious thoughts about this weekend. Are my friends going to be different around me now? What am I going to talk about? It's been years since I've done anything. What am I going to say when someone asks a simple question like "What's new?" What am I going to say if I have to talk to *Logan*? I'm not going to be able to handle this. Or worse yet, maybe I will be able to handle this, but everyone will find me incredibly *boring*.

The conversation we had with Rich before he died pops into my mind. His boring pills were just about the only thing that could have saved his life. He might have felt as if he was boring when he took them, but at least he'd be alive. Maybe boring isn't so bad after all.

Once the car drops me off at the hotel, I text Chris to let him know I made it. I collapse the handle and sling the carry-on garment bag over my shoulder by its strap so it doesn't get caught in the revolving door at the front of the hotel. Checking in at the front desk feels foreign to me. It's been so long since I've had to check in for anything completely on my own. Luckily, my brain hasn't forgotten what to do. It goes on autopilot, making me feel as though someone else is answering the questions for me.

The front desk manager smiles warmly as he finishes checking me in, and then says, "Enjoy your stay, Mr. Arvali."

"Matty!" Jess shouts from the other side of the lobby as she hears the attendant call out my name. I throw my bag off my shoulder when she sprints toward me.

I hold out my arms wide, and she plunges her arms under mine for an enormous hug. Josh, a few paces behind her, barrels right on top of her to hug me, too.

I breathe in deep and feel a calm wash over me. I haven't experienced something this familiarly comforting in a long, long time. The hug breaks up, but Josh and Jess stand intertwined, his arm around her shoulder, hers around his back.

"I can't believe you guys didn't tell me about this sooner."

"Well," Jess hesitates, "I tried to, but—"

"We're really glad you're here, Matty," Josh interrupts.

"Me too." I glance behind them for a second and catch the eye of another familiar face. "Is that Lex?"

Josh's sister waves back at me, and I nod a hello in her direction. She works in publishing now and always dresses immaculately, as though she could close the biggest deal of her life at any moment. Her hair is tied back tightly, and she has clipped in a long ponytail extension that makes her hair hang well beyond her waist.

When we approach, Lex gracefully leaps from the bar-height chair, and her tall heels lift her to my eye level. She places a hand on each of my biceps and squeezes tightly, giving me a pretend kiss on each cheek. *A real kiss would smudge her lipstick.*

"Shit, look at you," I say.

"It's been a long time, Matty," she croons.

Lex and I dated for a couple of months when we were kids. Back in middle school, when love was awkward and new and uncertain. We figured out pretty quickly that we were better as friends. But she still gets a lot of enjoyment out of exchanging flirtatious remarks with me. She likes to say something sultry and then playfully remind me that she's way out of my league. I used to fire back a suggestive remark or send a flirty smile her way. But it would be pathetic for me to play that game with her now.

"What have you been up to?" Lex takes a sip from the martini she is drinking, piercing her eyes into me. She once told me she hates martinis but loves the way she looks while drinking them. I can see why.

"Not a thing." I tilt my head with a sarcastic smile. "But you knew that already, right?"

I match her martini sip with a sip from a water bottle that I bought at the airport.

"Joshy has told me a little, yeah," she pouts.

"Are we doing that again, Alexis?" Josh interjects, protesting the nickname.

She ignores Josh and turns back to me. "I'm sorry. I didn't mean it to come off like that." Although we both know she probably did. "I guess I meant to ask you how you were doing with everything, that's all." She places a hand on my forearm, her eyes drilling deeply into my soul.

She's wearing a very large ring on her middle finger, a huge gemstone in the center with plenty of real diamonds all around it. I'm sure it cost thousands of dollars, maybe even tens of thousands. Her wrists are similarly adorned in gold bands of varying sizes.

"Yeah," I lie, "it's been great."

"Great." She gives my arm a little double tap, as if she's petting a dog, and then pulls her arm away. "You're living with your brother and his family, right?"

I nod. It's another question I'm sure she already knows the answer to, but I let her crush me with it anyway.

"So you're kind of like an au pair, then?" she teases.

"Alexis . . ." Josh interjects again.

I wave him off. I can stand my ground with Lex. "Yes," I say, with fake enthusiasm. "I am exactly like an au pair."

She smiles, satisfied that I'm willing to play the game. She leans toward me, resting her chin on her palm, careful to show off her opposite hand so I can inspect the full set of jewelry on this other arm.

"Do you enjoy living with them?" She nods subtly after she finishes the question, as if she is telling me the appropriate way to respond.

"They're great," I say sincerely. "Especially his kids."

"That's really great, Matty. I'm so envious of all that time you have." She smirks. "With your family, I mean."

She takes one last sip of her martini, then gracefully places both her hands on the table and says, "Well, we're going to have so much time to catch up this weekend while we hang out in

Cleveland,"—she says it as if the mere thought of being in Ohio leaves a bitter taste in her mouth— "so I'm going to go upstairs and unpack before anything wrinkles. But I'll be right back because I don't know what else I'm supposed to do here besides drink."

She stands, touching my arm with her million-dollar hand once again. She narrows her eyes, and puckers her lips suggestively. "It was so great to see you, Matty." Then she leans in closer to whisper in my ear, "It's been way too long."

I place a hand on her waist as she leans in and whisper back in her ear, "Hurry back."

She pulls away and runs her teeth across her bottom lip for a split second. Then she winks as if to say, *Welcome back.*

I keep my eyes fixed on the table because she wants me to watch her leave, and the only way to win this silly game we play is to not do that.

"Wipe that stupid fucking smile off your face," Josh says, snapping me out of my momentary trance. "You've done a lot of stupid shit, but that would be the biggest mistake of your life."

"We're just messing around." I raise an eyebrow at him as I take another quick sip of my water. "I thought you knew that?"

He shakes his head at me. "You guys are both so fucked up."

Ignoring Josh's protests makes him even more uncomfortable, and that's part of this game, too, so I quickly change the subject. "What's the timeline for this weekend?" I ask, mostly directing my question to Jess, who was known for having multiple planners at one time in her past life.

She runs through the whole agenda with me in more detail than I bargained for. The bachelor party, the rehearsal dinner, the ceremony, the reception, and a morning-after brunch before everyone leaves town. She mentions when a few key people are expected to arrive: some of Josh's college friends, Jess's sister, Josh's parents. She expertly does not make any mention of when Keelie and *Logan* will arrive, and I know I can't ask that question, no matter how much I'd like to. It doesn't keep me from imagining what Keelie and *Logan* will be doing along every point of Jess's timeline.

They're combining the bachelor and bachelorette parties into one big outing. "June can come," Jess adds. So that means *Logan* will be there. It's impossible to think about being sober while he's around. What if he tries to make small talk with me? *So you're Matty, huh?* I cringe even thinking about hearing him say my name. What if she never even mentioned me? She had to have, right?

The rehearsal dinner will be a handful of family and friends. Keelie and *Logan* will sit next to each other, eat off each other's plates. She will rest her hand on his inner thigh as she's done to me a thousand times. I'll watch them from across the room with envy.

Keelie will most definitely cry at the ceremony. She cries so easily for happy things. And I'll long to pull her in tightly for a hug, wrap her up in my arms, and tell her it's okay when she laughs at herself for crying. But instead, I'll get to see her look to *Logan* for comfort.

At the reception, they'll both have a few too many drinks. They'll sing and dance and laugh. They'll start by keeping their affection classy, a soft touch or a quick kiss. But once Keelie approaches her limit on drinks, she'll hold on to him a bit tighter, kiss him a bit longer, laugh a lot louder. Then he'll whisper in her ear as I've done a thousand times, and they'll duck out early to go back to the hotel room they share. He'll unpin her hair, unzip her dress, pull her down onto the bed.

I know how every moment will play out because I have been him for thousands of days with Keelie. Over three thousand of them. Three thousand days of laughing and holding and kissing. Maybe not quite three thousand of them, actually. There weren't as many good days toward the end.

"I think you've lost him," Josh whispers to Jess before she's able to talk about plans for brunch. I blink a few times to push the images of *Logan* out of my head.

"I'm listening," I assure her. *And it's all burned deeply into my mind.* "I think I'm going to go toss my stuff in my room," I say, pointing a thumb toward the elevator. "But I will be back down here by five"—I point both index fingers at Jess to prove I was paying attention—"to say hello to Momma Parker, whose flight lands at four and who will be picked up at the airport at four thirty and brought back here . . . around five."

Jess smiles approvingly.

"You sure you're good, Matty?" Josh asks.

"Yes," I say, much too confidently. "Positive."

Jess holds out her arms. "Okay then, one more before you go!"

I step off my chair and give her a hug and a kiss on the cheek, like always.

She says, "Love you, Matty. Thank you for being here."

"Wouldn't miss it, babe," I reply.

She lets me go, and Josh holds out a hand to pull me in for a hug next. "See ya later, okay?"

I nod, then head toward the elevator, taking the room key out of the front pocket of my bag to look at the room number again—744. I jump in the elevator and press number seven.

The elevator dings and the doors open on the seventh floor. I step out as a door at the end of the hallway opens and *Keelie* exits her room.

Panic consumes me as she takes a step in my direction, not yet meeting my eyes. *Of course she's walking toward you, idiot. Where else would she be going?* Turning on my heels, I press the elevator button, hoping to jump back on unnoticed. But it's too late. Someone has already claimed it. I'm stuck.

II

Thursday, September 20th

With my back to her, I strain to listen for her feet in the hallway, but it doesn't sound as if she's there anymore. Maybe she saw me and turned the other way to wait it out in her room for a couple of minutes. Maybe she went to get *Logan.*

No. Don't say it like that. I say his name in my head a few times, trying my best to erase the sarcastic snarl I have attached to it. Logan. Logan. Lo. Gan.

Am I about to meet him? Already? The confrontation I've been dreading. Here in the middle of the hallway, where everyone walking by can witness the horrific discomfort a conversation with him will cause me.

My heart races, sinking heavily into my chest. A lump crawls up my throat. I still don't hear Keelie. Maybe she went back to her room. That would be for the best, right? To avoid seeing her and *Logan* for as long as I can. Not *Logan,* just Logan.

I'm not ready for this. I don't know when I am going to be ready, but it's definitely not now. I need to—

"Matty?" Keelie calls out my name as if it's a question, as if maybe she doesn't recognize me, although there isn't any

189

amount of concealment that would keep her from recognizing me. I know this for certain because there is absolutely no amount of concealment that would keep me from recognizing her. I know every inch of her.

My face flashes with my best fake surprised expression, a quick practice for when I turn around, but as soon as my eyes meet hers, there is no need for a fake expression. I *am* surprised. My eyebrows peak at the sight of her and then melt into a look of familiar longing. She's even more magnificent than every version of her that has flashed through my memory in the two years that we've been apart.

She's tied her hair into her signature loose ponytail. Her oversize sweatshirt slumps off one shoulder. She's wearing leggings that cling to her skin. The urge to pull myself closer to her pulses through me. An urge to brush aside the loose curls that have fallen across her face and press her forehead to mine. To rub a finger on her neck, just behind her ear. To feel her breath brush against my face with every soft whisper.

"Hey, Mia," I say breathlessly. She crinkles her nose at the much too familiar nickname, snapping me out of my trance. "No, I'm sorry. Keelie," I apologize, then stupidly add, "Old habits, I guess."

She smiles kindly, although she probably thinks I'm a moron. The elevator dings, finally arriving on our floor. She points toward it and asks, "Are you . . .?"

She had spotted me heading toward the elevator, so I nod. I'll have to go back downstairs. Taking a step forward, my hand brushes against the bag still slung across my shoulder. I shake my head, pulling myself from the mesmerizing trance Keelie has me in. "No, I forgot. I have to put this in my room."

"Do you want me to wait for you?" she offers.

"Sure, thanks." *Sure?* Why did I agree to that?

I dash down the hallway, brushing off my stupid decision to accept her pitying invitation, fumbling with the room key outside of room 744. The key reader flashes a green light, signaling for me to step inside. Cracking open the door the smallest bit, I toss my bag inside and jump back into the hallway.

As promised, Keelie is still waiting by the elevator. When she sees me heading her way, she presses the elevator button again, and this time it's there waiting for us. She holds her hand inside the door, keeping it captive on our floor until I step on, with her following closely behind.

What will I do back in the lobby, only a few minutes after I told Josh and Jess I was headed upstairs to unpack? Josh will no doubt mention that they just saw me, fully confirming for Keelie that I was attempting to avoid her. Once the elevator arrives in the lobby, I will have to pretend I left something important in my room to make an excuse to head back upstairs.

Keelie and I are alone in the elevator the entire ride down, which makes the silence between us even more apparent. We're standing as far apart as we ever have inside an elevator. Keelie used to make a game out of our elevator rides, pushing me up against one side, pressing her body against mine, kissing me until the elevator doors dinged open again, then composing herself as if nothing ever happened. Now we stand far apart, as if we're complete strangers.

"Listen, Matty," she blurts out, breaking our silence, "I don't want things to be weird between us this weekend. For Josh and Jess."

"I don't either," I agree, gloomily.

"I was heading down the street to grab a coffee. Would you want to come with me?" She adds with an uncomfortable smile, "We can catch up on the way."

Every fiber in my body screams out for me to say no. Pricks bubble on every last surface of my skin. The lump in my throat triples in size. Maybe my heart has jumped clear out of my chest and lodged itself in my esophagus. *Say no. Say no. Say no.* The words echo in my head, but my stupid, dumb, disconnected mouth says . . .

"That would be great."

The elevator dings at the lobby level. We both walk off at the same time. Josh and Jess are sitting in the same spot they were a moment ago, Josh facing toward us. We meet eyes, and he immediately puts his beer to his mouth to take a sip, then turns his attention back to Jess. Maybe he didn't notice us.

The second I step into the revolving door at the front, my phone buzzes from inside my pocket. On the other side, I pull it out to check the message. There's a text from Josh on my screen: *What was that?* Fighting back the happiness I feel, preventing it from showing on my face, I pocket my phone without a reply.

Keelie cuts to the left, toward the intersection at the corner of the hotel. Cars zip by as we wait at the curb for a walk signal. With a warm grin, Keelie turns to me and says, "You look fantastic, Matty. Healthy, I mean. They might not even recognize you."

It's as if she's implying we're in a secret club, me and her against the world. *They might not recognize you, but I always will.*

"Thanks," I reply sincerely, "that means a lot." Her words fall tensely over me, more weight than I'm sure she had intended them to have.

"You've come a long way," she says, placing a comforting hand on my forearm. "I'm really proud of you."

My mouth refuses to formulate a reply. Instead my mind fixates on her hand touching my arm. Pinpricks surge through my body, all immediately rushing to my heart, which is once again beating out of my chest. Suddenly aware of the effect she's had on me, she releases my arm from her grasp, pretending she didn't feel a bolt of electricity pass between us at her touch.

"I know it wasn't easy," she says, trying to pass this exchange off as normal.

"Still isn't," I admit, searching my brain for other words to say so it doesn't come off as cold, but I come up empty-handed.

"Did you drive here?" she grasps for something, *anything* to carry the conversation.

In good Matty Arvali fashion, I put my foot in my mouth by replying, "I don't drive anymore." Desperately trying to lift the tone, I add, "Apparently, if you get too many DUIs, they take away your license. Wish someone would have told me sooner."

"You know, I have heard that," she smiles politely. "Sorry, stupid question."

"I don't know why I said that. I shouldn't make jokes about it. That last one probably should have killed me." Clearing my throat to start over and brightening my tone, I conclude, "No, I flew in this morning."

She tosses a quick acknowledging glance my way and then lets her expression drop. "Your mom told me about it. That must have been terrifying."

We stop at another intersection. What Mom hasn't told her, what Mom couldn't have known to tell her, is that the only thing that truly terrifies me about wrecking my car is that Keelie could have been in the car with me. A sad sigh escapes my lips, one that could have easily been mistaken for a short laugh, but Keelie immediately recognizes it as a sob and touches a hand softly to my shoulder. Sending an appreciative smile her way and blinking a few times to fight back tears, I admit, "I don't remember it." I push past the flashing images of the mangled passenger side of my car. Not knowing where to transition this conversation to, I say, "Anyway."

The light changes, we continue forward, and Keelie shifts our conversation into safer territory. "She also told me you're living with Chris now. How's that?"

I swallow hard, trying to dispose of the remnants of the previous subject. "Really great. It's nice being able to spend so much time with Luci and Katy."

"Four and six, right?" she remembers.

"Luci just turned seven."

"Wow." Nostalgia washes across her face.

The brief lull in conversation pushes me to address the fat, ugly elephant in the room before it's too late. I need to be the first to mention it. My heart drops heavy in my chest again, a huge gaping hole forming there. My breathing goes shallow.

"In the spirit of not making things weird," I start, immediately grabbing her attention, "Josh told me about Logan. And I want to say that I'm really happy for you. And that I'm really looking forward to pretending that I have been looking forward to meeting him." The words spill out of my mouth quicker than intended. It sounds rehearsed but hopefully not insincere.

"Thank you, Matty. Really." After a moment of hesitation, she adds, "I hope you do get to meet him someday."

I freeze. Actually freeze. Physically stop walking. My feet turn into two cement bricks that can no longer be lifted off the ground.

"Someday?" I choke out.

"He wasn't able to make it after all," she replies too quickly. "He had to work."

A weight lifts off my shoulders. The moment I have dreaded for weeks is suddenly gone.

"That's too bad," I say, way more excited than I would have liked. "So then you drove ten hours overnight by yourself?"

Keelie stops at a glass door with vinyl stickers pasted to the outside, one that I almost blow right past. She pulls the handle, opening the door for me, and tilts her head, directing me inside.

As I walk past she adds, "Sam's here."

"Sam?" I try to keep my voice light as the lump returns to my throat. My vision sways slightly. "Like . . . your brother?"

She beams as if she's completely oblivious to the tension between Sam and me. "That's the one."

Standing in line at the coffee counter, waiting to put in our order, hair stands up on the back of my neck and tiny beads of sweat prickle to the surface. I beg my brain to find something to say so it isn't completely obvious I'm clamming up at the thought of seeing Sam.

"Well, that's going to be a disaster." I laugh nervously. "I would have preferred six to eight hours with my therapist before confronting this situation." I flash a sly look her way so she knows I am attempting to make a joke—one that is mostly just the truth told in a light manner.

Things hadn't ended well between Sam and me. The last time I saw him, he was throwing me out of the apartment I shared with Keelie, after a night of cleaning up messes I had made. Checking my pulse to make sure I hadn't overdosed as I lay passed out on the bathroom floor. Searching my car for damages after I drove it when I shouldn't have. Keeping Keelie calm as she paced around our apartment, worried I might never wake up. Helping her call my brother when she finally decided she'd had enough of my bullshit.

Keelie has always been warm, kind, and understanding. But Sam? You can't burn Sam and get away with it. He holds grudges with the best of them, and he doesn't care if he hurts your feelings in the process. The moment I see Sam again, he's going to wring my neck.

"You are more than capable of handling Sam," Keelie says encouragingly.

"It's been way too long since you've been stuck in the same room as me and him," I remind her. "No one will be immune from that fallout."

The barista calls us forward and in a chipper voice asks, "What can I get ya?"

Keelie looks my way as she responds. "Two lattes?" I nod, then she turns back to the barista and says, "Yeah. Two of those."

"Syrup?" the barista asks.

"No, thanks," Keelie answers without needing my approval this time.

She gives the barista her name, pays for both drinks, and steps aside to let the next person in line step up to the counter. As she zips her wallet shut, she apologizes, mimicking my earlier sentiment. "Sorry. Old habits, right?"

With a breathless laugh, I reply, "Yeah," longing to be back in the days of the old habits. The days when we could admit that we knew each other's thoughts as clearly as we knew our own. A time when we didn't have to uncomfortably apologize for knowing each other too well. A time when I could be so completely, unabashedly in love with her and not have to hide it.

If this had been then, I would pull her tightly into my side, give her one kiss on the crown of her head, then rest my cheek there as we waited for our coffee. She would have an arm around my back and her hand resting on my hip bone. It's so familiar that I can feel it, even as we stand apart now.

Keelie feels my gaze on her and looks up to meet my eyes, expertly continuing our conversation in a hushed tone, trying to ignore that she caught me staring at her. "I'm glad you're seeing a therapist. Opiate addicts are at higher risk of depression."

"Oh yeah?" I ask smugly. "What do you know about it?"

"Keelie?" the barista calls out. Keelie steps up to the counter to grab our drinks.

She extends one to me, but clenches onto it a second longer, as she confronts the question in a low grumble. "Quite a lot, actually. Considering I'm a licensed counselor with a master's in psychology."

She releases her grip on my latte, gives me a fuck-you grin and walks off before I'm able to reply. I take a few quick strides to catch up with her.

"Keelie! That's so amazing!"

She's walking faster than before, as though she's suddenly in a hurry to get back. Reaching for her hand, I stop her in her tracks. "Hold on," I beg, giving her hand a slight tug so that she is turned around to face me.

She comes to a stop much, much closer than expected. Every speckle of color in her eyes is visible at this distance. The urge to pull her in for a kiss is overwhelming, and it takes every ounce of restraint in me not to.

"What?" she demands angrily.

"Will you please tell me more?"

"What do you want to know?" Her forehead wrinkles slightly as she looks up at me. She's so close, she has to look up to meet my eyes. I glance down at her lips for a second, then meet her eyes again. This brings her attention to how close we're standing, or maybe it's just inappropriate enough for her to use it as an excuse to take a large step backward.

"When did you finish?" I ask her.

"Last year," she replies impatiently.

"You finished early."

"I had a lot more free time on nights and weekends after you left," she says bluntly. "Ironically, it was easier to pour myself into work than it was to think about you being gone. Worked out in the end, though."

"I wish I could have been there." It's the only thought my brain can form. I swallow a dry gulp, fighting back the heavy feeling that is settling in around my eyes.

"So do I." She snatches away a tear that rolls down her cheek as quickly as it forms.

There's nothing I can say to make any of this better. It's stupid to even try. I say the only thing I have left to say. "Keelie, I'm so sorry."

She nods, scrunching her eyebrows, blinking a few times. She's doing everything she can to grasp for a tiny semblance of composure. "Yeah. Well." But for once, she has nothing else to say to me. What else could she say? She tilts her head in the direction of the hotel and continues our walk.

After a long, painful silence, she takes a deep breath and allows us to move on. "I work for Calhoun Middle now."

"Are you the new Mrs. Murphy?" I ask, remembering the school counselor that we had to meet with after her dad died.

"I work *with* Mrs. Murphy." Her lips peel back to reveal a quick flash of teeth as we approach a Don't Walk sign. "Laura."

I turn to face her. "You're incredible," I say, genuinely in awe of everything she has accomplished despite my unintentional best efforts to destroy her. "Those kids are so lucky to have you. I'm sure they love you."

She shrugs. "It's middle school. They're moody and thankless, and they all drive me a bit crazy." She sips her coffee as she transitions. "But I love it. It's great. Just feeling like I'm doing something that could make a difference for someone like . . ."

"Like us?" I say, finishing her thought. "Yeah."

The light changes and Keelie changes the conversation along with it, not dwelling too long on the past. "Have you seen anyone else yet? I haven't been here long."

"Yes." The thought of telling her that Josh noticed us leaving together pops into my mind, but that doesn't feel like the right thing to say. "I was with Jess, Josh, and Lex about an hour ago. Hanging out in the lobby." I opt for the word *lobby* instead of *hotel bar*, although it won't be long before she figures out what that actually means. "They might still be there."

"It's been so long since I've seen Lex. All of them, really."

Her pace picks up again, this time with excitement instead of with a drive to get the hell away from me. I wish she would slow down, though. I want to savor every moment with her. My heart aches for her. How am I going to survive an entire weekend pretending I'm okay with ignoring the history we've shared?

Back at the hotel, Jess and Josh are exactly where I left them, and Lex has rejoined, sipping on another martini. Keelie asks if she can hide behind me as we walk in so she can jump out and surprise them. Surprises are her favorite.

"Hey, guys," I announce, approaching their table with my coffee in hand. "Look what I found."

Stepping aside for the great reveal, Keelie swings open her arms with a huge grin on her face. Jess bolts off her chair and they dive for one another, swaying from side to side to emphasize the love in their hug. She spins Jess around as they hug, trading places with her so she now stands closer to Josh. He stays in his chair, giving Keelie a side hug as she tucks herself under his arm.

"Lex!" Keelie says happily. "It is so good to see you!" The hug Keelie gives Lex is much less aggressive. Lex operates on a different energy frequency, and Keelie seamlessly shifts to match her output.

"So . . ." Jess kicks off the conversation slowly. "What are you two up to?" She emphasizes "you two" as if it is completely out of place to see us together. And although we were together for ten years, it must be a bit odd to see us together now.

I raise my coffee cup in response. Keelie does the same and then gives a small, uncomfortable laugh, likely unappreciative of the reminder that we are perfect for each other.

"Just catching up," Keelie explains, trying to ignore it.

"Uh-huh . . ." Jess replies suspiciously. "Okay."

"Hey, so, Matty. When's June getting here?" Josh asks in an over-the-top shout.

I mouth a fuck-you in his direction before all three girls turn their heads to look for my reply. "Really soon," I say, a thousand times more confident than I feel. "Her flight should have landed thirty minutes ago."

"Can't wait to meet her." He smirks.

"Who's June?" Lex jumps at the opportunity to continue her brother's torture.

"A friend," I reply stiffly.

"A friend," she mocks. "So then, did you guys each get your own hotel room, or did you get a room with two beds? Or, like, what's going on there?"

I sip from my coffee cup to give myself time to decide how to reply. The cup is practically empty. I do my best to imagine the weight it would have if it were full so it isn't completely obvious I'm pretending. Turning to Josh and Jess, I ask, "Which one of you idiots invited her?" and point in Lex's direction.

Josh rolls his eyes to play along. "Mom said I had to."

Lex jeers, "That's alright. Your nonanswer speaks volumes."

"Leave him alone, Alexis," Josh scolds.

"You started it," I say before Lex has the chance to likely offer up the same reply.

This isn't how I had imagined Keelie finding out about June. I wasn't expecting to talk to Keelie much this weekend. I was expecting Logan to be here, and I was planning on doing my absolute best to bury every ounce of chemistry Keelie and I had, so Logan didn't feel uncomfortable. Not for his sake, but for hers. I was planning on seeing her from across the room, maybe waving a quick hello, our interactions possibly ending there. Keelie would see June on my arm and pull Jess aside to ask about her.

That was supposed to be the end of it. Never once as I dreamed up this plan did I imagine the possibility of having to address the June situation in front of Keelie. It was foolish to think things would work out that cleanly.

Maybe Josh did me a favor by blurting it out as though it weren't a big deal. Because it isn't a big deal, right? If I can be happy for Keelie, she'll be happy for me. Even if my relationship with June is a sham.

Jess is the one to transition our conversation away from June. She starts talking over wedding-weekend plans with Keelie. That is about the time I take my cue to leave, saying, "I need to go unpack," when actually I want to go find Sam.

I count the number of rooms down the hall, taking my best guess as to which one Keelie stepped out of earlier. I knock on the door, quietly so I don't wake him up if he is sleeping after driving all night, but loud enough so that if Sam is awake, he'll hear it.

A light from the other side of the door illuminates the peephole. It suddenly goes dark as someone looks through. The light comes back a second later as the person on the other side steps away. I knock once more, a little more forcefully this time.

"She doesn't want to talk to you!" Sam yells from the other side of the door.

"I just grabbed coffee with her," I inform him. "She told me you were here. I really want to talk to you, Sam."

He doesn't respond, but the dark figure blocking the light from the peephole doesn't move either.

"Please?" I beg.

Another uncertain pause makes me worried he won't come out. Right as I'm ready to give up, he slides the safety latch across the door so it's able to open only a crack, playing it a bit dramatic if you ask me. "What?"

"Can I come in?"

"Absolutely not," he scoffs, as if I made a hugely offensive request. "That crosses every one of our boundaries we've set for you this weekend." He says "our boundaries" as if Keelie is in on it, too.

"Do you mind telling me what those boundaries are so I can better prepare myself?" I try to see if joking with him will help.

"No." He smirks, taking the bait only slightly. "Not telling you about the boundaries *is* one of our boundaries."

"Okay, well then, can you at least come out?" I plead. "Or open the door more than three inches?"

He shuts the door in my face and flips the safety latch open. He opens the door just far enough so that he can wedge his body perfectly between the door and its frame. With his arms crossed, he glares at me.

"What?" he says again, even more bitterly than before, which seems impossible, but he does somehow sound *more* annoyed the second time around.

"I don't like where we left things." I shrug. "I was hoping we could talk."

"There isn't anything I want to say to you," he says coldly. And that's fine. I don't deserve anything but cold responses from him or Keelie.

"If you don't mind, I have a lot I would like to say to you."

"Such as?"

My confidence trails off. "I know it's not much, but I'm five months sober, and I want to make things right. Can I take you out tonight so we can talk, just you and me?"

"Whatever you have to say to me, you can say right here." He isn't budging.

"I can, and I will if you really won't come out with me. But I'd so much rather not do this in the middle of a hotel hallway."

His face softens a bit. "Eight tonight? Downstairs?"

"Yes! That would be great!" Calming my tone to a more somber voice, one slightly more appropriate to the situation, I add, "Thank you, Sam."

He locks his glare onto me for a second longer before taking a step backward into the room, letting the door fall off his shoulder and shut in my face without another word.

As I pull my phone out to check on June's status, I notice that a text from an unsaved number is waiting in my notifications: *Five minutes away.* I immediately save this number into my phone as *June* before tapping the message bubble to see when she sent it. Four minutes ago. Probably right as I knocked on Sam's door. I rush down the hall, into the elevator, and back down to the lobby.

June is fumbling with her bags, fighting the revolving door. The front desk manager jumps up from his desk to help her. As I approach, she looks up at me with an angry glare and huffs her hair out of her face. I wave a quick apology her way.

"I'm going to say something to you that you will *never* hear me say ever again," she snarls. "I needed you to come thirty seconds sooner." She lets out a loud cackle at her own joke.

"I'm sorry, I just saw your text."

"Don't save that number," she snaps in her *real* voice, before switching back to her seductive voice to add, "I have missed you so much, baby. I'm going to get us checked in, and then I'm going to ravage you."

"But we're already—"

She holds up a finger, telling me to hold on, and she walks toward the front desk.

I make a sideways glance to my friends. All four of them have their eyes fixed on June and me. I lock eyes with Josh and shake my head. *Don't let them come over here.* Jess throws her head back in frustration as Josh turns to her and says, "Don't." Lex gives me a little flirty wave. And Keelie, whose opinion is the only one I really care about, looks on with genuine, kind curiosity.

"Hi there." I overhear June charming the man at the front desk as she digs in her purse, retrieving a crisp fifty-dollar bill. Laying the bill flat on the counter, she points to it and says, "This is for you," but she keeps her sharp manicured nail on the edge of it for a moment longer, placing her credit card on top of it. "And this"—she places her sharp nail on top of the credit card next— "is the card I would like you to use for our room." She turns back to look at me for a second. "What room number?"

"744."

She smiles as she turns back to the front desk. "Room 744 is currently reserved for Mr. Arvali, over here." She overemphasizes each syllable as though this man might have a hard time understanding her. "I'd love it if you could please completely remove his name from the reservation and put the nights he had reserved in room 744 under my name *only*, and charge it to this card right here."

She slides the fifty-dollar bill and the credit card across the counter before continuing. "And that"—she taps on the bill—"is for you, because I know you are going to handle this with absolute care and discretion so that there is no way to trace that Mr. Arvali and I both occupied room 744. Can you do that for me?"

"I would be happy to."

Turning back to me, she says, "All taken care of," then taps me on my nose delicately. "My treat."

"You draw so much more attention to it by doing that," I inform her, sneering at her behind her back as she grabs one of her two suitcases and struts toward the elevator. I take the other and follow her.

In the elevator, she presses her entire body against my side and whispers in my ear, "I've got something very special for you in the front pocket of that one."

She points to the suitcase I have clenched in my hand.

"We need to talk about that, actually," I croak and set the suitcase down.

"What's there to talk about?" June purrs at me. "I did what you asked me to. Now it's your turn."

June runs one of her sharp nails down the center of my chest, over my belly button, and along the length of the zipper of my jeans. She crosses over to the front pocket of the suitcase that rests next to me and unzips it in one quick motion.

My eyes catch a glimpse of the bright orange pill bottle. The *full* bright orange pill bottle. Their phantom chemical taste fills my mouth almost immediately. The feeling of their grit sliding down my throat. Peace washes over me as my fingers touch the smooth plastic. I part my lips and gasp for air. I was naïve to think I could be done with pills. I'm not ready to say goodbye. I just need one of these. Not even one. Half of one.

"Why don't you have one of those and relax, baby?" She scratches all her nails down my arm softly. "You need it."

I drum my fingers against my leg, contemplating. "Maybe later," I decide.

She steps back to get a better look at me. "Maybe later?" she repeats, surprised. "Are you feeling okay?"

"No, I told you, I need to talk to you."

"Let's talk after you fuck me, alright?"

The elevator door dings, and June struts off confidently, without once looking back at me. Regret over inviting her floods into my mind as I shuffle my feet down the hall behind her. Not only inviting her, *begging* her to come. If *Logan* were here, I would feel differently. I would have been glad to have June here.

But now? Now every second with June is a moment I could be spending with Keelie.

As June unlocks the door to room 744, my heart drops in my chest. I need to tell her what's going on. I need to tell her all the things that have changed since the last time we spoke.

"June . . ." I sigh, slumping into a seat on the bed as she stands by the closet, hanging up each piece of clothing after she takes it off, until she's stripped down to her underwear. The bra she's wearing has at least eight extra straps. Two thin straps making an X at the center of her chest, two tracing the shape of each breast. Two more crossed over her ribcage. One extra across each shoulder.

She straddles my legs, lowering herself slowly as she perches on the tops of my thighs. Tossing her hair to one side, she puffs her chest out toward me. With her sharp nails she traces the straps that cross her chest, drawing my eyes to it.

Smiling suggestively as she watches my eyes trace the lines, she says, "If you like this, wait until you see what I brought to wear to the ceremony. *Everyone* is going to be thinking about fucking me." She scratches a finger along the side of my neck and leans into the opposite ear to growl, "*Especially Logan.*"

My gaze snaps to meet her eyes. She pouts her lips and raises an eyebrow at me as she runs her fingers along my arm. She grasps my hand, which I now recognize is still gripping tightly onto the pill bottle. So tightly that if I squeezed any tighter, I would likely break the plastic. June raises my clenched fist to her mouth, sucking on the back of my knuckle as she wrestles the pill bottle free. She twists off the lid and pours two pills into her palm.

I clasp her hand shut, forcing her fingers to curl around the pills, constricting my view of them before I catch a glimpse. She bites a pill between her teeth and leans in close to me, enticing me to snatch it from her. One corner of her mouth curls encouragingly. Her look eggs me on, making me want to taste how the faintest hint of vodka on her tongue mixes with the bittersweet taste of oxycodone. With my eyes fixed on the pill pressed between her teeth, I lean in so close to her that I can feel my breath bouncing off her cheek and back onto my face.

"June. Stop," I snap, my eyes refusing to look away from the pill.

June pulls away, sitting back on her feet. She sucks the pill into her mouth and sneers back, "What the fuck is wrong with you?"

She climbs off me, off the bed, and saunters into the bathroom, where she pours herself a glass of water to gulp down the pill with.

I let out a slow exhale before muttering, "I don't take pills anymore."

She scoffs in disbelief as she returns from the bathroom, giving me a patronizing glare.

"I mean it," I say with only slightly more confidence.

"Are you worried about wasting pills on stabilizing? I can get you more if that's what you want."

A longing sigh escapes my lips. My whole mouth waters. *More.*

"No." I lose all strength in my words. "That's not what this is."

"Will you spit it out already?" she groans, digging a silk robe out of her suitcase and wrapping herself in it.

"I'm five months sober," I grumble, not meeting her eyes. "Ever since I moved in with my brother. I thought I hated it, but being back with everyone—I don't know—I guess I've been thinking about everything I gave up when the pills took over."

Her eyes burn through me as she examines me, trying to gauge whether I'm messing with her. I glance up to meet her eyes, nodding to assure her it's the truth.

"You're fucking serious?" she spits out with a laugh.

"Yes," I choke.

"And when you say sober . . .?"

"All of it. I'm done drinking, too."

"Fuck, Matt," she snaps. "Why didn't you tell me this before you dragged me here?"

"I wasn't sure what I wanted to do about it yet."

"Oh, right, and now you've got it all figured out?" she taunts me.

"Yeah," I say, matter-of-factly. "I do."

"And what exactly is your plan?" June asks, turning her attention to her suitcase and hanging the rest of her clothes in the closet.

"I want to get Keelie back."

She lets out one single punch of a belly laugh. "What else is new?"

"Logan isn't here. She brought her brother."

June twists her body to face me, intrigued. "Trouble in paradise?"

"She said he had to work last minute."

"Huh," she chimes back. "I'm not sure I believe that."

"Me either."

She sits on the corner of the bed looking to me for our next move. "What can I do to help?"

"Maybe lay low for a bit," I say, scratching my chin, "at least until I figure this out."

She smiles kindly. "You got it."

III

Thursday, September 20th

Sam is hunched over a drink at the hotel bar when I get off the elevator. I yell out "Starting without me?" as I approach, and immediately regret it.

"You're late," he growls, taking a sip from his drink and not yet meeting my eye.

"You said eight, right?" I pull out my phone to check the time. I still had ten minutes to spare.

"I changed my mind," he sneers. He stands from his barstool, puts his drink to his mouth, but then recalls it. He meets my eyes, raises an eyebrow at me, then lifts his glass to cheers me before throwing it back. "Where we headed?"

I tell him about a place that Keelie and I walked past earlier while we were grabbing coffee. He nods immediately, as if he's familiar with it, despite having never been to Cleveland before. He takes off out the front door without another word, leaving me a couple of paces behind him until we get to the first crosswalk. There's a stiff silence between us the whole walk there. Sam's face is riddled with circulating thoughts. I wait for the moment when he opens his mouth and says what's on his mind, but his brow crinkles deeper as he holds back.

The sign at the front says Please Seat Yourself. The bar is relatively empty except for a group of friends seated on barstools, a couple that looks to be on a first date seated at the front booth, and another couple making out in the corner booth, two untouched beers sitting on their table. It's so dimly lit in here, it's hard to tell if they have any lights on at all or if the entire place is being lit solely by the fireplace opposite the bar.

Sam snags a booth at the side, settled between the two couples. He gets to face the first-date couple, while I have the couple making out in my immediate eyeline. A waitress approaches to take our drink order as we sit.

Sam turns his head in my general direction but doesn't look directly at me as he asks, "What's your drink?"

I address the waitress. "Club soda with lime?" She nods.

Sam shakes his head. "No, before. What was your drink?"

"Jim Beam Black," I drill off, as if it's one word instead of three.

Sam turns to the waitress. "One of those?"

She nods, then asks, "Rocks?"

Sam looks to me for the answer. I reluctantly shake my head.

"No, thanks," Sam replies to her, and she runs off to put in our order.

Sam slumps back in his seat. He turns his head and looks around the bar, fixing his eyes first on the friends who sit at the barstools, laughing as though they've had more than a few drinks, then to the awkward couple on a date. Finally, he leans his elbows on the table, looks me right in the eyes, and asks, "Who's the girl?"

"Who are you talking about, Sam?"

"June?" he asks sharply. Keelie must have told him.

"She's a friend," I reply. Sam scoffs, already writing me off as a liar.

There's no way to win back Sam's trust other than being completely honest with him, even if he will undoubtedly repeat back to Keelie every single word I say.

I amend my answer. "I'll tell you the truth, but you won't believe me."

"Try me," he challenges, his arms crossed, staring down his nose at me.

"She's my supplier."

"You're right, I don't believe you," Sam says. "You're five months sober and stupid enough to bring your drug dealer as a wedding date?"

"She's not—" I try to decide how much of my arrangement with June is necessary to divulge. "She's not a drug dealer. She's a friend. Barely a friend."

"'Barely a friend.' Who you get high with *and* that you are now sharing a hotel room with, far away from anyone who is holding you accountable to sobriety?" He studies my face intently, looking for any sign that I might be hiding a relapse.

I dispute his suspicions. "I'm not high, Sam. June being here won't change that."

He scoffs at me, not believing a word I'm saying.

"I can prove it," I assure him, "but I need you to do me a favor first."

"Of course you do," Sam replies, disinterested. "What is it?"

I reach into my pocket and pull out the completely full pill bottle, and I slide it across the table to Sam. "June gave me these, and I need you to get rid of them."

"What the fuck, Matty?" he snaps, snatching it off the table and immediately burying it in his lap. He glares up at me for a second before flicking his eyes back down to the bottle, unscrewing the lid. "Shit, there are like fifty pills in here," he says, as if I didn't already know.

"Thirty-seven," I correct him. "I can't stop thinking about them."

"Why did she give you this?"

"She didn't know."

"She didn't know you were *five months sober*?"

"Not until today."

The waitress returns with our drinks. Sam bolts upright, quickly shoving the pill bottle under one of his legs as if she's an undercover DEA agent. She places the soda water in front of me and a very generous pour of bourbon in front of Sam. With a kind smile she says, "Let me know if I can get you guys anything else," before bubbling away.

Sam takes a slow, hesitant sip from the glass in front of him. "Yikes." He lets out a light cough when the alcohol hits his tongue.

I shrug, craving that deliciously smooth taste. I fish an ice cube out of my glass and drop it in his.

Sam takes another sip, coughing again. "So, how much do thirty-seven of these cost?" he whispers, looking back down at the pills as he retrieves them from their not-so-secure hiding spot to inspect them.

"I don't know," I admit. "A lot, probably. I don't pay for them."

"She just gives these to you?"

I nod, grateful that Sam doesn't seem to want to read between the lines on that.

"Okay, so before June, how much did this cost you?"

"Maybe six hundred."

His jaw drops. "Six *hundred* dollars?"

Sheepishly I add, "Probably more."

"No wonder you guys were fucking broke."

Saying we were broke is generous. Drowning in debt would have been more accurate. "I wasn't taking quite as many when I was footing the bill."

He twists his glass around in his hand. "How long would these last you?"

I take a slow sip from my soda water so I don't have to answer that question too quickly. "A week."

"Fuck." His jaw drops again. He looks into his brain as he extrapolates that number into monthly and yearly figures. When he gets his final number, he shakes his head and mouths the word *fuck* one more time for good measure.

He shoves the pill bottle deep into his pocket, and suddenly a panic washes over me as my inner addict connects the dots on what has happened. *The pills are gone. Sam is going to get rid of them.* A shuttering crawl starts in my forearm. I slap my hand against it without conscious recognition, digging my nails into my skin, trying to make the feeling stop. Sam's face scrunches as he takes note. I close my eyes briefly, inhaling and exhaling slowly, before meeting Sam's eyes again.

"You know what, I shouldn't have given you those," I say, brightening my tone. "They're June's. She doesn't know I have them. I really need to give them back to her. I'll just tell her to hide them." I hold out a hand to take them back.

He sneers at me. "June can come get them from me if she wants them back."

I nod, agreeing with him, before trying another defense. "Sure. But she doesn't know you, and she might find it weird to have to come ask you for *her* pills back. I appreciate you looking out for me, but I'm fine, Sam. Just let me give them back to her."

He scrunches his brow, lips curled into a snarl. His face shows exactly how disgusted he is with me. But then he softens, flashing a brief wince before replacing it with a painful look of pity. "I'm not going to do that, Matty."

"Why not?" I demand, a little more forcefully than I intended. My hands clench into fists, my foot twitches uncontrollably. A sudden craving brought on by the phantom taste of oxycodone in my throat mixes with an overwhelming dread that overtakes my body. *The pills are gone forever.*

"Because, unlike *June*, I care about you enough not to let you torture yourself with this shit," he snarls. "If you told her you were five months sober, why did she let you keep them?"

My gaze drops to the table, my eyes fixing on the exact spot where the pills would be if I could see through everything blocking my view to them. "She's not sure I'm serious about being sober."

"Are you?"

My eyes snap to his immediately. "Yes," I reply without hesitation.

"That was a stupid question to ask." Sam laughs to himself. "That's the problem with addicts, Matty. If you believe a single word an addict tells you, it means you're a *fucking idiot*."

"You can believe me, Sam," I promise him.

He lets out another gut-punching laugh. "Believe you? I don't even fucking know you anymore."

"You know me," I grumble back. "You've known me your entire life. You know exactly who I am."

"No, I don't. Not anymore."

I lean back in my seat, returning his judgmental stare.

"I'm Matteo Arvali. *Matty*. Your dad gave me that name. But you didn't like that he called me Matty because you told me it was a girl's name, so instead you called me *Moog*."

The change in Sam's expression is subtle. His lips remain taut, but the furrow of his brow softens as recognition flashes in his eyes.

"You've been more of a brother to me than my own brother," I continue, leaning on the table so I can lock eyes with him. "And that's saying a lot, considering my actual brother put his own family on the line to—"

My lip curls in a quick, uncontrolled quiver. I inhale a deep breath through my nose to tamp down the sudden flood of sorrow that chokes me, determined to continue this confrontation.

"—Put his own family on the line to give me another chance." Tears well up in my eyes, forcing me to break eye contact with Sam. I prop my head up on my elbow, using my arm to block myself off from the rest of the people in this sad, empty bar on a Thursday night. "He probably saved my life."

I let out another heavy exhale, thinking about all that Chris has done for me, recognizing the sacrifice he and Michelle made for me. Recognizing how fucking ungrateful I've been to them.

"And how do I thank him?" I direct my question to Sam. "By giving him the number two slot on my brother roster."

Noticing Sam's empty glass, our waitress returns to ask him if she can grab him another. "One of these for each of us," Sam replies, raising his empty glass.

Stopping her would require lifting my gaze and making eye contact. Revealing to her my eyes welling up with tears, my chin dimpling with a frown. Instead, I let her run off to grab a pour of Jim Beam Black for both Sam and me.

"Does that mean you're putting Jake as third?" Sam asks slyly.

"If Chris found out I put him at number three behind you guys, he'd probably reconsider our living arrangement."

"I won't tell," Sam assures me.

Out of instinct, Sam grabs for the glass on the table, something to occupy himself with, a reason not to have to be the one to continue this conversation, an excuse to not offer a genuine reply. But when his hand touches the glass, he remembers it's empty and pushes it across the table and away from him in frustration.

"How are they?" I ask, my tone practically begging him to update me. "Jake and Em."

Sam glares at me, annoyed, as though he isn't ready to let me back into their lives. When he opens his mouth, I'm almost certain he's going to tell me to fuck off, but when he meets my eyes, his face softens again. "Jake graduated college last year. He has a job with a start-up as a web developer. And he makes these stupid fucking app games on the side." Sam shrugs, overemphasizing how stupid he thinks they are. "I don't get them. Like, at all. But he's got one that's, like, the eighth most downloaded game of last year. He's as weird as he's always been, but now people pay him to be weird."

I know exactly what he means about Jake. Smart, overly analytical, not always the best at reading a room, but when he gets in his element, there's no stopping him.

"And Em is graduating high school this year. She received several scholarship offers to play lacrosse because she's that good. She's terrifying, really. She can whip a lacrosse ball so fast it could knock you out. And I know that for a fact because I've seen her do it. She's so different from the last time you saw her. You probably wouldn't even recognize her anymore."

Sam doesn't look at me. He nods his head a few times, as though he's still trying to think of something else to say. I wait patiently, giving him all the time he needs to think.

"Em was four years old when you and Keelie started dating." He shakes his head in disbelief. "*Four.* She doesn't remember a time when you guys weren't together. Except for, you know, like now. It really fucked with her head when you left."

The waitress returns with the two drinks Sam ordered. Sam looks up at her to say thank you as she sets a glass down in front of him and another in front of me. I keep my eyes locked on Sam, waiting for her to gain the appropriate distance from our table before continuing. "I didn't *leave.*"

He continues on as if he didn't hear me. "You told Em you were going to teach her how to drive. Do you remember that? Because she does. And you promised Jake we would all come take a trip to see him at school. *You* promised him. But you were too much of a sloppy mess to ever remember our plans. Keelie and I went without you." He shakes his head at me. "You removed yourself from their lives long before we removed you."

He lets that one sink in for a minute, leaning back in his seat again and taking a slow sip of his bourbon. Giving me all the space I need to contemplate the weight of what he said. Even though I didn't physically leave, mentally I was gone for years. He was right about that. Of course he was right.

"Do they know what happened?" I ask quietly. "Or do they just think I stopped showing up one day?"

"Jake knows," he says coldly. "Keelie didn't tell Em everything, but she gets the idea."

"She gets the idea? What does that mean?"

"She knows it was drugs, but she doesn't know what, or how long this shit has been going on." This time, when Sam picks up his drink, he throws back the whole glass in a few large gulps. "Em was actually pretty mad at Keelie for 'giving up' on you. Keelie had every opportunity to run your name through the mud"—Sam ducks his gaze and raises his eyebrows to accentuate his point—"but she didn't. After all the shit you put her through. She actually *covered* for you so that Em didn't find out you were a piece of shit."

Sam shakes his head, disgusted at me.

"She didn't have to do that," I say in a low grumble, uncertain of what else I could possibly say in reply.

"Trust me, I know that. I told her not to. I told Keelie to tell Em every shitty detail about all of it. But it was Keelie's decision, and she didn't have the heart to ruin you."

"I don't know what to say." I stumble on my thoughts. "Other than, I'm sorry. I'm a fucking idiot."

"You *are* a fucking idiot." He takes another swig, then crosses his arms. "But that's the problem, Matty. You can't just say you're sorry and have that make up for all the things you've missed. You can't just make up for it anymore. You can't make up for not teaching Em how to drive. You can't make up for missing Jake's graduation. That's gone. So, what are you going to do now?"

"I guess that depends." I sip the bottom of my club soda. "Are you ever going to let me see them again?"

"That's Keelie's decision, not mine."

"I'm asking *you*," I emphasize. "What would *you* say?"

"I'd say no! I'd say they've already figured out how to get on without you." He takes a large gulp of bourbon, then mumbles into his glass, "I just wish Keelie would."

"What do you mean by that?" I press, maybe more hopeful than I should be.

"You heard what I fucking said," he spits back, the alcohol running thick on his voice.

I might have heard what he said, but I wanted him to say it again and again. More directly. Leaving no possibility of improper interpretations. *They've figured out how to get on without you. I just wish Keelie would.* Warmth fills my chest. She still thinks about me. She still talks about me to Sam. She hasn't given up on me.

"I'd love to have the chance to make things better with Jake and Em. And I want to make things better with Keelie, too." Quietly pleading, I add, "I would do anything to make things better with Keelie."

"Not anything," Sam cuts me off, thinking of all the countless times I let pills come between us.

"I would now," I assure him. "*Anything.*"

Sam's eyes lock on me, and he points down to the glass of bourbon in front of me and asks, "Do you want to drink that?"

"Of course I do, that's my fucking drink," I snap back bitterly.

"Then do it. Free pass. No one knows but you and me."

I want to drink it. I *need* to drink it. I don't deserve the clarity that sobriety brings. I deserve to let this kill me. That's exactly what Sam expects me to do. It's what I've always done. For once, maybe I can prove that I am not a complete piece of shit. I shake my head. His poorly thought-out plan won't entice me. For good measure, I confirm my decision out loud with a firm "No."

Sam studies me, pressing his lips firmly together. He snatches the second glass of bourbon off the table and pours it into his glass, placing the newly empty glass in front of me so it appears I drank it.

The waitress makes note of my empty highball, and she returns to our table to take them.

"Can I get you another soda?" she says, shaking the tall glass.

I nod. "Thank you."

"What about another round of the Jim Beam?"

I attempt to say no, but Sam cuts me off again. "Two more would be great, thanks."

Sam takes another large swig from his glass. Two this round, plus the first one, and the drink he had at the bar. *That makes four*, I calculate. The next round would be six. He sways a bit as he fixes his eyes on me.

But before he can say anything, I suggest, "Maybe you should slow down a bit, Sam."

He laughs, a full laugh, as though I had told him a hilarious joke. "*You* of all people do not get to decide that."

His words slur, but I don't argue with him any further. The last thing I want to do is piss him off and make things worse.

"What is it going to take for you to trust me again?" I ask him.

He scoffs, "I'm never going to trust you again." He has to focus his eyes on me with intention because, I would guess that when he doesn't, his vision spins.

I am very familiar with the place he is at. It's my favorite place to be. The kind of drunk where you have the most fun, have the most confidence. The place where the world makes the most sense. The next round of drinks is going to press his limits.

"You used to trust me," I remind him, as if that might help.

"Of course I did," he seethes back in a whisper. "But then I saw how much damage you could do and how little effort it takes for you to destroy it all."

"I'm done with all of that this time," I assure him.

"You ruined everything," he says, ignoring me. "I will *never* trust you not to do that again."

"I'm done," I repeat with a little more confidence. "No matter what happens, I'm not going back to that person I was."

Sam lets out a soft chuckle. "We'll see."

The waitress brings over another set of drinks. She sets the two bourbons in the middle of the table, then hands the soda water to me. I study Sam as he grabs his fifth drink of the night. His cheeks are flushed, his eyelids heavy, his posture sinking into the table. He's fading way too fast, but is perhaps at the perfect spot for me to press a new set of buttons.

"Why isn't Logan here?" I ask.

"He didn't want to come," Sam spits as he grabs the second glass of bourbon from the table, pouring it into the other. Then he laughs coldly. "He never wanted to come. He was just pretending he would be here."

"That's pretty shitty," I reply, saying what he was thinking, trying to coax more information out of him.

"Yeah, well, you know what I always say—" Then he looks at me, surprised, as if he had forgotten I was sitting there. He covers his mouth with a slight grin and shakes his head.

"No, no. It's okay, tell me. What do you always say?"

"The only guys Keelie's interested in are—" Then he pauses, takes a sip of his drink, and adds, "Fucking. Idiots."

I smirk. The description doesn't thrill me, but at least he'd roped Logan in there with me. It certainly levels the playing field a bit. Not that there is a playing field. It's a game I've already lost.

"You don't like him either, huh?"

"Who, *Logan*?" Sam uses the same sarcastic tone that I do. "No. Not really."

"Why not?"

His smile blooms. "None of your fucking business."

"Okay." I hold up both my hands in surrender, promising to back off. "But will you at least tell me why he didn't want to come?"

Sam lifts his hand and mimes zipping his lips. "I'm not supposed to talk about it."

"I won't tell."

"You better not," then he adds, "fucking idiot."

"Promise."

Sam swallows a huge gulp of bourbon. Then he shakes his head. "He didn't want to meet you," he lies.

I could always tell when he was lying, but I nod anyway, accepting his answer for now.

Our waitress comes back over as Sam drains his glass.

"Can I get you guys another round?" she asks sweetly.

I quickly jump in with a "no, thanks" right as Sam is about to spit out an "absolutely."

"Could you close us out?" I ask, then gesture toward Sam. "This guy is done."

"No! No, no, no, no," he sputters out, halting the waitress in her tracks. He turns to her with a smile, the same dangerously charming smile his dad had perfected in his short life. The smile that made you forget the irrational outbursts. The smile that Sam was hoping would make our waitress forget he just spit out his words like someone who has had way too much to drink. Then Sam makes an annoyed face at the waitress, as if he is begging her to excuse me for *my* behavior as he says, "Could you bring me one of those?" and gestures toward my drink.

"Soda with lime?" she asks.

Sam nods and says, "Thanks."

"Not done with me yet, huh?" I tease.

He scowls. "Not even close."

Good, keep talking.

Sam leans back in his seat again, crosses his arms across his chest, looks down his nose at me. I lock eyes with him, leaning in, waiting for him to continue grinding me down.

But he doesn't. He doesn't say anything. He keeps his intimidating stare fixed on me and waits for me to say something.

"How's your mom?" I ask hesitantly.

He nods slowly as he thinks about it. "She's dating." He lets out a soft chuckle. "That's been fucking weird." He shakes his head to backtrack. "I mean, it's not *weird*. It's fine. It's about time. We're just a hard family to join, you know? And we've had a lot of duds come through."

The waitress returns and places two sodas on the table. Sam snatches his glass and takes a quick sip.

"You would not believe how many of these guys think they're auditioning to be my new dad." He rolls his eyes. "Guess that's not their fault, though. Most of their kids are barely teenagers. It's hard for them to remember we're in our midtwenties."

"Or late twenties."

Sam raises an eyebrow at the thought, as if to say, *How did that happen?* "Mom's been having Kiki and me filter them out before they get to meet Jake and Em, but it should probably be the opposite. If they know how to not be weird around a high schooler, then they can meet her adult children next."

"Have you liked any of them?"

Sam nods. "*Paul.* He's young. I mean, he's only a few years younger than Mom, but he's basically just as much older than Keelie as Keelie is to Em." Sam shrugs. "He's cool, though. He's meeting Em this weekend, actually. And she can be pretty aggressive, so we'll see if he's even still around by the time we get back."

I smirk. "Good luck, Paul."

Sam raises his glass to cheers to that. Then his face drops into a frown. He fidgets with the straw in his glass, spinning the ice cubes around in a circle a few times. "She's seeing a specialist about a bipolar diagnosis." He bites the inside of his cheek, not making eye contact with me.

"Emmy?" I ask, mostly out of disbelief.

He glances my way, only for a second. "She was supposed to be the normal one, you know? The only one of us who can't remember any of this bullshit. We did everything we could to give her a normal life. And then she still gets fucked by genetics."

"You can't do anything about genetics," I remind him. "And she couldn't ask for a better family to support her."

He scoffs at this, covering up his own trepidations, as though he believes he could have done something more. He pushes the straw aside and takes a large drink straight from the rim. He flags down the waitress as ice from the bottom of his glass crashes against his lip.

She bounces back to our table, and Sam grumbles out, "Can I get a pint of whatever you have that is equivalent to a Budweiser?"

"Sure thing, sugar. We've got that on draft."

"Thanks," he flashes a quick smile, much less charming than before. He props his head up with his arms, meeting my eyes this time. "I was supposed to be there to 'mediate' this weekend, to make sure everything went well." He glares at me, as if this is also my fault.

"I'm sure it will be fine. Makaela can handle it," I say, not sounding very convincing.

He smirks and shakes his head. "Nah, she can't. No one gets Em like I do. Except for maybe you. When you were around."

And just like that, he's back to hating me.

The waitress brings over his beer, and I try hard to resist adding to Sam's tally, but my brain jumps in before I can stop it. *That's seven.* It's none of my business. Like he said, I'm the last person who should tell him to slow down. I'm the last person who should keep count.

I decide to ignore Sam's latest insult. "If you're so worried about it going badly, why not move it to another weekend?"

"Because Mom and Em said they'd be fine, and I didn't have a whole lot of time to argue with them before I had to come here."

"How long have you known you were coming to Cleveland?"

"Since Tuesday," he replies sharply.

"As in two days ago?"

He flashes a sarcastically jolly smile before dropping his expression. *Yep.*

"What happened?" I press.

"Matty," he warns, "fuck off. It's none of your business."

Could I believe that Keelie was supposed to be here with *Logan*, but then two days ago he found out he had to work and couldn't make it? Sure. I could buy that. But something about this situation makes Sam so defensive. It isn't that simple. There's more going on than what he's telling me.

Despite my suspicions, I diffuse the situation. "Okay, I'm sorry. You're right. It's none of my business. I'm—" I let out a huge sigh. "I'm not used to not knowing everything that's going on with you guys."

"You're not used to being *conscious* of not knowing everything that's going on with us," he corrects. "You've been out of the loop for a long time."

"Will you bring me up to speed?" I ask, trying to turn the conversation back around. "How have you been?"

He scoffs at me, "We're not friends."

"Yeah, okay, Sam." Then, under my breath, I say, "Stronzo." *Asshole.*

Sam cracks a slight grin. "I know what that means."

"I was counting on it."

He picks up his beer, and just before it reaches his lips, he asks, "Do you remember Sarah?" Then he takes a drink.

I shake my head. "No, who's that?"

Sam narrows his eyes at me. "I've been dating her for *three* years." He shakes his head and adds in a friendly "Stronzo."

I rack my brain, trying to remember Sarah, but draw a blank. "In my defense," I plead, "I was only there for one of those years. And you basically had a new girlfriend every time I saw you back then."

He squints his eyes and curls his lips up into a guilty smile. "I wasn't that bad."

"Kind of," I tease.

"Well, whatever. Remember Sarah. She's staying."

Our conversation remains mostly friendly after that. Sam orders two more beers, which I again try to resist counting as numbers eight and nine. When he finally surrenders to closing our tab and heading back to the hotel, he is more than a little clumsy.

We stumble back to the hotel, Sam's arm slung around my shoulder, weighing me down with his drunken heaviness. When we make it back to the front of the hotel, Sam insists on entering through the revolving doors, even though there is a regular door a few steps away. He rides around the revolving door twice, and as he flings himself out of it on his second go-around, he assures me the first revolution was "just practice."

He leans heavily against the wall in the hallway as we make our way back toward his room, his body slowly creeping closer and closer to the floor. I grip onto his arm and help him stand straighter, but he immediately rips his arm from my grasp and insists, "I've got it."

I laugh at him. "You don't got it."

He busts out a mildly disruptive cackle as he realizes he is once again a couple of feet shorter than he should be. He stops in his tracks, stands straight, releases pressure from the wall beside him, and shakes out his head a few times to get his composure back.

And then he stumbles on his very next step, which sends us both into a fit of laughter again.

A door at the end of the hallway opens, and we immediately fall silent, concerned we might soon be the recipient of a glare or a rude, albeit much deserved, comment from another guest. But when Keelie pokes her head out into the hallway, Sam and I exchange glances and double over again.

"What are you guys doing?" Keelie stage-whispers.

"Trying to figure out how to walk," Sam admits with another gut-busting cackle.

She rushes to his side and grasps one of his arms. "You've woken up half the floor. Get inside before someone gets mad."

"Tell them to chillax," Sam replies coolly. "Do you guys remember *chillax*? I'm going to bring that one back."

Keelie can't help but soften her furrowed brow at that one. "I've missed chillax," she humors him.

"It's coming back!" he shouts.

Keelie shushes him as she slides her room key into the door slot. Sam leans heavily on my shoulder as he waits for her to prop open the door. I keep an arm around him and walk with him into the room. Suddenly, he stops in his tracks and turns to me with an angry glare.

"Wait, no," he says to me. "Get the fuck out of here."

Keelie flashes me an apologetic glance and pleads with her brother. "Sam . . ."

I wave her off. "Hey, stronzo," I snap back at him with a grin, "chillax."

He lets out a soft snort that melts into a hearty laugh. "It's coming back!" But then he shakes his head, remembering. "No. You're not supposed to be in here." He traces an imaginary line in the air. "Boundaries."

"I thought not telling me about the boundaries was one of the boundaries."

"Fuck. You got me." Then he turns to Keelie and repeats, "He got me." He collapses face first onto a bed and mumbles into the mattress one last time, "Yuh go murh."

Keelie widens her eyes at me. *What is happening?*

"Sam's been drinking."

"A lot!" he declares loudly.

I gesture a hand toward him. *Told you.*

"Enough to bring back chillax?" she teases.

Sam bolts upright momentarily as he defends his stance on the word again—"It's coming back!"—before collapsing once more into the mattress.

Keelie steps closer to me. *Too close.* So close I can feel her breath caress my cheek as she whispers, "He didn't mention he was going out with you." Then she pulls back slightly so I can see the way her face lights up with joy. "How did it go?"

"Really well." I return her smile, hoping it doesn't reveal how deeply I want to kiss her right now. Hoping she doesn't notice the slight squint of my eye or the soft crinkle of my nose as I look back at her. It is a look of admiration I reserve only for her. "All things considered, it went really well."

"Matty!" Sam shrieks. "Come here!"

Keelie smiles appreciatively as I yell back, "What do you want now?" I move to the edge of the bed by his feet.

"No, come down here," he slurs, smacking his hand against the mattress, "where I can see you."

I swing my arms back and give a full-force flop onto the bed next to him. His body lurches into the air a couple of inches. When he lands, he grips the sheets with one hand and his stomach with the other. He holds like that for a few seconds before flopping his head to look at me, whispering, "Don't *ever* do that again."

"Sorry. It was pretty funny though, huh?"

"Not even a little bit." He holds up his pointer finger and thumb, pinching them together to show me how little. Then he places that same hand on my cheek and stares at me.

"What are you doing, Sam?"

"Shh!" he snaps immediately. "Give it a minute."

I wait, and he keeps his hand on my face.

Finally, he says in a hushed voice, "I love you, Matty."

I place a hand on his face. He wrinkles his eyebrows like he's confused and asks, "What ar—"

"Shh!" I cut him off. "Give it a minute."

He snorts. "That's what I said."

"Shh," I shush him again. "I love you, too, you fucking idiot."

He laughs and yells, "You're the fucking idiot. Now get the fuck out of here before I take back what I said!"

Instead of taking my hand off his face, I push his head into the bed as I stand up. He swats a hand at me but doesn't move another muscle. I'm not sure that he's able to.

Keelie leans against the dresser as she looks on with satisfaction.

"Looks like you guys worked through the 'fallout.'"

"Maybe," I say, stepping closer to her. Drawn to her. "Hard to tell for sure. Will you ask him again tomorrow and let me know what he says?"

"I can do that for you," she agrees. My heart skips a beat at the words "for you." The weight of it is so much heavier than I'm sure she intends. But when she says "for you," it implies sacrifice, love, unity. I can't help but feel overwhelmed by it.

I nod, choking on my reply, placing a soft touch on her shoulder as I walk past her toward the door, saying, "Goodnight."

She touches her fingers to mine, just for a second, as she replies, "Goodnight, Matty."

I can't even hold myself together long enough to make it to the door without tears welling up in my eyes again. I don't turn back to look at her as the door shuts behind me, even though I so badly want to, because I don't want her to see the effect she's had on me.

IV

Friday, September 21st

"Everyone who's not Matty or Jenna, come take a shot!" Lex shouts out, lining shot glasses along the edge of a round table in the corner of a crowded bar. The place is huge, and it's absolutely filled to the brim with people. There's a large built-in bar on the back wall with shelves upon shelves of booze, cocktail books, and knickknacks, giving the place a cozy, homey vibe. It's exactly the type of bar Keelie and I used to look for when we visited new cities. I can tell by the way she points to objects on the shelves as she nudges Sam's shoulder that she is just as smitten with the look of this place.

Keelie and Sam line up along the edge of the table with everyone else. Josh and Jess. Lex. Josh's friends Frankie and Nate from college. Jess's friend Aimee. And Jess's brother-in-law Andy. Jess's sister Jenna, who is five months pregnant, hovers off to the side with me. Everyone else has a shot glass in hand, waiting for the signal.

Lex tosses a glare my way and snaps, "Matty, where's June?"

I wave her off. "She's on the phone."

Lex scrunches up her face as if she's sucking on a lemon. "On the phone? This is a party. Go get her."

"She'd want you to have it."

She shakes her head, shouting, "That's not how this works." Then she stomps over to me, her heels clicking loudly with every forceful step. She huffs, "Everyone has to drink their dues. And she owes me double because she's drinking for you."

"She'll get in on the next round," I mutter. "She's talking to her kids."

She raises an eyebrow at me like she thought she might have heard me wrong. Shaking her head in disbelief, she scoffs, "You would date a mom."

"First of all, *not dating*. But also, what the hell does that mean?"

She rolls her eyes at me to say, *Like you don't know*. And without humoring my stupid questions any further, she turns back around and joins everyone else around the table, picking up her shot glass and sliding June's to Sam. Sam's closed-mouth smile stretches the full width of his face as he fills his other hand with a second shot glass.

They clink glasses and simultaneously throw them back. Coughing and laughing as the alcohol burns down to their bellies. I wish I could join them.

"Don't go anywhere!" Lex shouts out. "I'm grabbing another round."

Lex clicks her heels toward the bar. Frankie follows closely behind her, his eyes tracing her figure as he does. An airy chuckle escapes from my lips. If he tries any harder, he's going to push her away.

"What?" Keelie asks, eyes wide, studying me curiously. She snuck up on me, and now she's standing right next to me.

I shake my head. "Nothing."

"Tell me," she demands, knowing I saw something she didn't.

I nod my chin toward Frankie and Lex at the bar. Frankie has his hand on the small of her back, but Lex can't lean any farther away if she tried, at least not without physically walking away from him. And yet, she still flashes him a seductive glance, stringing him along.

Sam shuffles toward us, then follows our gaze. "Are we talking about how Frankie wants to bone Lex?"

Keelie buries a snort into my shoulder as we try to keep from drawing too much attention to our laughter.

"He's trying too hard," Sam says. "It's getting creepy."

Lex turns around with a tray full of their second round of shots. Frankie offers to take them from her. She ignores him and continues walking. The three of us exchange glances, doing our best to keep our composure.

"Round two! Ready up!" Lex announces. "Sam, you're covering June again!"

Sam grins as he strides over to the table to pick out both of his shots.

"Oh good." Keelie flashes a sarcastic look my way.

She takes a step closer to me, close enough that I can breathe in her soft scent longingly. So close that I tilt my head down fully to meet her eyes.

With a scrunched nose and a slight curl of her lip, she asks, "Hey, is it alright if I tag along with you tonight?" Her shoulders jump in a quick shrug. "I miss hanging out with you."

I tamp down the pure joy that bounces within me, settling on a tamer reply. "I'd like that."

"Okay . . ." she hesitates, leading her thought by getting even closer to me still, touching her hand to my arm and sending sparks pulsing through me, jolting me to life. "In that case, if any of this feels like it's too much for you, will you please tell me?"

My eyes get hot and flooded, and I smile graciously at her. "You don't have to do that, Keelie." I gulp down the emotions rising in me. "I'm not your problem anymore. You don't have to keep looking out for me."

"I want to," she rasps. Her eyes lock on me, clinging to me.

"Okay," I agree. I press my forehead to hers, letting out a deep sigh as I say, "It's already too much for me."

"Keelie!" Lex barks out.

Keelie pulls away from me slightly but doesn't look away.

"Come get your shot! We're waiting on you!" Lex snaps.

Keelie gives my forearm a light squeeze, and then she puts on a big cheery grin and skips to the table to join everyone else for round two.

Out of the corner of my eye, I catch a glimpse of June walking around, searching for us. I wave her down, and she bolts to my side with a drink already in hand. She wraps her arm around my waist, leaning into me as she takes a sip.

"How's everyone?" I ask.

She glares at me. "We're still not doing that."

"Having a conversation?"

"Talking about my family," she says harshly.

"Fine," I grumble back. "You're two shots behind everyone else."

"Good thing I had him make this one a double." She lifts her glass high, bringing it up to my eye level as if that will help me see what she's talking about.

Keelie bounces back to us, her face scrunched from the alcohol still burning her throat. She puts on a big fake smile when she sees June. So big her cheeks push her eyes into a squint.

"Hey," she says cheerfully, "you're June, right?"

June nods as she takes a sip from her drink. *Is she high?*

"It's great to meet you. I'm Keelie."

June freezes midsip. She glances my way, slowly taking her arm off my waist and taking a tiny step to the side, as if she got caught doing something she shouldn't have. She's definitely stoned.

"Keelie?" June's grin grows so wide it looks like it could push clear off her face. "*Val* has told me everything about you."

I close my eyes in a wince, then give her an unmistakable glare. "June," I snap, "be cool, ostrega." *Oh my God.*

Keelie looks to me as she says, "All good things, I hope."

June snorts into her straw, sending bubbles through her drink. "Are you kidding? He adores you."

"Mi fai morire," I mumble. *You're killing me.*

"You speak Italian, don't you," June asks Keelie, more of a statement than a question.

Keelie nods. "Some, yeah."

"Thought so," June says, satisfied.

Keelie smiles suspiciously at her. "Why?"

"Matt has never once spoken Italian around me, and he just did twice in a row." June glances my way, now signaling for me to *be cool.*

"I'm so glad you guys could finally meet." I laugh uncomfortably.

"Oh stop." June gives a knowing glance to Keelie, implying that they share a common bond over me, and greatly oversimplifying this entire situation. "I'm giving him a hard time. You know that, right?"

June doesn't look to Keelie for a reply, but instead glares in my direction, as if directing the comment toward me.

I give my nose a quick flick, signaling for June to get lost. June presses a hand to my shoulder warmly, then abruptly says, "I'm going to go grab another drink. I'll see you guys around." She bounds off toward the bar, freeing me from this mortifying situation, if only for a moment.

"Sorry about that."

"She called you *Val*," Keelie states, the hurt she's hiding seeping into her words.

"She's never called me that before today," I assure her. "Do you remember the photo frame from Sedona?"

A happy look of recognition washes across her face. "Of course."

"You wrote *Val* on the glass. That's where she saw it."

"Okay, but she also called you *Matt*," Keelie whispers like an accusation. The name sounds sticky on her tongue, as if she doesn't know what to do with such a strange word. Her expression sinks into a hint of sorrow. "Are you *Matt* now?"

"*No*," I snap back immediately. "I will always be *Matty*."

"Good," Keelie says, satisfied. "I could never get used to calling you Matt."

"She calls me Matt because she knows I hate it."

"How kind." Keelie laughs.

I raise an eyebrow at her, acknowledging exactly how annoying June is to me.

Keelie nods her head toward a table and says, "How about you go snag us a table, and I'll grab us some drinks. What can I get you?"

"Club soda with lime?" I deflate.

She places a soft touch to my forearm, exuding nothing but kindness, encouragement, compassion.

A deep pain fills my chest at her touch. If she touches me like that again, my heart is going to explode. I wish she would stop. On second thought, I wish she would touch me more. I just wish it meant more to her.

"Be right back," she says.

Keelie leans against the bar next to Sam. He's joined by Lex and Frankie. Sam turns his head toward Keelie for a second as he points to the long line of shots they had in front of them, offering one up to Keelie. She waves off his offer. Sam and Lex are going to be a dangerous combination this weekend.

The two drinks Keelie returns with are identical. Highball glasses, clear carbonated liquid, paper straws. The only difference is that one is garnished with a lemon, while the other has a lime. She places the lime glass in front of me.

I slump my shoulders and give her a crooked frown. "You don't have to not drink around me, you know."

"This one has vodka in it." She raises her glass as if that might demonstrate.

"Let me taste it," I call her bluff.

She scrunches her face. "No." She's right. Bad idea.

"Let me smell it then," I challenge, raising an eyebrow at her.

This time, a sly smile forms on her lips. Narrowing her eyes at me, she repeats "no" with a slight laugh. *Busted.*

"You really don't have to do that," I beg. "I want you to have fun."

She studies me, giving me a lopsided grin. "Matty, I *am* having fun."

"Sure, maybe," I say, "but you're not having as much fun as Sam."

I take a glance toward the bar. Sam and Lex have a shot glass in each hand. Frankie yells out for them to hold on, but Lex taps her shot glasses against Sam's and throws them back, one after the other. Sam quickly trails behind Lex before Frankie has his second shot in hand.

"No one is having as much fun as Sam this weekend. It's actually a condition for him joining me. No one can have more fun than he does."

While I really want to ask *Why did Sam join you in the first place?* I think better of it. As I stir the ice cubes in my glass around in circles, I settle on saying, "It's good to see him."

"Want to know a secret?" Keelie asks with a whisper. "He said the same thing about you this morning." She leans back in her chair, taking a sip from her soda with lemon, a smug look on her face. "But don't tell him I told you that. He's still trying really hard to hate you."

"We had a good time." I nod. "Felt a bit closer to how things used to be."

Keelie beams at this. "I'm really glad."

With my arms crossed on top of the table, I lean in closer to Keelie so that I can whisper, "Can I ask you about something Sam said last night?"

She studies me suspiciously, trying to gauge where this question could be leading. Squinting her eyes at me, she replies, "Sure."

"What's going on with Emmy?"

Keelie smiles proudly, an insincere, tight-lipped smile that she uses to fool everyone but me. I can tell she's about to evade the question she knows I'm asking. *I know you too well for this, Keelie.*

"She's graduating in May," Keelie says, "and she's got a scholarship to play lacrosse next year."

I hesitate a moment, acknowledging what she said. Then I lean in even closer to whisper, "Sam told me she's been seeing a bipolar specialist."

Her body goes stiff, and she scrunches her eyebrows at me. Her fake smile melts into a frown. "Sam wasn't supposed to tell you that."

I slump my shoulders, pleading, "Mia, come on."

"No," she snaps at me, making it clear that I have crossed a line. *A boundary.* "She doesn't want people to know, and Sam should have respected that."

"I'm not 'people,'" I remind her.

"You are now," she snarls. I trigger something inside her that sets her eyes glowing with fury. Just like that, I remind her of every single moment I've ever betrayed her, and she's right back to hating me all over again.

"That's not fair."

"You're right," she hurls back, "it's not fair. Em trusted you more than anyone else. She would have really loved it if you were there for her. But you're not."

My brain floods with ways to fight back. To tell her she's wrong. To point out that the only reason I can't be there for Em is because *Keelie* cut me out. *Keelie* walked away. I wanted to be there. I didn't want to leave, but she forced me to go.

Then Sam's words echo in my mind, reminding me that even when I was there, I wasn't actually *there*. I removed myself from their lives long before they removed me. This isn't her fault, it's mine.

I know Keelie can see the anger simmering inside me. She reflects the same furious expression back in the look she's giving me. She furrows her brow. Her eyes turn red from fighting back tears. Her lips pull taut until they're almost gone completely.

She probably thinks I'm about to fire back a defensive reply, igniting a fight like the ones that tore our relationship apart. The battles fought between Keelie and *the addict.* The addict who lied. The addict who stole. The addict who defended his decisions at all costs. That's not me anymore. I know it isn't. Instead of fighting with her, I take a deep breath and extinguish the flame, letting it go.

"How are *you* feeling about all this?" I whisper.

The anger melts from her face. Her lips soften into a slight frown, and her eyebrows droop in heavy slopes. She looks off to the side, not meeting my eyes. "I'm scared for her," she chokes.

I place a hand, palm up, in the center of the table. She eyes it, suspiciously, then scowls at me. *Really, Matty?*

I give a knowing glance, then nod my head toward my hand. *Come on, Mia.*

She places her hand in mine reluctantly, but as soon as I curl my fingers around her hand, she squeezes mine tightly. Tight enough that I can feel every ounce of frustration she is feeling, and all the pain she's been holding, melting away. She tightens her lips, closes her eyes, and takes a centering breath. She clasps my hand even harder as she pushes every last bit of air from her lungs.

She opens her eyes again with her next inhale, and something has shifted in the way she is looking at me. Her eyes sparkle with appreciation, and all I can return to her is a look of longing. A longing to be back in her life, a longing to be able to talk with her like this again. A longing for her.

Keelie gives my hand one last squeeze and lets go, placing her hand back on her drink glass.

"Mia Mae," I whisper, "Em is so lucky to have you looking out for her. It's early. And she's going to figure out how to manage this and have a completely normal life. You don't have to be scared for her. She's incredibly resilient. Just like her sister."

Keelie turns the corner of her mouth into a slight smile, her bottom lip quivering as it fights off a frown. Her eyes glaze with tears primed to fall. I wish she would let me hold her in my arms.

Jenna steps up behind Keelie. I lean away slightly and give a quick glance in Jenna's direction to signal to Keelie that we're not alone. Keelie winces, then blinks her eyes slowly, willing her tears to evaporate instead of fall. Then she puts on that big fake smile again.

Jenna places a hand on Keelie's shoulder, but eyes me before she leans to meet Keelie's gaze. "I'm going to grab a drink. Do you want to come with me?"

Keelie lets a breathy laugh escape her lips. "Thank you, Jen. I'm okay."

"You sure?" Jenna replies rigidly, taking a glance to study me again. I sink down in my seat.

Keelie smiles warmly at Jenna. "Yes," she replies confidently, "I'm alright."

Jenna looks at me and says, "Sorry, had to check."

I try not to feel offended by this. "Did Jess ask you to keep an eye on me?"

Jenna's stern look breaks as she admits, "Alexis." *Of course.* "Do you mind if I join you guys?" Jenna asks.

How do I say no to that question without sounding like a jerk? How can I say, *Thanks for looking out for Keelie. Now kindly get lost?*

Keelie jumps in before I get the chance to formulate my reply. "Sure." A sharp pain pierces my chest. I hate hearing Keelie's fake happy voice. I hate knowing she's hiding how she's feeling. I want to hold her hand in mine again. I have missed that so much.

Keelie slides her chair over, making room for Jenna to sit. I keep my eyes fixed on Keelie. She catches my eye and gives me a quick smile. *It's alright.*

"Remind me, when's your baby due?" Keelie asks Jenna, her incredible conversation skills helping her navigate a rocky transition once again.

Jenna glows as she replies, but her response is lost on me. I can't focus on anything but Keelie. I want to know more about how she's feeling. I want us to be able to talk like we used to.

"Jen!" Jenna's husband, Andy, comes stumbling over to our table. "Jen, come on! There are games upstairs! They've got shuffleboard."

Jenna lets out a kind laugh, trying her best to return Andy's enthusiasm. She stands from her chair and hovers for a minute. "Do you guys want to come?" She aims her question directly at me as a peace offering for her earlier defensiveness.

But before I get the chance to jump in and accept her offer, Keelie replies, "We'll come find you in a minute." She fixes her eyes on me, her look telling me she has so much more she would like to say to me.

Jenna gives a chipper smile, and she and Andy retreat to a set of stairs in the back corner of the room.

"I'm sorry," Keelie whispers hurriedly, once we're alone.

"For what?" I practically laugh out my reply, wondering what she can possibly think she has to apologize for.

"For snapping at you about Em. I should have told you yesterday."

I scrunch my eyebrows at her and shake my head. "I should have been there." I duck my head as I meet her eyes. "For all of you."

She drops eye contact, instead looking at the table. I'm nervous she is going to end this conversation. Shut down and shut me out. But I need this. I need her to keep talking.

Sitting patiently across the table from her, I wait for what feels like hours for her to be ready to talk. She bites down on her lower lip, finally blinking her eyes to meet mine. But instead of replying, she places her hand on the table, palm side up, and offers it to me.

A confusing combination of joy and sadness pulses through me. I clasp Keelie's hand, ignoring all the feelings swirling inside me. Happy, *so happy*, to be here with her. To be holding her hand. To have the chance to talk to her at all. And filled with a deep pang of pain thinking about how far we've fallen, how many days we will never get back, how much I've missed.

"I heard what you said earlier, and I want to go back to that." Keelie squeezes my hand tightly. "About you feeling like this is too much for you?"

There are so many things I love about Keelie, and I feel them all at once right now as she holds on to my hand. Her warm smile, her calming presence, her incredible selflessness. I pinch my eyes shut for a moment, absorbing all she has done for me. *I have done nothing to deserve someone as amazing as you.*

"It's not quite as overwhelming anymore," I say, feeling my heart surge with love for her. "Thank you."

She brushes her thumb along the backs of my knuckles in one quick but distinct motion. I curl up the corner of my mouth, intrigued, but her face is completely unreadable. She's lost in her thoughts, leaving me to crave the smallest taste of what she's thinking. With her jaw clenched tight, she gives my hand one last squeeze. She takes in a deep breath, and when she lets it out, tears well up in her eyes. She resets by returning to her big fake smile once again.

Don't do this to me, Keelie. You can put on a front for the rest of the world, but don't hide how you're feeling around me.

"We should go find everyone else." She releases my hand, and I have no choice but to regretfully pull mine away, too.

I force myself to agree. "That's probably a good idea. We promised Josh and Jess we wouldn't make this weekend weird. I think crying at a bar during a bachelor party counts as making it weird."

A laugh rises in Keelie's throat, popping as it surfaces in one quickly stifled burst. "We can talk more later," she confirms.

"Yeah," I try to say but choke on the word. "I'm going to tell June where we're at and then we can head upstairs."

As soon as I stand, I spot June sitting at the bar, flirting with two guys who look as though they're probably still in college. She glimpses at me, trying her best not to draw attention to it as she meets my eyes. I point to Keelie and me, then point to the stairs in the corner. June brushes her hair out of her face to give herself the opportunity to take a quick glance toward my point. She raises an eyebrow subtly, then gives it a quick scratch with her perfectly manicured nail before turning her attention back to the meatheads she's talking to, throwing out an over-the-top laugh.

Keelie lets out a snort. "She got 'meet us upstairs' from that?" Her nose crinkles suspiciously. "Are you sure she was even looking over here?"

"She gave me the signal. She knows where we'll be."

"*What* signal?"

"She—"I hesitate, suddenly embarrassed to have this conversation with Keelie. "She scratched her eyebrow. It's her thing. She knows."

Keelie snaps a quick tap against my arm as she connects the dots. "Was that nose thing a signal, too?"

"What nose thing?" I ask innocently.

She perfectly imitates the quick nose flick I directed toward June earlier. A guilty smile washes across my face.

"Matty! Did you tell June to fuck off with that signal?"

"It's more along the lines of 'Get lost,'" I finally admit.

"You shouldn't have done that!" Her shout barely rises over the noise of the crowded bar.

"She's done it to me a thousand times," I say, shaking my head. "Trust me, it's not a big deal."

"Are you like her wingman, then?"

"Not exactly." I sigh, hoping Keelie doesn't ask any more questions about the time I've spent with June.

"And you're not dating?"

"Definitely not," I reply instantly. "She calls me Matt. It would never work out."

Keelie snorts, accepting that as a legitimate response. "Teach me the other signals."

"It's not its own language. There aren't that many."

"Then I'll be able to learn quickly."

"Okay," I agree. "The eyebrow scratch is like saying 'okay,' or maybe 'I'm fine.' Basically, anything affirmative."

Keelie scratches her eyebrow in the same way June had done. "You're a natural. The nose thing means 'fuck off.' You know that one already."

"Uh-huh," Keelie confirms, giving her nose a quick flick.

"A lip tap means 'order me a drink.'" Depending on the context, we could also use it as a signal for "meet me in the back," but Keelie didn't need to know that particular detail.

She taps her lip to demonstrate.

"And a jaw scratch is like 'SOS, get me the hell out of here.'"

Keelie traces a finger down her jawbone, and for one fleeting second I long to trace that sharp line with the soft touch of my lips.

"That's all of them." I shrug, pushing the thought from my mind. "You're an expert."

"So to be clear, you're not dating, but you guys have this elaborate secret code?"

I burst with a laugh, amplified by the echoing walls. "Can I retrace this logic for you so you can see how ridiculous it sounds?"

"Break it down for me, Val."

A rush of air escapes my lips, hearing her call me *Val* again. I quickly suck the breath back in, doing my best to play it cool.

"If I was dating June, do you really think I would have tried to communicate with her in a secret code while she's getting hit on by Kappa and Gamma over there?" I raise an eyebrow at her as we make it to the top of the stairs. "Or do you think maybe I was communicating to her with secret code so I didn't go in there like a wet blanket, putting a damper on whatever the hell she was doing with those guys? Like a friend."

"*Barely* a friend," Keelie replies with a smirk.

"Ostrega, Sam is such a nark." I laugh. "Did he give you a play-by-play of our entire conversation?"

"He did." Even though I know she is joking, her starkly serious expression makes me question it.

The second floor is much less crowded than the first, but it still gathers crowds that most bars would envy. Bar games line the outer walls of the room. Darts, shuffleboard, and pool are scattered throughout. Jess waves to us dramatically from across the room, where a series of ringtoss hooks line the walls.

"She *is* a friend," I confirm for Keelie. "I just don't know that much about her. She doesn't like to talk about herself."

"Have you tried Googling her?" Keelie asks. "Maybe she's secretly a murderer."

Still listening to true crime podcasts, I see. "I have not checked Google to see if she's a secret murderer. But that's only because usually you only Google the people you're dating. Not your friends."

"*Barely* friends," Keelie corrects.

"Barely friends," I agree.

"A trip to Cleveland would have been a pretty good time for her to murder you, so you're probably in the clear on that front."

"Who's murdering Matty?" Jess asks as we approach.

"No one any more. Keelie put a stop to it." I put an arm around Keelie's shoulder in a move that feels way too friendly. "She's a hero."

Jess dives for Keelie, saying "I'm so proud of you" as she gives Keelie a big, over-the-top hug. The two of them teeter slightly. It is too early in the night for teetering. Keelie gives me a wide-eyed look over Jess's shoulder.

"Hey, Jess," I call out as she sways Keelie from side to side. "Where's Jenna?"

"She's playing Skee-ball." Jess shakes her head, correcting herself with a mumble, "Shuffle ball."

I grin. "Shuffleboard?"

A giggle ripples across Jess's face. "Shuffleboard," she confirms with a guilty smile.

"How many shots have you had?" I ask quickly.

"Eight," she replies casually.

"Eight?"

Jess scrunches her face as she thinks about it. "Maybe nine?"

Pushing Jess's response from my mind, I look to Keelie and say, "I'm going to go grab a few pitchers of water."

When I step up to the bar, I feel as if I'm crossing an invisible barrier, and at any moment I might get zapped for stepping too close. But nothing happens. Nothing is different. I carefully place my hands on the edge of the bar, half expecting it to shock me. It doesn't.

The bartender approaches. Nodding his chin in my direction, he asks, "What can I get you?"

Air is forced from my lungs. I forget how to form my words. With a long, grounding blink and a hard swallow, I turn my attention back to him. "Two pitchers of water and, uh, maybe ten glasses?"

"We don't do pitchers, but I can line up ten glasses of water for you," he offers.

I bob my head in appreciation.

"There you are," Lex calls out. She presses the front of her hip along the side of my leg and puts one hand on the small of my back. Her other hand is on the bar, the only thing holding her upright.

"Have you had nine shots, too?" I ask.

"Who's had nine shots?" She laughs, then narrows her eyes at me, slurring, "I'm being very responsible."

"Jess said she's had nine."

Lex closes her eyes, turns up her nose, and shakes her head. "She's getting married tomorrow. Do you really think I'd let her have *nine* shots?" Then her mouth twists mischievously. "Sam, on the other hand . . ." She shrugs.

The bartender places three glasses of water in front of us.

"Drink that, please?" I beg her.

"Matty," she replies firmly, "this is a party. Water is for quitters."

"Water is for people who don't want to puke during the ceremony tomorrow."

"Listen," she purrs softly, moving her hand from my back and rubbing it down the length of my arm. I glare at her. Ignoring my protest, she continues, "I'm going to be as irresponsible as I want to be this weekend because I don't get to do that anymore. I came here to have fun."

"You came here to be in your brother's wedding," I remind her.

She shakes her head skeptically. "How much do you remember from *your* brother's wedding?" she teases, still holding my arm.

She's got me there. "I saved the excessive drinking for the reception. Not the night before."

"I plan to save all *my* excessive drinking for the reception, too." She winks.

Shaking my head, I ask, "Can you dish out some of these waters with me?"

With a bratty scowl, she clenches one in each hand and saunters off to deliver them.

I wedge three of them between my arm and my chest, grab a fourth one for my hand, and head over to the dart boards where Josh, Nate, Frankie, and Sam are playing a round of 301, each with a beer placed on a nearby table.

"Water break," I call out, handing a glass to Sam.

"You're not supposed to be babysitting tonight, Matty." Josh reminds me, "Jenna said she would take care of it."

"Uh-huh." I squint my eyes at him. "How much water have you had tonight?"

"Does vodka count?" His voice is low and coarse.

"No, it does not. Therefore, Jenna has been relieved of babysitting duties." I shove a glass into his hand. "Drink this."

"Where have you been?" His words are still extremely gravelly, even after he takes a sip of water.

"Have you guys been smoking?"

Josh lets out a huge, guilty laugh. "How can you possibly know that? I'm feeling so level right now. What gave me away?"

I mimic his low grumble. "Because you talk like this when you're high."

Another laugh bubbles from inside him. Then he draws his eyebrows in, speaking much slower, trying to force his words to sound more sober. "Do I really?"

I pass glasses of water to Nate and Frankie. "Yeah, that's exactly how a sober person talks."

"Where have you been?" he asks again.

In a low whisper, I reply, "Talking to Keelie." I glance over his shoulder at Sam.

"Is that why she looks like she's been crying?" Josh asks accusatorially.

"You know that's not my fault."

He nods, allowing it. "Is everything okay?"

"As good as it can be. At least we're talking."

"Didn't I always tell you that if anything happens I'd make you guys friends again?"

Air bursts from my mouth as though I just got punched in the gut. "Except I don't want to be her friend."

"You do," he assures me. "Don't push her away by making it more than it is."

With a slow blink and a sigh, I say, "Drink your fucking water," which we both know means *You're right and I don't like it.*

He raises his eyebrows at me as he takes a few large gulps.

"Don't let me interrupt your game," I plead, gesturing back to the board.

It's Sam's turn. He throws his first two darts so hard they bounce off the target. His third one doesn't even hit the board, piercing the wall instead. It's the only dart he manages to stick to anything.

He turns around, cackling hysterically as though it's the funniest thing he's ever seen. Josh shouts, "A two-hundred-point gap isn't funny, Santiago," which only makes Sam crack up more. Josh leans into me and gruffs, "I know it's hard to tell now, but Sam was phenomenal about twenty minutes ago."

Frankie steps up to the line. With an ornate amount of focus, he sails three darts swiftly into the board, bumping fists with Nate as the scoreboard knocks off another sixty points. Frankie plucks the darts from the target and passes them off to Josh.

Sam leans heavily on the table across from me, his smile so wide it pulls his lips into two thin lines.

I laugh at him. "How are you feeling?"

"Moog, I am feeling fine!"

My jaw drops slightly. "What did you just call me?"

"Your name," he bumbles. "Mat-tee."

"No, you didn't. You called me Moog."

"Well, whatever," he stammers. "Not on purpose. I'm a little fuzzy right now. Ask me tomorrow and I'll tell you I said *Matty*."

"Okay, Sam," I allow, turning back to watch Josh's throw and doing my best to disguise the grin that's fighting its way to my lips.

We stay out until last call, but probably should have left thirty minutes prior. Heads droop and feet clomp as Keelie, Jenna, and I wrangle our drunken counterparts into ride shares and ship them off to the hotel. June and I share a car with the Santiagos, and Keelie sleepily rests her head on my shoulder as we ride back in silence. My pulse races and my heart aches as she leans against me.

When we pull up to the hotel, the four of us walk to our rooms together. I wave goodnight to Keelie and Sam as we arrive at our doors. Once inside, I point back toward the door and say, "I've gotta go call my brother."

June lets out a muffled sound as she collapses onto the bed. I duck back out to the ground floor and grab a spot on the bench out front.

I send off a text to Chris: *Checking in. All good here. Call if you want.*

As I wait for his reply, I open a web browser and type "June Nelson" into the search bar. There are so many results. I scroll through the top few. None of them are her. I try "Juniper Nelson," and none of them appear to be her either. Not one of the Juniper Nelsons I find appears to be a murderer either, so we're off to a good start.

I type in "Juniper Nelson Remington Realty," and the top result says *About Us: Juniper Nelson, Commercial Realty Agent*. I click the link and am transported to a bio page. My nose crinkles into a smile as her professional headshot fills the screen. This version of June is a stranger to me. But it's unmistakably her.

The bio vanishes into black, then my phone lights up with Chris's name.

"I didn't think you'd still be awake," I state as I answer the phone.

"Still awake," he grumbles in a low voice that suggests he had been asleep. "How was going out with your friends?"

"I spent a lot of time with Keelie," I blurt out. "I miss her."

"I know, Picco."

"She's all that's on my mind. If you don't want to hear me mope, I can let you go sleep."

"What was it like for you to be at a bar again?"

"It was fine," I answer, contemplating the question. "I don't have a problem with drinking."

"Matteo . . ." he booms in a scolding voice.

"*But*," I deflect, "I understand how it contributes to my addiction, and I am *not* drinking. Okay?"

"Are you parroting, or do you mean it?"

"I mean, I don't miss it. That's all," I explain. "I don't feel a pull toward drinking. So it was fine to be at a bar and not drink."

"Okay," he replies, still skeptical.

"And," I continue, "it also helped that Keelie wasn't drinking."

"She wasn't? Did you ask her to do that?"

"No! Of course I didn't," I reply defensively, "she just didn't want to."

He releases a soft *hmm* that's barely audible through the phone.

"What?"

"Nothing," he replies. "I can hear the enthusiasm in your voice, and I don't want you to get your hopes up."

I take a huge gulp of the cool, late-night summer air and release it in a huge breathy sigh. "We're working on being friends. That's all. Okay?"

"Okay," he says, not believing me but not awake enough to argue.

"I have to be up early tomorrow, so I'm going to go," I attempt to break off.

"Have you been sleeping at all?" he quizzes.

"No," I sigh, "hardly any. So I need to go now so I can hopefully get in a solid four hours of staring at the ceiling tonight."

"Have fun tomorrow."

"Grazie, Cristiano. Buona notte." *Goodnight.*

"Ciao."

When I pull the phone away from my ear, June's professional headshot is staring back at me once again. I scroll, looking for any indication that she might actually be a serial killer.

Graduated from the University of Missouri–Columbia with a degree in Business Administration.

Native to the St. Louis region.

Lives in Kirkwood with her two daughters and her husband, Randy.

I suddenly choke, the cold air going from refreshing to stinging my throat.

With her two daughters and her husband, Randy. I read it again. And then a third time to make sure I didn't miss the word *ex* anywhere in that sentence. Why even mention an ex-husband in a bio? I swallow hard as I process the answer to that hypothetical question. *You wouldn't.*

My foot twitches uncontrollably as I contemplate what my next move should be. I should storm up to our room and confront her about it. *What the fuck, June?* But she's been drinking all night. She's high on I-don't-even-know-what. So not tonight, then. But tomorrow is the wedding. There isn't exactly an ideal time. Tomorrow night at the reception? After the reception? Will I be able to not say anything for that long?

I'll have to try.

V

Saturday, September 22nd

According to Jess's timeline, the girls are supposed to start getting ready at seven, which means Josh gets kicked out of his hotel room at six thirty when Lex shows up to drag him from under the covers and yell at him to get lost. He calls me not even ten minutes later, jolting me awake. We didn't get back until almost two last night, which, as far as bachelor parties go, is pretty tame. But considering the fact that we're all almost thirty and we had to wake up early, it now feels as if staying out late was a bad idea.

I watched the clock turn over every hour all night long. I couldn't get to sleep, something that is going to take a long, long time for my body to relearn. At some point, I must have fallen asleep though, because when Josh calls me, he wakes me up. Before I even answer his call, I'm already mad at him for disrupting the little sleep I could get.

"What?" I snap, my eyes closed.

"Hey," he says with a laugh. "Are you awake?"

"Fuck off," I grumble.

"Jess kicked me out. Come hang with me."

"You're not off to a great start, are you?" I sit up against the headboard. June stirs when I move, but she stays asleep.

"Come on, Matty," he begs. "I'm outside of your room right now."

"744?" I ask. When he confirms, I add, "Oh, okay. Cool. Go three more doors toward the elevator. That's Frankie's door. He's probably still up from last night. I'll meet you guys in two hours, when you *said* you were going to wake me up."

"Matty," he whines.

"Vaffanculo," I groan.

"Come on," he sings into the phone, already knowing he's won.

I hang up on him without saying anything more but slump out the front door a moment later. He has a huge grin on his face to contrast my apathetic scowl.

"There he is," he chimes. "Let's go find you some coffee."

Downstairs in the lobby, I throw myself down in a plush, overstuffed lobby chair, still half-awake. Josh pours us two coffees and hands one over to me. I give him one more glare before I reluctantly accept it and then drop the act.

"You're getting married today. How the hell did that happen?"

His whole face glows. "To Jessica Mitchell." He contemplates how that sounds and smiles even wider as he adds, "I'm cutting off the beard."

He turns his gaze to me to gauge my reaction, which is encouraging. I know it will make Jess happy. Lex and his mom, too, but especially Jess.

"I told her I wouldn't. I made her so mad at me last week telling her I wouldn't get rid of it." He laughs as he remembers. "She was so mad. I just wanted to surprise her."

I laugh back. "You're a dick."

"I know," he confirms. "It'll be worth it."

Josh says he discussed his plan with Lex, and she had made us an appointment at an upscale barbershop down the road because she didn't trust Josh not to "fuck up his face." The image of a barbershop that I had in mind is much different than the place that Lex had booked us. The outside is painted a dark, matte charcoal color, and the interior is covered with warm, inviting dark wood and leather chairs. Shelves along the back wall are lined with bottles that remind me of whiskey. Upon closer inspection, I can see that it *is* whiskey. Bottles and bottles of top-shelf stuff. A display case in front of the shelves is full of cigars. There's a putting green in the front window. I'm slightly in awe that a place like this even exists.

Josh's dad, Jeff, confidently strides up to the person waiting to greet us at the front counter and announces, "Parker," as if that's the only thing he needs to say to explain who we are and why we're here.

Jeff is like that about practically everything. A bit pompous, fairly pretentious, not even remotely self-aware. Lex wouldn't hesitate to describe him as a moron, but Josh is a bit more tolerant of his dad's arrogance. Most of the time, I tend to side with Lex on the matter. The Parker parents divorced a short time after I first met them, almost twenty years ago. Jeff moved back to Los Angeles, and I didn't see much of him after that.

The man at the front counter smiles kindly at Jeff Parker and replies, "The wedding party! Congratulations! Which one of you is the groom?"

Jeff slaps a hand on Josh's shoulder with a beam of pride. The man nods a hello to Josh and says, "Right this way, gentlemen," showing us to a row of leather barber chairs.

Jeff immediately eyes the wall of whiskey, and Frankie quickly jumps in for a debate about which is the superior bottle, without having ever tried any for themselves, only knowing what they've found on the internet. Jeff calls out, "Let's get six pours of that Woodford Double Oak."

My mouth waters, instantly remembering its oaky vanilla flavor. "None for me," I cut in, gloomily.

"Nonsense!" Jeff barks. "Everyone's gotta have one! You'll love it."

I smirk, trying to play it off coolly. "I know I'll love it. That's the problem."

"Matty doesn't drink anymore, Dad."

"Well, why the hell not?" Jeff demands. "Did that girlfriend of yours make you quit?"

A puff of air escapes my lips in surprise. A cringe takes over Josh's face.

"No," I reply sharply, "my brother, actually. He said if I get any more DUIs, he'll make sure I serve jail time."

Jeff lets out a loud belly laugh as though I made a hilarious joke. Josh gives me an apologetic shrugs his shoulders. *That's Dad.*

"Five is fine," I say to the barber slash bartender. "Do you have any coffee?"

"Yeah, I got you," the man replies.

Josh is the last of us to be steamed, shaved, and cut. By that time, Nate, Frankie, Andy, and Jeff are a few drinks in and messing around on the putting green at the front. I sit in the empty barber chair next to Josh.

"How much of this are we taking off?" The barber asks Josh, running a comb through the mess of beard on his chin.

"All of it," I jump in before Josh gets the chance to reply.

"Not all of it," Josh protests. "I'll look like a child."

The barber pulls out a binder from a shelf next to the mirror and hands it to me. I flip it open to the first page and a mug shot of Al Capone looks back at me, with the word Cuts underneath it. The tab on the edge of the page is labeled similarly, and the other tabbed pages of the binder are labeled Beards and Mustaches. At the start of the beards section is another early-1900s mug shot of a man with a floppy hat, beady eyes, and long, out-of-control beard. Each subsequent page behind this tab is filled with more antique mug shots featuring other types of beards. Some are authentic, others are modern images made to match the old.

"This one," I say, pointing to one that is longer than stubble, but not quite a full beard. It would require lobbing off close to four inches of the unruly beard Josh has now. The barber pauses his combing to lean over and look.

Josh doesn't so much as think about looking, even after the barber invites him to check it out. "Nah," Josh replies confidently. "I trust him. He's going to have my wife and sister to answer to if he's fucking with me."

His wife. I grin.

June is still asleep when I get back. I realize it too late and let the door to the room slam shut behind me, causing her to stir. She groans angrily at me.

"Less than three hours until the wedding if you're still coming," I inform her.

She rubs a hand across her face. "I'm going to sleep until we get to the part where I can start drinking again."

"That's fine." I open the closet door and push aside all June's clothes to retrieve the only piece I have hanging, the suit.

"No," she mumbles, "the dress I bought for the wedding was very expensive and I want to have lots of time to wear it."

Instead of offering her a reply, I push open the curtains, allowing a bright, crisp light to fill the room. She burrows back under the comforter, shielding herself with yet another groan.

I toss the suit on the bed, pulling each piece apart one at a time to put them on. June emerges from her bundle of blankets as I finish fastening my top shirt button. I lift the tie in her general direction and say, "Help me with this," tossing it back down at the foot of the bed and tucking in the edges of my shirt.

She crawls to the edge of the bed, sits on her feet, legs splayed open. Her eyes scan me in a once-over as she picks up the tie. She gestures for me to step closer so she doesn't have to move any further, and when I do, she rises up to my eye level.

After flipping the tie around my neck, she rubs a hand along my jawline, admiring the crisp lines of my stubble beard. "Keelie won't know what to do with herself when she sees you," she says encouragingly, driving heat to the surface of my cheeks.

As soon as I'm dressed, I ride the elevator up to the fourteenth floor and knock on the door of the room where the girls are getting ready. Lex opens the door. She's already wearing heels and has on a satin robe that she has allowed to dip off one shoulder. Her makeup is completely done, but her hair is still tied into a knot on the top of her head. She presses one hand near the top of the door frame and leans away slightly to give her body a slight S shape.

She looks me up and down as she says, "You clean up nice."

I ignore her compliment. "I need to talk to Jess."

Lex scrunches up her face to show her doubt in my request. Then she leans in close to me, resting a hand on my chest as she whispers, "Are you sure you wouldn't rather I go find Keelie?" She winks at the suggestion as she pulls back to her previous stance.

"I'm here on official groom business. I need Jess."

Lex scrunches her face again, this time with a new look of disgust. "No," she scoffs, "no boys allowed." She closes the door.

"Alexis!" I shout back at her before she's able to shut me out entirely.

She laughs, opening the door fully, a look of shock on her face. "Did you call me *Alexis*?" she asks as if it was the strangest thing she's ever heard.

"It's your name, right?"

"It sure is, *Matteo*." Her face scrunches as though it's just as foreign for her to say my full name. She's right. It's strange.

I look past her, trying to get a glimpse of anyone who might help me get past the bouncer to see Jess.

"Is that Matty?" Jenna calls out from behind the wall that Lex had built.

Lex purses her lips and narrows her eyes at me, stepping aside. I lock eyes with her as I enter past her, teasing her inability to keep me away.

Their hotel suite is easily larger than the apartment Keelie and I shared, and this huge room has thirteen-foot ceilings and floor-to-ceiling windows. The suite has its own entry hallway with a coat closet and a table by the door with a big glass bowl at the center, where more than one person has tossed their keys and purses for safekeeping. The main room has a large couch with two additional chairs and a coffee table, all directed toward a large TV.

There's a full-size dining table to one side and a large kitchenette on the other. The counter in the kitchen is lined with barstools and someone, presumably Lex, has put out a mimosa bar. There's a plate of pastries on the table, which I gladly help myself to as I continue to gawk out the windows that reveal a panoramic view of downtown Cleveland.

"Did you just stop by to steal our food and views?"

Keelie is standing right behind me. I say to her, somewhat guiltily, "You guys have a much better set up than we have downstairs."

My light tone quickly fades when I turn to get a better look at her. She's wearing a deep ruby red, off-the-shoulder dress that makes her look stunning. Her hair is pulled back loosely, with curls spilling out methodically, one bunch coming to rest on her shoulder. Her lips, stained in the same dark red color of her dress, are succulent and glossy in a way that makes them completely irresistible. Her long, stick-on eyelashes continually pull my attention back to her eyes every time I try to look elsewhere. That is, until I notice her floor-length dress has a slit that lands high on her leg. The smallest hint of skin peeks out, making me want to rub my hand across her thigh.

I stare at her a moment too long, causing her lips to curl into a smile as she waits for me to offer the real explanation for what I'm doing here. When my words don't come, she blinks her beautiful long lashes at me, parts her glossy red lips and says, "You look very handsome, Val."

The urge to take hold of her has never been stronger. Desire pulses through me as I think about clasping a hand along the nape of her neck and kissing her until every last bit of lipstick has been completely rubbed off.

I bite the inside of my lip, hard, grounding myself back into reality. "We both clean up pretty nice, huh?" I smirk, keeping the compliment as casual as possible.

She accepts the compliment with a crinkle of her nose, turning back to the window to look out at the street below. I return my attention to the street, too, although I'd much rather continue staring at her. We stand as close together as we possibly can without touching. After a long, agonizing minute of silence passes between us, I find the smallest bit of courage to rub a finger softly against her forearm. Not lingering, not forceful, just one quick swipe across her arm to let her know I'm still here.

She responds by resting her head against my shoulder as she had on our ride home last night, only now she can't use the excuse of exhaustion to justify it. The only reason she has now is that she wants to.

I turn my head, my lips barely brushing against her forehead as I whisper, "You look amazing, Mia."

Lex's voice erupts from behind us. "What are you doing here, Matty?" We both bolt upright, stepping apart and turning away as if nothing happened.

"I need to talk to Jess."

Lex eyes me suspiciously. She licks the front of her teeth and lets out a disbelieving "uh-huh."

"Jess is busy," Jenna cuts in. "What do you need?"

"Ostrega! How many levels of security am I going to have to pass through?" I laugh, raising my voice in response. "Josh sent me to give her something."

Jenna and Keelie exchange a heartwarming glance. I scrunch my face. *Don't get your hopes up.*

"I'm in here, Matty!" Jess yells out from a door to my left, revealing her position in the labyrinth of the bridal suite.

I head toward her voice and nudge open the door to reveal an insanely large bedroom that has its own couch and sofa chair, a bench against the end of the bed, and a table in the corner. There is an equally massive bathroom attached, and I can barely catch a glimpse of the glass shower that resembles the one we have in our room but is easily twice as large. *What a way to spend a wedding night.*

The plush, king-size bed is haphazardly put back together after being slept on a few hours ago. Josh and Lex's mom, Annie Parker, sits on the edge of the bed, despite the plethora of other seating in the room. Jess's mom and friend Aimee sit on the nearby couch and the two of them shout bubbly conversations across the room to Annie and Jess. Keelie and Jenna follow in close behind me to catch a glimpse of the gift I have from Josh. Lex is nowhere to be found, probably glued to her phone, thumbing through her growing pile of emails despite her incessant promises not to do exactly that at any point this weekend.

A stylist with a handful of bobby pins stuck to a magnetic bracelet on her wrist twists and places ringlets of Jess's freshly curled hair into the perfect spots. Jess widens her eyes at me, as if to apologize for not being able to greet me.

"Matty!" Annie breathes excitedly, not even pretending to drink a mimosa, as she waves around a full flute of champagne.

"Hey, Momma Parks," I say as her hands caress each side of my face, placing a soft kiss on my cheek. She's already well past buzzed.

I wrap my arms tightly around her shoulders, completely engulfing her tiny frame.

"I am so happy to see you, my stupid, beautiful boy," she says, giving me another buzzed kiss on the cheek. "How are you?"

"Grateful to be here, lucky to be alive," I whisper back to her.

"You and me both, darling." She flashes a warm grin.

"I actually stopped by because that handsome son of yours sent me to give his bride a gift." I pull the box out of my pocket and flash it at Annie, speaking loudly enough for Jess to hear. My arm still wrapped around Annie's shoulder, I whisper, "You're going to like this, too, I think," before releasing her and presenting the box to Jess.

The hair stylist stops her bobby-pinning frenzy momentarily as Jess extends a hand to me to take the box.

"Jessica Mitchell, this is the most disgusting gift that I have ever had to give to anyone in my entire life. And the absolute worst part about it is that I know you're going to love it."

She fully snatches the box from my hand. There's a folded note card carefully taped to the top of it. She lifts the card flap and takes a peek, then quickly shuts it and glares up at me, tears already forming in her eyes. Then she rolls her eyes back in her head, takes a long, centering blink, and smiles at me with a quivering lip.

"You haven't even read it yet!" I say, protesting her tears.

Her eyes trace the words, and her hand covers her mouth as she reads the note Josh scrawled on the card. I don't need her to read it out loud to know what it says. I helped him write it.

The top half of the card has a small photo of the two of them from the year Jess and her family moved to St. Louis. A photo from spirit week, tie-dye day to be exact. Josh and Jess sported matching tie-dye shirts and sweatbands on their heads. Jess had the worst haircut—she'd be the first to admit it—with sharply angled bangs she had cut herself. Josh's hair was long and flippy, almost as long as Jess's. He had braces and proudly showed them off.

Under the photo is the note from Josh that reads:

When I first met you fourteen years ago, my heart skipped a beat. I didn't know what to do with that feeling, so, stupidly, I ignored it. If I had known that someday you would make me the happiest person alive, I never would have ignored what I felt for you. Fourteen years seems like an eternity now that I know what I've been missing. I can't wait to see you today and every day for the rest of our lives. I love you, Jess. Then, today, and forever.

Jess lets out a huge sigh and looks up at me with another smile that quickly melts into a quivery frown, a tear streaking down her cheek.

I nod at her to open the box. When she does, she reacts with an appropriately annoyed tone as she squelches out an incredulous, "Oh my God, Josh." She flashes me an unamused look, as if this were my idea.

"I told you it was disgusting," I defend myself.

"It's not a dick pic, is it?" Annie asks.

"Mom!" Lex shouts, now joining us in the doorway. "Don't ever say that again!"

"Come on, Alexis. I'm a single woman, too."

"Stop!" Lex whines again.

Keelie and I exchange looks of amusement. Having known Annie Parker for so long, that assumption seems pretty on par for her. Hopefully Jess's family already knows what they're getting into with the Parkers.

Jess snatches the note off the top of the box and keeps it for herself, reading it over and over again. She hands the closed box to Annie so she can finally see what all the fuss is about. Annie narrows her eyes at me, looking for some indication of what is inside.

"I do love a good prank," I admit, "but a dick pic would probably be a step too far, even for me."

"Matty. Stop," Lex huffs again. I flash a mischievous smile her way.

Annie opens the box and lets out a deep laugh.

Lex cautiously looks over her shoulder and then says, "Ew! Is that beard hair?"

Josh had kept an almost four-inch piece of his scraggly beard and placed it inside the box. Jess wrinkles her nose and sheepishly admits, "You were right, I love it." Then, with a flash of horror, she asks, "You didn't let him do anything stupid, did you? He's not going to show up with, like, massive Elvis sideburns or a giant patch of hair that's just in the middle of his chin, right?"

I shake my head. "He looks good, Jess."

Her face lights up. "I can't wait to see him."

"He feels the same way," I promise her.

I smile for my friends because I am so incredibly happy for them. But the happiness I feel for them gnaws at me. I could have been this happy, too. I *should* be this happy, too. Me and Keelie. The phantom oxycodone flavor fills my mouth, offering solace from losing her. Assuring me there's nothing I could do to win her back. Begging me to taste that bitterness again and find some peace.

The ceremony venue is close to the hotel, a quick drive down the shore of Lake Erie. It's a large old industrial building that has been converted into an event space. The rooftop ceremony will have stunning views of the Cleveland skyline on one side as the cool breeze rolls off the lake on the other.

Jeff Parker rented the most obnoxiously huge vehicle he could find to drive while he was in town for the weekend. He insists on driving "his guys" to the venue in this large, freshly waxed, champagne-colored Infiniti SUV. Jeff cracks open the sunroof just because he can, and he instructs me to dig out a couple of bottles of booze he has stashed in the center console wedged between Andy and me.

"Matty doesn't drink anymore, Dad," Josh huffs a quiet reminder his way.

"Really?" Jeff asks, as though he hadn't already heard that a few hours ago. "Sorry, I completely forgot."

"Still got both my hands, though." I smirk, taking out the bottles anyway. "More than capable of passing the fun around."

I gently hit Josh's shoulder with a bottle. He accepts it, flashing me a sympathetic sorry. I wave it off and hand the other one to the back seat for Nate and Frankie to split. Josh takes one swig to appease his dad, then hands it back to Andy. Andy accepts it and clamps it between his legs for the rest of the ride, not taking a drink himself.

When we arrive at the venue, we park toward the front of the lot. Jeff's SUV is too big to be contained by one parking spot, or so he says, so for good measure, he parks in the middle of two spots. As we climb out of the car, Josh and I exchange a knowing glance as we think about Annie's reaction when she sees his thoughtless parking job in a prime spot.

The inside of the building is full of exposed brick mixed with newly plastered walls. The windows still have the original hand-blown wavy glass that slightly obscures the outside world, but the perfect view of the Cleveland skyline is still apparent. Every handle and railing is made of old black iron. Cement support beams shoot up through the floors. The ceilings are made up of wooden slats, the floorboards of the room above us. Old chandeliers hang from the wooden support beams every few feet, and café lights swing back and forth between them. Round tables fill the room, and a team of vendors is already busy setting everything up. Annie and Jess's mom both hover nearby to make sure everything is done as instructed.

"This place is great." I smile at Josh.

"Wait until you see the roof," he replies, already leading the way toward the iron staircase that spirals up to another doorway on the far side of the room.

On top of the building, there are rows and rows of chairs being set up, and a large golden hoop at the center, to which a florist is fastening flowers. Cleveland, the city where they fell in love, as their backdrop. Josh looks on with pride, as if he single-handedly created it all.

He paces to the other side of the roof, looking out at the lake view. A couple of lone boats are drifting by. His expression drops from prideful to contemplative as he looks out at the water.

"How are you feeling?" I ask.

"Jittery," he replies almost instantly, "like my heart is about to beat out of my chest."

I know the feeling.

Then he turns to look at me. "Eager to get started, but sad that tomorrow it's all going to be over."

"Tomorrow is day one."

He nods, taking in a deep breath of the breeze blowing off the lake.

The vendors slowly vacate the rooftop as they finish setting up, and guests trickle in. I hover close to Josh as he says hello to old relatives who have made the trip from St. Louis or even California, or members of Jess's family that he has only met in passing, who have driven in from the Cleveland suburbs.

June finds her way to the rooftop and her stunningly sleek dress reminds me why I had invited her to come along in the first place. She stops by for a quick hello, giving me a kiss on the cheek. Then she takes a lap around the patio, making friends with people she doesn't even know.

I stand at the center of it all, trying my best not to feel self-conscious about being alone. Then a hand presses against my back and a voice behind me says, "Don't you check your phone anymore?"

No, Mia, I haven't had a phone in five months. I slide my phone out of my pocket to take a peek as I turn around to face her. I have two texts from her. "What's going on?" I ask without reading them.

She leans in close to me, so close I could kiss her neck if I were allowed to. Her delicious scent pricks my nostrils and a calm washes over me. She whispers, "Do you have the rings?"

I lean away from her slightly so I can see the worried look on her face. With a smug grin, I dig a hand in my jacket pocket and produce the box she had been frantically searching for a moment ago. In the snarkiest voice I can muster, I reply, "Of course I do."

She places a quick touch to my arm and lets out a sigh of relief. "We have been looking *everywhere* for those." Then she adds sharply, "Don't tell Jess."

"You should have asked me sooner."

She throws a playful glare my way and retorts, "You're right, I should have texted you."

"Sorry." I laugh.

She raises an eyebrow at me as she retreats to the doorway where she had emerged a moment ago.

If anything else caused a scare during the ceremony, I was oblivious to it and, hopefully, so were Josh and Jess. As instructed, Josh keeps his back turned when Jess enters the rooftop. He's not allowed to turn around until the music changes. Jess is absolutely beaming with happiness as she walks up the stairs. A soft murmur spreads across the guests. Josh drops his head and smiles, knowing exactly what's going on behind him.

Jess has her arms linked with both of her parents. She immediately starts crying as soon as Josh turns around to reveal his new look. He scrubs a hand across his chin bashfully. Josh hugs Jess's mom, does a handshake-turned-hug with her dad, then extends an elbow to Jess to walk her the rest of the way. Instead of taking his arm, she places a hand on his cheek. Her eyes grow as wide as her smile. He whispers something in her ear, a moment just between the two of them, and she nods her head back at him. Then they stand in front of the rest of us, holding each other's hands, and vow to love each other forever.

Keelie bubbles out a few sobs with a big smile plastered on her face as Josh and Jess exchange vows. She dabs her tears on the back of her hand and blinks a few times in vain. No matter what she does, her tears keep falling. When the minister announces them for the first time as "Mr. and Mrs. Parker," Josh and Jess walk down the aisle together, and all heads turn to follow them. On cue, I extend an arm out to Jenna and she links her hand through. Dipping a hand into my inside jacket pocket, I pull out a tissue I stashed away earlier for this exact moment and pass it off to Keelie.

She bursts with a quick embarrassed laugh, her eyes full of gratitude as she meets mine. The smoldering stare I return to her is meant to remind her that there's no one in this world who knows her better than I do. She holds my gaze for a long, agonizing moment, her eyes squinting at me with the tiniest bit of passion hiding behind them. Jenna gives my arm a gentle tug, signaling our time to walk, and I give Keelie one last suave smirk as I break her gaze.

At the very end of the rows of chairs, June mouths the word *smooth* as I walk by.

VI

Saturday, September 22nd

June has been schmoozing and making friends with strangers all day, people I don't even know. It must be pretty easy when you're fabricating every element of your life the entire weekend. Everything but her first name is a sham. That's assuming she's actually telling people her name is June. But for the first time tonight, I find her sitting alone at a table, and I feel guilty seeing her by herself, so I join her.

"Can I grab you another drink?" I ask.

"You don't have to babysit me, you know. I'm fine taking care of myself. I know you'd rather be over there." She nods her head toward Keelie, who is across the room, doing a choreographed line dance I'm not familiar with.

"I don't mind," I lie, sitting down next to her.

"Are you kidding me? You've spent every day I've ever known you blubbering about how much you love her, and now you're sitting over here with me?" She places her hand on my knee. "Really, Matt. It's okay. Go be with her. Go ask her to dance."

"That sounds like a primo way to get rejected."

She shrugs. "It's just a dance, don't overthink it."

I nod. She's right.

"Can I ask you something first?" June asks ominously. "What's the story with Jeff?"

"Jeff Parker?" I laugh before realizing she's asking seriously. "You're into Jeff?"

Her fulminating glare indicates she is not interested in responding to such a childish question. I scan the room, finding Jeff at the bar with Frankie and Nate, doing what I can only imagine is not their first round of tequila shots. He has already completely ditched his suit and is down to a pair of pants and his white dress shirt with the sleeves rolled up to his elbows and the buttons undone halfway down his chest. His white chest hair is almost luminescent against his tanned skin.

Lex had argued with him this morning, trying to get him to wear a suit at all. He made a last-ditch effort to wear something "less stuffy." But on behalf of Jess, who seems to be much kinder to her new father-in-law, Lex told him that if he didn't "put on the fucking suit," he could sit out every family photo they took, and none of them would ever have any way of remembering he had actually come.

When Jeff had pretended to take a moment to consider this, Lex yelled out, "Oh my God, I can't believe you!" And Jeff laughed lightly, making an offhand comment about how much she reminded him of her mother, which Lex understandably took offense to, considering her parents rarely had a nice thing to say about each other. Lex stormed off in a huff, choosing not to engage.

At that moment, I regretted being the next closest person in the room to Jeff, because he immediately met my eye, looking for affirmation from me that he hadn't completely lost his mind. I shook my head at him and said, "Jeff, if I were you, I'd put on the suit." He closed his eyes as if it brought him great pain, then nodded and said I was right, as if it were the first time the suit was suggested.

If that's what June was interested in getting tangled up with, who was I to stop her?

"What do you want to know?" I bring my attention back to June.

"They're divorced, right?" she asks, taking a sip from her drink.

Before I can stop myself, I blurt out, "More divorced than you and Randy."

Her expression grows sour. "What did you just say?"

"You heard me."

She doesn't meet my eyes, stirring the ice around in her drink. Barely audible above the music, she whispers, "How did you find out?"

"I fucking Googled you. Saw it on your Remington bio."

She glares at me. "Why?"

"Keelie made a joke about it." I shake my head. "It doesn't matter."

She takes a deep, heavy breath, then a long sip that drains her drink. "Please don't tell him."

"What?" I spit out at her, surprised. But then I see it. I see the tables turn. June used to hold all the power. She was the pills, the transportation, the funding. Suddenly, I am in control. I hold the power to destroy her life. To take it all away. And that terrifies her. "I wouldn't do that to you. We're friends, aren't we?"

She turns to face me, suspiciously. "Yeah, I guess so." A smile forms at the corner of her mouth. "Would you be mad?"

A soft desperate plea fills her expression, as though she might die if she doesn't get the chance to hook up with Jeff Parker. She has a husband and a family that she's willing to put on the line. And for what? Because it feels good. Because it gives her the chance to live in a world where things seem better than they actually are. A momentary, all-consuming rush. And then it dissolves, and all she's left with is an emptiness, leaving her searching for that moment again.

"No, June," I say, understandingly. "I wouldn't be mad."

I stand up and place a hand on top of her shoulder to show her I'm not holding any hard feelings toward her, that I'm not out to ruin her. She smiles back at me and says "Thanks, Matt" in her silky voice as I walk away.

The music slows and the dance floor clears of the mob of guests who were covering it a moment ago. Couples pair off and take the floor, Josh and Jess at the center of them. Josh has gotten rid of his jacket, vest, and tie, and has loosened the top couple of buttons on his shirt, sharing a resemblance to his dad that I'm sure makes his mom and sister furious.

Keelie and Lex are en route to the bar when Jenna stops them. The three of them make their own circle at the edge of the dance floor. My heart falls deep into my stomach and races a million miles an hour. My whole mouth goes dry; I'm afraid I won't be able to speak. I swallow a few times as I approach her.

I stand directly behind Keelie, holding out my arm parallel to hers, with my palm facing up. I catch Lex's eye for a split second, and the corner of her mouth grins suspiciously.

When Keelie's eyes glance toward my hand, I whisper in her ear, "Dance with me."

Nerves swell inside my chest. It took every ounce of confidence I have to whisper those three words, and every second that passes without a response leaves me second-guessing myself. Leaves me wondering if Lex and Jenna, standing only a couple of feet away, are about to witness the most excruciating rejection of all time.

Keelie turns further to meet my eyes, even though she knows my hand from every other hand in the world and my voice from every other voice. Just as I know her. When she looks at me, she doesn't show a drop of emotion on her face. Not happy or sad or annoyed or completely disgusted that I thought to ask her. She stares at me for what feels like an eternity.

So when she finally places her hand in mine, my knees go weak. I'm not sure I can even move. But as I curl each of my fingers around her hand, I feel electricity pass between us, and I quickly find my strength. Lowering our hands to our sides, gripping her hand tightly in mine, I lead her to the dance floor. There are plenty of eyes watching us as we make our way across the room, but I keep my eyes on Keelie as if there's nobody else around.

With her right hand in my left, our fingers become intertwined. More old habits, it seems. She places her hand on my shoulder, and mine finds its home at the very top of her waist. We fall into the beat of the music, and I am lost in this moment I have dreamed of for years.

She leans in close, her chin coming to rest right next to her hand that grips my shoulder. I can feel her soft breath sweep across the side of my face, her mouth inches from my ear. My face nuzzles up alongside hers.

"Is it just me, or are people staring at us?" She lets out a light laugh as she likely questions agreeing to dance with me.

I look around. There are a few sideways glances directed at us. Sam is keeping watch from a distance. Lex and Jenna are not even remotely trying to hide their stares. I catch a glimpse of Annie looking our way, and that's the handful of people that I'm able to see. I'm sure there are as many eyes on us from Keelie's direction.

But I shrug. "I didn't notice. I've been too busy staring at you, too."

She gives my hand a quick squeeze. "I *have* noticed that," she whispers, then pulls away from me slightly, taking her head off my chest. She doesn't release my hand though; she doesn't stop dancing. She separates herself further from me to signal this isn't anything more than a dance.

I shift my hand in hers, and change the speed of our feet, pulling us from a drifting sway to getting lost in the tempo of the music with an actual rhythmic step we had once practiced together. She lets out an airy laugh as she recognizes the pattern, following along as though it has been days since we've last done this, not years. It has been at least three years since I've been alert enough to dance with her like this. *Why did I ever let this get away?*

I smile at her as I catch her eye, but I'm fighting back tears, thinking about how much I love her and how stupid I was to give this up. I softly squeeze her hand as a signal, then I lift her arm into the air to spin her. The edges of her dress brush up against my ankle as she twirls. When she reels herself back into my arms, she stands closer to me once again, her cheek pressing against mine, her breath brushing the tip of my earlobe.

I nestle my face back into her hair, looking down at the floor so I don't have to meet anyone else's eyes. I don't want to think about anyone else at this moment but my Mia Mae.

"What's on your mind, Val?" she whispers in my ear. So close, her lips practically dance across my cheek as she speaks.

"I've missed this so much," I reply softly. I opt to say "this" instead of "you," but we both know what I mean. I miss the touch of her skin, the soft whisper of her voice, the feel of her heart as it beats against mine. I've missed all of this. *All of you.*

I don't expect for her to say she missed this too, but I do hope she will say something. After a long, agonizing pause lingers between us, she softly whispers, "I've been keeping a secret from you."

Chills prick the back of my neck as I think of all the crushing-ly disappointing secrets she could unleash on me right now.

"Tell me," I demand cautiously. I want her to be able to talk to me again. I'm just not sure I'm going to like what she has to say.

She shifts away from me, creating enough space between us to look me in the eyes as she says, "Logan and I broke up. That's why Sam's here."

My expression softens, and my heart races. If she wanted this to be a secret from me, why tell me right now? Or ever? She *wants* me to know. And only me. And her fingers are twisting in my hair, and her hand is gripping onto mine tightly. She's sending me a signal. A guilty smile spreads across her face, confirming that she has meant this as an invitation for more.

I kiss her without hesitation. Right here in the middle of the dance floor, with all sorts of eager eyes watching us. I kiss her with a hand on her waist, pulling my body close to hers, and she kisses me back, brushing her fingers along the base of my neck. We stay like this for only a moment before the song ends and our attention suddenly snaps back to reality. She pulls her lips away from mine, but her mouth stays slightly parted in a way that makes me want to kiss her again.

She keeps her gaze locked on me as she shakes her head. "That was a really bad idea."

With her fingers still entwined with mine, she gives my hand a firm, unmistakable squeeze. Then her face softens into an apologetic frown that eats away at my chest as she releases my hand and walks away. Dumbfounded, I don't know what else to do but watch her go.

Josh comes up behind me, probably having witnessed the whole exchange. He places both his hands atop each of my shoulders in a firm, comforting clap. Jess walks past at that exact moment, turning to say "What the hell, Matty?" as she continues on to catch up with Keelie.

Nate approaches, oblivious, holding a cigar in hand. "Let's go celebrate." He raises a glass to cheers us as he wraps an arm around Josh's shoulders and pulls him toward the exit, with Frankie following closely behind.

"Come on, Matty!" Josh yells back to me as they usher him out the door. My instinct tells me to stay inside, to go find Keelie. But if she wanted to talk, she would have stayed with me instead of walking away. So I follow Josh, Nate, and Frankie instead.

There is an old retaining wall, about six feet high, just outside the side exit. I'm the only sober one in the bunch, and I still decide it's a good idea to scale the wall so I can sit on top of it. Gripping my fingers along the top edge, I slowly scale the side. Josh extends his hand to me and I brace him as he runs his feet up the edge to join me. We tower a few feet above the other guys.

"Hey, Frank," Josh yells. "Go find Andy."

Frankie, chomping on an unlit cigar between his teeth, walks back inside to search.

"I think Frankie's got an eye on your sister, man." Nate smacks Josh's knee.

"Here's the thing about Alexis," Josh explains. "She wouldn't give Frankie the time of day if she didn't already have him picked out. He's playing into *her* games, and she's going to eat him alive."

"I think that's what he's hoping for." Nate cackles.

Josh smacks him on the back of the head and snaps, "I'm the only one who gets to take cracks like that, alright?"

"Matty's been hitting on her all weekend, and you don't smack him," Nate whines.

Josh wraps an arm around me. "They're just messing around, right Matty?"

"Bullshit," Nate spits back, swaying slightly. "I heard how you guys talk to each other. You've either fucked her or you want to."

I shake my head. "It's not like that. We talk like that around Josh because it pisses him off."

I flash Josh a cheeky grin, and he gives me a sideways glare, then rolls his eyes jokingly and takes a big sip of his drink.

Frankie returns with Andy and Sam. All three of them have a glass of whiskey in their hands.

"Hey, Frank-kay!" Nate yells, even though he isn't that far away.

"What do you want?" Frankie yells back.

"You fucking Josh's sister tonight?"

His smile admits guilt as he looks at Josh. Josh snatches a small rock from the landscaping behind us and chucks it at Frankie's shoulder.

Frankie cackles as he grips the spot where the rock got him.

Sam lifts his hand in my direction, for help scaling the wall, too. I grasp his hand as he runs his feet up the side and flips himself around to sit before he softly grumbles to me, "Those guys are so fucking annoying."

I snort a quick laugh, glad that they're equally as annoying to someone who's been drinking as much as Sam has. At least sobriety isn't my reason for being a stick in the mud.

Frankie pulls two more cigars out of his jacket pocket and passes them around. He flicks the Zippo he had stashed in his other pocket and lights the cigars for us, one at a time. I suck in enough air to help light mine, but after one disappointing, highless hit, I hand it off to Sam. When he offers it back, I wave him off, so eventually he stops offering.

Nate notices this and feels the need to chime in. "You don't get high off cigars, man. It's not against sobriety to smoke a cigar." He's so drunk, his words flub together.

"Leave him alone, Nate," Josh steps in.

"Sorry, I'm just saying—"

"Fucking drop it, alright?" Josh interrupts again.

Nate takes a drag from his cigar and glances in Frankie's direction, searching for backup.

"So, Matty," Frankie starts, "I saw you macking on Keelie during that last song. What's going on there?"

I toss a sideways glance at Sam to see him intently looking my way. "It's a long story."

"History there, huh?" Frankie nudges my leg with his elbow as if we're longtime pals.

Andy awakens from his drunken stupor long enough to blurt out, "They dated for like ten years."

"No shit?" Frankie asks, but in a way that feels as though he doesn't believe I was ever the kind of guy Keelie would go for.

"Yeah," I reply shortly, not wanting to get into this with him while Sam is around and available to provide his own version of events.

Frankie raises his glass to me. "Good luck." Then a corner of his mouth jumps into his cheek for only a second, as if to say, *You're going to need it.* He turns back to Nate to start a new conversation, but by now, I'm too busy thinking about Keelie again to pay it any attention.

Sam takes a few quick puffs of the cigar, and then, with a gravely, smoke-muffled voice, he grumbles out, "She told you, didn't she?"

"Yeah," I whisper back to Sam, "she told me."

"Told you what?" Josh jumps in.

I shake my head. I don't want to be the one to spread that rumor, even though I'd love to tell everyone. I'd love to pull some great, rom-com–caliber gesture—running inside, stealing the microphone from the band, announcing to everyone that I love Keelie, and hoping she falls into my arms and we live happily ever after. Maybe if I had been drinking tonight, I would have done exactly that.

Josh leans past me and points a finger at Sam and repeats, "Told him what?"

Sam takes a long sip from his drink and looks to see that the other guys aren't paying attention to our conversation before whispering, "She dumped Logan."

She hasn't exactly told me that. I didn't know that she *dumped* him.

Josh leans back toward the bushes behind us. His eyes wide, kicking the heels of his shoes against the retaining wall a few times like an excited toddler, he says, "Well, shit."

"Don't read too much into it," Sam huffs to Josh. It's obvious from his tone that this is meant for me. It's too late, though. Josh is already reading way too much into it on my behalf.

"So what now?" Josh asks me.

"What now?" I laugh. "Nothing. I overstepped and got rejected."

"You're probably lucky she didn't smack you," Josh notes, shoving an elbow into my side.

"That's Sam's territory." I smirk, turning my gaze to him.

Sam holds the stub of a cigar between his teeth and lifts his chin so he can look down his nose at me. "It's about to be."

Josh laughs, interpreting Sam's statement as more of a joke than a threat, but I'm not as certain. "Sam, you're coming out with us tonight, right?" Josh asks.

"I believe the word Lex used was 'mandatory.' But yeah, I'd love to. Thanks."

Josh stamps out the last bit of his cigar, then stands up on the edge of the wall. My heart races at the potentially bad outcome that looms. Stumbling and falling, breaking a leg, busting open his face, or anything else that might leave Jess resentfully spending their honeymoon in the hospital instead of on a beach. He swings his arms back and lands with both feet firmly planted on the ground, much more gracefully than I expect after how much he's been drinking. He offers a hand up to me and I push against it as I jump off the wall.

Sam leans forward and lets himself do more of a fall back down to the ground. He prevents himself from toppling over by catching himself against my arm. Then he wraps his arm around my shoulder and sways slightly as he walks, his heavy feet dragging me down and making us fall behind everyone else.

"I just fucked everything up, didn't I?" I groan at Sam as I think about what to say to Keelie.

Sam lets out a single, forced laugh. "I think you're probably okay." Then he adds with a huge grin, "Chillax, Moog."

"What the hell do you know, you fucking idiot?"

"I know my sister," he replies harshly, "and so do you. So why are you second-guessing that all of a sudden?"

Sam yanks open the door to the reception, the music growing loud as we are engulfed in that world once again. He ushers me inside, not giving me a chance to dispute what he's said, before running off to the bar and leaving me alone to figure out what to do next.

VII

Saturday, September 22nd

We're quickly approaching the portion of the evening where laughs are replaced with uncontrollable giggles, words are spoken in shouts even when they don't need to be, and conversations happen with only a few inches of space between participants. My lonely sobriety has become very apparent. So apparent that I even get asked about it. "Hey, Matty, how are you holding up?" I put on an enthusiastic smile, raise my sad, booze-free drink, and cheerily say "I'm great" before changing the subject as fast as possible.

I'm not great. I'm actually pretty miserable. There's nothing quite like being the lonely sober guy during the second half of a wedding reception. Even June's company would be comforting right now, but she's at a table in the corner flirting with Jeff, slamming back vodka sodas at an alarmingly fast pace as she casually touches his arm and laughs. It takes every ounce of my attention not to look over at June and Jeff. Being the pathetic, lonely, sober guy idly watching as his fake date gets swept away by the father of the groom would be an all-time low for me. Ignoring them seems easy enough, but then my brain pings with a series of questions, all mostly of the what-the-hell-is-she-thinking variety, and just like that, I'm back to making sideways glances at them.

Leaving now would be best for everyone. My friends could stop asking about me, June could get on with hooking up with Jeff, Keelie wouldn't have to worry about me trying to kiss her again. Everyone would benefit from me leaving. So why am I still here? Because I told my friends I would be. Because I need to prove I can handle this.

Instead of deciding for myself to leave, maybe I can talk Chris into making that decision for me. I'll call him, tell him how I feel, and with any luck, he'll encourage me to leave. He'll say that being overwhelmed by sobriety is dangerous and that I should get myself out of this lonely, pathetic situation. I can blame the decision to go on him and make my exit.

My feet slowly shuffle up each of the black iron steps on the spiral staircase that leads to the rooftop, moving as casually as possible so as not to draw attention to myself. All the chairs that were set up on the roof earlier have disappeared. The golden hoop is gone; all that's left is an empty rooftop and the sparkling lights of the Cleveland skyline.

The heavy metal door slams shut behind me, and the sound of the reception below is dramatically muffled. Instead of facing the city, my usual go-to in a setting like this, I gaze out at Lake Erie. The almost pitch-black waves ripple in and crash along the shoreline, the soft sound barely audible beneath the sounds of the city. The cold breeze that blows my way is not quite as refreshing now as it had been earlier. My hands press down on the short brick wall that encircles the entire rooftop, my forehead against the taller glass panels that extend the barrier. Did some drunk moron have to fall off this roof before they put up the glass?

Leaning against the brick ledge, I pull my phone out of my pocket and start a text to Chris: *Can I call you?* I'm about to hit send when the door to the stairs slams shut once again. Someone followed me up here. Before I get the chance to look up to see who it is, she announces her presence with a shout.

"Can we talk about what the hell just happened?" Keelie yells from the other side of the roof. She takes hurried steps toward me.

"I'm sorry. It was stupid," I apologize.

"It was very stupid," she shouts back. With one kiss, I've ruined all the progress we've made this weekend toward being friends again.

"Can we forget about it?" I beg. "Please?"

She shakes her head as she stomps closer and closer to me, angrily. I stand from my seat on the ledge and take a step closer. Even in her fury, I'm drawn to her. She makes no hesitation, allowing her angry strides to bring her mere inches from my face. The soft sounds of Lake Erie on one side of us, the Cleveland skyline on the other, the lights from the city giving her face a soft, warm glow. She clenches her jaw, her nostrils flaring with each deep breath she takes as she glares at me.

Keelie lifts a hand as if she might slap me right across the face, but instead she presses it firmly along the side of my head, her fingers burrowing into my hair, as she pulls me into her and kisses me hard and sloppily, and so intensely it sends chills down my spine. I gasp in a deep, surprised breath through my nose and am immediately hit with the scent of whiskey fresh on her tongue mixing with the sweet smell of coconut lingering in her hair. A smell so tantalizingly comforting, I wish I could capture the scent of this moment and live in it forever.

I grasp her hip with one hand and wrap my other arm up the middle of her back, my hand falling between her shoulder blades, pressing her even closer to me. She leans heavily against me in reply, pushing me up against the short brick wall, my back leaning against the glass. Her hand drifts down to the small of my back, dipping under my jacket. A soft grunt escapes my mouth, muffled by her lips. I can't help it. This moment is so incredible that my brain shuts off and forgets to tell my mouth not to release strange noises in its absence.

She leans into me with such intention that one of her feet completely leaves the ground, her knee squeezing slightly against the side of my leg. My hand wanders down her thigh, toward the start of the slit on her dress that has been plaguing my mind all day. With my hand down low on her leg, just above her knee, I grip onto the bare skin of her thigh, testing the waters. Keelie's deep, tongue-twisting kisses and clawing hands don't seem to be the slightest bit fazed by my wandering fingertips. Slowly, my fingers inch higher up her thigh, the opening of her dress getting narrower the further I get. The top of the slit rests on the back of my wrist, and I hesitate for only a moment to see if this is the threshold we aren't able to cross.

Instead, Keelie only pushes further, untucking my shirt so she can tuck her hand into my waistband, her nails scratching parts of me that haven't felt her touch for almost three years. This is a clear invitation for my hand to continue its own journey. I push beyond the slit of the dress, the entire skirt rising as my wrist lifts it. My hand explores the circumference of her leg, my fingers tracing the crease at the top of her thigh. She lets out a soft moan and sucks my bottom lip. Her sound vibrates through me. I would do anything to hear that sound again.

Leaning back even further into the wall, I grip the back of Keelie's leg and lift it against mine. Her straddling stance becomes a necessity for standing, as does keeping one of my hands firmly gripping onto her to maintain her balance. Wrapping all the way around the back of her leg, my other hand explores the soft, warm skin of her inner thigh. She pulls away from my kiss, and I bring my wandering hand to a halt. Instead of telling me to stop, she drops her head forward against my shoulder and lets out a soft moan, encouraging me to keep going.

My fingertips press into the back of her leg, just below her butt cheek. With every stroke of my fingers along the innermost portion of her thighs, every *accidental* brush against the center of it all, Keelie lets out a soft breath of warm air that whispers in my ear. I softly kiss the top of her exposed shoulder. She throws her head back, away from my chest, so I can continue the trail along her neck. Her hands are climbing inside my shirt, her fingers digging in deeply to the soft skin of my back, her warmth radiating through me.

As I kiss the small, hidden space behind her ear, she lets out another soft moan that sends a shot of pleasure through my veins, the same wonderful feeling that oxycodone brings. With that jolting reminder, a warning bell triggers in my head. I pull my lips away, pressing my forehead to hers. Our chests rising and falling in tandem. Keelie's hands grip tightly onto my rib cage, feeling every breath as it enters my lungs. She scrunches one side of her face slyly, her lips still parted, then dives back in, her mouth coming over mine. I allow myself to be distracted by her hurried kisses and wandering fingers for only a moment longer before I pull away again.

"What are we doing, Mia?"

She lets out a few heavy breaths. "I think we're hooking up on the roof." She grins slightly, amused by her own answer.

Before she stuck her tongue in my mouth, I was thinking about the possibility of falling off the roof, and now we are leaning against the thin glass barrier at full force, seriously tempting fate. My hesitations, however, have nothing to do with falling from the roof and everything to do with the fact that Keelie and I are not at all on the same page about this sudden reunion. I loosen my grip on her, but my hand stays firmly planted on the back of her thigh. I can talk to her while still pressing her pelvis into mine, right?

Keelie jets her chin straight into the air. "Val!" she groans without me needing to say anything at all.

I smirk at her. "Mia?"

"If you're going to get in your head about this, can you at least not let it distract you?" She tightens her grip on my ribcage, pulling herself closer to me.

"No can do."

She sighs, pressing her forehead against mine, resigning. "I know."

"We can continue this *later*," I promise, unable to resist stealing another kiss, "back at the hotel. Just one more hour."

Keelie presses her lips to mine again, then biting down on my lower lip, she growls through her teeth, "I want you now."

I choke on the words as she says them. My heart lurches from my chest and finds a new home in my dick, which now has a pulse of its own. Keelie's leg gently presses against it, begging me to take back what I said and continue touching her.

"One hour," I repeat, trying to convince myself as much as I'm trying to convince her. There's nothing I want more than to take another soft bite out of her neck, to explore further beneath her dress, to feel myself inside her right here on the roof, surrounded by the lights of downtown Cleveland and the sounds of Lake Erie. But I'd also love to hold her in my arms, nuzzle into her neck, fall asleep with her by my side.

"Fine," she says softly, reading the pleas in my eyes. "One hour." The corner of her mouth curls into a grin. She presses a finger to my lips to shush me as she whispers in my ear, "*Our secret.*"

I kiss her finger in agreement. She gives a quick wink, then takes off for the stairs, returning to the reception and leaving me standing alone on the roof in disbelief.

I am the biggest moron in all of Cleveland. By the time I'm actually able to make it back down to the reception, each of my footsteps fall heavy on the black iron stairs, dragging like cement blocks. I'm utterly baffled at what an idiot I am. Keelie had her fingers in my hair, her hands under my shirt, and her tongue in my mouth, and I told her to stop. What the hell is wrong with me? My moronic status doesn't end at the Cleveland city limits.

I'm likely the stupidest guy in all of Ohio, possibly the entire country, maybe even the world.

One more hour. In one hour, I will be redeemed. I will trade the possibility of a hurried rooftop encounter for hours with her. Undressing her. Touching her. Tasting her. Everything I have been missing since she left will be mine again. *As long as she doesn't change her mind.*

My mind flips to autopilot to help me cope with the thought of potentially giving up my only shot to be with Keelie. Without conscious recognition, my feet take me straight to the bar.

The bartender greets me, "Hey, Club Soda Guy." Her words are a shock to my system as I realize what I'm doing—finding my way back to the bar to bury my fear. A couple of shots of whiskey will make all my worries about Keelie vanish. Most likely because if I have a couple of whiskey shots, any chance of being with Keelie tonight will vanish, too.

"Better make this one a double," I beg her with a pained smile.

While the bartender scoops up some ice, my eyes scan the room for Keelie. She's back on the dance floor, her hands in the air as she sways her body from side to side. She's loudly singing along to the song. Almost the entire room is singing along, it seems. But then she catches me staring, and she holds onto my gaze with an unmistakable fire burning in her eyes. She places one hand on her thigh, hooking a finger on the slit of her dress, and raises it slightly before quickly dropping it, giving me a quick flash of extra skin.

My lip curls into a smile and I shake my head at her slowly, subtly. She is so fucking incredible. I cling to her tantalizing gaze, only breaking our stare when the bartender turns back around and places a glass in front of me with two lime wedges instead of one.

"Double club soda," she announces.

"Thanks," I say, accepting my disappointing drink.

By the time I look back up, Keelie is no longer looking my way, leaving me eagerly awaiting the next moment that our eyes meet.

I pace around the room with my double club soda in hand. If I sit, it will be obvious that I'm alone and on the sidelines, but if I keep moving, I might build a facade of being included, of having a good time. As I stride past the dance floor, Lex spots me. After a brief chin nod to recognize her, I keep walking as if I have somewhere important to be.

Her tall stiletto heels make a few loud clacks behind me as Lex takes large strides to catch up to me. She tugs on my forearm, bringing me to an abrupt stop.

"What are you doing?" she snaps, her sentence flubbing together like one big word instead of four individual ones.

"What do you mean?"

"You've walked past here three times now," she points out. "What are you doing?"

"Keeping myself busy so I'm not tempted to drink."

Lex snatches the glass from my hand and takes a sip, her lipstick leaving a smudge on the black straw.

I sigh. "It's club soda."

She squints her eyes at me, handing it back. "Why don't you keep yourself busy by dancing? It's a fucking wedding reception, Matty."

"I'm only good at dancing when I'm drinking."

"No one's good at dancing when they're drinking," Lex snatches the drink from my hand once again and sets it on a nearby table. "Let's go."

She seizes my arm and drags me into the crowd. Small specs of white light spin around the room, illuminating faces for the briefest moment before scrolling onto someone else.

Lex immediately begins swaying her body to the up-tempo music, arms in the air. I give her one last pleading glare, begging her to let me go back to walking circles around the room. She shakes her head, and when I don't immediately take up the beat, she jerks my hands toward her and forces me to dance along. It takes less than a minute for the nervousness to subside and joy to settle in. Soon I am dancing without any coaxing from Lex at all, spinning and twisting and enjoying myself all at the same time.

Lex takes my hand for a spin, but instead of allowing me to spin her, she spins me around, catching me against her shoulder and giving me a forceful shove away from her and straight into Keelie. Keelie's taken-aback expression is quickly washed with one of recognition. I place an apologetic hand on her shoulder and shout out a "Sorry!" into her ear, turning my head to throw a glare in Lex's direction, but Lex has already vanished.

We share an almost silent laugh, knowing that Lex was attempting to set us up for a connection that is already well on its way. Keelie clasps my hand in hers, places her other hand on my shoulder, and takes quick steps to the beat of the fast-paced song. For this one song, we spin and dip and turn like we used to, quickly rediscovering every move we had forgotten. The speckled lights that dance around the room light up her face. The smoldering flame burning behind her amber eyes, the way her lips part to reveal a glimpse of her teeth, the feel of her body brushing against mine. It all leaves me excited for what's to come.

When the song changes, she gives my hand a squeeze, takes a quick glance down at my lips as she takes a short step backward, adding distance between us. She nods her head to the side of the room where our friends have gathered in a small circle of dancing. I reluctantly follow her in joining them, and spend the rest of our time at the reception catching Keelie's eyes from across our group.

When the band announces the final slow song of the night, they invite all the couples back out onto the dance floor for one last chance to "dance with the one you are leaving with tonight." Keelie's eyes dart straight to mine. A mischievous grin tugging at the corner of her mouth, my blood pressure skyrocketing. I *am* the one she's leaving with tonight, aren't I? But then she quickly looks away, tapping on Sam's shoulder and probably saying something like, "I never got to steal a dance with my date," because he smiles, throws back the last of his drink, and holds out a hand for her.

This last slow dance should have been mine. Another chance to hold her again, pull her hips close to mine, nuzzle my face against hers. *Soon*, I remind myself. *Soon I will have all that and more.*

Josh steps onto the dance floor with Annie. Jess is nowhere to be found during the last dance of her own wedding. But then two arms wrap around my waist from behind, and Jess ducks under my arm. With a blissful, alcohol-smoothed tone, she reminds me, "You still haven't gotten a dance with the bride."

"Jess Parker, can I have this dance?" I offer my hand to her.

The sound of her new name brings a blissful bubble of happiness to her face as she releases her grasp on my waist.

"Don't look now," she teases as she offers me her hand, "but I think Jeff is stealing your date."

Jeff and June have skipped the last dance and still sit at the table in the corner, June sipping from her never-ending vodka soda. Jeff leans in close to her, talking in her ear in a low voice, unbuttoning a fifth button on his shirt as he does. There aren't many more buttons left before he's simply not wearing a shirt at all. *That* would make Lex lose her mind.

"That's alright," I assure her. "My heart belongs to someone else."

Instead of simply acknowledging what I said, she dives in deeper, asking suspiciously, "Can we talk about that kiss?"

I shake my head. "There's nothing to talk about. I got the wrong read on the situation and shouldn't have done it." Keelie's eyes meet mine from the other end of the dance floor. A heavy sigh escapes my lips. My eyes remain locked on Keelie as I continue this conversation with Jess. "What did she say about it?"

"Pretty much that." She shrugs. "That she thinks she might have been sending you mixed signals. She's not mad about it."

She's definitely not mad. Keelie's smoldering gaze from across the room makes the urge to put my hands on her all the more overwhelming. Jess continues to speculate, continues to let me know more about her conversation with Keelie, but my mind is elsewhere. My eyes lock on the flirtatious glances Keelie is passing me from the other side of the room. I'm doing my best to conceal the smile creeping across my face, hoping to prevent Jess from catching on. But then Keelie takes her hand off Sam's shoulder and gives her jaw a slow, deliberate scratch, June's signal for "Get me the hell out of here." My heart surges in my chest—it might explode. I can't suppress my happiness any longer, especially not after Keelie snaps her eyes to mine once more, softly raising an eyebrow to make sure I caught on to her secret code.

"Matty?" Jess laughs. "Who are you smiling at?" Before I'm able to respond, Jess shifts her body and spins us around, her eyes meeting Keelie's from across the room. She furrows her brow, suddenly suspicious of us. "What was that?"

The look I give Jess in reply is one that attempts to assure her it's nothing, but Jess doesn't buy it.

"She asked if we could share a ride back to the hotel," I explain, wishing more than anything that I could have come up with a better lie than that.

Jess deflates. "She's not coming out with us?"

"I guess not. First I'm hearing about it, too." I feel a small pang of guilt about lying to Jess. It's the smallest fraction of guilt that will quickly melt away as soon as I get my hands back inside Keelie's dress.

Jess narrows her eyes at me for a moment longer before dropping it. "Are you sure *you* don't want to come out with us?"

"I am incredibly grateful for the offer, but I'm going to turn in after this. I've had much more than I can handle in one weekend." This truth is enough to erase my guilty feelings.

She nods sympathetically. "Thank you so much for being here, Matty. We're both so happy you could make it." She squeezes my hand softly. "Everyone is. Lex and Annie were so excited when I told them you were coming. It's been really great to see you."

The song fades, and the band starts up one last peppy song to get everyone excited for going out, going home, or otherwise getting the hell out of here.

Jess presses a soft kiss to my cheek and says, "We'll see you tomorrow, right?"

I nod. "Absolutely."

The guests who are drunk enough to want to continue the party for a few more hours rendezvous on the dance floor during the last song. Keelie gives a sympathetic nod to Jess, who has already confronted her about turning in early. Jess throws one last suspicious look my way as Keelie approaches me.

"Hey, I'm turning in. I've got a car coming to take me back to the hotel. Wanna share it?" She makes sure she speaks loudly enough that anyone nearby who wants to can hear it.

"Sure, thanks," I reply equally as loudly, though I'm certain we're fooling no one.

She lifts a foot, then holds out a hand to me for balance. Offering my elbow to her, she grasps it with one hand as she uses the other to undo the straps on her shoes, kicking them off altogether. The touch of her hand sends a surge of heat down my spine.

Once we're out the door, away from the eyes of the rest of the wedding party, Keelie glances around for anyone that might recognize us. When she doesn't see any familiar faces, she stands up on her tiptoes and steals a quick kiss. Latching a hand onto her waist, I pull her toward me, taking a kiss more like the one I have earned after an hour of watching her make eyes at me from across the room. She swings her arms around my neck, her shoes lightly tapping against my back as she does.

She kisses me hurriedly, her breath sweeping across my face every time she pulls away. Without warning, she suddenly pulls back and stands next to me as if nothing happened. She cautiously slips her hand under my jacket, wrapping her arm around my waist and nuzzling her temple into the side of my chest. With my arm around her shoulders, I pull her in tightly to me, taking in a deep breath of her whiskey-and-coconut scent. The familiarity of it makes me feel at home.

She carefully untucks the tiniest portion of my shirt so she can stroke one finger along my skin just under my waistband. As soon as our ride shows up, I'm going to be all over her, further exploring beneath her dress before we even make it back to the hotel. Reading my mind, she lifts her phone to check our ride status impatiently. Our driver is still two minutes away.

"Hey, guys!"

We both jump, turning to see Jenna and Andy approaching. Andy is stumbling over himself, even more drunk than he was last night.

Keelie casually removes her hand from my waist as if it were never there at all. After Keelie returns their hello, Jenna offers us a ride back to the hotel. I attempt to get out the kindest "no, thanks" I can muster, as Keelie exclaims, "That'd be great!"

Jenna laughs, and I reluctantly change my vote. "Sure. Thanks, Jenna."

Keelie cancels the ride request, and we follow Jenna to their car. Andy needs my help to climb into the front seat. I'm very familiar with the struggle of tall cars and clumsy, drunken legs. In the back seat, Keelie sits with her legs outstretched toward my side of the car. She's allowed her dress to ride up, the slit showing off a good portion of her leg. If we had gotten a ride from a stranger as planned, I would be saddled up next to her right now, with my leg pressed against hers, my hand under her dress, my lips running across her chest. Instead, we sit on opposite sides of the back seat, leaving me only to imagine touching every inch of her.

The short drive back to the hotel feels so long that a few minutes might as well be a few hours. We pull into the parking lot next to the hotel. I assist Andy in climbing out of the front seat. He places his hands firmly against the side of the car until Jenna is able to walk around and give him a steady hand of support.

Keelie stops short of the entrance and says, "I think I'm going to go check if that place down the road is still serving food. I'm starving."

"I'll come with you," I offer casually.

Andy pipes in, "I could use a snack," and my heart drops.

"I think what you really need is sleep," Jenna reminds Andy, who can hardly keep his eyes open anymore. He grunts out an agreement, and they step into the lobby without us.

Keelie's hands are full of her belongings, but that doesn't stop her from placing both her hands on my chest, her shoes tapping against my arm on one side, her wallet clutch tapping me on the other. She says, "I don't want food. I just wanted to ditch them so I could do this some more." She rises onto her toes and kisses me again. My hands grasp onto her, one on each side of her waist, pulling her close to me, so grateful that we have found our way back here. As she pulls away, she runs the backs of her hands down the length of my arm, tucking her wallet under one arm so she can grab my hand and lead me into the lobby.

When the doors to the elevator close behind us, Keelie presses her body against mine, pushing me up against one side. I snatch her wallet from under her arm, shoving it into my pants pocket, freeing up her arm to snake around my back and untuck a portion of my shirt, her hand diving under my waistband. With my hands low on her hips, I pull her pelvis into mine. When the elevator dings, she pulls away, running her free hand along the edge of her hair and standing next to me as if nothing happened.

Keelie strides off the elevator confidently. Once she has the chance to look around and see that the hallway is empty, she extends a hand back to me, lacing her fingers in mine.

"Sam went out with everyone else," she explains to me in a hushed voice as if he were right around the corner. "He won't be back for at least a couple of hours." She glances back at me, looking for a sign of protest before she squeezes my hand tighter, striding right past room 744 to her room at the end of the hall.

She releases my hand as we approach her door, plucking her wallet from my pocket and unzipping it. She flips through all its contents, all loosely tossed inside in search for her room key. This isn't new for her. She used to constantly lose things in the unending depths of her wallet. I press my body fully against her back as I, rather impatiently, wait for her to find the key. Placing my hands on the front of each of her thighs, I pull her body closer to mine, my chin pressed alongside her ear, my breath brushing the top of her shoulder. She momentarily pauses her search to reach backward and wrap a hand around my neck. I kiss her shoulder again, and she gently tosses her head back in pleasure.

Nuzzling my face along hers, I whisper in her ear, "You know if you actually used the card slots, you would have found your room key by now." My lips place a soft kiss behind her ear.

She spins around in place, her back against the door, my body falling into hers. She holds the room key up to my face to show me with a proud grin. "Don't start on that again, Val."

I snatch the room key from her hand and kiss her softly, using my hips to press her harder against the door. Without looking, without pulling my lips from hers, I fumble with the room key at the door, trying to get it to line up with the slot and get the door unlocked.

She gives me a gentle shove, snatching the room key from my grasp once more and says, "You know, if you just used the card slot, you could be unzipping my dress by now."

The urgency to get to the other side of this door becomes unbearable. It is no mystery to either of us what is about to happen, but hearing her describe it without any room for misinterpretation sets me on fire. She spins back around, facing the door. I grip her forearm, pulling her hand toward the card reader, but she twists her wrist at the last second, creating a T shape between the card and the card reader. I let out a reflexive groan, and she responds with a soft laugh.

"Oh, did you . . .? Did you want to get in *here*?" she teases, turning sideways to glance back at me.

I place a hand along the far side of her face, roughly pulling my mouth toward her nearest ear and grumbling out a breathless, "Yes." With my palm flat against the front of her thigh, I pull my body closer to hers with one unmistakable thrust. "Adesso." *Right now.*

She effortlessly swipes the card into the card reader. It lights up green and lets out a quick beep to let us know we can proceed.

There is hardly time for the door to slam behind us before Keelie drops everything in her hands. Her wallet, phone, and shoes all clatter to the floor. She snorts a quiet laugh, satisfied with her efficiency, as I press her up against the door. Bracing myself with one hand pressed onto the smooth wooden surface, and the other grasping the round curve of her hips, I slide my touch around her to the crease at the top of her thigh. Keelie sinks her hands down the front of my chest, wrapping each hand around my sides, then up to my shoulder blades. Her hands guide the sleeves of my jacket off each arm, and I release my hold on her momentarily as the jacket falls off me and into her hands. She tosses it across the room with another small snorting laugh.

The sound snaps my mouth to hers like a magnet, and I'm stealing hungry tastes of her lips again.

She breaks off my kiss, pressing her forehead to mine, her lips still parted and calling to me to kiss her again. Just as I'm about to take another taste, she turns, tearing her lips out of reach, flipping the deadbolt, then the safety latch. I trace a finger down the curve of her exposed shoulder before proceeding into the room without her, kicking off my shoes and loosening my tie as I walk.

"What are you doing?" she snaps at me playfully, her body leaning against the door, fingers splayed open, pressing evenly into the wooden surface like claws.

I respond by giving the loosened end of my tie a tug and pulling it from around my neck, presenting it to her. She takes a few quick strides toward me, snatching the tie from me as she says, "I wanted to do that." She tosses it in the same direction as my suit jacket, stealing another sloppy kiss as repayment.

I laugh an apology into her mouth. "You're going to have to be quicker than that," I challenge.

She wastes no time scrunching her hands along my stomach, untucking the bottom of my shirt and immediately getting to work plucking open each of the small buttons, taking a few backward steps as she goes, pulling me further into the room.

I unbutton the ends of each sleeve, but before I'm able to pull my arms out, she falls onto the bed, pulling at the edges of my shirt to take me down with her. Her hands trace the length of my arms, sliding off each sleeve as her lips meet mine again.

My hand latches onto her leg above her left knee, eagerly digging my fingertips into her soft flesh before skating softly up her thigh, pushing past the slit in her dress once again, gathering the skirt up around her hip on one side.

Her fingers dance across my chest, across my heart beating rapidly into her touch, before she continues drawing lines down my stomach to the clasp of my pants. Not even one second passes after she has them undone, before I flip over onto my back and slide them off my hips, briefs and all.

My eagerness brings a smile to both of our faces, her lips hurriedly meeting mine, telling me she's feeling that eagerness, too. Without backing off on the force of her kiss, she lifts the ends of her dress above her knees so she can straddle my stomach, one knee pressing into each side, her curls falling around my face, like a flowing curtain settling after a gust of wind.

Unsatisfied with our uneven standing, me naked while she is still fully clothed, I pinch the zipper of her dress between my fingers, slowly dragging it down to her hips. My focus shifts when the dress doesn't immediately fall open, I sit up on my elbows, confusion likely overtaking my face.

Keelie rolls off me with a laugh, reading my frustration, turning away from me and pointing to her back. "There's a clasp."

"Cazzo," I curse, sitting up, gingerly opening the small metal clasp that stands between me and Keelie's naked body.

Once I have it undone, she stands, allowing the dress to fall to the floor, encircling her feet. A tiny burst of disappointment surges through me, as I'm faced with another layer of fabric standing between me and her soft, warm skin. She crawls toward me, meeting my lips, as my hands search for a way to remove the torso-crushing contraption keeping her from me.

"Get rid of this," I grumble between kisses, her mouth coming over mine before I am even able to finish the thought.

She pulls back, looking at me with a grin so tantalizing I want to kiss it right off her face. "What's the rush, Val?"

With my fingers tangled in her hair, I pull her to me with the strength of every ounce of bottled up *lust* I had felt for her tonight. Every time she made eyes at me from across the room. Every mischievous smile that pricked her lips. Every second that passed between the moment I first saw her in the hallway to right now, as I feel her touch on my skin once again. Sitting up, pulling myself toward her, pulling my mouth toward her ear, I whisper back, "Ho bisogno di te." *I need you.*

She lets out a breathless gasp just before my lips take hers, a kiss she quickly breaks off as she springs off the bed once again to get rid of the only thing keeping her from coming in full contact with me. This time, when she crawls across the bed toward me, about to straddle my stomach once again, I grab her by her hips and flip her onto her back, determined to enjoy every second of this.

My palms feel her legs, the soft skin of her hips, the curve of her waist, and the peak of her nipples. Every bit of her that I haven't felt in almost three years. I want to savor every inch of her, *taste* every inch of her. My hands dig into her sides—my fingers holding her tight, but my thumbs brushing softly against her skin. My mouth drags across her hip bone, down her thigh, before slowly retracing each careful step, finding its way back to her lips once more.

Her fingers grip the back of my neck as my hips slide between her thighs. Each kiss is deeper, hungrier than the last. We're enjoying each taste as if it might be our last. Pulling my lips away, leaving her desperately clawing at me for more, I taste the length of her neck, feeling her throat vibrate beneath my lips as she lets out a satisfied moan. That sound lights a fire inside me. I can't bare the thought of stalling this for even one second more. I lift her thigh to my hip, slowly pushing into her. We return to this familiar place as though we've never been away. Finding our rhythm together as though it's where we were always meant to be. She takes a fistful of my hair, pulling me to her mouth for another tongue-twisting kiss before pressing her cheek against mine as she presses her hips up into me. Our heavy breaths whisper in each other's ears until breaths turn into breathless gasps, then back to desperate, hungry kisses. I lose sight of everything around me, focused only on the euphoria that engulfs us. The oxycodone-like euphoria that surrounds us.

The phantom taste pricks the back of my throat. It infiltrates my life, even now. In this moment, when I have everything I've ever wanted, oxy slithers its way in, reminding me that one pill can make me feel like this and *more*.

But I don't want more. I have everything I want right here. *For now*.

I grip onto Keelie's leg tighter, pressing into her harder, faster, trying to outrun the oxy craving, trudging through it, leaving it behind. A moment ago, the world had been nothing but me and Keelie. Now it's me and oxy. The taste of oxy in my throat, the bliss of oxy in my head. I don't even notice as Keelie hits her peak, until she grips one hand into the back of my neck, the other digging into my hair once again.

I lose all tempo, all speed, all rigidity after that. There's nothing left for me to give, my mind has been lost to thoughts of oxy.

Keelie runs her hand down the side of my face, pressing her mouth to my opposite ear, whispering, "Come back to me, Val."

I smile at her apologetically, pressing my lips to hers once again, my mind returning to Keelie. Her breathless whispers, the soft touch of her fingers across my back, the sweet smell of coconut in her hair. Keelie's beautiful smile, the way she snorts when she laughs. The way she reads my mind, knows my thoughts, knows everything about me. Remembering all the things I love about my beautiful *Mia Mae* is enough to bring me back to this moment, to push oxycodone out of my mind long enough to collapse into Keelie's arms.

My body refuses to move once we finish. I can't leave the comfort of being wrapped in her embrace. I feel safe here, with my forearm framing her head, her heavy breaths whispering in my ear. I burrow my face alongside hers, my nose brushing against her diamond-studded earlobes. This is where I belong. I don't need *more*. I don't need oxy.

She traces one of her fingers down the center of my back, then back up, sending a shaking chill through my entire body.

Her cheek presses into mine as she smirks, satisfied at the reaction she is able to elicit from me. Then she does it a second time, running her finger down the center of my spine and slowly back up, another wave of chills rippling through me.

"That trick still works, huh?" She laughs as her finger descends the length of my back once more.

I push away from her, grabbing the wrist of her teasing arm, pulling another deep kiss from her lips as I pin her hand to the bed.

"Quit it," I growl through smiling teeth. My lips hover so close to hers that they brush up against them as I form my words.

A guilty laugh bubbles from her lips. She bites her bottom lip contemplatively.

Being here with her fills me with an overwhelming bliss. Feelings of happiness, calmness, and joy fight for a place in my mind. And then, all these bouncing feelings converge, and all I feel for her is love. A love that consumes me, wraps me up, fills every inch of me. I love her. I've always loved her. I always will love her.

But that doesn't matter. Not anymore. *I've lost her.*

The look of happiness melts off Keelie's face as she asks, "Where'd you go?" and then tilts her head so she can look at me out of the side of her eye, suspiciously.

An uneasy laugh bursts from within me as I try to evade her questioning, try to avoid admitting something I know will crush her. Admitting that while her legs wrapped around my waist and her fingers tangled through my hair, I couldn't stop thinking about oxy.

"What do you mean?" I ask cluelessly.

"You're in your head," she accuses, before softly asking, "What were you thinking about?"

Leaning my forehead against hers, I melt into her, feeling every inch of her against me. "I've missed you," I whisper to her, still trying to evade her question. Then, to avoid the rejection that might come by waiting for her reply, I add, "I guess I let that distract me."

It horrifies me how easily I'm able to fall back into lying to her. Not even three days and already I've shut myself off from her, lying to Keelie in order to protect my addiction.

"I know you better than that, Val," she reminds me.

A heavy sigh escapes my lips as I lower myself onto my side, settling into her shoulder. I run a hand down her side, over the ridge of her hips, down the front of her leg, and then retreat, bringing my hand to rest on her chest, with my arm resting along her sternum and my finger carefully tracing the line of her collarbone.

I hesitate, trying to decide the least hurtful way to tell her the truth, because I *need* to tell her the truth. I need to let her back in. I sheepishly admit, "I was thinking about pills."

Keelie's lips twist into a frown for a second before she kindly asks, "Did something trigger you?"

I scoff out a laugh. "Basically, anything that makes me happy is a trigger for me. Anything that reminds me of how I used to feel with oxy."

She nods her head a few times, contemplating what I've said, before simply replying, "Thank you for telling me." She presses her arm into my back, pulling me in for a hug. "I can't help you if you don't let me in."

"I'm trying. I am."

"It'll get easier," she assures me, and although we both know she doesn't have any idea what this will be like aside from what she's been told by words in a textbook, her comforting encouragement does make me feel better.

"I hope so," I sigh.

She traces a finger down the bridge of my nose, across my cheek, down my jawline, and over my bottom lip. Then she asks, "How'd you get the scar?" as she runs her finger across the rounded white line that slices through my upper lip.

Her soft touch sends chills down my spine. When her finger meets the center of my lips, I catch it in a quick kiss before replying, "I tripped on the porch steps at Mom and Dad's. Hit my face on the door frame."

She let out the softest gasp, one I wouldn't be able to hear if I weren't only a few inches from its source, as she familiarizes herself with this new piece of me.

"I didn't feel it at least," I say slanting my eyebrows at her apologetically so she knows that I know it was my own stupid fault. That *all of this* is my fault.

A grin pricks at the corner of her mouth as she fixes her eyes on mine, then drops her gaze to my lips. She stops tracing my scar with her finger and instead traces it one time with her eyes, before pressing her lips to mine for a kiss.

"It's weird that you have a scar I didn't know about." She squeezes me tightly into her side. "I don't like not knowing everything."

"You didn't miss much, trust me," I promise her.

She shakes her head. "We've both missed so much."

Keelie presses a kiss to my forehead, lingering there so I can feel every breath she takes against my skin. My whole body flutters with warmth. I might be able to win her back yet.

But then she whispers in my ear, "It was really great seeing you, Val." The way she says it gives her words the weight of a goodbye. It sends anxiety pulsing through me, reminding me once again that this doesn't mean anything to her. A quick nostalgia trip before she returns to her real life. This new life she's built without me.

I squeeze onto her tightly, pushing that thought out of my mind. At least for tonight.

VIII
Sunday, September 23rd

My head is mostly tucked under the plush comforter when I wake up. I stretch my leg across the bed to see if June has made it back from her night out. She isn't there. Light shines brightly into the room. Surely she should be back by now. Despite my typical level of apathy toward June, a slight panic washes over me. *Where is she?* She has a husband and a family, who will be looking for her. They might not even know where she is. Why didn't she come back? The slightly irrational thoughts consume me. I bolt upright, tossing the covers from my head.

Everything around the room is a mirror image of what I was expecting to see. There are two beds, not one. Instead of the bottles of alcohol that June had lined up on the dresser, there is a makeup bag, scrunchies, a few necklaces laid out. A luggage rack in the corner has a duffel bag, similar to the one I left at home, splayed open.

I'm still in Keelie's room.

"Mia?" I call out. There's no reply. I hesitate for a moment before trying again, not wanting the other occupant of this room to reply. "Sam?" I ask with much less confidence.

Nothing.

My phone isn't on the side table where I usually leave it. I throw off the overstuffed down comforter fully, and the cold air from the room crashes against my warm body that was wrapped inside the cocoon of sheets. I'm still completely naked. We fell asleep. I haven't slept for months. *How the hell did this happen?* My pants lie in a pile on the floor, my phone still in my pocket where I left it. Anxiety prickles every inch of my skin as I tap the screen on. I have three missed calls from Chris, with just as many text messages:

Where are you?

You owed me a call by midnight.

We had a deal. Call me now.

His last text came through at almost two in the morning. *Fuck.* He is going to be so mad. It's possible he won't ever let me leave the house again. Can he do that? He can as long as I want to keep living with him. I'm going to be confined to the walls of his home for a long time after this.

I quickly fire off a text to him: *Cristiano, mi dispiace tanto. Sto bene. I'll call you as soon as I can. Va tutto bene.*

I'm so sorry. I'm fine. Everything is fine.

My text is received with an immediate call back from him, but I don't have time to talk to him now. Right now, I need to find Keelie.

One by one, I collect each article of clothing that was thrown about the room. My suit jacket that Keelie had tossed far off into the corner with a soft snort of laughter. The shirt that she untucked from my pants with slow, scrunching fingers pressed against my hips, her fingers digging deep into the flesh of my back right before she pulled the shirt off me all together.

My tie somehow had landed in Sam's bag. Sam has enough clothes for a few more days. He is an overpacker, just like his sister—the result of being raised by a man who was always completely underprepared. They're leaving today. Surely Sam wouldn't mind if I borrowed something. He'd understand why a layer of deniability would be necessary as I walk down the hallway to my room. At least until I have the chance to talk to Keelie.

I place my pile of clothes neatly on the edge of Keelie's bed. Right about the same spot where she pulled me down on top of her and muffled her soft, tantalizing moans into my mouth. Her dress is still on the floor, lying in an O-shaped puddle where she stepped out of it. I carefully lay the dress across the bed, wishing Keelie were still here, lying on the bed in its place. *Why'd you leave, Mia Mae?*

I cautiously pull a pair of sweatpants and a shirt out of Sam's bag. My room key is still shoved inside my suit pocket. I dig it out and run down the hall. The door to Keelie's room slams shut behind me just as I realize I left my phone on the dresser. Chris would have to wait for his returned call.

When I slide the room key into my door, the green light flashes and the door makes a beep, but it doesn't budge. June turned the locks. Keelie did the same last night. Why didn't I hear her unlock them? Or hear Sam come back last night?

Shoving the key back into my pants pocket, *Sam's pocket*, I practically run to the elevator. The car dings at the lobby level, and as I round the corner, both Sam and Keelie are sitting at a table with coffees in hand. My stomach twists when I see her. *Why didn't she stay?* A heavy sinking feeling settles inside me.

She regrets this. She doesn't love you anymore.

The skin on my arm starts to crawl, and my hands shake.

She left you.

I press my tongue to the roof of my mouth, taking a deep breath through my nose before slowly letting it escape through my mouth. The phantom taste of oxy coats my throat. But oxy can't help me now. Only talking to her will make this better. With each exhale, I imagine the jitters in my hands pushing out of my body through the tips of my fingers.

My eyes are fixed on Keelie as I make my way across the lobby. She catches me out of the corner of her eye and raises her gaze to meet mine. Her soft whispers from last night echo inside my head, a rising fire pushing the doubtful feelings away.

Uncertainty washes over me again as I nod a hello in her direction and she sends her fake smile back before quickly turning to Sam. I'm too far away to hear her, but her lips make out the words *He's here.* Sam immediately jumps from the table and the sinking feeling in my chest returns.

He starts to ask, "Do you—" but then he quickly recoils, getting a better look at me and scowling as he changes course. "Are you wearing my clothes?"

I smirk guiltily and say, "This isn't going to affect us being bros again, is it?"

He considers, not looking too pleased with me, then with a lightness in his voice he says, "I'll let you know."

He holds his coffee cup out to me, nudging his forehead toward the pot close by to demand a refill as he grumbles back, "Go take my seat."

I shake my head. "It's okay, Sam. I can come back later."

He raises both eyebrows at me to emphasize the seriousness of his words as he replies, "I'm not the one asking."

My eyes dart to Keelie. She's not looking over at us. The sinking in my stomach turns into a twisting feeling. My stomach ties into knots that quickly spread to my lungs, cutting my breathing short.

"What's the temperature like over there?" I beg, "Give me something."

Snatching his newly filled cup from me, he says, "You'll be fine." He looks me up and down, examining the clothes once more. "You better give those back."

Without waiting for a reply, he walks off. Keelie gives him an appreciative glance as he passes. Then she sets her eyes on me. It's nothing like the look she gave me last night. Now, her expression is calculated, stiffer, friendlier. Before she even opens her mouth, I know this is not going to be the conversation I hoped to have with her.

My hand shakes return. The twist in my stomach chokes me all the way to the top of my esophagus. Any air I can take in is shallow and unquenching.

I take another breath through my nose and slowly push what little air makes it to my lungs out through my barely parted lips in a silent buzz.

"Can I sit?" I ask her nervously, taking another gasp for air.

She looks up at me, creating big sad eyes that pierce me right through my heart. A crooked smile forms on her face. "Of course you can," she whispers.

Her hands tightly grip the sides of her coffee cup, fidgeting with it, shifting the handle from one side to the other and back again. Instead of looking at me, her eyes follow the rim of her mug as it spins. She stops suddenly, raising her eyes to mine once more.

She tucks her bottom lip inside her mouth, sinking her teeth into it contemplatively, reminding me of each playful bite she drove into *my* bottom lip last night. As she releases her bite and her lip springs forward, I suction my tongue to the roof of my mouth, imagining I am sucking it again. Her mouth twitches into the slightest smile as she registers how I'm staring at her. But instead of telling me to stop, she carefully places her hand on the table, palm side up, offering it to me.

It doesn't matter if she means to take my hand with romantic intentions, or if she's trying to comfort me as she lets me down easy—I'll accept any excuse to touch her. Even if she wants to tell me this was all a huge mistake, I'll still cling to her grasp and hold her tight.

"Matty," she starts, but then immediately stops her thought to give my hand a squeeze. It's beginning to feel more and more like a slow, comforting breakup. Not that what we are doing can even be called breaking up, because that would require being back together.

She crinkles her brow, and her lips turn into a frown, as if she might cry at any moment. I squeeze her hand tighter, offering her all the comfort I can give, even if this conversation makes me want to run and hide. When she struggles to find the words, I give her a start to the conversation she wants to have. "Why'd you bail this morning?"

She guiltily sucks both her lips into her mouth, letting them loose with a light smack. "We never unlocked the door." She laughs. "I woke up this morning to a series of drunken texts from Sam, all to the effect of 'You're dead to me.'"

A soft, guilty laugh bubbles across my face. She gives my hand another squeeze.

"And the last one just said"—she clears her throat before she recites it from memory—"'I'm sleeping out in the hallway, whenever you and Matty are done *catching up*.'"

My guilty look grows. "So much for not telling Sam."

"It gets worse." Her smile matches mine. "Lex knows."

"What?" I groan, "How?"

"They shared a ride back to the hotel, and she was still in the hallway when he found out our door was bolted shut. She let him crash in her room for a bit." Her guilty smile fades to something more somber. "He said he wasn't out in the hallway long, but I still thought I owed him an apology." She squeezes my hand tighter. "I really did want to stay."

Rubbing my thumb along the back of her knuckles, I reply softly, "I wish you would have."

She drops eye contact. "Are you sure about that?"

"Am I sure?" I say with a slight laugh. "Of course I'm fucking sure."

My words echo inside my head. I hear how much I sound like Rich when I say them. Keelie's crooked smile indicates she recognizes the similarity, too.

She lets out a slow sigh, her eyes fixed on the table. "I thought that maybe . . ." She pauses as tears well up in her eyes. I want to jump up and pull her into a tight, comforting hug as I used to. "Maybe I didn't think it all the way through. I don't want to be a distraction to your recovery."

"I think about you every day, Mia Mae. You have always been a distraction to me, but you have never once kept me from sobriety."

She lets out a soft noise, a mix between a sob and a laugh, stifling it quickly. She meets my eyes again, a bit of the fire she had in them last night returning. She gives my hand another squeeze as I lift her hand to my lips, giving her a soft kiss on the back of her knuckles.

"We can't pick up where things left off," she says, then corrects herself, "*I* can't."

"What do you want to do?"

She takes in a huge breath of air, sighing it out slowly, her shoulders rising and falling, making me want to wrap my arms around her so I can feel her chest lifting against mine. She whispers, "I want to figure it out after this weekend. Right now I can't stop thinking about you kissing my neck."

A burst of electricity surges through me as her words bring the image back into my mind. Brushing her hair aside and kissing every inch of her bare shoulder up to the soft, untouched skin behind her ear.

Tilting my forehead to her, squinting an eye into my suspicious smile, I whisper back, "I don't want to be a distraction to you."

She lets out a soft, beautiful laugh and replies, "I'll try not to let it interfere."

She takes a slow, steady sip from her coffee mug, never parting her gaze from mine.

"I want to kiss you so bad right now." My mouth blurts out the thought before I get a chance to reel it back in.

She glances over my shoulder, looking at all the faces behind me to see if she recognizes any of them. "Then do it," she challenges me.

Scanning every face behind her, I determine the coast is clear. With my elbows firmly planted on the table, I lean into her. Her lips curl into the slightest smile as my lips meet hers. This kiss is softer than any we shared last night. Less blind passion, more loving familiarity. It's a long, steady kiss like the ones that came right before she left for work in the mornings or when I got home at night. The soothing, comfortable kiss of someone you've been sharing kisses with for over a decade.

Heat slowly fills my body, starting at my lips and melting me all the way down to my toes. Even after I pull away, I still feel the warmth growing inside me. My hand still grips hers tightly, never wanting to let her go.

"Are you sure we can't talk about this now?" I beg, hoping to get a clearer idea of where things stand between us.

She shakes her head confidently, knowing for certain only that she is not certain enough to make any life-altering decisions right now. "I need time to think about it."

"Why?" I reply instantly, begging her to give me an answer.

"Because," she snaps quietly, something shifting in her tone. She pulls her lips into her mouth and releases them with another *pop*. "Because it has nothing to do with how I *feel* about you. My feelings for you have always been the same."

She stops short of saying she loves me. She doesn't have to say it, though. I already know that's what she means.

She squeezes my hand tightly. "I know what life with an addict looks like and I need to decide if I'm ready for that again."

"I'm not that person anymore," I promise her.

She looks down at our hands intertwined between us. "I genuinely believe that you want to be done with pills. But we both know there's more to it than that. It's not a yes or no reaction."

"I don't just *want* to be done with pills," I plead with her. "I *am* done with pills. It's so much different this time."

She raises an eyebrow with a slow, disbelieving blink. She lifts her gaze back to mine, her eyes turning red with each deliberate blink, fighting off tears. "You've said that before."

My shoulders deflate at her harsh, albeit true, response. Now it's my turn to drop her gaze, not able to look at the fury building in her stare. "I know," I choke. "This time I mean it."

A tear streaks down her cheek. She quickly snatches it away. "You've said that before, too."

I wince. "What can I say to make you believe me?"

She swallows hard, stiffening her lip. "Nothing." She shakes her head. "There isn't anything you can say that will make me believe you. Not right now."

"Please, Mia," I beg, squeezing her hand.

"I don't want to fight with you about this, Val," she sighs, never one to agree for the sake of agreeing. The anger and fortitude on her face melt away. Her eyelids droop heavy, and she pinches her lips in tight to prevent a frown. "I have to go pack. Sam wants to leave soon."

Just like that, she's shut me out. She's ready to head back into her life without me once again.

"Okay," I attempt to say, but the words get caught in my mouth, making no sound at all.

"Okay." Keelie gives volume to the word I couldn't get out. "Do you still have your stuff in my room?"

I nod. Attempting sounds would be pointless.

She tilts her head toward the elevator, then walks away from me, away from our life together.

We stand far apart in the elevator once again, much as we did the first time we rode it together. But then she turns to me, and when I meet her eyes, a sob bursts from her lips and her hands jump up to her face to swipe the sorrow away.

I hold an arm out to her, inviting her to curl up under my arm one last time. She dives into my arms, burrowing her face into my side. I press my hand to her back, pulling her in close, feeling her breath quiver as she stifles a cry.

The elevator dings on our floor and she breaks away from me, wiping her eyes, letting out a deep exhale, pushing me out of her mind. Then she puts on that big fake smile of hers and confidently strides off the elevator as if she doesn't have a care in the world.

I take hurried steps to catch up to her. She fumbles with her room key at the door, and as I stand there behind her, I swipe one finger across her shoulder, brushing aside her hair so I can kiss her neck again. Something to remember me by. Her body sinks into mine. She reaches an arm back and burrows her fingers in my hair as she swipes the card in the card reader.

Sam is directly in our line of sight as the door opens. He looks up briefly, eyes focused on Keelie's reddened eyes and swollen lips. He doesn't meet my eye before digging through his duffel bag, folding and refolding the four things that are left.

Keelie hands me the stack of clothes lying on her bed. Another text lights up on my phone screen as I retrieve it from the dresser. I don't even look at it before shoving it into my pocket. Keelie stands in front of me, waiting.

"Let me know when you're leaving," I beg.

"I will."

She hooks a finger on my pants pocket, pulling me into her. I tuck the pile of clothes under my arm and place my free hand along the side of her face, gliding my lips across hers and then kissing her as if I'll never see her again. *Will I ever see her again?*

She breaks off our kiss, resting her forehead against mine, her fingers tracing the line of my hip bone. I give her one last quick kiss, then add distance between us once again.

I raise a hand to wave goodbye to Sam, and he turns up his head as if he just noticed we were here, waving back. Keelie gently brushes my arm as I step out the door and into the hallway —her silent but powerful goodbye.

"Where the fuck have you been?" Chris demands, the phone not even making a full ring before he answers.

"Mi dispiace tanto," I plead. *I'm so sorry.*

"Dove ti eri cacciato?" he repeats, angrier.

"Is Michelle there?" I ask, without answering his question.

"She can't help you, Picco."

"Please?" I beg. "I want to talk to both of you."

Chris's silence on the other end is more threatening than any words he can say. The anticipation of what he might do to me is scarier than anything that actually comes out of his mouth.

"Miche!" he yells out, a bit more angrily than intended. He calms his voice and adds, "It's Matteo!"

From a distance, Michelle says, "I'll be right back," likely to Luci or Katy, as she shuffles her way to Chris's side. "Hey, Matty," Michelle chimes in solemnly, likely having listened to Chris yell about how much he'd like to wring my fucking neck all night last night.

"Okay. What happened?" Chris asks, waiting for me to dig my own grave.

"I kissed Keelie last night," I say.

"Oh my God," Michelle gasps, "at the wedding?"

"At the reception," I correct her, "and after."

"After?" Michelle asks suspiciously. When I don't reply, she connects the dots and repeats, "Oh my God, really?"

"Yeah," I reply breathlessly.

"That's great!" she exclaims, then loses all confidence when Chris and I don't return the same excited sentiment. "Right?"

I sigh. "I think it was a onetime thing."

"Oh."

After another long and brutal silence, Chris finally asks, "Does this feel triggering to you?"

"No," I state confidently. "I didn't do this for Keelie."

I can hear the enthusiasm in his voice as he attempts to coolly reply, "That's good."

"Hey, so I've got this brunch thing I've got to go to with the Parkers . . ."

"Go," Chris allows. "Have fun with your friends."

"I'm sorry I didn't call last night," I apologize again.

"I'll see you at the airport tonight," Chris says, ignoring my apology, allowing us to forget it. "Five thirty."

"Grazie, Cristiano," I say. "Bye, guys."

They add a "See you tonight, Matty" and a "Ciao, Picco" before hanging up.

Back upstairs, I hover in the hallway outside of the room I share with June, hoping this time the door will be unlocked. More importantly, hoping she's alone, not wanting to add "awkward encounter with Jeff" to my list of activities for the weekend. As I slide the card into the card reader, the light on the door knob lights up green. Chills surge through my body at the sound, as it brings to mind the image of pressing Keelie up against her door last night.

June has unbolted the door. It swings open freely when I press down on the handle this time. My eyes stay glued to the ground as I slowly step into the room, searching for signs that June might not be alone. Everything looks to be exactly how it was yesterday morning. The shower is running in the bathroom. Pushing the door open a small crack, I search the reflection in the mirror to catch a glimpse.

With only one figure moving behind the frosted glass, I push the door open further and announce myself. "Hey, just me," I say, stepping into the bathroom and leaning against the granite countertop.

"Hello, stranger," June sings back, the extra emphasis on her *hello* acting as a verbal wink.

"Did you guys have fun last night?" I ask.

June shuts off the water as she laughs, either because she remembers something funny or because she blacked out and doesn't remember anything at all. "Your friends are a lot of fun."

While part of me is dying to know what she means by that, a smarter part of my brain knows better than to ask for any extra details about her night.

She pushes open the shower door a crack so she can feel for her towel and keep as much warm air in the shower as possible. Then she emerges with the oversize towel wrapped around her body and slung over her shoulder like a toga.

She struts out of the bathroom without giving me even the slightest glance. I follow her like a lost puppy, as she's trained me to. By the time I realize with disgust what I'm doing, it's too late to do anything about it.

She opens the closet door, examining her clothes, as I toss myself down on the bed, instantly regretting my chosen spot. *Jeff might have been here.* Maybe I do want to know the details of what happened with him last night after all, so I can stop thinking about it.

More than asking her about Jeff, I want to talk to her about Keelie. I would prefer to actually be with Keelie, but right now, all I have is June.

"Did you have fun with *Keelie*?" June asks, her voice almost mocking me.

"Yes," I reply vaguely.

"Are you serious right now?" She turns around, hand on her hip, looking annoyed with me. "You never shut up about her, and now you're clamming up? Details, please. All the juicy ones."

"I think she's going to break up with me again." I sigh.

"Break up with you? When did you guys get back together?"

"You know what I mean."

June plucks a blue shirt with billowing sleeves from the closet and lays it out on the bed. She strides across the room, over to the dresser, and lifts the handle of vodka she still has there.

"Well, if she does 'break up' with you," June patronizes me, "vodka will help."

She's probably right. Drinking myself into darkness could make this better. So could pills, if she could get them back from Sam before he leaves. Once Keelie goes back to her new life, I can get back to the way things used to be.

But then again, what do I have left of the way things used to be? I don't live in my parent's basement anymore. I live with Luci and Katy, who see me every day, who look forward to spending time with their uncle. I can't hang out with June anymore, at least not like we used to, not now that I know about Randy. About her family that is very much together, her family that she abandons for alcohol and pills time and time again.

A text from Keelie buzzes my phone: *Meet me in the lobby?*

I slide off the bed, crossing to June. She lifts the vodka bottle in my direction, but I gently push her arm back down, lowering the temptation away from me.

"That's not me anymore," I assure her. Then I gesture my phone in the general direction of the door. "Keelie's leaving. I have to go."

"Good luck, Matty," June says, for the first time choosing not to call me *Matt*.

She twists off the cap and takes a swig straight from the bottle.

The second the elevator doors open to the lobby, my eyes are immediately drawn to Keelie, who is standing at the front desk. She is in the midst of a conversation with the desk manager and doesn't look my way, but Sam does, nodding a hello in my direction as I approach. I softly scratch a hand on the small of Keelie's back as I step up to them, immediately regretting being so presumptuous. She turns her head to flash a quick smile at me. Everything inside me is heavy and aching.

"Thanks for helping us take everything out to the car, Matty," Keelie says, raising an eyebrow as if to say, *Get it?* It's not immediately apparent why she needs a cover for this interaction, but I nod anyway, holding out a hand to take a bag from her and slinging it across my shoulder.

Jess comes pattering around the corner a second later, adding a bit of clarity to the discretion, shouting out, "Don't leave yet! I'm here!" She swoops in on Keelie in a quick flash for a big animated hug.

Josh strides up behind Jess a few paces back. He laughs as he smacks a hand against Sam's shoulder. "I do not know how you are vertical right now."

A guilty laugh escapes Sam. "There's no such thing as too much fun."

Josh gives me a knowing glare. "Is that true, Matty?"

"There is absolutely such a thing as too much fun," I confirm confidently.

Josh and Jess swap places, Josh giving Keelie a barreling hug, and Jess giving Sam a quick hug as he thanks her for letting him tag along.

Jess turns to Keelie one last time. "We have to go finish setting up, but please let me know when you make it home?"

Before they leave, Josh adds, "Matty, we'll see you in an hour. We gave June all the details last night, so don't even think about trying to skip out." He adds in a quieter voice, "If we have to be there, you have to be there."

Jess snickers, peeking behind her to make sure no one overheard.

"I'll be there."

They wave goodbye, then Jess steals one last hug from Keelie before they run off to the banquet hall from which they emerged a moment ago.

"You have five minutes," Sam grumbles in my direction. At first his tone feels cold, angry almost, but then he nudges his chin in Keelie's direction. He's giving me one last chance to talk to her.

Keelie places her hand softly on my elbow to signal that we are going to walk outside before talking. Far away from prying ears, far away from anyone who can rescue me as she breaks me. She releases my arm, spinning through the revolving doors and leaving me to chase after her. Her feet slow, allowing me time to catch up. When I do, I extend an elbow to her. She loops her hand through, gripping tightly onto the top of my forearm, where it meets my elbow.

"It was really great to see you this weekend, Val," she says softly as I tuck her hand against my side.

"'Great seeing you.' That's what you want to say to me?" I tease.

She nods, then adds, "I had fun catching up with you."

She snorts a small laugh, gripping my arm tightly. She looks away for a moment with a reminiscent grin floating across her face, leaving me dying to know which part of last night she has running through her head right now.

"When do we get to talk about all this, Mia?"

"I don't know," she replies defensively.

"Is there anything I can do?" I plead, holding on to her hand.

She squeezes back tightly, but replies, "No. I need time to think about it."

"What are you going to do, make a pros and cons list?" I smirk at her.

She feigns offense. "I might."

"Can I add something to your pros list?"

She stops in her tracks, studying me. Maybe trying to decide whether the words I used were a coincidence, or whether I remember the night we first kissed as clearly as she does. I raise an eyebrow at her, awaiting her reply.

The corner of her mouth turns up in a smile, her eyes wide as though I told her something exciting is about to happen. She jokingly drops her expression to something more serious, ready to hear the incredibly useful pro I have to add to her list. "Go ahead."

Placing one hand firmly on her waist, and the other softly on the back of her neck, I pull her into me. As her lips fall over mine, her body sinks into my arms. If I weren't standing here, she might collapse onto the ground. When I pull away, I return her playful, inquisitive stare. *What do you think about that, Mia Mae?*

She clears her throat and nods once, gazing off as if she's contemplating it. "How very presumptuous of you to add that to the pro list," she decides, continuing her walk toward the car as if that never happened. "I'll give that point some consideration."

"Okay." I nod, accepting that she needs time. "So when can I see you again?"

"Well . . ." she trails off for a moment, "we do family dinners every Tuesday. Do you want to join us?"

"Your whole family?" I ask skeptically, not sure her mom would be too thrilled to see me.

"Me, Sam, and Em," Keelie says, reading my mind. "And Sarah, Sam's girlfriend. Jake's usually too busy for us now."

"And that's this Tuesday?"

"It's *every* Tuesday." She backpedals. "It's not too soon, is it?"

"This afternoon wouldn't be too soon," I assure her.

Her face lights up, and my heart can't help but ache with longing for her.

Sam has already settled into the passenger seat of their car by the time we approach. I've never seen this car before, but I immediately know it must belong to Keelie. Before I can stop myself from blurting out the thought in my head, I say, "Did you give your old car to Em?"

"I did." Keelie eyes me suspiciously. "How did you know that?"

I grimace, realizing I've said too much, but it's too late to go back on it now. "Because *Ol' Rudy* has been parked out front at your mom's house for a while now."

"What a totally normal and completely-not-creepy observation to make."

"Yeah, I kind of backed myself into a corner on that one." I smirk. "Sorry, I really wish I didn't say that."

"Too late." She winks.

Sam has left the trunk popped fully open for us, creating a shield from anyone in the hotel with wandering eyes.

Keelie places the bag she is carrying in the open trunk. She extends a hand out to me, offering to take mine. Instead of handing her the bag, I take her hand in mine, sit on the edge of the bumper, and pull her close to me. She stands between my legs, her hands resting against my chest, and mine cupping her elbows. She won't meet my eyes. Her gaze locks to the side of my face. She blinks frequently, her eyes turning red.

Rubbing my thumb across the divot on the side of her elbow, I smirk at her. "Mia Mae, we're heading back to the same place. And I'm going to see you on Tuesday, okay?"

She furrows her eyebrows and shrugs, suddenly apathetic to the entire arrangement. She sometimes gets mad when she means to be sad. She used to say that her emotions could be "inside out." But in reality, it was her dad whose emotions were inside out, and Keelie learned these confused reactions from him. It sometimes helped her to talk through how she was feeling, and sometimes she just needed more time to process it.

"Don't shrug." I shift my grasp to her waist. "It's not up for debate. You're going to see me on Tuesday and so many other days after that. You're going to see me so much you're going to be so fucking sick of me. I promise."

A laugh bubbles out through a blubbering sob as her emotions finally shift into place. A tear rolls down her cheek, and my thumb quickly snatches it away, and then sticks around to softly trace the line of her cheekbone a few times.

"I'm never going to get sick of you," she mumbles out in a hoarse voice.

My heart surges with a fluttering pulse; smugness curls across my lips. "We'll see about that."

The car engine starts up and the whole body of the car shakes under us. Keelie twists her mouth in disappointment. "Guess our time's up."

"Let's see how long before he starts honking." I smirk.

She gives me another soft kiss. This time I can feel the plushness of her lips, which swell up when she cries. She replies, "I should go."

I nod, even though I don't want her to. I step away from the car bumper, sliding the bag off my shoulder and closing the trunk behind me. She loosely holds my hand and leads the way to the driver's side of the car. She opens the door, jumps inside, then signals for me to wait as she rolls down the window.

I stick my head inside the car to kiss her again, trying to think up another way to stall our goodbye. I reach my hand across the front seat and out to Sam, making eye contact with him. It's the first time he acknowledges I'm at the car with them. He clasps my hand and gives it a quick squeeze.

"Good to see you, Sam," I chime.

"See you Tuesday?" he asks, the slightest grin pricking at the corner of his mouth says it all; inviting me to dinner was Sam's idea.

"I'll see you Tuesday." I raise my eyebrow at him, thanking him for his help. Then, turning back to Keelie, I add, "Text me to let me know when you make it back?"

She nods. "I will."

I hold her gaze for a long, aching moment, looking for more that I can say, but I can mutter out only a "goodbye, Mia."

She studies me, searching for more. I brush my hand along the side of her face, hovering there, searching for permission for one last kiss goodbye. The smile that darts across her face from ear to ear is the only response I need. Her lips find mine, coming together slow and deliberately. Her teeth brush over my bottom lip. Her tongue tastes mine once, then again a bit deeper. She burrows her fingers in my hair as I press into her further, pushing her head into the headrest, biting down on—

Honnkkkk!

The loud noise startles me enough that I hit my head on the roof of the car. Sam releases his hand from the horn and settles smugly back into his seat. Keelie lets out a guilty laugh as I retreat from the car window.

"Suck face on Tuesday," Sam snaps. "We have a ten-hour drive that will more than likely turn into a twelve-hour drive as soon as this hangover catches up to me. We have to *go*."

I lean in for one last kiss, swatting away Sam's hand as he reaches to honk the horn again. I duck out of the car window one last time. Lifting a hand to wave to them both.

"Bye, Val."

Tears well up in my eyes as she pulls out of her parking spot and drives off. For a second, I keep my eyes fixed on the ground to try to fight through the tears that are threatening to fall, but then I decide I don't want to miss the last glimpses I can steal of Keelie's eyes in the rearview mirror, so I look up at her and wave as they pull out of the parking lot and turn down the street and out of sight.

IX

Sunday, September 23rd

Annie Parker and Jess's mom hosted the postwedding brunch later that morning. To say that the idea completely exhausted Jess would be an understatement. Like the rest of us, she was about at capacity for the amount of fun that could be shoved into one weekend. But in her usual fashion, she gave zero indication that she was feeling overwhelmed.

When June and I arrive, Jess is making the rounds with relatives, Josh loyally standing behind her with a hand placed on her shoulder, smiling along to the conversation. I raise an eyebrow at him for a soft hello as we meet eyes, but then June and I are immediately swept up by Annie, who undoubtedly has already had more than a few mimosas while setting up for the party.

Blissfully bubbly, Annie hands a mimosa to June, then to me. I wave it off, but then Annie winks as she informs me, "I made this one with Sprite."

"Thanks, Annie." I accept the flute graciously, take a sip, and instantly regret it. The fizzy orange juice immediately makes me crave a boozy buzz.

June scrunches a hand through her hair, giving it a quick fluff, then she touches my arm and leans into me to whisper, "I'm going to go check out the breakfast spread. I'm starving."

As she makes her way there, she casually catches the eyes of Jeff, and he slowly makes his way across the room to stand next to her at the serving table. She wasn't after food at all but was starving for the attention of anyone ready to fawn all over her.

As soon as he sees me alone, Josh casually steps to my side, following my gaze to June and his dad. "So what's going on there?"

"I didn't ask."

"You didn't ask?" he scoffs disbelievingly.

"Didn't ask, don't need to. It's pretty obvious." I shrug. "Also, I don't really care. It's none of my business. We're not together."

"Yeah, and it's a good thing, too," he says as I take a sip from my fauxmosa. "If you guys were together, you probably wouldn't have had sex with Keelie last night."

I immediately snort the fizzy orange juice back into the glass. Coughing, I reply, "What?"

"Don't 'what' me."

"Did Jenna tell you that?"

"No, what the fuck does Jen know about it?" His eyes dart across the room to his sister-in-law. Jenna and Andy are locked in a conversation with an older relative.

"She gave us a ride back last night."

"And then what?" he presses further.

"And then nothing," I say over my glass. "And then I went to sleep."

Josh nods like he believes what I am saying, leading me to think this conversation is behind us. And then he adds, "It's funny though, Lex said Sam slept in *her* room last night because he was locked out of his." Josh sucks his teeth. "It seems kind of weird that Keelie went back to her room alone and still locked Sam out overnight."

I shoot a fiery glare in Lex's direction. She sits at a nearby table, flirting with Frankie. Her bare, tanned legs are crossed and sticking out to one side so they don't have to be hidden under the table. Each arm is fully adorned with a whole new set of jewelry.

"I'm not sure I buy that," Josh adds with a suspicious stare. "Unless, of course, she wasn't alone."

"You don't like your sister, do you?" I say with a grin. "Because I'm going to kill her."

Josh beams. "Now do you want to talk about it?"

"There's nothing to talk about," I plead, drooping my shoulders in protest.

He takes a long, slow sip from his drink, turning his head to take another glance at me. "Sworn to secrecy?"

A small, guilty smile cracks across my face. "Something like that."

"Thought so." Josh lifts a hand to wave down Jess's attention. When he catches her eye, he points to me, and then gives her a thumbs-up.

"What part of 'sworn to secrecy' did you not get?"

"*I* was not sworn to secrecy," he says. "And you didn't tell me anything. You didn't have to. I see it all over your face."

"You do not."

"I do too," he confirms. "You absolutely have a tell."

An embarrassed chuckle is the only reply I'm able to give him.

Jess comes sashaying across the room, eyes locked on me. "What the hell, Matty?" Her tone is angry, but her eyes show excitement.

"What?" I laugh back.

"You know what you did."

"Maybe. But I don't know why that's making you mad."

"I'm not mad," she says, angrily. "Confused. Surprised. A little excited. Definitely not mad. How are *you* feeling about it?"

I repeat back, "Confused. Surprised. A little excited."

"A *lot* excited," Josh amends.

"Pretty fucking stoked, actually." I laugh. "Trying not to get too excited. She's thinking about it."

"'Thinking about it' on a ten-hour car ride with *Sam?* You're fucked." Josh grimaces jokingly.

"I'll call her from the airport," Jess promises. "I should be able to undo any doubt that Sam sews in her."

"Thank you," I reply appreciatively. "But I think Sam's on my team this time around."

"That's huge," Josh says.

Jess puts a hand on Josh's shoulder, and he nudges his head in her direction. "We need to keep doing rounds before Mom yells at us again. But I think Alexis would probably appreciate the company." He darts his eyes from me to Lex, then back again as if to say, *You'll see what I mean.*

I follow his glance over to Lex, and it is now very apparent what he means. Her body language is so obviously disinterested. Her turned-out legs facing away from Frankie, and she turns only her head as she responds to him. And yet, she still flashes him her big eyes, a flirty closed-mouth smile that pushes her lips forward into a puckered kiss, and an incredibly forced laugh, as though she's trying hard to impress him.

Her entire body lurches toward me when I sit down next to her, her hand clinging to my knee like she would cling to a buoy in the middle of the ocean.

"Hey, Matty," she coos.

Frankie glares in my direction, lifting Lex's mimosa glass off the table and offering her a refill. She nods appreciatively, still stringing him along.

"What the fuck did you do?" I growl at her in a whisper.

"I'm sorry," she snaps back playfully, "you're welcome?"

"Yes, thank you so much for telling everyone."

"I didn't tell *everyone*." She shakes her head and glares my way as she says it, then she puts on another stupid smile, lifts her chin, and gently places her hand under it as if she has something important to ponder. "But I may have mentioned it to my brand-new sister."

With a frustrated, airy laugh I reply, "Which you already know is the same as telling everyone."

She tilts her head, keeping her chin firmly attached to her fist. "I think what you mean to say is, 'Thank you, Alexis, for selflessly giving Sam a place to stay last night so that I could fuck Keelie.'" Then she tilts her head back the other way and widens her eyes at me.

My brain runs through all the ways to dispute what she is saying, the suggestive remarks I could fire back at her to keep up with this never-ending game we play. Instead, I narrow my eyes at her, release the glare with a deep sigh, and say, "Thanks, Lex."

She smiles, satisfied. Then suddenly, the look in her eyes shifts from devious to something kinder. She squeezes my knee again and says, "You're welcome." Genuine. Sincere.

Frankie returns with her fresh mimosa. Lex sends a pained glare my way, then turns and to thank him, giving him only the slightest sliver of attention before turning back to me. Frankie takes the hint and joins up with Nate.

"Thank God," she deflates, whispering to me, "not interested."

"I think what you mean to say is," I repeat her own words back to her, "'Thank you, Matty, for giving me an excuse to tell Frankie to get lost last night.'"

She grins. "It was mutually beneficial." She takes a sip of her mimosa. "But for the record, I don't need an excuse to tell Frankie to get lost."

"Then why are you letting him hang around? He's a creep. Tell him to fuck off."

"He's Josh's friend—God knows why—and I'm not going to make enemies out of his friends at his wedding." Lex lifts her phone off the table, tapping it a few times to flash me a long line of texts from Frankie, all unanswered. "But if he keeps this shit up after this weekend, I'll tell him exactly where he can stick it."

"And where's that?" I ask.

"The fucking garbage disposal," she snaps back starkly, making me wince at the thought. Lex chuckles, amused by my pained reaction.

"That's good to hear. You can do way better than Frankie."

"You don't think I know that?" she scoffs back, then adds in a disgusted whisper, "Of course I can do better than Frankie. That guy's a moron."

As she taps her messages from Frankie closed, another message on her phone catches my eye.

"Why was Sam texting you about me?" I ask, craning my neck to get a better look at the preview text before she flips her phone over and out of view. It looks like a series of drunken typos: *Hres teh link to Matty thig.*

Lex gave another closed-mouth smile, puckering her lips out once again. "What happens in Cleveland, stays in Cleveland."

"That's not a thing," I protest. "Why is Sam texting you about me? Since when do you talk to Sam?"

"Sam and I had a lot of fun this weekend, okay? And what we talked about at"—she glances down at her phone for the time stamp—"four thirty this morning is none of your business."

"Oh, I very much disagree."

Lex props her head up on her elbow so she can lean in closer to me. "I know Sam tries to make you think he doesn't like you anymore, but once you get twenty-six ounces of straight alcohol in him, Sam likes you a whole lot."

"I have noticed that about him."

She nods with wide eyes to further emphasize it. "I started talking to him about my job. And he told me I should be working with you. He practically chastised me for not thinking of it first."

"Working with me on what?" I ask with a laugh.

Lex scowls at me—*Like you don't know*—and opens the text from Sam, clicking on the link that he drunkenly sent over to her at four in the morning.

When the page loads, it flashes with a familiar website that is recognizable but foreign all at once. It is an outdated portfolio website created the same year I dropped out of school. I was working with a few local companies on some packaging design projects at the time, and Keelie encouraged me to put a website together to share with potential clients. It's been years since I have even thought about it.

Mortified, I reply, "I can't believe he showed you that."

Lex shrugs. "Drunk Sam really cares about you. Don't let Sober Sam tell you otherwise."

"Sober Sam is warming up to me again, too. I think he's the reason I'm seeing Keelie again on Tuesday."

"That's great, Matty." A small grin curls across Lex's face. "I'm happy for you. Both of you." Lex strokes my cheek with the back of her hand, and scrunches her mouth contemplatively. With all the sexual tension Lex enjoys building between us, this move is far from that. It's caring, comforting. She holds my gaze as she says, "She loves you, you know. She just has to decide if she forgives you."

My eyes roll back into my head with a slow blink. I'm doing everything in my power to keep from crying in the middle of this casual brunch that is supposed to be a happy celebration of two of my best friends and not a blubbering freak-out about Keelie.

Jess's mom raises her mimosa glass and clangs it with a fork a few times to get everyone's attention. Annie Parker is standing by her side at the front of the room. They thank everyone for coming, then each takes a minute to give her own quick toast to Josh and Jess. I try to focus on what they're saying, but my brain spirals into thinking about Keelie. A huge wave of despair washes over me as my brain churns out a horrifying thought.

What if you destroy it all again?

My heart races and the lump in my throat returns. My breathing grows shallow. Air won't fill my lungs.

You're never going to make her happy. You're ruining her life all over again.

My throat clamps shut as the slow, bitter taste takes over my mouth once again. I can't swallow. I press my tongue to the roof of my mouth, desperately trying to get air back into my lungs, but no matter how slow and steady I try to force my breath to be, my throat clamps down tighter to cut me off. My eyes desperately scan the room, searching for a conversation I can cling to as a distraction. Anything that will help me break my mind from this cycle.

Stop being selfish. You're not good enough for her.

The phantom taste floods from my mouth, down my throat with that familiar chewed-pill grit, sinking deep into the pit of my stomach and jolting me with a sudden burst of nausea.

You'll never make this work.

Annie. Focus on Annie.

You're pathetic.

My vision gets blotchy and my body sways slightly. The lump in my throat grows larger, threatening to cut off my air flow enough to make me pass out.

"Matty?" Lex whispers.

Her voice jolts me back to reality. I inhale sharply and blink a few times, trying to focus on Lex.

She squeezes my knee, then asks softly, "Are you okay?"

"Yeah, I . . ." The words get tangled up inside me.

She nods knowingly, then takes a few deep breaths with me. I smile at her, grateful to have people in my life that know me well enough to not need an explanation. Taking a few deep breaths, I'm finally able to get air back into my lungs.

"You're going to be okay, Matty," she assures me, then she returns to her usual, snarky self so we don't have to linger on what just happened. "Try not to stress too much about the omelet bar situation. I'll walk you through it."

I roll my eyes at her with a laugh. Then I place my hand on top of hers and add, "I'm really worried there won't be feta."

Lex cackles a bit too loud, earning us a glare from Annie, to which we promptly respond by waving our hands in apology.

Annie takes a slow, annoyed blink as she turns her attention back to the room, a smile cracking on her face, as though she was expecting us to cause problems before she even started talking. She continues her toast without losing a beat.

Lex makes a sideways glance at me like she used to when we were scolded as kids. But now, we're two adults in our late twenties, still too immature to keep quiet for five minutes while the real grown-ups talk.

I've missed Lex. I've missed all these guys. Every single person who I pushed out of my life in favor of lying around high on oxycodone. Giving up these relationships feels much more daunting now that we're all in the same room, where my clear, sober mind can see exactly what I lost—it was so much more than my relationship with Keelie.

I lost touch with my best friend, missing out on the beginning of his budding relationship with someone we had both known for a majority of our lives. I could have stayed up late, waiting for his text after their first few dates to hear how it went. I could have been the one he talked to as he grappled with the decision to move to Cleveland. We could have talked through his nervousness the day before he proposed. I regret missing out on all of that.

I completely lost touch with Lex, and although I would never admit this to her, she's more than just the sharply intimidating little sister of my best friend. She herself is one of the best friends I have. That I've ever had.

And even though Jess tried her best to stay in touch, never cutting me out completely, I completely drained my relationship with her. Whenever we spoke, I drained her of every ounce of energy and never gave anything back in return. Even when I was high, I knew that was true.

I am going to be better for every one of these people to make up for the fact that I lost sight of how important they are to me. I'm going to hold on to them tight and never let them slip away again.

X

Sunday, September 23rd

June and I say our goodbyes at the gate as soon as we get off the plane. We both know it's a permanent goodbye. I thank her for coming, and she says, "I'm glad it all worked out for you, Matt."

A goodbye is weird when you know it will be forever. Sometimes you can try to make it better by saying, "I'll see you again someday," even when you both know it's not true, but neither of us is that kind of person. We knew this was it. So we stood by the gate for a few minutes, awkwardly stumbling through our departure. She wrapped me up in a hug and added one last "It's been fun." Then she left, heading toward the front of the terminal as if she never knew I was there at all.

I power up my phone. When it turns on, a text buzzes through from Chris: *In the pickup lot. Let me know when you land and I'll drive around.*

Knowing my brother, I'm sure he is watching the flight tracker and knows exactly when our flight landed. He is probably even estimating how long it should take me to walk from one end of the airport to the other so he can figure out whether I made any stops on my way to the car. He'll never admit to that, though.

I text back a reply to let him know I've landed: *Sono qui.* Then I slowly walk toward the front door. I fire off a text to Josh and Jess next, letting them know I am back, finishing my message with: *Congrats guys! Can't wait to see you again soon.* I want to text Keelie, too, but if she's still driving, Sam will be the one to read my message to her, and he'd fire back a dictated reply. I'd rather wait for her to text me when she's home.

Outside, Chris's car barrels up the ramp in the distance. I step up to the curb. When he pulls over, I crack open the back passenger door, toss my bag inside, and climb into the front seat next to him.

As he pulls off the curb, I catch a glimpse of June being greeted by her kids. The man I assume to be Randy stands close by looking on. I look away quickly, feeling guilty. Instead, I ask Chris, "How are the girls?" He tells me they missed me, and I wonder whether that includes Katya, or whether she's going to continue to be her apathetic self toward me.

He asks what's going on with me and Keelie, and I tell him I don't know yet. He laughs. "Well, you better figure it out quick because Michelle has been dying to talk to you about it."

"Maybe she should talk to Keelie and let me know." I smirk.

"Give it time," he says, looking away from the road for a second to glance my way.

"Yeah," I sigh. "Would it be alright if I hung on to my phone for a bit? Keelie's supposed to be letting me know when they make it home."

He nods. "Keep it."

"All the time?" I say, surprised.

"Sure. You've proven you can handle it. Don't give me a reason to change my mind."

The girls are fully animated, running around and shouting the second we step through the front door. Even Katya seems excited to see me. Luci takes hold of my arm and says, "Zio Picco, we made something for you!" and pulls me into the living room while jumping up and down.

Taped to the wall is a makeshift banner made up of pieces of paper tied together with string. Each paper has its own block letter, which Michelle and Chris had drawn out and the girls had colored in with scribbles of crayon. The letters spell out "Bentornato." *Welcome back.*

I thank her, and I ask which letters she colored. Katy eagerly joins the conversation, letting me know which she had done, too. I lift Katy up so she can point.

"I did this one. It's red," Katy explains to me.

"Sono rosso," I repeat back to her in Italian.

Then Luci says, "Zio Picco, I want to come up, too."

I scoop her up onto my other hip. Luci points to each of the letters and repeats the colors back to me. "Rosso. Verde. Blu. Nero." She pauses and looks puzzled by the next one. "Um. Orange?"

"Arancione," I remind her.

"Oh yeah," she says, embarrassed. I raise an eyebrow at her—an expectant stare, encouraging her to repeat back, "Arancione."

Once Luci runs through all the colors, Katy wants to join in, so we do them all again in Italian and English. Michelle and Chris look on with smiles.

"Zio Picco?" Luci rubs a hand over the stubble on my chin as she asks, "Can you read me a story?"

"Solo se me lo chiedi in italiano," I reply. *Only if you ask me in Italian.*

She looks to her dad for help, but Chris shakes his head at her. *You don't need my help for that.* So she turns back to me and thinks about it for only a second.

"Mi leggeresti una storia?"

"Certo, scegline una." *Yeah, get one.*

I set Luci and Katya down on the ground, and they immediately take off running for the stairs to search for the perfect book.

Michelle lets out a huge sigh. "I've forgotten what it is like to only have two adults in this house. It's good to have you back, Matty." Then in a low whisper she says, "And I'm very much looking forward to hearing about your weekend in detail once the girls are asleep."

The memories of this weekend are already floating away like a dream. How much longer am I going to be able to hang on to them before I convince myself it never happened at all? It doesn't feel real.

I pull the garment bag that is slung across my shoulders up over my head and tilt my head toward my room. *Be right back.*

It's almost alarming how much everything looks the same. It feels like a lifetime has passed in one weekend. I toss the bag on the floor. I'll unpack it later. Right now, my eyes are drawn to the photo of Keelie and me, still sitting on the side table as always, now with a large crack glued together in one corner.

My heart flutters with the same joy I felt when this photo was taken. Only now I don't need oxy to help me remember what that moment felt like. I remember. That feeling is no longer years away, buried by long, foggy weeks lost to drugs. I felt it this morning when I was back in her arms. The memory of Keelie's smile, her laugh, her touch, are all fresh in my mind.

My brain pulls my attention to the vent behind the side table, the place where I found my yellow pill. The yellow pill that could have reversed everything. That could have convinced me to take those pills from June. That could have ruined everything that happened this weekend. The phantom chemical taste returns to my mouth, reminding me why it would have been worth it.

Remember how good they feel?

I can't shake their taste; I can't push it from my mind. I don't want to think about them. I don't need them anymore.

You can't handle sobriety. You're never going to make this work.

I sit on the edge of my bed as I pull my phone out of my pocket. I tap into my contacts, hovering a finger over June's name.

She can get you more.

I take a few deep, contemplative breaths, trying to figure out what I could possibly say to June to convince her that everything that happened this weekend was just a fluke, that I've made a huge mistake. Instead of tapping to call her, to leave her another voice mail at work, I tap the three dots in the corner and then Delete Contact.

Are You Sure? The dialogue window pops up on my screen, begging me to reconsider. I tap Yes before I have time to think about it. Before I try to talk myself out of it. I scroll through the rest of my contacts list, deleting names of people I don't even know. Names that can only serve as temptations when the phantom flavor fills my throat. A knot forms in my chest; I'm immediately regretting what I have done. The addict inside me regrets what I have done. I trudge through those feelings of regret, breathing out every negative thought that spikes in my mind.

When this happens, Adam suggests I make a mental list of all the things I stand to lose if I take pills again. I would lose these moments with Luci and Katy and Chris and Michelle. I'd lose the tiny bit of forgiveness my parents have extended my way. I would never hold down a job. I might never have a home. I would lose my real friends, the people I have known for almost my entire life.

I would definitely lose Sam, whose patience for me is barely hanging on as it is. I'd never get to see Em or Jake again.

I would lose Keelie. I would break her heart, and I wouldn't get another chance to make it right. I can't lose her again.

Making this list is supposed to help me remember all that I have, even when it feels as though I don't have anything at all. More importantly, it serves as a distraction to the craving, occupying my mind long enough for it to pass.

"Zio Picco!" Luci shrieks out. "Sbrigati!" *Move it!*

Her feet come pattering down the hallway. She pokes her head into my room and repeats her frustration. "Adesso!" *Now.*

"Per favore!" Chris yells down the hall as a reminder to her.

"*Please*?" Luci repeats, annoyed.

"Vieni," I whisper to her, waving her over. *Come here.*

She throws back her head, annoyed that we still aren't reading a story. I pick her up by her armpits and set her down on my knee, wrapping my arms around her to give her a huge, crushing hug.

"I missed you this weekend," I tell her, squishing a kiss onto her temple.

"I missed you, too," she agrees, putting one of her little arms around my neck. "Dad sucks at reading stories."

"We'll teach him," I promise.

"Right now?" she groans.

"If you want to."

"No," she sighs back. "Just you tonight."

I agree. "Okay. Just us tonight. Show me which one you picked out."

She takes off running for the living room. I follow behind her, much slower. My phone dings in my pocket as I walk down the hallway. *Keelie.*

We're home. It was great catching up with you this weekend, Val.

My grin is wide across my face when I join everyone else in the living room. Michelle immediately notices. "What are you smiling about, Zio Picco?" she teases.

I send my reply to Keelie, *I've missed you, Mia. See you on Tuesday*, then toss my phone to Michelle for her to see.

I scoop Luci into my arms and make her shriek out in laughter as I rub my scratchy beard against her soft cheeks. Her giggles intensify as I hang her upside down by her ankles, above the couch, threatening to drop her before slowly lowering her down onto the couch cushions.

I snatch up the book she picked out and settle in with her curled up by my side. Katy sits next to me on the other side, from a more reserved distance. Chris and Michelle break off to a secluded spot on the porch, taking a moment for themselves. I wrap an arm around Luci as I crack open the book, squishing her tightly into my arms, remembering how nice it feels to be a part of our family once again.

EPILOGUE

Friday, April 19th

Every morning, I get stuck in the same loop. I wake up with my face mostly buried under the fluffy down comforter, enveloped in a high–thread count sheet that feels like satin on my bare skin. The smallest hint of the emerald-green fleece blanket peeks out from the other side of the bed where Keelie left the corner turned down when she got up this morning. She should have left for work twenty minutes ago, but she never woke me up, never said goodbye. I snatch my phone off the side table, looking for a text from her.

Instead of a text from Keelie, there is a flood of notifications from Lex, already filling my to-do list this morning:

Revisions call at noon. My time.

Need to make it fast, though. I have a lunch meeting. Can you look at markups before our call?

Remind me to tell you about Harper Tonelli.

I lean over the edge of the bed and retrieve my laptop, which I keep stashed below for mornings exactly like this one. Mornings when Lex has flooded my inbox with work, while I sleep. Mornings when I have to spend hours digging myself out of the long list of rapid-fire thoughts she's sent my way.

My email is still pulled up from yesterday afternoon, and my inbox is already fifteen messages deep. I scan the list of familiar names, the majority being Lex, but also Trish, Jordan, and Bailey. My *clients*. It still feels strange to call them that.

One message from an unfamiliar name catches my eye. Erika Gavin. The thread of messages starts with an email from Lex.

> *Hey Erika,*
> *It was great seeing you yesterday. Let's get something on the books again next month! Matty Arvali is the designer we worked with on Tiny Yellow Fires. I've cc'd him here so you can chat with him directly about layouts. You'll love him.*
> *Talk soon,*
> *Alexis*

Erika's reply came through almost immediately after.

> *Hi Matty,*
> *So great to e-meet you! Do you have time this afternoon for a call about a project with Tanya Allison? Looking forward to it!*
> *Erika*

I open the calendar app on my phone. I have two deadlines next week and three the week after that. The work keeps piling on, the weight getting heavier. I don't know how Lex and her friends can keep up this pace. This nonstop parade of networking and hustling and happy hour drinks. Am I cut out for this?

The familiar tightness builds in my chest. I close my eyes and take the slowest stream of air into my lungs before opening the side table drawer and retrieving a pill bottle. The label on the outside is crisp and new, the ink on the sticker an unfaded black.

I twist off the lid and pour one out into my hand. This pill is a green and white capsule. It used to come in the form of a little green tablet, but I asked Adam to switch me to something in capsules. The tablets were triggering me. I would grind the fluoxetine tablets between my teeth when I got anxious, and then the phantom taste of oxycodone returned to the back of my throat, and it would take hours to clear my mind of it. Capsules are much better. I can't chew them, I can't taste them. Nothing about fluoxetine capsules reminds me of oxycodone, except for the comforting familiarity of twisting off the cap of the pill bottle. A habitual comfort I'm not ready to let go of yet.

Keelie nudges open the door slowly, peeking her head inside slightly, then pushes it open fully when she sees I'm awake.

"You're late for work," I say, dropping the pill bottle back into the drawer.

"I took the morning off," she admits, sitting down on the edge of the bed, wrapped up in the shirt I wore yesterday. "What time's your first call today?"

"I'm talking to Lex at eleven," I reply, laying a hand on her thigh and softly brushing it with my thumb. "And someone new this afternoon."

Her eyes light up. "That's great, Val." She narrows her eyes at me. "What time?"

"Not sure yet."

"Can it be before four?"

"Sure," I reply suspiciously. "What's going on at four?"

"A surprise." She smirks. "I'll pick you up at four."

The arch of her eyebrows and the slight curve of her smile are contagious. I can't help but return the look of excitement on her face.

"What do you have planned, Mia?"

"It's a surprise," she repeats firmly.

"I told Em we'd be at her game tonight."

"That's not until six thirty. I promise we'll be done by then."

"Sam wants to get there at five thirty so he can get 'his' spot back."

Keelie snorts. "He's such a baby."

Sam has been feuding with a parent of one of Em's teammates over a patch of grass on the sideline for this entire season. At least, it's a feud in Sam's eyes. Every week, he arrives earlier and earlier to stake his claim on the prime piece of sideline real estate.

"Are you picking me up at four so we can steal Sam's spot from him?"

"No," Keelie replies shortly, not even entertaining the idea. "This is much less stupid than that."

I take her hand in mine, lacing my fingers through hers. "I can't wait to see what you're hiding, Mia Mae."

Excitement bursts across her face. She collapses into my shoulder to disguise it. When she emerges, recomposed she asks, "Do you have time for breakfast before your call with Lex?"

"Sempre." *Always.* "What's the occasion?"

She looks down at our intertwined hands, sandwiching my hand between two of her own and giving it a tight squeeze. "I know what today is, Val."

I know what today is, too, but it doesn't feel real until she says it. *One year sober.* I've never been here before. I haven't spent a full year of my life sober since I was thirteen years old. Not even during my one-year outpatient rehab program. "Relapse is part of the process," they had said, and I took that as permission to relapse, instead of its intended forgiveness for relapsing. But now I'm here. For the first time ever, one year sober *by choice.* Well, more like four months by force and eight months by choice, but an entire year nonetheless. Thinking about it brings a smile to my face.

"How'd you know?" I ask.

"I know everything," she says with a playful glare, then amends her reply. "Chris told me."

I wrap my arms around her, pulling her into my embrace. She burrows her face in my chest, and I whisper "I love you, Mia" into the top of her head.

"I love you," she whispers back softly. "I'm so proud of you."

A soft sob catches in my throat. I squish my cheek hard against the top of her head, pulling me tighter into her still.

At eleven o'clock, a video call comes through from Lex. Without wasting any time on formalities, she snaps, "Did you look at the markups I sent?"

"Good morning to you, too."

"Hi, Matty," she scowls. "I'm very busy today. Can we get to it, please?"

I study her frantic look for a second, before I figure out what she's hiding. "You have another lunch date with that greasy music producer, don't you?"

Her face softens, and she fights a surfacing smile. "He's not greasy," she defends.

"What is it, like, the fifth date?"

Lex sucks her lips into her mouth and bites down on them, as if hiding her lips is the only way to hide the childlike joy that is completely drowning her expression. She nods sheepishly, confirming this will be date number five.

"Finally, someone has beaten my record."

"Fuck off!" she yells out with a smirk. "Can we talk revisions, please?"

"I'm opening the file right now," I assure her, activating screen sharing so she can see the file loading.

"I hate the color palette," she states bluntly, not waiting for it to load. Her fingers are rapidly firing off a text as if they function as an independent entity from the rest of her body.

"It's the exact same one you approved last week," I remind her.

"Okay, well," she sputters, "I hate it. Fix it, please."

"You got it."

"Deeper reds," she contemplates, fingers still fluttering against her phone. "Something sexier."

"Is that a note for me or for your music man?" I smirk.

She drops her phone like it's on fire, her eyes finally meeting her laptop screen. "For you. Darker reds. The best-seller list is covered in that awful burnt-orange trend right now. I need a cover that's going to stand out, alright?"

"Oh, you wanted something eye-catching? You should have said so."

She glares at me, not amused.

"Lex, I'll work off the notes you sent over this morning, and I'll call you if I need clarification on any vague critiques you scribbled on my design. You should go get ready for your 'lunch meeting' with the music man."

"Ernie."

Before I can tamp it down, a laugh bursts through my lips. "You are *not* dating a guy named Ernie."

She grins. "I swear!"

"What's his real name? Ernest?"

"I don't know," she admits, "probably."

"How was that not the first question you asked him?"

She narrows her eyes at me and purses her lips before she replies, "There wasn't a lot of talking on our first few dates."

I shake my head in disbelief. "Your life is so much more interesting than mine."

She smiles mischievously, offering more details than I asked for with just a look.

"Do you want to tell me about Harper Tonelli before you go?" I change the subject.

"Briefly." Lex shifts back to her professional self. "She's writing a book set in Tuscany, and I need you to do the cover. I don't have any other details. But I want you to work directly with her so you guys can geek out about being Italian together and keep me out of it."

"Send her my info."

"I will," she says kindly, then takes on a harsher tone. "*After* you get those revisions over to me. Deadline is Tuesday."

"I'll have it to you tonight," I assure her.

"Thanks, Matty. I'm going to go. Talk soon."

She ends the video call without waiting for my reply, eagerly running off to her lunch meeting.

I click open the markups she sent over. A sea of red lines are scribbled across the cover design I sent her earlier this week. Some are positive, sections of the design circled with a note like *Love this*. And other notes are sarcastically hostile, demanding a change. But every time, no matter how many or how few changes she makes, Lex always scribbles *Thanks, Matty*, with a little heart next to it in the margin.

I spend the rest of the afternoon making updates to Lex's design, working on something new for Jordan, scheduling calls with Erika, and updating my calendar with deadline changes for a project I'm working on with Trish. Four o'clock comes before I know it. Keelie comes in through the front door, right as I am writing out a list of all the things I need to remember for tomorrow, before I do this all over again.

To pick me up, Keelie has to drive all the way back to Sam's house in the city to get me, only to drive back to the highway in the direction she had just come from. She says she doesn't mind, that she's been doing this drive every day for the almost three years she's been living in Sam's guest bedroom.

But once again, this arrangement forces Keelie to double back. She drives us almost all the way to the neighborhood where she works, a couple of miles from where our parents live and right down the road from Em's game this evening—back to the small St. Louis suburb we've called home for most of our lives.

"I was joking when I said we should get there early to steal Sam's spot, you know."

"We're not headed to the game yet," she says.

"Okay, then, where are we going?"

She doesn't reply, instead turning into a quiet neighborhood with lots of tall trees canopying the road. After a few twists and turns, she pulls into the driveway of a house I don't recognize. An olive-green split-level home with a black iron railing leading up to the front door. Flower bushes are starting to bloom around the entire front of the house. In a few weeks, this earth-toned house is going to light up with every vibrant color of flower imaginable.

Keelie keeps her eyes fixed in the rearview mirror, as though she's waiting for someone else to pull up.

"What are we doing here?" I ask.

"It's a surprise," she snaps back playfully.

A pearl-white Cadillac coasts onto the driveway and parks directly behind us. Keelie presses the seat belt release button and jumps out of the car without explanation. Hesitantly, I follow her. Keelie greets the Cadillac driver, a woman in a bright red pencil skirt and a black blazer, holding a black leather folder. She has on bright red lipstick, the exact shade as her skirt, and gold beads are clipped into her small braids, all pulled tightly back into a ponytail.

"You must be Matty," she greets me.

I crinkle an eyebrow in Keelie's direction before turning to the stranger with a confused expression. "I am."

She shuffles the folder from one arm to the other so she can extend a hand to me. "Jasmine. Great to meet you." She turns back to Keelie and says, "Shall we?"

Keelie glows with excitement as she gives one quick nod of her head. Jasmine places a manicured hand on the iron railing and walks up the front steps.

"What are you up to?" I whisper to her.

"You'll see."

Jasmine holds her phone against the keypad at the front door, triggering the locks to turn open and ushering us in. On a small landing inside, there's a sign that requests we kick off our shoes. A mirrored closet reflects the light from the outside window, a chandelier hangs overhead, stairs go both up and down from here. Keelie tilts her head toward the direction of the stairs going up, and I follow her. Tall vaulted ceilings, tons of natural light, and inviting, warm wood floors, but there is no furniture anywhere. The entire place is empty.

I let out a small laugh as I stand behind her, squeezing my hand on each of her arms and burrowing my face in her hair so I can whisper in her ear, "What am I looking at, exactly?"

"An empty house," she retorts smartly.

I give her a kiss on her cheek. "What are we doing hanging out in an empty house?" I ask her, even though I already know the answer she's hiding.

She turns around, places a hand on each of my hips and whispers back softly, "Starting our lives together."

"Mia Mae," I whisper softly, feeling wrapped up in the warmth of her words. Feeling humbled by her forgiveness. Feeling hopeful for our future. I didn't need to say any of this to her, the look on her face says it all. She feels it, too.

That's the beauty of being with someone for so long. After fourteen years of being in love with Keelie, she didn't need to say anything at all. I can read her thoughts with just a look.

I wrap her in my arms as my eyes search the empty room, imagining our life here. Then I mumble into the top of her head, "I said I didn't want to make a big deal out of the whole one-year sobriety thing. How are you going to top this next year?"

She pushes away from me, a friendly look of annoyance washes across her face. "I knew I should have gone with a cake. You're right, we should go."

She takes two steps toward the stairs before I snatch her by the wrist and pull her back into my arms. "Show me the rest."

She spins out of my grasp, barging straight ahead into the kitchen. "It could use some improvements here, but I was thinking"—she presses me up against the corner counter by the kitchen sink, then presses her back to me so I can follow her point—"we move the stove over there, extend the counters out that way, cut out those cabinets, and put in an island. Eventually."

She tilts her head backward to gauge my reaction. I wrap my arms around her shoulders and give her a tight squeeze. She grasps my hands, ducks out from under my embrace, and leads us further into the house.

"This room first," she says, jumping to the room all the way at the end of the hallway. It has thick, plush carpets, two large windows, and twin closets. "This one is our room."

Keelie picks a spot at the center of a wall and sits down on the ground, tugging my arm to join her.

"Bed right about here," she explains, snuggling up into my shoulder, "and soft, flowy curtains on the windows to diffuse all the bright light coming right through here every morning."

She pauses a minute to gaze out the window before jumping to her feet and running across the hall.

"And this one"—she spins around in the center of the room—"is your office. We'll get you a real desk, so you have lots of space to work. Maybe a big desktop monitor, too."

She pulls me into the next room. This one is already painted as though it once belonged to a small child. She wraps an arm around my waist and looks around. "This one will be Sam's room, obviously," she says with a playfully pensive face.

"Of course." I laugh.

She takes my hand and leads us out of the hallway, back into the wide open main room and then down the stairs at the front, to the bottom level. Another wide open room with a large fireplace in the corner.

"Big comfy couch with lots and lots of blankets down here." She tilts her head as she pictures it. "All snuggled up in front of the fireplace in the wintertime. And then . . ."

She leads us back to the landing, through the garage, and out the back door to an expansive backyard with a large oak tree on one side.

"We've got all of this." She holds her arms out wide, presenting it to me. There is a deck attached to the top level, a bricked patio on the lower level, and lots of grassy space. Keelie looks over it all, already so in love with everything about it.

She turns to me and asks, "What do you think?"

Uncontrollable joy curls across my lips. I place a hand on each side of her face and press my forehead against hers. "It's perfect."

"Yeah?"

"Yes," I assure her. "I love it."

"It's not too much, is it?" she asks, crinkling her nose, making sure I know what she means. *Is it too soon to take another leap forward?*

The familiar chemical taste pangs the back of my throat once again. More time with sobriety doesn't make that haunting craving go away, but it does allow me to reframe the phantom taste. It serves as a bitter reminder of everything I stand to lose by falling off this path. A reminder to reflect on why I'm staying sober. As the bitter flavor fizzles in my throat, I let out a slow, steady exhale.

"It's not too much," I say calmly. "As long as you're sure it's what *you* want."

Keelie takes my hand in hers, giving it a squeeze. "I've been waiting *years* for this."

Sam already has chairs set up along the sideline before we pull up to Em's game. He's wearing reflective aviators and slumps down low in his seat, arms crossed on his chest. His girlfriend, Sarah, is nowhere to be found, probably embarrassed to have arrived so early to a high school lacrosse game.

"He's unbelievable," Keelie scoffs as she catches a glimpse.

"Just a dedicated fan."

Em and her team are running drills on the field, and the other team is starting to arrive. She throws a quick wave our way as she sees us heading over to Sam. Em turns to her coach and then takes off running toward us, keeping her high-knees formation.

"Did you guys go look at your new house?" Em shouts excitedly.

"Em!" Keelie snaps, furrowing her brow into a look of disbelief. "Oh my God!"

"What house?" I ask, playing along with Keelie's game.

Em drops her jaw, eyes wide, as she tries to figure out how she's going to backpedal her way out of this one. "Umm . . . You know . . . the . . ."

"Em, we're fucking with you." I crack a smile. "We just came from there."

She snaps a slap onto my forearm. "That's not funny!"

I give a quick shrug. "I don't know, the horror on your face was pretty hilarious," I tease. "Have you seen it?"

"Yeah, that one and like *forty* other ones."

Keelie rolls her eyes in my direction. "We looked at *eight*."

"Okay, well, it felt like forty. And I promise, we found the only good one in the entire Calhoun School District. Trust me." Her sass melts into curiosity. "Did you like it?"

"It's perfect."

"Em-me!" Em's coach bellows out for her to return to their warm-up.

Em huffs an invisible piece of hair out of her face. "I've gotta go." She dives into my chest for a quick hug. "Thanks for coming, Moog."

She does the same to Keelie, as Keelie says, "Don't clock anyone tonight, please."

"No promises," Em replies mischievously, running off before Keelie has the chance to reply.

"Em!" Keelie shouts out after her.

Em waves a hand above her head as she runs off, dismissing Keelie's concern.

Sam doesn't move from his slumped-down position, his eyes impossible to see through his aviator glasses, his stare fixed straight ahead. I sit down in the chair next to him, and he doesn't move a muscle. *Is he asleep?*

I tap a hand against his shoulder, jolting him to nod a hello in our direction. He *was* asleep.

"Where's Sarah?" I ask.

"Hiding in the car. Afraid of a little fight," he replies, shifting in his seat.

"It's grass, Sam," Keelie snaps.

"It's my *fucking* spot, and he knows it!"

"You've lost your mind," Keelie confirms quietly.

"You sound like Sarah," he grumbles.

"Reasonable?"

"Shortsighted."

Keelie snorts out a laugh.

"Don't listen to them," I egg Sam on. "Stand your ground."

Keelie lets out an audible sigh. "Between Em's frequent illegal hits and you starting fights on the sidelines, people might start to believe that *we're* the problem."

"Let 'em talk." Sam smirks.

"I'd rather they *didn't*," Keelie protests. "I still have to work in this school district, and I'd rather not be known as the counselor with the crazy family."

"I've got bad news for you, Kiki." Sam glances at her from overtop his aviator sunglasses. "You've always been the one with the crazy family."

"Hey, guys." Sarah emerges from her hiding spot, finally feeling confident enough to be seen around Sam. "How was the house?"

I turn my gaze to Keelie. "Did you tell everyone already?"

"Michelle doesn't know." Keelie grins. "She can't keep a secret."

"Mom and Dad?" I ask.

Keelie nods.

"*Your* mom?"

She nods again.

"Paul?"

Keelie laughs. "I don't know. Probably."

"Everyone knows, Moog," Sam cuts in.

The referee blows his whistle, clearing the field from warm-ups before the game starts. Em stands on the sidelines, rocking her stick back and forth between each hand. She notices I'm looking her way and raises her stick high into the sky as a hello.

"Do you guys want to come hiking at Castlewood with us on Saturday?" Sarah asks, leaning her view across Sam and me and looking directly at Keelie as she asks.

"We can't." Keelie places a soft touch on my arm as she responds, "We're going to be in Elmwood with Luci and Katy this weekend."

"Again?" Sam hums. "How long are you going to be there?"

"Until Tuesday," Keelie replies.

"Uh, okay," Sam grumbles, "but you guys are still on dinner duty this week, don't forget."

"We've got it taken care of," I cut in. "The girls are going to help us make gnocchi this weekend. *Chillax*, Sam."

Sam glows with pride. "You know, there will come a point when you realize that you're no longer making fun of me, but actually saying 'chillax' unironically. And that's the moment when you will see I was right." He throws a sideways glance my way. "I just hope that day comes *before* you move out of my house so I can bask in the glory of it."

The feeling I get being back in Keelie's room is the same familiar feeling of being back home. The comfort of being surrounded by everything Keelie is a luxury that I had taken for granted before. Something I won't take for granted again.

Sam's house is mostly nondescript. Gray walls, charcoal couches, dark wood tables, a couple of plants, generic artwork, no photos. It could be anyone's house.

But when Keelie moved into Sam's guest bedroom, she turned this small corner of his house into something that was undeniably Keelie. Something warm and familiar, the walls and shelves littered with photos, mementos, and personal touches. It mirrored the feeling of stepping into the apartment we once shared. This space was ours. It was what our house would soon be.

The blue velvet chair and the tall golden floor lamp. The oakwood dresser we took from my parent's house. A bookshelf in the corner, stuffed to the gills with books. In front of each row of books were many small souvenirs of life outside this room. Seashells, rocks, small figurines. Some things I remember collecting; others look unfamiliar, mementos that Keelie collected on her own.

That night, after Emmy's lacrosse game, I scan the objects on the shelves as I do often, digging through the layers of moments she has encapsulated here. Tonight, my eyes are drawn to a tiny hand-carved wooden box on a lower shelf that I have yet to inspect. The carvings match the photo frame we bought in Sedona—the frame that now lives on Keelie's dresser. The corner is glued back together, but the glass is still missing. It now has a new note, penned right onto the photo this time. *I love you, Val.*

I turn the tiny wooden box in my hand a few times, curiosity getting the best of me as I flick open the tiny golden clasp latching it shut. A bundle of gold twisted metal hides inside.

My gaze snaps to meet Keelie's. She's curled up under the covers, watching me discover what she already knows is inside.

"I can't believe you still have this," I say, jaw dropping open, dumbfounded.

"Of course I still have it." A small smile pricks her lips. "It's my engagement ring."

I gently pull the twist of metal from the box, as if it's an artifact that might disintegrate in my grasp. In a way, it is an artifact. A relic of another lifetime.

I offer the metal prosecco ring to her once again, a silent assurance that I fully intend to fulfill the promise I made to her that day. Only the next time I make her a promise like that, I'll have something made of *real* gold to present to her, not a golden twist of aluminum. Next time, I'll *ask* her to spend the rest of her life with me, too humbled by losing her once before to ever assume, even if I think I already know her answer to my question.

She takes the ring from me, placing it on her own finger, and giving the metal tab a couple of quick twists to bring it down to size. She locks eyes with me as I join her at the top of the bed, our backs resting against the headboard. She looks away to examine her ring finger, holding her hand far out in front of her to get a better look.

"It's beautiful, Val." She grins.

With my forehead pressed to her temple, I get lost in her coconut-scented curls, whispering softly back to her, "Only the best for you, mia vita."

Acknowledgements

This story has been living in my heart for over a decade and it is so surreal to have watched it finally come to life. I couldn't have done this without my partner in all things, Jason, who dedicated many weekends to reading very rough drafts or breaking down plot until we got it just right. Huge thank you to my editor, Lila LaBine, who transformed this mess of a manuscript into the beautifully polished novel you hold in your hand, and who reluctantly looked the other way as I turned all the *all right*s back into *alright*. My Italian translation editor, Maddalena, who received the strangest abridged version of this story and didn't once question why extremely colorful language and red-sweater-wearing penguins occupied the same space. Emily, my beta-est of beta reader, who provided feedback and encouragement even when this story was carrying the weight of two hundred extra pages — we've come a long way. And thanks to Courtney, Hannah, and Jessie, who endured countless rounds of anxious questioning as I figured this whole thing out.

While this story is a work of rose-colored fiction, the opioid epidemic is very real. For anyone struggling, please take care of yourself, be kind to yourself, and remember you are a very important piece of this world. Mental health disorders and addiction are both treatable medical conditions. For more information on finding help visit: findtreatment.gov.

Kelly Piazza lives in Saint Louis, Missouri, where she is often mocked for the way she pronounces the name of her native land, "Wis-CAN-sin." Kelly is a lover of romance novels and finds herself fortunate enough to be living in a romance novel of her own every day thanks to her rockstar husband and adorable rescue pup. Other favorites include strong coffee, Midwest road trips, and spending endless hours clicking that pesky "Add to Cart" button on Etsy.

Connect Online
KellyPiazza.com
@KellyPiazzaWrites